"I will not go easily to Avalon..."

Elizabeth glanced at the Angel of Death and saw the woman smile as if in recognition. *Well, my Lady of Darkness,* Elizabeth thought, *if it be my time I will go. But I warn you, I will go west fighting, and if necessary I will fight even you...*

The Dark Lady of Death nodded her head as though, even with her deafness to the pleas of those she came for, she had heard Elizabeth's thoughts. She spread her hands in a gesture of acceptance. Then, furling her wings closely about her, the angel leaned back against the oak tree to watch, as the first of the horsemen burst through the encircling trees into the clearing...

WITCHDAME

KATHLEEN SKY

BERKLEY BOOKS, NEW YORK

WITCHDAME

A Berkley Book/published by arrangement with
the author

PRINTING HISTORY
Berkley edition/January 1985

ISBN: 0-425-07449-8

Acknowledgments

The author would like to thank Karen Trimble and Karen Willson for transcribing this manuscript and my notes for it; Ian Myles Slater for his excellent research; Joyce Odell for listening to me blather and offering excellent criticism; and my doctors, for keeping me alive while I wrote this book.

This book is dedicated with much affection to

JOYCE ODELL

because she has managed to keep
her wit, wisdom, and style
in a mediocre world.

Author's Warning:

This book is a work of fiction, not a grimoire. Many of the spells and magical recipes mentioned in this book are extremely dangerous, if not deadly, and I do not recommend their use. There are no woodwitches or witchlords left upon the earth, and only they had the true knowledge to deal with *their* magic.

Chapter 1

The queen was dying. The wall hangings whispered the words down the long galleries. The staircase thrummed with it, and the carved wooden heraldic beasts were only too willing to pass the message along. The Great Hall echoed with it, and in the three unfinished towers of the rose brick Palace of Witchdame the sounds of the carpenters' tools carried the dismal comment to the waves of the river Theames lapping at the watergate stairs. But the stairs had heard that same message for years. It had been built into the foundations nearly seventeen years ago. The queen had been dying for a very long time.

In the south tower of the palace—the only one completed of the four magnificent towers that would eventually grace the building—the sun was turning the glass windows on the western side a deep crimson, staining the air in the queen's chambers the color of blood.

The honey-gold of the oak linenfold paneling was darkened

by the light, and only the large silver candelabrum gave enough illumination to prove that the table it was on was made of oak instead of ebony. The table had a scattering of objects carelessly arrayed across its surface. There were bits of colored string, candle ends, bundles of dried herbs, a stack of papers covered with the queen's delicate handwriting, and a large parchment document held in place with a seastone said to be from the cave of Merlin himself. The document was a will, signed and sealed by the queen. At the bottom of the scroll was a green blob of wax with her signet ring imprint, and even in the dim light it was possible to make out the queen's device of a rowan tree with a crescent moon caught in its upper branches.

The tile floor of the room was covered in overlapping layers of rush matting to keep out the cold, and in the shadows massive clothespresses loomed like dark square-shaped ghosts.

The gigantic bed, carved for a queen long dead, was large and shadowed, its woodwitch green velvet hangings only partially pulled back. The tiny body of Queen Dianne of Englene could hardly be seen among the satin and lace pillows, piles of goosedown comforters, and the red and blue embroidered velvet coverlet decorated with the gold ships and leopards of the arms of Englene.

The queen was a tiny waxen doll. Her black hair, once glossy, now lay matted and dull across the pillows; her face, once rose and snow, was now the color of old tallow. Her eyes were closed, and only the gentle stirring of the covers over her spare chest indicated that there was still life present.

The door to the chamber opened. The queen turned her head to see who might wish to visit her, alone, on her deathbed.

"Bess," she whispered, her voice frail in the large room. She watched her daughter approach, her eyes widening in horror at the girl's appearance.

The Princess Elizabeth, heir apparent to the throne of Englene, was dressed in pale blue velvet; the deep, square-cut neck of the gown was most unflattering to her shoulders, made broad by many hours of work in the tiltyard and in swordplay. Her skin was the rich boiled pink of a redhead who has been too long in the sun. The princess was tall, six foot one inch at the measuring at her last birthday, and the round waist of the gown made her torso appear overly thick. The gold brocade of the kirtle visible in the deep inverted "V" of the overgown's skirt was of a large cabbage rose pattern. As Elizabeth approached the bed, the queen could see only too clearly the jeweling around the neckline of the gown, pearls and sapphires in a design of forget-me-nots.

The queen closed her eyes for a moment, as if to shut out the sight of so much misplaced daintiness. "Child," she said, her voice now losing its feeble edge, *"who* picked that gown for you? I'm not yet dead and already you've forgotten everything I've taught you about taste."

"I knew you were shamming, Your Grace." Elizabeth swept her mother a deep curtsy. "When I heard the whispers that you were again dying, I thought I'd best put in an appearance so that I could lay the rumor low at this evening's feast. There are many people who will be so disappointed to find it's not true."

The queen reached out, patting the edge of the bed to indicate that her daughter was to sit. There was a great creaking of the roped mattress as Elizabeth obeyed, and her mother winced slightly at the excess weight. There was nothing slight or woodwitch about this daughter of hers.

"Oh, you'll find the rumor true enough by morning, my dear. I intend to go out with the tide. This time the queen will die."

Elizabeth turned to her, shocked at the confirmation in her eyes. "You really mean to do it? After all these years, you mean to let them win? You—a woodwitch—are going to give in to *them?"*

Queen Dianne smiled, pleased for the moment that her daughter had remembered that she was a woodwitch. "There are reasons; you are now old enough to look out for your own interests, and I have no wish to still be here for the initiation on your eighteenth birthday. I'm too high-stomached to easily stand the sight of you in one of *their* circles." The queen paused for a moment, breathing deeply. "And there are other reasons. You, my child, must be the next ruler of Englene. There can be no other. And with my dying, I will make sure of that."

"The Lady Anne thinks otherwise. She and my father will be between your sheets before they're barely cold, and by next Midsummer's Eve we will be celebrating the birth of a prince."

"I do not think so, daughter. You and you alone shall be the next ruler of Englene. The Mother Goddess herself gave that promise at your birth. Even if your father takes to his bed a hundred women like the Pemberly, he *will* have no other heir but Elizabeth of Englene. I and the Mother of All wish it so to be."

"So mote it be," Elizabeth said dutifully, though she did not believe it.

There was a brisk knocking at the door and the queen rose slightly on her pillows, hope plain on her face. "Richard?" The name was almost a plea.

The door opened, but it was not the king—only his sister, Marguerite.

Princess Marguerite was a sturdy woman in her forties, long past any claim to youth or beauty. Her height and stocky body proved her relationship to the Princess Elizabeth, but Marguerite was no warrior. Her battlefields were parchment, pen, and books. She wore a court gown of black velvet with a matching hood; her red hair straggled in wispy tendrils out from under the jeweled biliment, and her turned-back sleeves were spotted as much with ink as with ermine tails. The brocade of her silver kirtle was equally stained, and a small leather-clad book dangled on a chain hanging from her girdle. She bustled across the room, her red leather slippers scuffing and ruffling the matting.

"Well, Your Grace, they say you're at it again. Dying, of all things. And me with the herbal only three-quarters done. You know, Dianne, it's very inconsiderate of you. You promised to wait until the book was finished so that you and I could gloat over it together. The work was more than half yours.

"I won't have it. I tell you, I simply won't have it! You've been meditating on dying for the past seventeen years, and you might as well wait another seventeen to do it."

Dianne waved a small hand to quiet the woman. "I die when I must, Marguerite. I am not something you can put a wax seal at the bottom of, declaring *me* finished." The queen again eyed her daughter's outfit with disapproval. "Tell me, Marguerite, what think you of the way my daughter is dressed? Is it proper and right for her?"

"Oh, you know I pay no attention to such fa-las. I merely stand and let my ladies-in-waiting throw on my body what they will," Marguerite laughed. "I couldn't tell if she were wearing a fashionable court gown or a barrel."

"Green, child. You must wear green, the queen's color."
There was a sharp intake of breath from Marguerite, but the
queen ignored it. "And have your neckline a little less spread
out to the shoulder; and wear your shift high, to the neck. The
bosom should not be so exposed. Also the waistline should be
pointed—it narrows the waist—and your skirts spread wide
and smoothly over the hips. And wear a feathered bonnet over
a pearl caul. That touret makes your face look round as a
Cheshire cheese." The queen tapped one beautifully shaped
nail against her upper lip. "Green," she repeated. "The woodwitch's color. Pale delicate green for spring; green baudekin,
tafity, or velvet for high state—and for mourning, the dark
deep forest green of the pine tree. Wear no black for me,
Elizabeth. If you honor me, and you have the courage to remember that I was a woodwitch, you will wear green in my
memory."

The princess nodded dumbly, unable to speak. Green was
not a color acceptable at her father's court. It was a woodwitch
shade, and naught but a woodwitch would wear it. But it was
her mother's wish, and something that the queen would not
ask of her except that she was truly dying.

"Remember that you are half woodwitch," Dianne continued. "When the time comes, go deep into the Heartwood and
find there the old woman named Nerthus. I know you will find
it hard to do as I ask. But for your sake, and the sake of
Englene, you must. Do not consider it as a promise to me, but
as a promise to yourself. Will you go?"

Elizabeth nodded slowly. It was clear from the set expression on her face that she wanted to deny this request. She knew
only too well in what ill repute the woodwitches were held at
her father's court.

The queen closed her eyes and seemed to be willing all her
energies toward simply breathing. She gave a small mewing
sigh, and again opened her eyes. "Marguerite, don't make her
forget what she is. Make her be my daughter as well as Richard's. Let her be strong for the land that we both love. I beg
this of you as the one person at this court that I can truly trust."

"You have my word, Your Grace." Marguerite's voice carried the conviction of a vow.

"Too, I want you to be the one to see to my funeral. Don't
let the Pemberly ruin it for me. I want to be buried in my green

velvet gown, the one with the silver oak leaves and acorns around the neck and sleeves. I also wish paste copies of my pearl earrings—the court jeweler has those—and the paste crown as well. He had that made fifteen years ago when they were so sure I would die of the ague from the northwind and I surprised them no end by getting well again." Dianne laughed mirthlessly. She knew only too well how her many illnesses had been helped along by the neglect of the court physicians.

"The green and silver," Marguerite nodded in acceptance. "And for your pall?"

"Dark green silk embroidered with rowan blossoms. That too has been provided. You'll find it at the bottom of the coffer in my privy chamber. I embroidered it myself. There will be no black at this witchqueen's funeral! You *will* see to that. Let Richard weep and wail about court etiquette, and the Pemberly pout; I will go to my death as a woodwitch and not as one of them."

Marguerite leaned across the bed to gently tuck the coverlet around Dianne's thin shoulders. "Sleep, Your Grace; all will be done as you wish." There were tears in the woman's blue eyes. Dianne smiled up at her sister-in-law and obediently closed her eyes—brown eyes, woodwitch eyes, the same color as Elizabeth's. Marguerite straightened and turned to her niece; her eyes were bright, but the tears remained unshed. "Go to the feast, Bess; you've very late and your father will be angry with you."

"But aren't you expected at the table, Aunt? You anger the king fully as much as I do," Elizabeth said.

"Nonsense. I am too unimportant to be noticed by Richard anymore; and as for his leman, the Pemberly . . . well, I am no challenge to any royal brat of hers," Marguerite answered.

Dianne reached out her hand and touched her daughter's sleeve. "Go now, Elizabeth. Go to your father's table; but as you sit there, remember of what cause I died. Remember that unless you are strong, you too will die of it. We will not meet again, my child. But remember that I died a woodwitch, I will be buried a woodwitch—and that you are half my child. Now go to the feast."

Elizabeth rose to her feet and curtsied deeply to her mother, with the full reverence due an anointed queen. She backed slowly out of the room, step by step, pausing to curtsy again three times before reaching the door.

"Don't worry about Her Grace," Marguerite called to her niece. "She and I will sit here together quietly, two forgotten ladies in this glittering court, and we will talk a bit; and then when she is ready I will leave her, as we all must leave her when she goes on her journey."

Elizabeth nodded shakily, opened the door, and slipped out of the room. As she left the chamber she heard her mother say, "Now here are my plans to make sure Elizabeth is queen after Richard . . ."

Not wanting to hear more, she closed the heavy oak slab behind her and leaned against the carved surface for a moment. It should have been her father sitting there by the queen's bed, but Elizabeth knew that her father had tired years ago of hearing of the queen's imminent death.

She sighed and straightened herself, tugging the blue gown firmly down over her boned corset. She looked at the velvet folds and realized that her mother was right—the gown was ugly. She let go of the fabric and knew that never again would she allow Lady Anne to pick any dress that she might wear.

Elizabeth made her way down the darkened corridor, her eyes not focusing on the linenfold paneling, the tapestries, the painted plaster ceilings molded in intricate flowing strapwork. The tower gallery was as familiar to her as her own body; there was no need to observe it closely. She turned onto the main staircase leading downward toward the Great Hall, and was startled to see that most of the torches had been allowed to go out. The staircase was dark; only an occasional flash of the rising moon from a glass window outlined the magnificently carved and painted heraldic beasts squatting on the newel posts as the staircase zigzagged its way down the tower. The lifesize lions, unicorns, bears, and griffins were almost real standing there in the dim light, each one a little more terrifying because of the darkness. She'd known these figures for most of her life—but this night, with the queen truly dying, they took on a horror she had never seen in them before. She paused on a landing to catch her breath and calm her heart.

One of the beasts seemed to be clothed in a red, blue, and gold motley—strange for a heraldic figure. She tiptoed across the landing, her pulse hammering unpleasantly at her tight cuffruffles, to get a closer look at what this beast might be. It was a gargoyle, wrapped around a newel post, a creature all elbows and knees, with the face of an angel.

Suddenly, out of the dark, a jester's bauble twirled and stopped short a hand's-breadth from her face. Elizabeth screamed and grabbed for the stair railing, as with a mixture of relief and hysteria she recognized the being on the newel post.

The king's jester slowly unwound himself from the heavy post and sprang down onto the landing beside the princess. The man was short, shorter even than most humans; his crumpled back and long, spidery arms and legs made him look as grotesque as any carving. He was barely as tall as the princess's bodice, and had to tilt his head to look up at her face. Jackie Somers, the king's jester—from the neck up, the most beautiful man at court; from the neck down, the ugliest.

"Did I frighten you, poppet? I hadn't meant to. I merely came to serve as a warning. You're very late below, you know. Lady Anne is quite displeased."

Elizabeth reached out to touch Jackie's shoulder, almost as if to reassure herself that he was real. "I was with my lady mother; she lies dying, and I felt it wise to know what final words she would have for me."

"What, dying again?" Jackie rattled his bauble. "She's been dying for years, poppet. All the court knows it; it's nothing new. And it will not serve as an excuse to be late for the feast."

"Can you think of a better? If I should wish to visit my mother, isn't that my own business? Does it have to be the bibble-babble of the whole court?"

"Aye, and it does, for no one visits the queen the night of the Pemberly's birthday feast. Are you trying to show her direct insult by being late? Now come, take my arm and I will be your swain for this evening, and we will walk into the court hand in hand, like good lovers should, and all will know that you are late because you've spent the time tumbling in my bed." Jackie reached up and tweaked the heavily embroidered gold undersleeves of the princess's gown. "But I must say," he added, "that if I'm to go into the Great Hall with a lady, I think I should take one that's better dressed. You look like some servant girl out a-maying in her mistress's cast-off gown. It's most unbecoming." He fingered the velvet and then let it fall. "Pale blue isn't your color. But I can tell who picked it. It was the Pemberly, wasn't it? Pale blue suits her. Any shade of blue does. Why, the lady even has her undergarments made of blue silk."

"And how would you know the color of her shift? Did *you* just come from tumbling the Pemberly? The court is more likely to believe a tidbit of that sort than the thought of you spending the time in my bed."

Jackie laughed and said, "Alas, no. There are some things that the king does not allow his jester to taste first. And the Pemberly is one of them. Not that I miss it much. Vinegar and honey was never an appealing combination."

Elizabeth laughed and reached out to tweak the jester's golden curls, set like a halo on his head. She pulled his coxcomb hood higher, letting the ridiculously shaped ass's ears fall forward over his face. "That for the Pemberly. May she have an ass in her bed. And if my father has anything to say about it, she soon will."

"Look you, poppet," Jackie said, trying to be soothing, "the king's not been in her bed yet, as far as I know. There'll be no baseborn brat for the Pemberly, more's the pity. I have it from her lady-in-waiting that the moontime has come round for her again, so it proves she's not with child. That information cost me a kiss to the Pemberly's lady-in-waiting, who is a very ill-favored wench. Now the least you can do, my princess, is pay me a kiss in return."

Elizabeth laughed, reached down, and, taking the jester's head gently in her hands, kissed him upon the mouth, a soft, sweet kiss.

The jester sighed, and then pantomimed a lover covering his excessively beating heart with his hands. He only succeeded in swatting himself on one ass's ear with his bauble. "You know, Elizabeth, my one true love, there is a difference between kissing you and kissing any other lady in the court. Most of them store my kisses in a velvet box deep in their souls, as a reminder of their daring obscene deed. But you let yours fly free as a butterfly's thought through your mind. I find your kisses best of all for that reason, for I would be a butterfly, free in your mind."

The jester's voice made it clear he was being quite serious. In all his years at the king's court, the Princess Elizabeth was the only woman who ever treated him as though he were a whole man and not some amusing toy. They had known each other since childhood. He had been but three when his peasant parents had given him as a May Day gift to the king, thinking that his warped little limbs and back might prove to be an attraction at the court. He had been a child of six when the princess was born, and he had found her a fascinating toy. He devised his best jokes for her; his best clowning and his most witty mimes had been done for the little red-haired wench. As she had grown older, he found that his was her favorite shoulder when there was some childhood grief that must be vented. He took his role as jester to the king with great seriousness, but he treasured his position as confidant and friend to the princess far and above any honors the king heaped on him.

He smiled up at her and again extended his hand, and arm in arm they swept down the stairs, across the entrance hall, and into the long gallery that led to the dais of the Great Hall.

Chapter 2

The Great Hall of the Palace of Witchdame was an immense room, high-ceilinged, and as elegant as the artisans of the court could make it. Trophies of the hunt decorated the upper gallery, and the lower walls were covered by Queen Dianne's chief gift to the palace, a series of magnificent tapestries designed and woven by her ladies and herself. They showed the forests surrounding the capital city of Lundene, depicting trees, flowers, and small streams trickling over rocks. There were views of wooded clearings containing unicorns, roebucks or rabbits, and one particularly fine tapestry of a riverbank covered with wild strawberries. It was said by many that if you came close to the tapestries, you could hear birds singing in the trees, and listen to the streams laughing to themselves; and no matter what odor there was in the room—be it foodstuffs, perfume, or the scent of new rushes—the room was always filled with the odor of pine and bay and wild strawberries. It was as though the court dined in the middle of the forest itself.

The Hall was laid out around a circular firepit with two rows of immense tables up each side of the room; on the dais, a short table set at right angles to the long trestle tables was reserved for the Royal Family and such guests as might be shown preference. There were eight chairs of richly carved Moorish leather behind the damask-covered table. Three of them, to the right of the king—those of Queen Dianne, the Princess Elizabeth, and the Princess Marguerite—were empty. Seated in the one beyond Marguerite's was Thomas the Mage, Lord High Chancellor of all Englene. At the king's left, seated far enough away so that she was not truly under the cloth of estate, sat Anne Heywood, the Lady Pemberly; just beyond her, Elizabeth could make out the figure of Englene's primate, Aleicester, Archbishop of Avebury, Bathford, and Wells, a balding suet pudding of a man clad in the silver and gold brocade of his calling. With him was his wife, Mary of Richmond, bastard sister to King Richard. Their son, the Duke Charles, sat at the top of the left table, above the salt.

It was the king himself who dominated the table. He sat under the scarlet, blue, and gold cloth of estate, garbed all in pale blue and silver. Richard was an elegant monarch. In his forty-eighth year he was still flat of belly and trim of figure, though he was as big-boned as Elizabeth herself. His shoulders were broad, his neck a well-formed column; his complexion was as pale and delicate as that of a high-bred lady. Richard's cheeks were touched with pink, and his round face was made even more broad by his fluff of golden-red beard and his hair worn long and curling below the ears. His eyes were large and blue; a mouth that was warm and generous completed his face. He was a cheerful man, even-tempered, and lacking the red choler of many of his courtiers.

Elizabeth could not resist the feeling of pride and love which filled her at the sight of her father. She disagreed with him greatly on his treatment of her mother, but even so he was to her the elegant and perfect knight, the image of a king.

She moved soundlessly across the carpet-covered dais, pausing at intervals to curtsy. The king, intent on the capon upon his golden plate, did not notice her approach; but Lady Anne turned and watched the princess's stately series of curtsies, her face struggling to be bland and sweet even though her rigid posture made it clear she was very angry indeed.

Elizabeth finished her last curtsy by her father's chair. With her head still bowed, she murmured, "My lord, forgive my tardiness. I realize that my rudeness has been most inexcusable."

The king turned, startled to find his daughter so close. "Well, daughter, you have dallied overlong, and I have found it necessary to allow the feast to go forth. You have missed the first two courses. So sit, and do what you can with the food before you and that yet to come." He reached out and helped her to her feet, and then pulled out her chair and assisted her to sit.

Elizabeth was weak with relief that her father's reproach was so light. She was disappointed at having missed the first courses, but as she looked down the length of the high table, she could see that the other courses would provide an ample amount of food. At her right side was a large chine of rare beef; in front of her was a whole roast pig, a brace of pheasants in plumage, two chicken pies, a bowl of peas with bacon, a great sallet of crayfish, cucumbers, carrots, olives, and beets in oil, sugar, and vinegar, and a platter containing three well-larded hares. At a wave of her hand, the pageboy who had taken his place behind her chair stepped forward to wash her hands and place her napkin over her left shoulder. She indicated to him that she wished to be served from a dish of mushrooms cooked in eggs and cream sauce, the sallet, and then the beef. The king politely pointed out that the cook had provided a large supply of dormice covered in shredded almonds and cinnamon to resemble fur and with their tails braided together at the center of the plate, stuffed with dates, raisins and nuts—a dish he knew Elizabeth favored.

Still more food was brought to the high table by servants so that a choice of many dishes might be made. There was a peacock in all its glory, and a large stuffed breast of veal. There was a presentation platter of boiled turnips that had been carved into the shape of galleons, floating on a sea of fresh sorrel, and the Lord High Chamberlain, Henry Terrell, was about to dismember a stuffed heron.

The king accepted a leg of the heron, commented with pleasure on the use of cinnamon and nutmeg for spices, and began to chew delicately at it.

Jackie had waited in the background to make sure the princess would not be overly abused for her lateness. He then skipped to the table and placed himself in Marguerite's chair, where he began an elaborate jest on that lady's mannerisms at table. Marguerite was well known for her habit of trying to eat and read at the same time, so Jackie peered downward at his lap and pantomimed getting a leg of fowl caught in his headgear, then getting his hands mixed and trying to carve and eat a book. King Richard roared his approval as Jackie finished his act by standing upright in Marguerite's chair, kissing Thomas the Mage on one ear, and bounding across the table, performing a full somersault in midair before landing in front of the dais, at the foot of the table.

The king and Lady Pemberly applauded the jester's antics, and the mage threw Jackie a scrap of beef from his own plate. The jester received the morsel with deep bows and proceeded to suck at it with closed eyes, as though he were eating the food of the gods indeed.

"That was kind of you, my lord, after his taking such a great liberty. But then, you are always kind," Elizabeth said to Thomas as she quietly picked up a wooden trencher and began to fill it with the various foodstuffs before her.

Thomas smiled. His face was made for smiles. His lips were full and red, and his eyes, deep blue under his fringe of light brown hair, crinkled in a way that proved he smiled often. "Truly, Your Highness, I value that little human's wit—and his wisdom. Also, he is an excellent source of gossip, and no politician such as I could keep his place without full knowledge of what people are saying of him."

"But they only say the best of you, I'm sure," Elizabeth replied as she pushed the trencher to the far end of the table, within reach of Jackie's hands. Thomas smiled and bowed in acceptance of her compliment.

Elizabeth's page stepped forward to pour a rich red wine of La Bonne Terre into her goblet, which had a turquoise bowl held in the arms of a silver merman. He then filled a pewter tankard with ale for the jester.

It was not that Jackie did not appreciate wine, but he felt it necessary to keep his head unmuddled—for when the feast and banquet were over it would be time for more elaborate entertainments. During the feast itself, the minstrels up in the gallery and a troupe of small singing boys served as ample background for the sound of eating and drinking. And Jackie, between mouthfuls of food, would occasionally toss off a brief quip in the direction of the king.

The feast being finished, it was time for the banquet. Servants rapidly cleared the tables, removing heavy embroidered linen cloths now stained by food and wine, to reveal clean damask cloths beneath. To the sound of trumpets and drums, the banquet foods were brought into the Hall. On the king's table were placed large bowls of fresh cherries, apricots, and raspberries thickly covered with cream and sugar; there were pies of apples in custard, and jellies elaborately shaped as roses and dragons and mythical beasts. Bowls of moon and star frumenty, and plum pudding were placed within easy reach; wet suckets and dry, sugared nuts, and kissing comfits were distributed along the table. And then, with the sound of sackbut, drum, and horn, the subtlety was brought into the Hall.

Since this banquet was in honor of the Lady Anne of Pemberly's birthday, the pastrycook had labored long and hard to produce a confection to please that lady. It was a reproduction of the court gardens, complete with spunsugar trees, a duck-pond filled with rosewater and sugar ducks, and gravel walks made of finely chopped almonds. The lady applauded the subtlety and viewed it with great pleasure—particularly since everyone in the Hall knew that the gardens of Witchdame had been laid out by Queen Dianne. At the center of the garden, on one of the paths, stood an eight-inch-tall figure of the Lady Anne dressed in a blue gown which had been colored with turnsole. It was a beautiful portrait of the lady, and the king bent gracefully across the table to place a gentle kiss on the hand of the small figure. The court applauded the action, making it clear where its sympathies lay.

Lady Anne's page cut a slice out of the garden and placed it upon her plate. The base of the garden had been done with marzipan and rich fruitcake studded with plums and almonds, and it was much to her taste. The king dabbled his fingers in the rosewater pond, making the ducks bob and wobble. He laughed boyishly, and turned to flick his fingers, dripping with rosewater, at Anne. She appeared amused by this action, and she too began dabbling her fingers in the pond and spraying all within reach with the sweet, fragrant water.

Elizabeth sat still in her chair, her every instinct outraged by the fact that the garden so dear to her mother had been usurped by the king's favorite. Slowly she reached out her silver, ivory-handled dagger and, with great care, sliced a large wedge of marzipan out of the back of the figure of Lady Pemberly. There was a gasp from Anne as she watched the princess lift the slice of marzipan to her mouth and chew noisily.

"I'm very fond of marzipan," Elizabeth said blandly. "Although I do find it quite cloying."

"Ah, but Princess, this marzipan has been flavored with cinnamon and nutmeg and clove, and you will find it has quite a bite," answered Anne, striving for as bland a tone as the princess had achieved.

"'Tis true," Elizabeth said. "However, 'tis marzipan nonetheless—and overly sweet."

The king had either not heard or was ignoring the exchange. He was quite busy attempting to eat a spunsugar tree without getting any of the sticky substance in his beard.

Elizabeth, growing bold after the success of her first attack, reached again toward the figure, and with one deft slash of her knife beheaded it, catching the delicate morsel in her fingers and crushing it slightly as she popped it into her mouth. The lump of marzipan was rather large for her, and she moved it from cheek to cheek cautiously, trying not to choke and thus give amusement to Anne.

The lady, however, sat pretending not to understand the insult that the princess had attempted. She merely requested that the pageboy bring her another slice of the garden, this time a beautifully decorated piece of the flowerbed. But she could not resist a slight attempt to regain her position of power over the princess.

"I marvel," she said, "that your father has allowed you to come so late to the Hall without requesting some explanation for your tardiness. Do, I beg you, let us know what kept you from honoring me at my birthday feast by being on time."

"I was visiting my mother," Elizabeth said. "She lies dying, as you well know."

"She has been dying a long time, my daughter," the king said before Anne could answer. "I find that a feeble excuse for not being here at the start of the feast to honor the Lady Pemberly. Was there some special reason to tarry?"

"She was lonely, Your Grace," Elizabeth said evenly. "And I think it odd that she has only her daughter to comfort her, and not her husband by her bedside as well. But then, as you have pointed out, she has been dying a long time."

The king, his eyes clouded, did not answer. Instead he reached for the heron bone that still sat on the edge of his gold plate and had not been removed at the end of the feast. He picked the bone up and whistled sharply between his teeth. His grayhounds, which had been lounging by the fire, came to instant attention and began barking shrilly as they ran toward the dais. Jackie, pretending great distress, covered his ears and rolled himself into a small ball, as if to avoid being crushed by the large pack of dogs.

The king studied the dozen or so dogs gathered before him, and then threw the heron bone toward one particular ill-favored bitch. The dog had a reputation for bad temper and an unpleasant tendency to bite. She caught the bone expertly and ran off down the Hall with the other hounds in pursuit.

The king sat back in his chair and signaled for the steward to bring him a bowl of rosewater to cleanse the grease from the bone off his hands. "Elizabeth," he said over his shoulder, "if you ever come to rule this land, there are many lessons about the kingship that you must learn—and I have just given you an example in one of them. A king, to keep his throne, must know which of his charges to favor and which to ignore, lest they should take it into their heads to tear out his throat. The dog that caught the bone I generously gave her is the least attractive of all my hounds; but she carries puppies from a truly great and royal strain, and she must be favored—not for what she is, but for what she will do for me. Try to remember this lesson."

"His Grace has promised me one of the pups," Anne broke in, "and I am sure it will make a very engaging pet." It was obvious that she had neither understood the lesson nor had any wish to, though it had been partly aimed at her.

Princess Elizabeth said nothing. For her, the lesson had been well taken. The Lady Pemberly was useful to her father; her mother the queen had no further purpose. She sighed and picked an almond tart from a plate at her right hand and began slowly to eat it. It was tasteless in her mouth, and dry, and she wished there was some way to spew it out; but etiquette required that she finish it, carefully and with as much daintiness as she could manage.

The banquet having come to its end, it was time for mumming and masquerading. The tables in the Great Hall were pushed closer to the walls, and those people unfortunate enough to have been seated along the inside edge scrambled for positions close to the wall.

With shouts and the rattling of tambourines, a horde of raggle-taggle gypsies burst into the Hall—but their rags were made of silk and velvet, covered with gold coins and embroidery; their beards and long straggling hair consisted of silk threads and gold wires; and all their sparkling gems were real. They danced in the center of the room, the men leaping high into the air while the women clattered the tambourines and played upon small tabors as they sang of the joys of the free life upon the roads and byways of Englene.

The gypsies, Elizabeth knew, were probably members of the court—younger sons and daughters of noblemen—but they made a fine array, and their singing was a pleasant thing to hear. With one last rattle of their tambourines, they danced out of the room to the sound of applause.

Jackie rose slowly to his feet and made his way down the Hall, picking up a scrap or two of silken rag left by the gypsies. He came back to the dais and raised one piece of silk to his nose, sniffing at it.

"I find it strange, Your Grace, how these gypsies smell," he observed. "Did you know that they sweat violet and lilac and lavender? It's very odd. You must have more of them put about the court to sweeten the air."

The king laughed appreciatively, and then said, "Jackie, since it is the birthday of a lady, give us a dissertation on the joys of womanhood."

Jackie twisted himself into a particularly grotesque, gargoylish posture. "And what would a poor cripple such as I know of ladies, Your Grace?" he whined. "Alas, alas, none of them looks on me with favor. I am naught but a poor thing, kicked from room to room—and bed to bed—unloved, uncherished—but very satisfied." The court laughed appreciatively; Jackie's amorous exploits were legendary, and many a young lady hid a blush behind her hands, knowing that this grotesque little creature had very recently shared her bed.

"But if you would have me speak upon *women,*" Jackie continued, "I would have to say that I like my women large, Your Grace. They're warm in the bed. Those tall, thin willow sorts provide no fire; they burn very quickly. But give me a large log of a woman to warm my bed the entire night."

"And what of tiny woodwitch women?" asked Anne provocatively. "What do you think of them, fool?"

Jackie screwed his angelic face up into a grimace of intense concentration. "Why, my lady, I find that while small, they provide the most intense heat of a night—but unfortunately the flame goes out all too soon."

Jackie bowed mockingly in the direction of the king. He was treading on dangerous ground—but as jester, he had the right to say almost anything he wished, as long as he remembered that the emphasis was on the word "almost." To tweak the king too much about neglecting his woodwitch wife for Lady Pemberly could be a bit unwise.

"Now, Your Grace, enough of women; too many of them can be a bother both at night, and the morning after," Jackie said. "We have other entertainment for you. I have persuaded old Menadel to come out of whatever moldy little cell he resides in and perform for your edification some small sleight of hand." There was a giggle from the Lady Anne, which was echoed by many in the court. The wizard Menadel had an unfortunate reputation for having none of his magic tricks work very well.

Jackie skipped off down the hall and, with much flourishing and mimed pretense of playing a trumpet, ushered Menadel into the room. The round redhaired man came slowly up the Hall, bowing repeatedly to the king, whom he rarely saw in the normal course of his day. Menadel spent most of his time in an unused dungeon, attempting great feats of alchemy— most of which produced only horrendous, sticky, ill-smelling liquids and great scorch marks on the wooden trestle tables he used for his experiments. He stopped before the dais, bowed again to the king, made a small bow to Anne, and gave a warm smile to the Princess Elizabeth.

Elizabeth had always been raised to call Menadel "Uncle," although she was not quite sure if he was one of her grandfather, King Edward's, many bastards or not. The wizard had been her teacher for as long as she could remember. He might have been any age, from forty to four hundred. His florid face and fluff of untidy red hair and beard were one of the earliest visual images in her life, as he stood over her cradle waving some absurd rattle of his own devising in her face.

Menadel bowed again, and, pulling his mouse-colored robes more closely about his body, he stepped into the center of the Hall. In his high-pitched voice he announced to the court at large that he was going to attempt the great Firenza Fireball effect. He removed from the sleeves of his garment three glittering glass balls, which he proceeded to juggle—not very deftly—and then, at a guttural sounding spell from the wizard, the balls burst into flame and proceeded to juggle themselves.

The wizard stepped back and crossed his arms across his ample belly. A few members of the court applauded limply. The king leaned forward in his chair, intent on watching the elaborate patterns that the three balls of fire were weaving through the air.

And then disaster struck. Menadel, his face suddenly turning purple with effort, sneezed—a loud, honking sneeze. The balls paused briefly in midair and then, realizing that they were no longer under control, began to dash backwards and forwards through the Hall, frightening the ladies of the court and singeing the beards of the gallants. Menadel, his hands waving swiftly through the air, attempted to recapture the fireballs, but they ignored his commands. He cried out great oaths, screeching them at the top of his tenor voice; the balls continued to ignore him. They darted upward toward the hammer beamed roof, danced in the air, and swept downward to illuminate the various courtiers.

The laughter in the Hall, which had been directed at Menadel, changed to screams of fright and terror. The king, having watched this display with some amusement, pulled himself slowly to his feet. He raised his right hand, the hand that bore the copper and emerald ring Raziel, the source of his power—power so strong that a thought could level three counties.

With a negligent flick of his wrist, King Richard produced a large shimmering bubble, iridescent as the skin of a pearl; at his command it swept down the Hall and one by one collected the fireballs, then rose toward the ceiling of the Great Hall. The opalescent light illuminated the court, revealing the golden blond, red, and shimmering tawny of the curls of the witchlords and witchdames. There was not a brunette among them; no witchlord ever had hair of midnight black. It revealed the colors in their gowns: red, yellow, wine, saffron, black, bronze, orange and pink, violet, silver, gold, every shade of blue, all colors of the rainbow but one—the green of a woodwitch.

The globe swelled even larger until it burst with a loud popping sound, showering the court with flowers, comfits, sugared almonds, and small silver and gold trinkets.

There was much laughter in the Hall as the courtiers jumped and dove after the favors falling from the king's bubble. They were like children laughing artlessly in their play, snatching sweets out of each other's headgear, and diving for a particularly succulent bonbon in the bodice of a lady-in-waiting. And on the dais, Princess Elizabeth sat ignoring the hail of sweetmeats and gifts falling into her lap, while she silently damned all of these golden, beautiful people who were, by their curses, circles, and divers spells, causing the death of her mother, the queen.

When the Princess Marguerite left the queen's bedside, the candles were guttering and the quantity of moonlight in the room said that the tide was on the point of turning. Dianne sat up in bed, her arms wrapped around her knees. She knew the time had come to complete her last task on Earth.

She reached under the pillow and withdrew a small bag of potpourri. It was a harmless mixture of rose petals, sandalwood, cinnamon, and night jasmine. It would do to confuse the witchlords. Smiling, she poured it into the small brass bowl on the table beside her bed. With slender fingers she scattered a few of the petals across the tabletop. "Let that keep them," she murmured.

Then she extracted a second bag from under her pillow, and, reaching into the bed, she pulled out a charcoal-heated bedwarmer, its brass sides still hot to the touch. She opened the lid and gazed at the red-tinged coals. Then, from the bag, she removed a fine, white silk handkerchief. She knew it well. She had watched Elizabeth embroider it as a New Year's gift for Richard. The handkerchief was crumpled and stained. A trusted serving maid had obtained a quantity of Richard's sperm. Dianne found she had no wish to know how the girl had accomplished it; sufficient it was that it had been accomplished. Smiling coldly, she tied nine knots in the silken fabric. She laid the handkerchief on the coals and watched it scorch, little tongues of red flame nipping eagerly at the soft fabric.

As the flames consumed the fabric and sperm, she sprinkled onto it a mixture of dried orange peel, hemlock, vervain, white poppy, and wormwood. She began to mutter in an ancient eldritch language: *"Twine in three knots, Amaryllis, in three colors twine them, Amaryllis. Do and say, far sy far fa far fay u far eight na forty. Kay u Mack straik it, a pain for hun creig wel. Mack smeoran bun bagie."* And the brazier burst into blue flame. This was a spell of ligature; it could only be broken by untying the knots—and since the handkerchief was burned, it could never be undone. Richard would not have a child by any other woman.

Dianne watched the flames consume the cloth, and found that she was weeping. Weeping for the lost days at the beginning of their marriage when they had tumbled joyously in this same, big bed. And with her touch, she had enlivened him and brought him ready to her. That would not happen again, ever. Richard was now less than a man because of her spell. Sighing, she closed the lid of the bedwarmer. Its task done, she returned it to its place under the bedcovers.

The tide had turned.

She lay back on the silken pillows and waited. She knew her end was not far off.

"Well, have you finished everything you were to do?"

Dianne peered into the shadows in the corners of the room. The door had not opened—but then, the person in her room had not needed a door.

"Yes, Nerthus, I am done," Dianne said. "I have finished the chronicles of my life for my grandchild-to-be. I have saved the throne for Elizabeth, and I am ready. I have but two regrets: One, that I shall never see Bess on the throne, and the second, that I shall never see her child that you've promised will make all of this worthwhile."

"And what of the Towers you've not finished? Have you forgotten that only one tower is done? I gave you a command to do four." An old woman came out of the shadows. She was stooped and gray, her face wrinkled with a thousand, thousand cares. She was clad all in woodwitch green from the top of her gable headdress to the tips of her velvet slippers. She lifted her overly long skirt daintily into folds over her belly as she moved across the room.

"The Towers will either finish themselves or Elizabeth will do it with your help. I care not which it is to be," Dianne said. "Can't you see that the power is gone from me? If I had tried, with so little strength left in me, to finish Witchdame Palace, I would have broken or marred it."

"Excuses!" The old woman's voice was a catlike hiss. "That is all I have ever gotten from you—excuses!"

Dianne laughed weakly and said, "I am your child. My weakness is your weakness. Enough! Leave the work to Elizabeth. She will be much more to your taste, since she is so much more biddable than I. Have joy in your ordering of *her* life. I have ended mine. All my powers have gone into a curse on Richard's manhood. Richard is unmanned, and I have done it!"

Nerthus shook her head at the hate that filled the small queen's mind and body, and said, "In all the years I've known you, Dianne, I have never found you to be vindictive. I have found you petty, argumentative, quarrelsome, and, at times, petulant, but never vindictive. I must admit I am surprised, and as you know very little surprises me."

The queen rearranged the bolsters and pillows around her thin, bony shoulders. "If anyone has the right to be vindictive, it is I. I have suffered seventeen years of his neglect, and the hatred of his court. He did nothing to stop them! I could flay him alive and roast his flesh, and not even you could say that I was not justified in such a deed. Do not indulge yourself in sanctimonious hypocrisy, old mother. You know what I have suffered. Do you really think I am unjustified in it?"

Nerthus turned her back on the queen and stood looking down at the documents spread on the large oaken table. She picked up the large stack of papers that represented Dianne's gift to her unborn grandchild, the memoirs that she had spent so many weeks laboriously writing. "There is a great deal of truth here," Nerthus said, putting the sheets down on the table. "A great deal of truth and a great deal that is merely opinion. It doesn't matter. In the long run it is the opinions of people that become history, not truth. In time what you do here will become a truth of sorts. The great and mighty Queen Dianne so *loved* her husband that she would not suffer him to touch another woman. Oh, they'll sing ballads in taverns about it and lament the woodwitch queen who went lonely and unloved to her grave. But they will never sing that she was petty and mean-spirited."

Nerthus turned back to face the queen. "I will not stop you. It suits my plans very well. In fact, were I to look very deeply into my heart, I would probably find that it *was* my plan, and that's very discouraging. I thought *I* was less petty than that. Mark you, great queen of Englene—for Richard, next year is a year of a seven and a seven again. The years of his age and the years of his reign cross, and that is an evil portent for a king. Would you send him forth to the year of a double seven unmanned?"

Dianne stirred restlessly in her bedcovers, an expression of doubt on her face. She raised her fingers to her lips and focused her attention on a slight flake of skin beside one nail. She nipped it neatly off with her small white teeth and sighed. "His destiny is his destiny. It is not mine to trouble myself with. I do what I do, old woman, because I must. If it come that the year of a seven and a seven be the doom of King Richard, I have presented Englene with its hope and his successor. In my Elizabeth is my apology for any harm that I do this kingdom through my cursing of its king. Tell me, old mistress of meddlers, is not that *your* plan? Come, admit your part in my curse, and give me your blessing before I go down into that dark and empty tomb in Westmonasterium. Forgive me, and comfort me with your blessing. All my life I have done thy will, and have suffered for it."

Nerthus the woodwitch, Mother of all the woodwitches and spiritual head of them, stood beside the bed of Dianne, she that the woodwitches called Deerwydd Oak-seer, and did for her what she had done so rarely in her long existence—she felt pity mixed with love and regret for this, her own creation. Perhaps a flawed creation, but a creation nonetheless.

"May you be blessed in your living and your dying," the old woodwitch said. "May you be blessed in this your last spell and may it be, no matter what darkness it produces, of final benefit to Englene. And may it be as you wish, a way for your daughter to sit securely upon the throne of Englene. May she come to know the bitterness, anger, and pain that you and her father have wrought, and may she curse his name *and yours!* I, Nerthus, take upon myself the blame because I know that your deeds are my deeds and my deeds are yours. *Mea culpa, mea maxima culpa.* I, Nerthus, have said it."

Dianne accepted the blessing and the curse equally. The old woman's curse was simply one more drop of bitterness, and in an ocean what was one drop?

Dianne closed her eyes and waited for death to claim her. "I want to die. The time has come; let me die now, old mother."

"The time will be soon, child. I hear the wings of the angel."

The window shutters groaned and creaked in an apple-scented breeze that had sprung up in the western Isle of Avalon, and there was the sound of knocking at the window panes. The shutters broke open of their own accord and there, seated on the window ledge, stories above the ground, was the Angel of Death.

She was garbed in the rusty green-black of a crow, and her long black wings had much of the raven about them. Her hair was long and midnight black, her eyes jet, set in a dead white face. Her expression was sad, her mouth thin, still. She had no voice, for she was mute, and when Dianne cried aloud at the sight of her it was clear that she did not hear, for she was deaf to all pleas.

The angel slipped into the room and stood facing the bed of the queen. She spread her wings, shaking the feathers, and then settled them back against her shoulderblades. She held out her hands, white and thin, toward the bed and beckoned. She beckoned again and then, hugging Dianne to her, she wrapped her wings about the queen. And was gone.

Left behind on the bed was the body of Englene's woodwitch queen. The old crone bent, and closed the lids of Dianne's dark brown eyes; and Nerthus found, to her surprise, that she was weeping.

Chapter 3

"My lady, my lady. Wake up." The rattle of the heavy rings on the velvet curtains around Elizabeth's bed woke her abruptly. The clatter of metal on wood was far louder than the voice of Jane Howard, senior lady-in-waiting of Elizabeth's entourage.

"Your Highness, your lady mother, the queen, is dead." Lady Jane stood beside the bed, a concerned expression on her sweet, gentle face.

Elizabeth sat up in bed amidst stacks of embroidered and gold-trimmed pillows. She pulled the goosedown coverlet up over her knees and sat staring thoughtfully ahead of her. "Well, she said she would, and it appears she meant it. Lady Jane, have any preparations been made? My lady mother said that her pall was prepared for her and that her gown was ready. I should like those things that she prepared for her own funeral to be used. It was her last wish that she be buried as a wood-witch."

"Well, and so she shall be. It's very good that she was so prepared, my lady. Your father has declared that there is to be but one week of mourning for the queen."

"One week! Why, a stillborn babe gets more. Even a dead cat—why, Father ordered two weeks mourning when the Lady Anne's familiar died. How could he? One week for my lady mother who loved him!" Elizabeth could feel tears gathering, and she hastily stifled them. She could not cry in front of the lady-in-waiting.

"It does make a difficulty in preparing your clothing, my lady. I shall have to fetch the Mistress of the Wardrobe and see if she has suitable mourning-weeds for you. You'll have to be in full dewle. I know that for you, nothing less will suffice."

Elizabeth stretched and prepared to unfasten her nightshift. Lady Jane assisted her. When the girl stood naked on the rush matting beside the bed, Lady Jane directed various junior ladies-in-waiting in the task of first washing, and then dressing the princess in her corset and fresh shift. Elizabeth accepted the black velvet blanchet that Lady Jane slipped around her shoulders, and then moved across the room to a stool in front of the looking glass so that Lady Margaret Sheffield could brush and dress her hair.

"I shan't be wearing black or full dewle for my mother. I shall wear green. She asked it of me. I'm sure that if you check with Lady Mary you'll find that there is a green gown already prepared for me. Mother was always thorough."

"Green! Green!" There was a stirring of exclamations from her ladies. "But you can't wear green!" "Green is a forbidden color in this court. It's the color of a woodwitch!"

"I shall wear green," Elizabeth said with cold determination. "Send for the Lady Mary Hamilton and ask if my mother set aside a green gown for me. And send word to the Princess Marguerite that I *must* see her as soon as she will come to me." Elizabeth sat waiting for the arrival of her aunt.

Lady Mary and Princess Marguerite arrived at almost the same time. Both wore full black dewle in mourning for the dead queen.

Marguerite, on being informed of what the fuss was about, said, "Of course the child will wear what she pleases. Queen

Dianne did request it of her. I was there, and stand witness. No one, not even the king, will dare to question the wishes of his dead queen."

"'Tis true." Lady Hamilton proceeded to the princess's side and hugged Elizabeth reassuringly. "Your lady mother has prepared a court gown for you in woodwitch green. I have it ready and shall bring it to you if you wish it."

Elizabeth acquiesced and Lady Hamilton left the room, her ivory and jet girdle clicking against the front of her black kirtle and gown as she moved.

The gown proved to be a thing of great beauty, the workmanship exquisite. It was also clear that the queen had ordered the dress some time before her death. The embroidery on the sleeves alone would have taken months. It was of a deep forest green in a tabby silk grogram. The point of the busk was deep, making Elizabeth's body look almost slender. The white cambric partlet was high-necked, with a touch of gold lace about the standing collar. The skirt belled over her hips covering the kirtle of bronze and gold, picked with pearls and silver cord.

Her mother had not provided a cap to go with the gown, so Lady Hamilton picked out a black-hooded touret with upper and lower biliments of gold and pearls. "'Tis fitting that you wear this, my lady.' Twill please your father to see some black about you." When Elizabeth saw that most of her ladies and Princess Marguerite agreed, she accepted the black touret.

She turned to face Lady Jane. "Hear me, and hear me well. This day you will empty my closet of all gowns that are not green. Give them to my ladies, or to any that might want them. From this day forth, on my vow to my mother, the queen, I will wear naught but green."

The ladies-in-waiting ran with light-hearted giggles toward the princess's clothespresses. The spoils would be well worth while, and many a young maiden knew that she would look far better in the princess's gorgeous gowns than Elizabeth herself.

"Lady Jane," Elizabeth said, "be sure to give that blue velvet dress I wore last night to Jackie. I think he wanted it for mumming, or to give to some succulent maid servant. Either way, I have no wish to ever see it again. Do not let any of my ladies wear it."

There was a scratching at the door and Lady Jane moved to open it. Jackie stood there, looking unlike himself save for his crooked body, because he was clad completely in black. There was not the slightest hint of the jester about him. His bauble and bells had been set aside, and he was Jackie Somers, mourner of the woodwitch queen.

"My lady, His Grace the King wishes to see you." Jackie's voice was as solemn as his apparel.

Elizabeth found her father in the lesser library with Thomas the Mage in attendance. King Richard had just finished ordering the russet gowns for the poor women of Lundene.

"Your daughter, Your Grace," Jackie said, leading Elizabeth forward.

Elizabeth swept into a deep curtsy, her head bowed, before her father. Through her lowered lashes she could see that *he* was dressed all in black.

The king looked down at his daughter and was startled. "Tell me, daughter, is what you are wearing proper for my court? I gave orders for full mourning, and what is this?"

"Forgive me, Your Grace, and give me your blessing," Elizabeth said in a low voice. "It was my mother's wish. My Lord, I made my lady mother a vow. I vowed that I would ever wear green in her memory. I beg you to let me honor it."

Richard bent and helped his daughter to her feet. He held her in his arms and said, "Of course, my child. Honor your mother as she would wish. I give you permission to wear green as long as you should want." Richard turned his head to make sure that Thomas had made note of the remark, then turned back to Elizabeth. "If you feel I have given less to your mother than you, with your vow, there is a good reason why I have ordered only one week of mourning. That reason is you. I would not have your eighteenth birthday marred by mourning."

"But my birthday is not till the seventh of September, and this is but the first of August. There is more than a month that the court might mourn!"

"It takes a great deal of preparation to honor a princess of Englene on her eighteenth birthday," Thomas said. "You must understand, my lady, that there is your initiation to prepare for, the birthday tourney, and your dedication in the shrine at Bathford to consider. If the court were in mourning it would cause a great deal of talk among the populace. They would come to think that we mourn your presence in the Circle rather than rejoice in it as we should."

"Very well, since it is my fault that it is but a week, I must accept it," she said with a sigh. "But I want to dedicate a bell to my mother, to hang in the Palace of Witchdame, and it will take time to have it made. I think a tenor bell, with the inscription 'Voce nea viva detello cuncta nociva' will do. Will you see to that, Thomas?"

"I shall, my lady. And 'The voice of this bell will expel evil spirits' is a fitting motto for such a good lady as our late queen. I promise that the bell will be made as you wish." Thomas bowed to the Princess Elizabeth and then to her father. "If you would forgive me, Your Grace, my lady Princess, I have much to do before this evening, when the queen is to be buried. So, if you will bid me farewell I shall be on my way." Thomas bowed himself out of the room, leaving the king of Englene with his daughter, alone.

Elizabeth found she had very little to say to her father. She shifted gawklike from foot to foot. "I suppose Mother will be buried in the crypt with all of the other kings and queens of Englene? She at least deserved that. . . ."

"Of course! She was a queen of Englene, crowned and anointed. Where else would she be buried?" Richard's tone was a shade too hearty. He, too, was ill at ease. He fingered his beard, then adjusted his cap. "Child—" He picked up his gloves and put them down. "Child, there is something I wish to tell you. You know that the Lady Anne and I have for some time been touched by Cupid's arrow. We would wed, but I promise you this: no princess born of the Lady Anne shall be made heir before you. That is the most I can do for you."

"I understand, Your Grace. I will lead no rebellion against your marriage to Lady Anne. But I will grieve if you do manage to get a son by her. I will not grieve for myself, but for my mother." She looked up at her father, tears in her eyes. "I bid leave to go, Your Grace. I too have many preparations to make."

The royal crypt beneath the shrine of Westmonasterium was dark and dank. Every available niche and cranny was filled with the perfectly preserved bodies of the royal witchlord dead—

kings, queens, princes, princesses, dukes, noble bastards—
stretching back in an unbroken line to 1066, first year of the
coming of the witchlords from over the sea.

Elizabeth had always thought of this crypt as The Royal
Waxworks—and with good cause, for not all the bodies were
in coffins. Because the preservation was so perfect, it was a
custom to place many of the dead monarchs in a standing
position, arrayed in their coronation robes. They looked star-
tlingly alive. Elizabeth had often been sent here as a child to
study her ancestors, and had not enjoyed her lessons. There
had been something rather fearsome about the glassy gaze of
her grandfather, Edward the Just, and great uncle, Henry the
Hopeless. Henry and Edward had been placed side by side,
their heads almost touching. Henry's face turned slightly towards Edward as though they were sharing some other-worldly
jest on their still-living descendents.

But there was one corpse in the royal waxworks that frightened the courtiers and the princess more than any other. It was
the perfectly preserved body of William Marshall, chief coun-
cillor to King James Woodwitchbane. King James had reigned
in the twelfth century, and it was said that he had been re-
sponsible for more deaths in Englene than any king before or
after. He was a man who delighted in savagery. His wife,
Eleanor of Aquitaine, had died in childbirth, and many said
she was quite glad to be rid of her king and her life. It had
been rumored that the child had not been that of the king, but
of the Chancellor William Marshall. King James had devised
a particularly evil revenge against his chancellor.

When the queen was buried in the royal crypt, William
Marshall was placed in a position of prayer beside her glass-
topped coffin. His eyes were open and on his face was an
expression of abject terror, for William Marshall had not been
dead when he was placed here in the royal crypt. His body had
been preserved perfectly for centuries, but it was still possible
that his soul remained inside the body.

Fortunately, Dianne's little crystal casket lay some distance
from that of the unfortunate Eleanor. The alcove that Richard,
or the Lady Pemberly, had selected for the little queen was
quite some distance from the rest of the royal family. It was
almost as though someone had chosen the darkest, most out-
of-the-way corner for Dianne—a small hollow, barely big

enough for the chief mourners: Elizabeth, Marguerite, and Richard.

The casket was placed on the black velvet-draped plinth and the gorgeously embroidered green pall pulled back to reveal the queen's face.

Elizabeth arranged her green skirts carefully in a pad under her knees. The Princess Marguerite knelt beside her and, as Marguerite arranged her skirts, Elizabeth saw a flash of green under her aunt's black fur-lined blanchet.

The king, pale and shaken, moved to the head of the coffin to view the face of his wife. Lady Pemberly hurried to squeeze in beside her king. Richard glanced at his dead queen and then looked at Anne, much as a child might seek some comfort from a nursemaid. "I . . . I didn't really think she'd die. I didn't really think it would happen this way. I—I—I—I feel odd, dizzy. I'm not sure what's wrong. Oh, my head does ache. I've not eaten all day. I've fasted since they brought me word of her death." A tear ran down the king's cheek and splashed on his black velvet tunic, leaving a watermark.

Anne hastened to hand him her silken handkerchief and pat him gently upon the shoulder. "There, there, my lord. Don't grieve too much, you'll make yourself ill." She looked over at the stone-faced Elizabeth and Marguerite. "He's not very well, you know," she explained to the two princesses. "He shouldn't be in such a damp place all night. It won't be good for him. And it can't be good for Englene if the king comes down with lung rot. I think it best that he return to the White Tower. *I* will order a hot posset for him, and a warming pan for his bed."

"You don't look well, Richard," Marguerite said thoughtfully. "Perhaps it would be best. . . . Dianne was always concerned about your health. I'm sure she would understand. Go, leave us. Elizabeth and I will do vigil for her mother."

Anne assisted the king to his feet and the two of them fled the tomb of Queen Dianne in almost obscene haste.

The night wore on slowly. Elizabeth found her knees cramping. She sighed and shifted her weight and looked at the tally candle to see how many hours might be left till dawn. "Marguerite, are you awake?" She had noticed that her aunt had been nodding for the past hour, and that the older woman's head had gotten lower and lower into her black stonemartin collar.

"Uh? What? Awake? Yes, of course I'm awake." Marguerite's voice was irritable and cracking with the lack of sleep. The older woman shifted her weight, revealing again that flash of green fabric beneath the skirts of her velvet blanchet and plain black bombazine gown. "I'm not used to this sort of thing, that's all. Old bones and stone floors don't go well together. But I do this for your mother and I do not begrudge it."

"I see you don't begrudge her a green petticoat, either. That is green I see under your gown, is it not?"

Marguerite pushed aside her black blanchet and lifted the hem of her mourning gown to reveal a green brocade kirtle. "I have the king's permission to wear it," Marguerite said. "Did you think that you were the only one at court who really loved her?"

"I think you and I were the only ones at court who ever did," Elizabeth said. "Oh, my father may have loved her once back in the dark dim ages of the past when he was young, and I think Jackie cared more for her than he cared to admit. But as for love, yes, it did come down to you and me."

"I loved her from the day I first saw her. And she returned that love. That, my child, you had better keep in mind for your own future. How many people did your mother love in return? You and I. And we are all she has to mark her passing."

"She did love my father."

"Did she really?" Marguerite looked at the face of the queen. "For all that I do not understand of the marriage between Dianne and Richard, there is one thing I can say: I doubt very much that she loved him. Whatever purpose there was in their marriage, on her side it was not love. I wish I knew what it was, so that I might understand why she was willing to go through the horrors of these past years. I suppose I shall never know."

Elizabeth sighed and bowed her head over her arms. It had never occurred to her to think that there might not have been love on her mother's side. Why else had her mother stayed at court and fought to survive the death spells of the witchlord courtiers?

Nearby, in the White Tower of the Palace of BrynGwyn of the Blessed Raven, the Lady Anne of Pemberly lay naked on the white satin sheets of the king's great bed. Richard, with a glad cry, took her in his arms, crushing her body to his. Then he groaned, his body tense with anticipation. They lay intertwined for a moment, hungrily clawing at each other, both awaiting the deep thrust into her body. The thrust did not come. She was aware of the king trembling. King Richard of Englene lay in her arms, sobbing.

"Dianne, Dianne!" he wept. "My little queen. I didn't realize how much you meant to me until you were gone. Oh, Dianne." He rolled off Anne's body, his manhood limp. He lay beside her and wept for his dead wife.

And in the royal crypt a strange smile appeared on the face of the dead Queen Dianne.

The queen's curse had come to pass.

Chapter 4

The rumor of the king's impotence spread swiftly through the court. There were many who felt a great deal of amusement at the efforts of Anne of Pemberly. In the opinion of many courtiers the woman had been giving herself airs prematurely. And should *she* not be able to give the king a child, there were many other ambitious ladies of the court more than willing to try their luck.

Lady Anne had ordered Thomas the Mage and the Archbishop Aleicester to meet with her in the Queen's Solar at BrynGwyn. Both men felt it wise to obey the summons; even though Anne's star was shaky, it had not yet fallen.

"Gentlemen," Lady Anne said, "I require your help. As you well know the king has been experiencing some obstruction of late. I wish your aid in putting an end to it." It was a difficult admission for the Lady Anne to make. She was everything a

king should find desirable, but Richard continued to weep for
his dead wife.

"I am not sure how we might assist you," Thomas said.
"The queen may have laid some sort of spell on the king before
she died. We found flower petals scattered about her room;
she was a very powerful woodwitch. How else could she have
stayed alive this long?"

"That's quite so, good Thomas," Aleicester said. "But the
petals were nothing more than potpourri. There was no glow
of magic to them. Our king may indeed be mourning his wife."

"Nonsense." Lady Anne turned to face the archbishop.
"Nonsense," she repeated. "Richard hadn't loved that little
scraggly bag of bones in years—if he ever loved her. *I* am the
one he loves. This is some summer sickness that has fallen
upon him. He has the physicians with him now and I'm sure
they will discover the cause. But I wish your help, gentlemen.
I more than wish it. I *demand* it."

Thomas the Mage turned away from the blonde beauty, who
stood shimmering like a gem in the sunlight from the casement
window. Stroking his chin thoughtfully, he commented, "I, for
one, do not think I can help you, my lady. If it is, as we
suppose, the spell of the woodwitch queen, there is nothing in
the Three Realms that can help you. The curse or blessing of
a dead woodwitch stands forever."

"They say you are of woodwitch blood," Anne said sharply,
"and your own words convince me it is so!"

"Nay, my lady." Thomas's voice was mild. "I have no
woodwitch blood that I know of—but then, since I know not
who my mother and father might be, anything is possible."

"Bastard!" Anne spat in rage. *"My son* will reign in Englene,
I swear it! Don't be a fool and take the wrong side in this
battle, lest you be destroyed."

"My lady, my lady, do not say that," the archbishop inter-
posed quickly. "King Richard has declared that the Princess
Elizabeth is his heir until the birth of a son. And until you have
such a son it is unwise to set yourself up as the Princess Elizabeth's or Thomas's adversary."

"The archbishop is right," Thomas said. "After the ceremonies at Bathford and Avebury that woman will have an
enormous amount of power—far more power than you would

care to go against. Should you choose to oppose her there will
be many who will oppose you, including myself. And you do
not want me for an enemy, Lady Pemberly." Thomas's voice
was fast losing its mild tone.

With little ineffectual wavings of his flabby hands, Aleicester attempted to soothe the two combatants. "Now, now, now,
Thomas. You lack diplomacy. The two of you are both too
important to Englene to quarrel. I would that you be friends."

"Now, as to your problem, my lady. I have taken the liberty
of formulating a spell for you which *will* make a man potent.
You mix coriander, jasmine, and violet which was picked in
the last quarter of the full moon. Combine it with a goodly
amount of honey and the full ashes of a weasel. Anoint the
big toe of his right foot, and sing of your love as you do so.
In addition, the water in which a myrtle leaf has been seeped
for two days is to be rubbed all over his body. And," the
archbishop added with a smile of conciliatory conspiracy, "bathe
in warm water in which several fistfuls of dried rosemary have
been added. Then you rub your naked body all over with powdered orris root. I assure you the spell is a sovereign remedy
for the impotence and we should be singing the praises of a
prince before the tenth month from this time comes nigh."

"I thank you, my lord Aleicester. You have been of great
service. I will do the spell, and we will indeed rejoice in the
birth of a prince." She shot a look of triumph at Thomas and
then swept out of the room, her back straight and head proud,
as if she already wore the crown of Englene.

"You shouldn't have done that, Aleicester," Thomas said.
"There is no way to break Dianne's spell."

"There could be if you would help. When can I get you to
understand that you must be polite and diplomatic to royalty?
Just because you were raised in a shrine does not mean you
cannot learn proper manners of a courtier. I despair of you,
Thomas. You will lose your head if that woman has her way."

Thomas laughed. "You have made a serious mistake, Aleicester, in assuming she will win. She won't. My head is safe;
but yours, my friend, yours may be in danger. If you must
favor this woman, do it with neutrality. Because, by all the
portents, Elizabeth will win."

* * *

Elizabeth admired her reflection in the glass and turned to get a better view of the train of the court gown she would wear at Bathford for her presentation to the populace—a dark green brocade with turned back velvet sleeves latticed in goldwork. According to her mother's wish she wore a high white partlet with a pearl-edged standing collar closed at her throat. Lady Jane stepped forward to fix the emerald and gold chain around her waist, while Jackie hurried to Elizabeth's side to hand her the flat velvet cap, thick with ostrich feathers, which completed the ensemble.

"I do like green," Elizabeth mused. "It's foolish that this color has been barred at court; it's very flattering, especially to someone with my overly pink skin. Look how fair I am! Oh, I am so pleased with it. Mother was right."

She turned so that Lady Jane and her other ladies-in-waiting could assist in removing the elegant gown from her broad shoulders. In a moment she stood only in her corset and shift, waiting for her riding habit to be put on her.

"But that dress is for Bathford," Jackie said. "What will you wear for the ceremony at Avebury? Come on, Elizabeth, you can tell me. Is clothing that big a secret?"

Elizabeth glanced over her shoulder to see that the ladies-in-waiting were out of hearing range. "No, but tradition says that you don't tell humans about this sort of thing. It's a white robe woven by virgins, of pure silk from Cathay. I'm not to wear it until we get to the Circle at Avebury, so I can't even try it on." She shivered, not from cold. "Jackie, there is one thing that worries me. At Avebury, well . . . do you know what the Great Rite is?"

Jackie leaned forward, his voice low. "Yes, I do. It's the most powerful conjuring up of magic by way of the sex act, isn't it?"

"Yes, it's that and more than that. It's the making of my future power, much as a man and a maid make a child between them. But you see, for the initiation of a witchdame of my rank it must be done by the king. . . . I am frightened, Jackie."

"Then, my lady," Menadel's voice sounded from the window bay behind the heavy brocade curtains, "you should have spoken to me." He came out from behind the curtains and confronted the princess. "You have no right to discuss it with the fool. It's against all tradition."

"I'm sorry, Menadel. I suppose I should have come to you—but because Jackie is human, it doesn't seem to matter too much what I say to him."

"Ah, that's me," Jackie said, "a useless little dust mote in the corner that anyone can talk to and it's of no concern whatsoever." He made a grotesque face. "We humans are the dust of the earth beneath a witchlord's foot. Talk away, my princess. I am nothing but your puppydog."

"No, now, Jackie, you know you're more than that to me, and well you know it!"

Jackie laughed and did a handspring across the room, then attempted to crawl under Nan Butler's skirts. Elizabeth's ladies twittered and giggled and tried to remove the jester from underneath the farthingale of their companion.

Elizabeth watched the scene with amusement. Then she turned to Menadel. "Jackie and I have always been very close. That's why I spoke as I did."

"It's all right, Your Grace. I quite understand." Menadel patted her arm. "And as for the other, you need not worry if you will do as I say. I will make sure that the man in the Circle is to your taste.

"Now, listen carefully. When you go to the Shrine of Sulis at Bathford and make your offering, you must stand before the high altar, turn to the four quadrant points and invoke the Watchtowers. Then you will have a man worthy of you in the Circle."

Elizabeth stared at the wizard. "What! Invoke the Watchtowers before I'm fully a witchdame? You know I can't do that until after the Great Rite at Avebury. It's not until the blue flame goes up that I'm entitled to do anything of that sort!"

"I say to you, if you want a worthy man, then you must invoke the Watchtowers before the high altar of Sulis." Menadel bowed low to her and her ladies and took his leave of them.

Elizabeth nodded thoughtfully and stood still while her ladies-in-waiting, still laughing, brought her dark green woolen riding habit and fitted it around her. Her voice was somewhat muffled by the fabric as they slipped it over her head. "Jackie, do stop teasing my ladies and come and sit here at my feet like a good fool. And, if you behave yourself, I'll take you hunting with me."

Jackie, eager for the chance to spend time in the company of his princess, hurried to do her bidding. "Shall you be going alone my lady—that is, alone with me? Or will we have others with us—Duke Charles, perhaps?"

Elizabeth started in surprise, a flush staining her cheeks. She ducked her head in embarrassment. "Well . . . he did say that he would like to talk with me this afternoon. And it would be so pleasant. He is such a handsome, well-formed man. I do feel attracted to him, Jackie, even if he is my cousin." Elizabeth's face was an unpleasant shade of scarlet. She was not a woman who blushed well.

"And it's obvious he likes you, too," Jackie said. "For the past week or so I've kept tripping over him everywhere you go. I hadn't noticed such devotion to you before. In fact, I had the impression that Charles considered himself such a lord of creation that he had not time to bandy words with a mere princess. Ah well, Cupid scatters his arrows broadside and cares not where they strike. Methinks the lad is too fond of himself and too high in his own opinion."

"Oh, but he *is* handsome. His hair is the color of molten copper. And those *enormous* blue eyes of his! And he's almost as good a fighter as I am. Perhaps . . ." She glanced at Jackie, who stood leaning against the brocade curtains, his eyebrows raised. "Oh well," she muttered. "If Menadel won't tell me who he has in mind for Avebury, I'll do the spell anyway and hope."

Jackie made loud kissing noises that were quite vulgar.

"Stop that, Jackie. What is it to you if I should choose a lord of my father's court? You're but a servant; you have no right to comment on such things."

At Jackie's dismayed expression, Elizabeth was swift to apologize. "I'm sorry. I didn't mean that the way it sounded. You must understand that I'm all in a twit over my birthday and initiation; there will be so many changes in my life. I notice that my father is having Mother's rooms in the West Tower at the Palace of Witchdame redecorated. He didn't need to go to that trouble for me. I liked them the way they were. Mother had excellent taste."

Jackie would not look at Elizabeth, and the cluster of ladies-in-waiting were shocked into silence by the princess's assumption that the queen's rooms were for her. *Poor poppet,* Jackie thought. *The king intends those rooms for the Lady Pemberly. Someone will have to tell her after she comes back from Avebury, but she'll not hear it from me....*

Chapter 5

The journey to Bathford Shrine was a wondrous revelation to the Princess Elizabeth. For the first time she saw the people of Englene come out to honor *her*. The farmers and villagers crowded the roads and lanes; they threw sprigs of rosemary and flowers at the passing caravan. At the sight of the princess, men and women uncovered their heads and cried out, "May the gods bless thy fair face!" It was an outpouring of love and devotion, and even though Elizabeth knew it was directed to Elizabeth the princess rather than to Elizabeth the individual, she found herself enjoying it immensely.

The city of Bathford seemed to have been scrubbed and polished for the visitation; it glimmered yellow-gold in the sunlight like fine old ivory. And from the encampment on Widcombe Hill, the king and his daughter had an excellent view of the river Avone and the city beyond.

Elizabeth smiled at her father and said, "I hadn't realized

how overwhelming it would all be, to have a ceremony that centers around me."

"There will be others, my child. Your wedding day. The naming of your first child. But let us not talk of the future. Come, let us celebrate today!"

Richard slipped his arm around his daughter's shoulders and turned her so they might walk back into the camp as sweetly close as lovers.

The camp was a gaudy array of brilliantly colored silk pavilions. The royal pavilion was of gold brocade and had a canvas roof decorated with astrological motifs. Several ships's masts had been lashed together to form the center support of the structure. Tapestries and carpets had been brought from the Palace of Witchdame to cover the floors and some of the walls, and they gave it the air of an authentic court. The furniture was all covered in red and blue silk and bright embroidery work and decorated with gold. There were two fountains in the courtyard which poured forth white and red wine for anyone who cared to drink.

Horses whinnied and tugged at their tethers. There was the sound of men at arms, and cooks, and scullions; the cry of minstrels and peddlars of all descriptions. There was the rich laughter of high-born ladies, and the shrieks of their serving wenches as the younger squires attempted to use the occasion as an excuse for a bit of pat-and-tickle. There was the smell of damp earth, smoke, and spiced meat; the odors of meals to be and meals already eaten.

"We feast shortly," the king said as he led his daughter to the royal pavilion, "and then you must sleep, alone, on open ground where the river sounds in your ears, and hope for a dream. And may the God Sulis send you a worthy one, my daughter."

The night passed slowly. Elizabeth thought she would never sleep. She tossed and turned on the unaccustomed hard ground and stretched her long body, trying to find a comfortable position. The night noises were odd. She found herself straining to identify them. There were crickets, field mice, and other small creatures all around her. The splash and gurgle of the river was restful, but Elizabeth's warrior's mind could not help but think how that sound might mask the footfalls of an assassin. She had not really considered, until that moment, the thought of an assassin. But the court had killed her mother. Those very people had every reason to wish her dead as well. They had not wanted a woodwitch queen, nor would they wish her halfbreed daughter. This initiation was the first step on Elizabeth's road to the throne—or the last.

She turned and tossed, searching for comfort. Without realizing it she slipped over the border from wakefulness to sleep. The river sounds faded away, the noises of the camp, the chirping of the crickets close by her ear, all was stillness and quiet.

She saw clouds, nacreous like the inside of a seashell; they rolled across the deep night sky like playful kittens on a black velvet coverlet.

She saw a golden staircase descending from the Ethereal Regions to the earth, and angels upon it walking upward and downward. She saw the archangels of the God Sulis. Michael, Raphael, Gabriel, and Uriel, and the other angels of the zodiac with them—then the greater and lesser angels as they came down the stairway toward her and turned and returned upward. One angel alone stood at the bottom of the stairs, looking at her. She knew he was a great and powerful angel, but could not identify him. He pointed upward and she watched as a glorious being clad in gold and white samite fell, shrieking, down the stairs. He fell past the waiting angel through the levels of the Earthly Regions, down into the Nether Region itself, and he took to himself a crown in that place.

The angel spoke. "It is Ashmedai. He who was greatest of the archangels. Now he is of the least. He reigns as King of the Nether Region. Fear him, as thy seed shall fear him but will conquer him, even though he is a being of great power. But heed this lesson: he reached for a kingdom in the Ethereal and gained only that which is lowest in the Universe. He has power but he shall not see the light again, and a child of light shall bring him woe. You will have power, great power. More power than any witchlord king before you or after you. But do not reach too high, my lady, or you too will fall. Remember Ashmedai."

The staircase, the angel, and the clouds vanished. There was only the darkness of the night around the sleeping princess.

* * *

In the morning it was Thomas the Mage who came to wake the Princess Elizabeth. "Did you sleep well, my lady?" he asked, and before she could answer he said, "Did you dream?"

Elizabeth stretched, easing the kinks in her body. "I did dream, Thomas, a strange and wondrous dream of angels coming up and down a golden staircase unto the earth." She told him the rest of the dream, and watched the wondering, amazed expression on his face.

"Were you aware, my lady, that the Mage Oliver had such a dream of angels climbing up and down from the Ethereal Region and as a result—in your grandfather's time, I believe— he built the Bathford Shrine in honor of the angels and the great God Sulis? There are shrines to each of the angels you named, even one to Ashmedai. It is below the crypt at the very base of the shrine. It is but his head and shoulders attempting to dig his way out of the Nether Regions; but he is imprisoned there in stone forever."

"That's fascinating!" Elizabeth stood and stretched again, catlike, reveling in the feel of the sun on the sheer nightshift she wore. "Did he also dream what the angel prophesied about my descendents?"

"No, my lady, that part of the dream was vouchsafed only to you. Cherish it. The maiden dream on the morning of initiation is very often prophetic. You should remember that when you are queen." He smiled and kissed her hand. "Come, it is time for you to be dressed and about. The city of Bathford awaits you."

As Thomas turned and walked away from her, she called out to him. "Thomas, wait! Please, good Thomas."

He turned to face her, waiting to hear what she would say.

"Mage, do you care for me? Not just as a princess, but as a person?"

"Of course, my lady. I have both loved and admired you since you were but a babe."

Elizabeth twined one lock of her fine red hair around her finger. She looked down at it, studying the way the sunlight brought out the gold in its curl. "Then tell me, who will it be that performs the Great Rite with me; who will wear the sun mask of Sulis?"

"Why, His Grace the King. It is his by right, and by custom."

"You and I both know that my father is not capable of the act. I have heard the tales that have gone 'round the palace since my mother's death—how, when faced with a woman, he is unmanned. Tell me, true Thomas, who will be in the mask?"

"By law it must be His Grace, the King, or an acceptable substitute. Since by custom it must be the complete Great Rite, then a substitute will be chosen. But I cannot tell you who will be under the mask. In the old days it was customary that the substitute be slain after such a ritual, much as we still kill a failed god-king. But now we merely cloak the man's identity in secrecy."

"I don't ask this out of mere curiosity, Thomas, or a green girl's lusty imaginings. I have a *good* reason. If my reason is of import, will you answer me?"

"I would have to think on it, my lady, but tell me your reason."

"I do not wish it to be the Archbishop Aleicester—his hands are cold and wet, and he smells of stale suet! If I perform the Great Rite with him the very foundations of my body will seal up and the act will not be completed; I am likely to be sick all over him, at the sight of his sluglike body naked next to mine."

Thomas stifled a laugh at the image of a naked Archbishop Aleicester. "I see your point, but should a substitute be chosen, it would probably be your father who would make such a decision. I will of course convey your feelings to him, but *not* in the archbishop's hearing! That's all I can promise, my lady."

Thomas walked off toward the path with the Princess Elizabeth following close behind him. As they reached the edge of the encampment, Thomas could see the princess's ladies hurrying toward them. He spoke softly, reminding himself of Aleicester's suggestion. "They say the Duke Charles is a well-favored youth, and handsome withal...."

Elizabeth smiled and went forward to greet her ladies.

Chapter 6

When Elizabeth tried to remember her initiation at the shrine of Bathford, she perceived it dimly through swirls of color and sound as if in a scrying mirror. There was the impression of the vivid clothing worn by the courtiers who packed the shrine, the heralds in their bright tabards, and the flower-bedecked altars glowing with hundreds of candles. She could remember hearing the voices of massed choirs and the thunder of trumpets. But of the actual procession down the nave she remembered very little.

Her long cloth-of-gold surcoat, embroidered with the arms of Englene and her mother's moon and rowan tree, was heavy and the embroidery scratched. She feared that the young page boys would not manage to carry the twenty-five-foot train, and that she would fall over backwards from the sheer weight of it. Her gold Moorish leather slippers were a size too big, and flopped alarmingly. All the way down the length of the shrine,

51

and as she proceeded around the alter kneeling, rising, and bowing to kiss the sun disk in the priest's hands, her only thought was, "Oh dear, what if I lose a slipper?"

She could remember only too well the story of King William the Unlucky, who, as a young boy at his coronation, lost one of his slippers. As a result, the land had supposedly been cursed by Sulis. The Northmen had attacked, the grain had been blighted for seven years, and William had eventually been murdered by his own wife. Not a pleasant tale, and, true or not, Elizabeth wanted to run no risk. Being half woodwitch was viewed by many as being curse enough.

The altar was packed thickly with the various archbishops, priestesses, and mages of Englene, their attendants, altarboys, maidens, and assistants; and each one, it seemed, had some part to play in the elaborate ritual. Elizabeth was guided here, directed there, exhorted, lauded, praised. She drank wine, she ate cakes. She had a laurel wreath placed upon her head and then removed.

The ceremony seemed to go on for hours and still there was much yet to come. She felt tired, hungry, thirsty, and she was getting a blister from those wretched slippers.

Finally the high point of this phase of the ceremony came. Elizabeth was led forward to where a bier had been placed in the center of the aisle. Andrew the Mage, Bishop of Eboric, and his wife Aunt Catheryne, the High Priestess, lifted her onto the bier and arranged her limbs as if for her burial. Thomas the Mage came forward and anointed her hands, breast, feet, and forehead with sweet oil. Then Archbishop Aleicester of Avebury, Bathford, and Wells placed over her body a black and gold pall. She was now dead to her youth and magical innocence.

Through the pall she could hear choristers singing and the chanting of the funeral services. It sounded muffled and distant, as though she indeed heard it from the grave. Then she felt the bier being lifted and she knew she was being carried down the nave to the cross aisle which led to the chantry chapel of the Goddess Diona.

It was very stuffy under the pall. She resisted the urge to sneeze. She listened to what she could hear of the funeral service out in the nave and knew that her childhood was gone. Then, with a slight bumping, the bier was placed in front of the altar of the Goddess Diona and she was left alone while the organ boomed through the shrine and the service continued.

This time of solitude was very important, for in the quiet and dark of her pseudotomb, her adult name would come to her, the name she would use in the Circle or to speak to the gods. Her name of names, that came from the Goddess. She waited listening, wondering if the Goddess herself would speak to her, or only a priestess. She waited for what seemed like a long time.

Then the air seemed to lighten around her, and suddenly it was no longer stuffy. The pall was gone. She found herself bathed with a golden light and the chapel all around her was too bright to see; both the altar and the image of the Goddess were hidden from sight. There was nothing but silence and light. Elizabeth lay very still and tried to control her gasping breaths.

Then there was a voice—soft, gentle, and very young. It spoke sweetly to her of spring and all green, growing things. And it said, "Eliora, Eliora, Eliora." The Goddess spoke with the sweet voice of the chapel bells, and then was silent.

The light faded away and Elizabeth was again under the pall in the dark. Eliora, she knew, meant "The Lord my light." It was a good name and a good choice, and one she knew she would be proud to carry.

She waited for the attendants to return for her; but to her surprise the chapel again began to glow with light—a brilliant white light, blinding in its intensity. Then a voice in the bells spoke, the voice of a mature woman, her voice thick with the knowledge of all things sexual, and she cried out, "Eirene, Eirene, Eirene, thou art peace to us," and the voice was that of the Goddess also. There was no doubt of that fact.

The light faded around her. Elizabeth lay there in shock. Two names? Was she to have two names? How so? Eirene sounded Norse. What could it mean, why had she been given a human name that she had no need of or use for? The light faded away while she pondered this question.

But before an answer came to her, the chapel again brightened with the vivid green clear light of the inside of an emerald. The chapel smelled of strawberries and pine trees and small streams. There in the clear green light Elizabeth saw an old woman standing beside her, and the old woman carried in one hand a chalice. She extended it to the princess. "Drink, child, it will do you good."

Elizabeth took the chalice and drained it. The fluid inside tasted of spring and honey, winter and ashes; it was sweet and bitter, salt and sour, but the princess drained it to the dregs.

The old woman took back the cup and said in the woodwitch tongue, "Thou art Erica, for thou art the eternal ruler of Englene. Thy seed shall rule Englene for ever and ever and ever as long as the universe endures. Thou art Englene." The bell rang out loud and long as the light faded and the pall settled in place.

The old woman was gone, and Elizabeth was alone in the chapel of the Goddess. But she had her names, all three of them—witchdame, human, and woodwitch—and she did not know the meaning of it all.

The archbishop and the High Priestess returned to the chapel and lifted the bier with the princess on it. They carried it out of the shrine and through the cheering crowd of humans outside to the sacred Great Bath of the God Aquaesulis. This was the sacred pool of the Old Elf-Kings who had been the first rulers of Englene. The Bath was rectangular, like a tilt field, and deep as a man's waist. The floor of the pool was covered in brilliant mosaics of turquoise, jasper, carnelian, and gold. Overhead the roof was open to the sky, so that Sulis could look down and approve the events that took place at his chief shrine.

Elizabeth was deposited beside the Great Bath. The pall was removed and Thomas stepped forward to unfasten the surcoat and remove it, revealing her white silk shift. Elizabeth lay unmoving on the bier as Thomas picked her up in his arms and strode into the Great Bath. He lowered her into the warm water until every inch of her body was covered, held her there for a count of nine, and then stepped back as Elizabeth, like one come up from the grave, rose out of the water unaided by any but the God. Dripping wet, she returned to the edge of the bath where one by one the priestesses, archbishops, and high mages of Englene came forward to kiss the hand of a shivering, soggy woman half naked in a wet dress.

Then, with the sound of much rejoicing, she was taken to a small chamber where her ladies, chirping and chattering like so many peacocks, fell upon her to dry her, strip off the shift, and put on the green court gown that she had chosen for this ceremony. But as Lady Jane brought forward the sleeves to the dress, Elizabeth saw to her surprise that they were queen's sleeves sweeping down to the floor, their lining heavy with gold braid and pearls.

"What is this, Lady Jane? Who gave me leave to wear queen's sleeves?" Elizabeth reached out to finger the rich material.

" 'Twas your mother's wish, my child." Richard came out from behind a screen, laughing at his daughter's startled exclamation at finding her father there. "Take this, my gift to you on your first day of womanhood. You and you alone of all the women of Englene are entitled to wear the sleeves of the queen." He bent to kiss her gently on the mouth and she, with great joyousness, accepted his blessing and the sleeves.

Fully robed, she came out into the colonnade of the Great Bath where the courtiers waited, their cheering and applause silenced as they saw her fully clothed in the green brocade gown with the queen's sleeves she was now entitled to wear. With Thomas on one side and her father on the other she walked around the rim of the pool deosil to the cave of the underground spring, source of the water of Aquaesulis. The cave and spring were protected by a fence of black iron and bronze. Elizabeth leaned against the barrier and looked down into the rust red heart of Aquaesulis. The water sprang upward, wetting the hem of her gown, but she saw it as Sulis's blessing and was content.

Archbishop Aleicester stepped forward and handed her a small lead tablet and an etching tool. The tablet was to be inscribed with some wish and then tossed into the spring along with such childhood trinkets as would make an acceptable sacrifice to the God. It was well known that any wish made on initiation day came to pass. Therefore it was best to ask carefully, for there was no worse curse than an answered prayer.

Elizabeth knew what it was she wished for. Writing quickly she inscribed the tablet, "May the man I want and need be with me in the Circle tonight." Then, clutching the tablet to her heart and thinking unsacred thoughts of Duke Charles, she moved forward to the mouth of the spring and, after being blessed by Aleicester, she threw the tablet into the water. Then, one by one, she made sacrifice of her childhood jewelry and toys. Aleicester then led her through the small gateway from the spring and through the Bishop's Garden, back into the shrine of Bathford. There before the high altar he proclaimed her "Royal Maiden of the Circle" and full witchdame of Englene.

Remembering Menadel's command to her to do a premature circle spell to get the man she wanted for the initiation, she then faced the altar, bowed and, before the full multitude, began the rite of evoking the lords of the Watchtowers. Using only her naked hand, she traced a nine foot circle of blue fire upon the floor and then, facing northward, she chanted the invocation to the first Watchtower:

> *Northward stand I.*
> *My favors I pray.*
> *Grant them me, mighty prince of light.*
> *I pray thee, holy keeper Uriel.*
> *Up to the Ethereal Regions I pray,*
> *And down to thy Earthly Regions, I call thee!*

She then turned eastward and chanted:

> *Eastward stand I.*
> *Thy favors I pray.*
> *Grant them me, mighty prince of light.*
> *I pray thee, holy keeper Raphael.*
> *Up to the Ethereal Regions I pray,*
> *Bow down to the Earthly Regions, I call thee!*

She then turned slowly southward:

> *Southward stand I.*
> *Favor me, I pray.*
> *Grant them to me, mighty prince of light.*
> *I pray thee, holy keeper Michael.*
> *Up to the Ethereal Regions I pray,*
> *Unto the Earthly Regions, I call thee!*

And finally she turned to the west:

> *Westward stand I.*
> *For thy favors I pray.*

Grant them me, mighty prince of light.
I pray thee, holy keeper Gabriel.
Up to the Ethereal Regions I pray,
Come down to the Earthly Regions, I call thee!

A cone of blue light formed, pointing upward to vanish into the Ethereal Regions. There was silence in the shrine, a waiting. Then there was one clear, bell-like note, the circle of light faded, and Elizabeth stood bathed in a bar of sunlight in front of the high altar.

Archbishop Aleicester and Thomas the Mage both dashed forward and almost collided. Aleicester was gibbering and Thomas hissed to Elizabeth, "Why did you do that? It is not part of the ceremony."

Elizabeth lifted her head and spoke calmly to Thomas. "Menadel told me to do it."

And Thomas, to her surprise, made no comment, but simply bowed his head in acceptance. The Archbishop Aleicester picked up the threads of the ceremony and continued on as though the invocation of the Watchtowers had been meant to happen. The crowd of nobles in the shrine relaxed and soon flowed into the responses and prayers at the end of this portion of the initiation.

Now all that remained was the journey by torchlight to the Great Circle of Avebury, and Elizabeth's final consecration with the Great Rite.

The great stone circle at Avebury covered more acres than Elizabeth had years, and was one of the most sacred spots in all of Englene. It was believed that the universe had begun at the sacred circle of Avebury, and that the giant obelisk might possibly be the plug that kept the known world from vanishing into the chaos from which it was created.

Inside the great stone circle there were two smaller circles, to the north and the south. The north circle had, through time and custom, been dedicated to the initiation of the male. To the south was the female circle, and in its center stood that stone obelisk called "the Navel of the Earth." A temporary wicker and post hut had been built around the obelisk. It was the sacred place in which Elizabeth, heir to Englene, would be initiated in the blue fire of the Great Rite.

In the encampment on Sanctuary Hill, the procession for the initiation readied itself. There was no moon, but none was needed. There were thousands of torches and leaping bonfires lighting up the chalk plains until the whole area shone like the light of the day sky.

There were, as is the case with all ceremonies involving large numbers of people, the usual delays and personal problems: a court lady, annoyed over a question of precedence, complained bitterly to all around her; a small page who was missing was sought and found; and a horse who proved to be too fractious to use was exchanged for another. But slowly and carefully, the procession was formed.

The priestesses, swinging censers and scattering rose petals, came at last down the Kennet avenue. Then came the choristers singing sweetly of the joys of initiation. Then the courtiers chattering and laughing among themselves. Along the great avenue the musicians played trumpets and drums, sackbuts and harps. Bringing up the end of the great procession came Thomas the Mage, Chancellor of Englene; Archbishop Aleicester, Bishop of Bathford, Avebury, and Wells; and Catheryne, High Priestess of the Circle.

The courtiers ranged themselves in the area of the southern circle. Catheryne, Thomas, and Aleicester stationed themselves beside the door to the obelisk hut and then, to a fanfare of trumpets, the Princess Elizabeth and her ladies came down the great avenue. As she passed each pair of stones a trumpet sounded; one hundred times the sound filled the plain of Avebury.

Elizabeth shivered in the cold night air. She was clad only in the sacred garment, a loose white samite houpelande with a dark blue knotted cord tied around her waist. She stood at the door of the hut and asked first Catheryne, then Aleicester, and finally Thomas if she might enter, and they in turn replied, "Blessed is she that comes from the south, enter thou here." Elizabeth entered the wicker and post hut and stood with her back against the obelisk stone.

The stone was still warm from the sun and the heat felt very pleasant to Elizabeth. She tucked her bare feet deep into the rich altar cloths covering the floor and waited with apprehension for what must be done in this place. By the flickering torches she could see a screen on one side of the obelisk stone, and supposed it might be used to help in the substitution of the god-king. She could hear her father's footsteps at the lintel of the door and the ritual greeting and welcoming by Catheryne, Aleicester, and Thomas. She straightened, knowing the time had come.

There was a small clump of oak trees at the edge of the great Kennet avenue where the avenue joined the south circle. Two people stood in the shadows of the trees: the old woman Nerthus and a tall, elegantly made blond man.

"The king is entering the avenue," Nerthus said. "The time has come. Are you ready, my lord Michael?"

The Archangel Michael adjusted his gold silk houpeland appliqued with flames. He held in his hands the mask of the godking. "Yes," he said, "I am ready, but I wish it were not so. I wish she had not summoned me by way of the Watch-towers. Angels have no part in the ways of witchlords, wood-witches, and humans. The temptations of the daughters of man are strong for those of us who are sons of the Ethereal, and I fear that in time I may become too fond of her to leave."

"You'll not leave as long as she lives. She will own you, Michael, and you will be her slave. You and, in time, all the others of the Watchtowers. But you, the chief of the archangels, will be hers."

"I might be hers, and I know Gabriel and Uriel are with me, but I fear that Raphael grows restive. He's been in the power of this family for many a year. Can we be sure he will join our cabal?"

"He *must!*" Nerthus exclaimed. "How dare he think that he can damage my pattern? Does he want to be the next angel to fall from the Ethereal Regions? But to be sure of him, I will have Menadel tell her to do a deed of power in Raphael's lands, and that will give her control over him. So mote it be!"

Michael adjusted the golden mask over his face, muffling his voice as he echoed, "So mote it be."

Then he moved out of the shadow of the trees and onto the great avenue to serve as a substitute for the godking, Richard.

He stood in the doorway, tall and majestic, his face com-pletely hidden by a gilded sunburst mask of the great God Sulis. He was clad in a houpelande of yellow silk, dagged and appliqued with the leaping red and orange flames of the sun. The houpelande was cut open to his crotch and a few blond curls of pubic hair slipped over the top of the fabric. Embroidered in gold at the base of the open slit was the sunburst of Sulis marking the place where the root of immortality lay.

He moved into the room and stood a few feet from her. She could smell attar of roses and sweat. Catheryne, Thomas, and Aleicester entered the room and took their positions at the obelisk and on each side of the door. Aleicester lowered the pure white linen covering over the door and stood waiting.

Both men expected the king to slip behind the screen and then the king's substitute to reappear to perform the Great Rite, but this did not happen. The figure in the gold Sulis mask began casting the holy Circle, calling upon the Watchtowers and, when he finished, turned to face Elizabeth. He slipped the cord from around her waist and then removed her silken gown so that she stood naked before him. He reached down and adjusted his garments so that his own erect male member stood outside the clothing. He took her in his arms and gently lowered her to the altar cloths. He positioned her along a north-south axis with her head to the north and then waited while the High Priestess stepped forward to hand him a bowl of anointing oil.

Accepting the bowl, he began anointing every inch of Elizabeth's body with the ambergris and musk scented olive oil. His fingers left fiery trails as he anointed her, and when he had finished she was fully ready to receive him.

Spreading the houpelande over the both of them, he positioned himself in the traditional uniting of male and female principle, and all was ready for the final act of the Great Rite.

Elizabeth felt great joy pierce her body. A joy that spread through her until body and soul exploded with it. Again and again and again, the explosion continued to send out great waves of blue fire which filled first the hut, then the outer southern circle, then finally the Great Circle of Avebury itself until, with a great burst of his release and hers together, blue Aurorae Borealis danced on the hills of Englene and the skies over the entire kingdom flashed with blue lightning that could be seen far out to sea and from the distant hills of La Bonne Terre.

And as Elizabeth felt her body reverberate with the power of the Great Rite, filling her with its power as it filled Englene, she knew without a shadow of a doubt that the man in her arms was not her father. Whoever he was, there was power in him, and gentleness. Desire welled up in her and, as she embraced him, her hands clasping his muscular body to her own, she knew she must have him as her consort.

By the door, Thomas and Aleicester stared into each other's wondering eyes, while the High Priestess prayed aloud to the Goddess in thankful puzzlement. The man who performed the rite was *not* Duke Charles. But how could it be the king? Had the Goddess given him back his powers, and for how long would it last? They were sore troubled, and each knew that the subject would need much discussion on the journey back to the capital city of Lundene.

Chapter 7

The birthday procession of the Princess Elizabeth clattered triumphantly through Southwarke and turned onto the Lundene Bridge, bordered with large, magpie-timbered houses, spanning the river Theames. Windows and archways were hung with red and blue tapestries and carpets; the crowd, thick and smelly, waited anxiously to see the princess, the king, and other notables. The journey through Lundene took hours, but Elizabeth's smile never varied. She waved at the crowd and enjoyed herself. This was her city and her "good people." At the gateway to the Palace of BrynGwyn, she and her father dismounted and arm in arm walked into the large forbidding fortress.

Inside the White Tower in the center of the fortress, all was a state of bustle and organized chaos. Servants ran to and fro with bed linens, table covers, mazer-cups, bowls, and candlesticks; from the kitchens the odor of goose, swan, beef, and pork could be smelled perfuming the air; and from the chapel on the second floor there was a sweet sound of singing boys, practicing for the banquet that would follow the feast that night.

While the bustle continued, gossip could be exchanged. Those who had gone out to the great plain of Avebury could tell others what they had seen. The great blue flames, the fires dancing on the hills, and the amount of power that had been raised in the Circle by their princess were all topics of awed conversation. Of course, along with such discussions of the event, there was a great deal of speculation. Who had it been in the Circle with the princess? Who had been the man to raise such glory that it could be seen all over Englene? And was it really King Richard, his powers restored? It was amazing how swiftly the information managed to spread to every corridor and room that it had *not* been Duke Charles, nor had it been the Archbishop Aleicester or Thomas the Mage. The gossip took a decidedly vicious turn as they considered the failure of the Lady Pemberly to arouse the king's male member to action, and Elizabeth's obvious ease with *whoever* it had been with her. There was a certain amount of snickering in chimney corners, laughter behind bed curtains, all of it directed at Lady Anne of Pemberly.

Lady Anne was not amused. She fumed in her bedchamber—a bedchamber that had once been Queen Dianne's. Not only had the lady managed to acquire the royal bedchamber in the Palace of Witchdame, but she had also usurped the royal bedchambers at the Palace of Windleshore, the Palace of Eltham, the Palace of John the Mage, the Palace of Westmonasterium, and now the hallowed chambers of the Queen Elenora Regina at the White Tower of BrynGwyn itself.

Lady Anne directed her maidservants in the placing of her possessions, her voice sharp and hard-edged. "And when you finish here, bring me the royal seamstresses and what's left in Queen Dianne's clothespresses. I will have a dress made. A green dress. Perhaps it's the color green that attracts the king and only *that* arouses him. Well, if that be the case and the gown gives him power, we'll take down all this blue and may my bed be hung with green, may my sheets be green satin, and my nightgowns of deepest green. I *will* have a prince!"

Her ladies hurried to do her bidding. With the Lady Pemberly in that sort of mood, it was not wise to be slow or laggard in one's duties.

The king had heard the rumors that had spread through his court concerning his lack of prowess, and had been deeply disturbed by them. And since he could not deny the report, his fate rested solely on his privy member's abilities to rise to the occasion. The fertility of the king meant the fertility of the country, and a king with loss of vigor could find himself swiftly sacrificed to the Goddess at the Heartwood come next high summer. So the reports of Avebury Circle, even though he had no actual memory of it, were both comforting and of great appeal to his ego. If he had been so potent with this daughter of his, perhaps he would be equally potent with other women. He considered the possibility that failure with Lady Anne had been due to some fault of hers. She had, he admitted, been a virgin save for her initiation, and lacking in skills and ability. Perhaps he would welcome to his bed some Syrian dancing girl or a sleek-bodied Moor. He considered this possibility with lecherous delight and ordered the menservants of his chamber to procure some woman skilled in the 999 ways of pleasure in bed. He, Richard, was not ready to go to the Goddess yet!

The princess's bedroom was still at last. She had managed to rid herself of her chattering ladies-in-waiting by the simple ruse of pleading a headache.

She sat up in bed, pushing aside the heavy down comforter. Elizabeth smoothed her nightshift over her legs and, pushing her pillows about, created a nest for herself. Her back was against the ornately carved bedstead which proclaimed to all the world her royal descent from all the kings and queens of Englene by means of a plethora of coats of arms and assorted mottos. It was not a comfortable thing to lean against.

It was the same room she had inhabited at BrynGwyn Tower since her childhood. The fact that her mother's rooms had been given to Lady Anne gnawed at her vitals like a hungry fox. How could her father have done it? How could he have given that woman Dianne's rooms? By rights they belonged to her, Elizabeth. She had not entered the queen's chambers at any of the royal palaces since finding out that they had been given to Lady Anne. She couldn't bear to see the changes the woman might have made in Dianne's green bowers.

She knew from comments by her ladies-in-waiting that all the green had been banished from them. Lady Jane and Nan had managed to salvage a number of the queen's green possessions and were integrating them one by one into the princess's rooms. Elizabeth stroked her embroidered green silk comforter and knew she had cause to be grateful to Jane and Nan, and their love for her. Even with the difficulties and expense of obtaining new cloth, Lady Anne, had she been given her way, would have ordered all the hangings burned.

There was, too, her other problem—the one she had been gloating about for the past few days. Now she pulled it out like the last gift saved because it was biggest and best: that wonderful, exciting time of passion in the Great Circle at Avebury. Elizabeth could not help smiling. It had been glorious. She had never known that the physical coming together of a man and woman could be so splendid. Of course, one problem nagged at her like a sore tooth: Who was the man?

She knew it was not her father; regretfully, she dismissed the idea of Duke Charles. One by one she considered the possible men at court, and one by one dismissed them also. The mystery remained a mystery.

Elizabeth supposed that there must be someone at court who could tell her the name of her unknown lover. Someone had to have planned the substitution at Avebury—and of course the man himself would know. But *who* was he?

There was a gentle scratching at the secret door beside the fireplace. Elizabeth smiled, knowing full well who it was on the other side of the door, and she was sure that of all men at the court it could be guaranteed that Jackie Somers had not been the one in the Circle.

Getting out of bed, she padded barefoot across the rush mat covered floor and pressed the embossed rose beside the fireplace, then waited while the secret panel swung open. The passage had been built centuries before by a princess famous for her sexual appetites. Remembering that princess, Elizabeth laughed as Jackie, covered with cobwebs, slipped into the room.

Jackie dusted himself off and look around, taking in the green embroidered cushions on the chairs, the green hangings on the bed, and the green counterpane. "By the Gods, I've got the wrong room! I was looking for the bedroom of the princess of Englene, and instead I've stumbled into a woodwitch's bower. Does the king know of this?"

"He does and he has given me permission. Of course I would have preferred all these things to have remained where they were, but the Pemberly had other ideas." Elizabeth turned and walked back to the bed. She climbed in under her coverlet and pulled the sandalwood scented fabric up to her chin.

Jackie wandered over to the bed and stood beside it for a moment, then leaped into the middle, just missing Elizabeth's legs. When he came up from the welter of blankets and pillows he said, "She's done your mother's rooms up in particularly voluptuous shades of blue. Why *will* that woman try to make a cult of color? Only a woodwitch can do it well, you know. They say the Pemberly is planning to do them up again in green, but *that* will not make her queen or give her a son!" Jackie made a particularly hideous gargoyle face and wrapped his head in his arms. "A lot of good blue or green's going to do her! Even if she has all her sheets made of silk scented with musk and mandrake root, it's not going to make the king any more ready than he was before." Jackie untangled himself from his gargoyle position and stretched out full length on the bed. "Tell me, Elizabeth my love, just what did you do in that Circle to get your father's member so straightly up? From the rumors I hear, no mating in Englene has ever been like it. They say you scorched earth for miles about. I'm very impressed."

Elizabeth blushed a deep crimson. "I—I—I don't know. It just happened. But I will tell you this. The man with me was not my father." She sighed. "I have never known that mating could be such a joyous thing. I *must* find out who he was." She looked at Jackie appealingly. "Jackie, do you think . . . ?"

"No, I don't and I won't. If you think for one moment, poppet, that I'm going to go snooping about the court and lead in some bashful witchlord for your wallowing in bed, you've got wool for brains. My duties don't extend to that sort of thing." Jackie's voice was hard-edged. "Your problem is that you haven't been frolicking with the right sort of man. Who did get your virginity, some ham-handed stableboy or pimply page?"

Elizabeth laughed. "My! You've developed an acid tongue in your old age. I was just requesting some help of you. Besides, my interest in this man is completely innocent. I want to find out who he is so that I can ask my father for him as a husband. He did *delight* me so!"

Jackie made a rude noise. "I suppose if I stay here, I shall have to listen to you blithering on and on about the marvels of this randy witchlord all night. Did he have any intelligence, any wit and charm, or did you manage to consider anything above his waistline for more than one moment? As princess of Englene, if you want a bed partner you can choose anyone, but a husband—a husband is another matter. Bedding takes up so little time of a marriage that if the man doesn't have wit, outside of bed he'll drive you to yawns in bed before long. And as heir to the throne you must marry and beget heirs, a subject that often becomes very tedious. When you bring other considerations into the bed like the getting of children, a great deal of pleasure flies out of it, and that's why I shall continue on my way from bed to bed to bed without the slightest concern about marriage or heirs."

Elizabeth picked up one of her bedpillows and threw it at the fool. Jackie caught the pillow and returned the fire. Within minutes a boisterous pillow fight was in full battle formation.

The uproar in the princess's bedroom came to abrupt silence with the sound of sharp knocking at the heavy oaken door.

"Shhh," Elizabeth said, one finger to her lips. "Let me see if I can manage an opening spell. I've been wanting to try out some more of my skills."

She abruptly cleared away the bedclothes, leaving a bare space on the white linen sheets. Muttering, she began to trace with her forefinger the circles, triangles, and squares of the sigil for the standard door opening spell. At its completion there was a satisfying click of the doorlatch and the sound of the door swinging open.

"Ugh! This room stinks of magic." Menadel stepped through the doorway and closed the door behind him. He walked over to the bed and stood studying the princess's work. "Very good, very good indeed, but didn't I teach you to tidy up after yourself?" He passed his hand over the sheet and the runes and sigil disappeared.

"Speaking of magic, Menadel," Elizabeth said, "there was something I wanted to discuss with you."

"Oh no. Am I going to have to listen to more blithering about that besotted witchlord at Avebury? Please spare me, poppet, or I shall be sick here and now on your best Turkey carpet," Jackie said, heading toward the secret door. "If you stay around, old man, you'll have to listen to a lot of lovesick maiden's gibber on the delights of sex. You'd think the poor girl had been virgin when she went to Avebury! It's amazing how the sight of a virile male member will send some women mad." Jackie paused by the door to the secret passage. "I shan't be back, poppet, until you find a more interesting topic of conversation." With that parting shot he disappeared into the passage, and the door slid shut behind him.

"That was disgraceful," Menadel said. "Jackie's tongue will run away with him one of these days, and lead him straight to the block. I'm surprised your father gives him so much leeway. He should not have been discussing Avebury, and you should not have countenanced such a discussion—and don't tell *me* it's only Jackie! He's a human, and he's too clever by half; there are times when I distrust him greatly. Particularly when I find him ensconced in your bed."

Elizabeth shook her head and laughed. "Oh Uncle, if you had been here a few minutes earlier, you would have seen what we were doing. It was naught but a pillow fight! Certainly you don't think there's anything between Jackie and me, do you? Though, I must admit he did get terribly jealous when I was discussing the sacred Circle at Avebury. Or rather, not so much the Circle, but the man in it. Who was he, Menadel? Please, please, *do* tell me." Elizabeth placed her hands together and looked sweetly supplicating at Menadel.

Menadel sat down on the end of the bed, his finger idly tracing a few runes of his own. "That's something I can't tell you right now. I tell you this, though: It was no man of this court in the Circle, so you needn't go inviting them, one by one, into your bed to find out." He raised one hand to forestall the eager questions he could see forming on her lips. "No now, I won't tell you his name, but I will say this. He is a man ideally suited to you. He is the man that all Englene will consider suitable for you and fit to be the father of your children. I would see you bed with no other ever—but that is impractical, so I'll not demand it."

"If you won't tell who it was in the Circle, will you tell me how I can find him? Please, please, if you love me you'll tell me. I shall *die* if I don't have him!"

"Don't excite yourself. Jackie was right, there is something extremely tedious about the blithering of a young girl with love sickness. All right, all right, if you'll stop being a bore on the subject I'll tell you how to get him. Now listen carefully. The kingdom of Englene will be yours one day. It is traditional when one is given a piece of property to make it one's own by magic. This is done by way of the property walk."

Menadel's voice slipped easily into his pedagogue tone. "Now what you will have to do is, going deosil, you must visit each of the four quadrants of Englene, and in each of them *you* must perform an act of magic by your own power. Then you must go and fulfill your vow in the Heartwoods. This last is very important. You must have no unpaid vows or debts, or the spell will not work."

Elizabeth shivered a bit at the mention of the Heartwoods, the most mysterious place in all Englene. It was older far than the witchlords. It was older even than the woodwitch rulers or the Elf-Kings, dating back to the very dawn of time.

"Why the Heartwoods? I know my mother wanted me to go to Nerthus someday, but not until I'm queen—until I must go at the time of sacrifice! I fear it. I fear what might happen to me in that place."

Elizabeth shivered again, and drew the covers back around her body, pulling them tighter and tighter until only her nose showed in the swaddling of green. "I've dreamed that if I ever go into the Heartwoods I shall not be allowed to come out again the same person that I am now."

"You *will* do the property walk and you *will* go to the Heartwoods, or I promise you will live to be old and unhappy and barren. There is no other way."

Elizabeth poked her head out of her green cocoon and considered what the wizard had said. She considered it very carefully. She thought of Avebury and that virile young man who had been with her there. "I'll do it," she said fiercely. "For him it's worth it."

Menadel laughed and shook his head. He glanced at the runes he had idly scribbled on the bed, corrected one line and looked at them again. "Never underestimate the lustiness of a lovesick maiden," he said, passing a hand over the runes. "Of course, a persuasion spell doesn't hurt anything. . . ."

"You old trickster! Do you realize what you could have

done? I know how often your magic is apt to go agley. Menadel, you could have changed me into something loathsome! Don't do any of your spells on me ever again. That frightens me even more than the Heartwoods. Now, tell me about these rituals I'm supposed to perform at each of the four quadrant points."

Menadel smoothed his red fluff of a beard. "I can't be sure what form they'll take. I would tend to believe that the best method would be to see what rituals come to mind at each of the four cardinal points, a sort of impromptu magic." He glanced at the princess. "So! We will just see what happens at each of the cardinal points and follow where our inclination leads us. Very good."

"We? Did I hear you mention 'we,' or were you using that in the royal sense?"

"Oh, I intend to go with you. I'm not going to allow a child as innocent of the real world as you are to go forth alone. Of course there is the problem that a property walk is generally done nude. I don't think that's practical. It will take us some months to make this journey, and having you travel nude for such a time would be very uncomfortable. I suppose we can dispense with the nudity. Yes, the property walk is the important part. . . ." Menadel's words drifted away to a vague mumble as he considered the problem of his princess traveling nude around Englene.

Elizabeth simply rolled about on her bed and laughed. "Oh Menadel, Menadel. Nude!" She went off in a gale of giggles which ended with hiccuping little gasps. "Oh! Think of the sunburn I would get, and how chapped I would be. Lady Jane would never forgive me after all the almond oil and lemon she's rubbed into this terribly freckled skin of mine. Oh dear no, it's not to be considered. If the property walk will work without nudity, fine. But as for it being just you and me traveling abroad, I'm not sure that I approve of the idea. I'll need at least a lady-in-waiting to help me dress, and a journey of that nature will take several pack ponies for my clothing boxes and my good bedstead, my eating knife, spoon, ewer, and goblet, my harp, and rugs, bedding, and hangings, too—and of course a stable boy to tend White Surrey. Oh no, I couldn't possibly go alone, or even alone with you! Think of the scandal. The princess of Englene does not travel all over the countryside attended only by a wizard."

"But it must be done that way, and not just because of the spell. Think of the question of your safety. One young half woodwitch princess would be far safer alone with me in Englene than in the company of half the court. I would not put it past the Lady Pemberly to add an assassin to your train. No, it must be you and I, no others."

Elizabeth considered what the wizard had said and found herself reluctantly agreeing. It would be just like the Pemberly to decide that it was an excellent opportunity to rid herself of the princess. A little accident, a fall from a horse or a bit of bad eel eaten at dinner; it would take very little to rid Richard of his only heir.

Yes, Menadel was right. The journey must be for the two of them and no more. "All right," she said reluctantly. "I will ask my father if I may go forth on a quest; I'm sure he will agree to it. Then I'll leave him a note saying that I thought it best to slip away and perform mighty deeds unaided, like a great mage. But I do wish I could have at least one lady-in-waiting with me...."

Chapter 8

King Richard paced his privy chamber waiting for Thomas the Mage to come to him.

The message he had received that morning from the Palace of Witchdame disturbed him. The messenger had ridden hastily from the palace to Lundene to inform his king that the Queen-dowager Renee of Gaeland and her son had arrived to join in the festivities of the princess's birthday. But Queen Renee had not asked for permission to enter her brother-in-law's realm as the law required. Knowing Renee, Richard was sure she had felt no need to ask his or anyone's permission.

The thought of Renee of La Bonne Terre ached in Richard's head like a sore tooth. He always felt guilty in her presence, a feeling she did her best to use to her advantage. Princess Renee had been promised to him in childhood. It was she who should have been queen of Englene but Richard, in that first flush of delight at being king of Englene and free to give his heart where he would, had married the woodwitch Dianne. As a sop to Renee's feelings, he had married her off to his twin brother, King Robert of Gaeland. He had tried ever since to soothe his conscience with the thought that had it not been for the decision of their father to divide the kingdom between his two sons, Robert would not even have been a king. He would have been naught but a younger brother, no more, no less. And he, Richard, had been more than beneficent in allowing his father's will to stand after taking the throne at Edward's death.

Of course, the fact that Robert had been given the kingdom by word of Edward the Just, and Edward had in his lifetime made a great border of blue flame between the two countries, was something that could be conveniently forgotten. Renee was Queen-dowager by Richard's blessing, and she *must* not forget that fact. But now she and her son were on their way to his capital city.

He considered the possibilities of the visit and what might be gained by it. There was the question of his daughter's future, and who she might marry to strengthen her position. To be married to her cousin, Prince John, would not be too bad a thing for both kingdoms. Richard of course would wait and see how the boy had developed; the king had disturbing memories of John as a very spoiled little boy. It had been one of the reasons he had denied the child the crown of Gaeland until such a time as the young prince came of age. It was far better for Gaeland to remain in the protection of the king of Englene and his regent, Lord Hamilton, until such a time as it could be deeded to John without allowing Renee to get her hands on it.

The thought of Renee, and of what might have been, brought to mind another ache, an embarrassing one. The king blushed to recall the previous night. He had supped with the Lady Anne of Pemberly and had waxed merry over wine and other comforts, and had gone off to the lady's bed sure of fulfillment. Had he not caused the greatest flames in all of Avebury's rites? Was he not proven fully potent? Perhaps there had been a bit too much wine with dinner, or was it the green dress Anne had chosen to wear? It had brought to mind many memories of Dianne. And when he had found himself again unmanned in Anne's arms, he had wept on her bosom with grief for his lost queen.

He wished he could recall something of that magical rite he had performed with his daughter, but search his mind as he may there was not the slightest fragment of memory. He had performed rituals to return the errant thoughts, and had even attempted to cure his strange amnesia by use of the ring Raziel, but the results had not been satisfactory.

He remembered full well the events at the shrine at Bathford. He remembered the journey down to Avebury in the presence of the court and his daughter. He remembered also the magnificence of the camp overlooking the Circle, and even his robing in the fantastic costume of the God Sulis. But from the moment his foot first touched the great avenue, he remembered nothing until he came to himself again in his pavilion tired near unto death.

That fatigue was the one shred of evidence he could cling to. He had tired himself out with much raising of magic, and he had proven himself potent. This "fact" was something he found himself cherishing. He admitted to himself how much this lack of potency frightened him, for he, too, had dreams of the Heartwoods—bloody dreams.

He knew full well that he could never again enact such an event with his daughter. It was one thing to perform the Great Rite at a daughter's initiation, but it was another, most shameful, thing to take a daughter to one's bed for one's own pleasure or safety. The Great Rite was for the benefit of the God, and so it must remain. Elizabeth as his wife-mistress was not an answer.

He would have to make sure in his lifetime that Elizabeth was married to a strong man who would help her keep the throne of Englene. That finding of a suitable mate was a considerable problem, for should she marry a foreign prince, Englene might become simply a subsidiary of his kingdom; or should she marry one of her own courtiers, that would cause dissension and jealousies. There was the possibility of someone who was a younger son of a great king—but would he and his country attempt to take over Englene? It was very troublesome.

There was, of course, John. . . .

Richard was musing on this possibility when Thomas the Mage entered the privy chamber. "You sent for me, Your Grace? What would you have me do for you?" Thomas said, bowing deeply to his king.

"I am considering my daughter's marriage, Thomas. She's now of an age where such things become important—and since she is my only child, the matter of her husband is crucial to Englene. What think you of marrying her off to John of Gaeland?"

Thomas rubbed his smooth shaven cheeks, long fingers brushing his lightly sunburned skin. "Hum-m-m, an interesting thought that, Your Grace. With such a union Englene and Gaeland would again be united into one country. The people of Englene would like that and, of course, the presence of Prince John as king of Englene would please the Gaels. Of course, one must consider how the people of Englene would feel about having John as king."

"Oh, I only intended him to be a consort. Elizabeth will be queen." Richard spoke with a confidence which he admitted to himself he did not feel.

"What you might intend and what John and the Gaels might do could be two separate and distinct things. Have you spoken to the princess concerning her cousin? I do not believe they have met for a number of years."

"The Queen-dowager Renee refused to allow John to come to court anymore after he was about ten. Elizabeth bashed him about a bit too much on the tourney field, and Renee was afraid her brat might be damaged. But I've not spoken of the marriage to Elizabeth yet. There's a drawback to it. I would not wish a mother-in-law like Renee on anyone for anything. However, Elizabeth is strong minded; she would cope."

The king led Thomas over to a bay window and motioned him to sit on the cushioned windowseat. He himself took a place knee to knee with his chief counsellor. "Well, Thomas, you have not given me your answer. What think you of the marriage? I know you are not prone to give away answers— but then, this is not an easy question."

"Have you consulted the Archbishop of Aleicester about this matter?" Thomas said, attempting to see all sides of the problem. "I believe he has ambitions for that handsome son of his, the Duke Charles—and Charles too is Elizabeth's cousin. I will say that Charles's claim is not as good, but perhaps the princess would like to be given a choice between the two men. My answer to your question does come back to what does the Princess Elizabeth want?"

"I can't leave this to a young girl! Charles is handsome and charming, and Elizabeth has known him throughout her adolescence. The last time she saw John he was a fat little child with spots. If I give her a choice she will say 'Charles' naturally—and as to the choice being even between Charles and John, that is not so. Charles is of a bastard line, and John is to be king of Gaeland; as such, Prince John alone can be of advantage to the kingdom."

"In that case, since John and his mother are now in Englene, let Princess Elizabeth meet Prince John, dance with him, hunt with him, play the lute, sing songs and see what she makes of him, and then perhaps the choice will be as you wish. But a word of caution, my lord King. Do not fail to take into account Elizabeth's wishes. I doubt you would be able to force her into a marriage she does not want."

"No, I would not make her marry against her inclination. I understand too well what grief can come of that. My father did not force me to marry where I would not. The least I can do is to give the same consideration unto my daughter—but I cannot help but think that my marriage did not prosper, choice or no choice. A marriage with John of Gaeland would be wise. . . ."

The palace fortress of BrynGwyn was the largest of the king's palaces. It had been built back in the ages before the witchlords came to Englene by the legendary Elf-King Bendigeidfron of the Blessed Raven. It was said that his body lay under the west cornerstone and his head under the north cornerstone. Inside its massive gray walls were the Palace of the White Tower and a number of other towers which served as royal mint, armory, zoo, cannon foundry, and storehouse for the crown jewels. Two of the towers functioned as a royal prison; they stood side by side in the east corner near the royal mint, each one more grim than the other. Traitor's Tower was the tallest, but it was Queen's Tower, built by Isabel the She-wolf, that was the most fearsome. It was said that it was there she murdered her husband, William the Unlucky, by pouring molten lead into his ear while he slept. Whether the story was true or not, this corner of BrynGwyn fortress was considered unlucky. It had been built on the site of that spring where Edmund the Mage lost his foolish heart to the treacherous

watersprite Melusine. This corner of the palace also contained
the Gaeland Lodging—and considering the hoopla the Queen-
dowager Renee was causing in that section of BrynGwyn Palace
it was indeed unlucky for everyone she dealt with.

Renee and Prince John had brought with them an unwar-
ranted number of ladies-in-waiting, men at arms, courtiers,
cooks, servants, pages, and other hangers-on. Renee was trying,
with the help of Richard's staff, to house some two hundred
people in quarters built to hold perhaps twenty-five comfort-
ably.

The Lord High Chamberlain, Henry Terrell, was not amused
by the queen-dowager's efforts to take over the surrounding
towers. The Palace of BrynGwyn had been filled to the gunnels
by the visiting nobility who had arrived for Elizabeth's birthday
celebrations, and there was really no room for some two hundred
wild Gaels.

Renee was totally oblivious to the comfort of any but her
own people, and it was with much jockeying and losses of
temper that she finally managed to shoehorn all of her people
into empty nooks and crannies of the palace. But the result of
this effort sent her off to dinner in a very bad temper, an
unfortunate thing for her cause.

Prince John sat in the middle of the small circular chamber
that had been fitted up for him, and gazed at his golden embroidered hose with annoyance. His tailor stood trembling before him. John reached down, felt the heel of the offending
hose, and then shrieked, "There's a knot, you fool, a knot! I
tell you I can feel it right here at the heel. You stupid toad,
you've tried to give me a blister!" With that, he backhanded
the unfortunate tailor, knocking the little dark man end-over-
cookingpot across the stone floor.

Satisfied at having caused an uproar, and discomfort to
someone else, John pulled on his soft Moorish leather slippers
and stood up to swagger over to the mirror and inspect himself.
Every bit of elaborate material, tailoring, and jewels that could
be assembled to make a prince handsome had been applied to
his pearshaped body. It had not helped very much. At sixteen,
Prince John of Gaeland was stooped and slack of gut, hollow
chested, and knock-kneed. His hair was a lank, rusty red and
his skin, which should have been the peaches-and-cream of his

forbears, was marred by spots. His blue eyes were cold and piggy; that and his habitually petulant expression did nothing for his looks. But what John saw in the mirror was a prince, and that was sufficient for him.

Gathering his velvet gloves and clapping his eagle feathered bonnet on his head, he pronounced himself ready for dinner and strode out of the room, smack into his mother's arms.

"John! I wasn't expecting you to be still loitering around here," Renee said. "The king is expecting us at dinner and I do hope he will place you under the royal cloth of estate. It is your right by birth and kingship." Renee fussed with the gold lacing at John's collar and then placed his bonnet on his head at an attractive angle. Unfortunately, the eagle feather curled around one ear and tickled, rasping John's nerves. "Now, be sure you're pleasant to the king. We don't want to have to wait until you're eighteen before you're made King of Gaeland. And be nice to that woodwitch daughter of his. Remember, until something happens with the Pemberly, she *is* his heir."

John grunted and moved the hat to a less itchy angle. "Why do I have to be nice to Elizabeth? She isn't even pretty—and besides, if anyone should be heir to Uncle Richard it should be me. Then too, I should have been made King of Gaeland after Father died. It wasn't at all fair that Uncle Richard made me wait this long."

John's lower lip protruded. The very thought of all the tax monies that should have been his made him quite sullen. But then he reflected on the subject a moment and quickly decided that it would indeed be a very good thing if his Uncle Richard decided to let him be King of Gaeland two years before coming of age. A cunning look momentarily took the place of petulance on John's face.

"You're right, Mother. I will be very nice to Uncle Richard and his fat pink pig of a daughter. But just don't place me anywhere near Aunt Marguerite. She'll expect me to talk about books, and you know I never read anything."

The Great Hall of the White Tower of BrynGwyn had been lavishly decorated for the princess's birthday feast. The cloth of estate which hung over the king's head at the high table was made entirely of red and blue cloth-of-gold, liberally embroidered with gold, pearls, rubies, and sapphires. The banners

hung from the hammerbeam roof were of velvet and satin, silk
and taffetas, brocade and goldwork, and even the great trophy
heads of stag and deer had had their antlers freshly gilded and
draped with greenery.

King Richard stood beside his chair at the high table waiting
for the queen-dowager and her son. They were late. Richard
forced a mask of politeness over his feelings of irritation. He
turned to look at his daughter beside him and admitted to
himself that she looked very well. Her gown of sea green velvet,
powdered over with embroidery in a darker green and picked
out in pearls over a cloth-of-gold kirtle, was very becoming to
her.

"You look very well, Bessie. Your mother would be very
proud of you and, like me, glad to see you in green. Believe
me when I say that. It suits you. And I will make sure no one
criticizes your use of it."

"Thank you, sire. I am glad that you let me honor my mother
in this way. There was a great deal of green fabric available
in her clothespresses, so it was not at all difficult for my ladies
to make dresses for me. There was, however, a length of gilt
and green brocade that I had long admired. I was looking
forward to having a kirtle and foresleeves made of it, but my
ladies could not find it anywhere."

Before Richard could comment on the missing length of
fabric there was a fanfare of trumpets, and he turned to watch
the queen-dowager of Gaeland and her son enter the room. A
stillness fell over the Hall. This was the first time in six years
these courtiers had had opportunity to see Prince John—and
since many of them had been considering that he might make
a suitable king of Englene, there was curiosity as to what the
boy might be like.

There was a flurry of whispers as the prince and his mother
came down the length of the room. Renee drew many favorable
comments, for even in her late forties she was still a very
attractive woman; a bit thin and perhaps her neck a trifle scraggy,
her bosom lacking in the full roundness favored by the witchlords, but nonetheless in her gilt and pink and blue prettiness
she was every inch a suitable princess of La Bonne Terre.

Her son, however, was a bit lacking in personal charms,
and it was at that evening that some courtier—no one remembered who—christened him "John Lack-Grace." The nickname

was to stick and would go down in the chronicles of Englene as the reigning name of this Gaeland king.

Richard stepped forward to welcome his sister-in-law, taking and kissing her slender white hand. He led her to the place at his left under the canopy of estate, and seated her with the canopy over her head. John had followed in his mother's wake, and Richard almost collided with the boy when he turned back, thinking he would again descend from the high table and welcome his nephew at the place in the Hall where he had left him. Richard gracefully covered the awkwardness by inquiring after his nephew's health and leading him over to make his bow to the Princess Elizabeth. Elizabeth was seated to the right of her father, also under the canopy of estate, and when John was seated at her right the canopy did not cover him. It was a slight he noticed, and stored up as one more grievance against his uncle. There was another fanfare as the king seated himself, and then the courtiers took their places at the long banqueting tables. In that interval John and Elizabeth took the opportunity to study each other. Neither was impressed.

After perusing his cousin, John turned all his attention to the Lady Anne of Pemberly. He ostentatiously kissed her hand and inquired after her health. The Lady Anne, noticing the prince's snubbing of the Princess Elizabeth, proceeded to flirt madly with him.

Elizabeth observed John and the Pemberly and realized swiftly that her cousin was trying to annoy her. His shot had missed the mark. She felt that the Pemberly and John were well suited to each other, so her only emotion was amusement. Elizabeth's page helped her to some roast partridge. John was conveniently forgotten.

He was not, however, forgotten by either Renee or King Richard. "Don't they make a charming pair?" Renee said, beaming approval at her son.

"Who?" Richard asked, looking up from his baked eel and onion pie.

"Why, Prince John and your daughter Elizabeth. I do think they make a clever pair. We really must consider that pairing a little more closely, my dear brother-in-law."

Richard frowned at Renee's insolence in mentioning a matter of state at the dining table. He was fast becoming convinced that John would make a very poor son-in-law. So the marriage was simply something he would toss to the Great Coveyne and let *them* argue until it came to naught, thus saving face for himself and the Gaels. "He might make her a good consort, but of course there are so many claimants for my daughter's hand," he observed.

Renee chose to ignore the implications of Richard's remark. "Oh yes, there may be other suitable young men, princes or lords of foreign nations—but after all, my John is a king, or would be if you gave him Gaeland as is his right. I think he would make a splendid king of both Gaeland and Englene, and it would unite the country again. I think that would please all our people."

Richard scowled and looked about the Hall to see who had overheard the remark. Unfortunately, too many people had. He could tell the conversation had even been overheard at the side tables and was rapidly being relayed down the room. "I think, my lady, that this conversation would best be saved for another time," he said in a cold, even voice. "I am sure you are aware how easily gossip spreads, and I would not wish any of this to get about until my councillors had discussed the ramifications of the union."

"Oh, but I think it should be discussed, Richard," she continued in a loud, bright voice. "I would like to get this settled before John and I go back to Gaeland, and of course I would like you to have him made king. It would be such a shame to make the boy wait until he is eighteen."

"Your son will wait until the moon turns blue with cold, Madam!" Richard said between clenched teeth. "I request that you observe courtesy and cease this conversation. Remember, Madam, I am your king, and I command it."

Renee sputtered to silence. She realized too late her folly in pushing the marriage and John's kingship at table. She turned her attention back to her dinner, her flaming cheeks the only indication that she was seriously upset by the outcome of her attempts to ingratiate her son with the king.

Elizabeth had observed the conversation going on between the king and Renee, and she admitted to herself that it was vastly amusing. It made her understand a little more why her uncle, King Robert of Gaeland, had been foolish enough to go off and fight the Boggies in Faerie. Even though King Robert had been very unfortunate in his battles in that dank island—

unfortunate enough to get himself eaten by a Thing—it may well have been a lesser fate than spending the rest of his life with Queen Renee. Elizabeth vowed to herself that the moon would more than go blue before she married her cousin and had such a mother-in-law underfoot.

John had been totally oblivious to the conversation between Richard and Renee. He had devoted his attentions solely to Lady Anne, and they had reached a certain agreeable level where the lady had allowed him to place his hand upon her bare knee under her voluminous skirts. John was convinced that with a little more flirtation he might manage to sleep with the king's mistress and cuckold his uncle. The thought made the prince's eyes go small and piggy. His thick lower lip was dripping with the grease of the fat goose he had shared with Lady Anne, and there were crumbs on his tunic from the spinach and date fritters he had stuffed himself with. All in all, he was not a very pretty sight.

Anne seemed not too concerned over the slovenly dining habits of her companion. After all, he was a prince who would soon be a king, and a king was what she had been angling for. She had, however, noticed the quarrel between Richard and Renee and decided it would be politic to soothe her monarch.

Ignoring John's attempt to fondle her bosom, she leaned forward in her chair and addressed the king. "My lord, would it not be possible to show our northern visitors some of our entertainment here at court? Perhaps your fool would be willing to tumble for them, or to sing some witty song of the taverns. He is, after all, a very clever fellow."

Richard, glad of an opportunity to avoid further conversation with Renee, agreed swiftly to the Pemberly's suggestion. He signaled to Henry Terrell to find Jackie and bring him to the dining hall.

Jackie came prancing down the room wearing a long green and gilt brocade gown which he had inexpertly hitched up around his waist so that he would not trip over the voluminous folds of fabric. He stopped in front of the high table and paraded back and forth, showing off the glories of the pearl embroidered sleeves and heavily jeweled bodice. The court laughed at the fool's elaborate attitudes and effeminate posing until even Richard himself looked up to observe. He recognized the gown immediately and a dull pink flush crept up his cheeks.

Queen Renee leaned forward to get a better look at Jackie, and commented, "Why is your fool prancing about in the dead queen's dress? It seems a poor sort of joke to me, Richard."

"Aye, a poor joke indeed," Jackie said. "'Tis a woodwitch marlotte, 'tis woodwitch green. I'll tell thee a riddle, and give this gown to the one who guesses it. I found it in a maid's closet, and that maid had no woodwitch blood. Methought it was Queen Dianne's marlotte, but the skirts were far too long." Jackie spread the long shimmering skirt like a peacock's tail around him. "Then, said I, it must be the Princess Elizabeth's. She has taken to wearing green of late, in honor of her lady mother.

"But look, you, our princess is a bonny, buxom wench, wide in the shoulder and hip. The span of this gown would not meet at the back of such a hearty young warrior." Jackie smoothed the bodice of the gown over his own slender chest. "Methought it fit me quite well, for I am slender as a reed and have boyish hips and a boyish bosom; therefore it was my understanding that the gown had been made for me to fop about in and play the fool. If this is not so, my king, I will of course remove it." Jackie fitted his actions to his words, and removed the gown so that it fell in a green pool around his feet.

"Your jest is in very poor taste, fool, and were you mine I would have you whipped." The remark came from the high table, but it was not Richard who had made it. It was the Lady Pemberly. She had recognized the gown she had worn to try seducing the king, and she was sure the court could guess Jackie's riddle quickly. Then, realizing that too much attention was being focused on her comment, she swiftly altered its meaning. "Fool, you have no right to make fun of the wood-witches. It is not wise. In this kingdom we must be kind to all."

King Richard smiled at her in relief, and Anne knew that, for now, she had won the exchange of wit.

"Oh aye," Jackie agreed quickly. "Kindness must be extended everywhere, from the highborn in their palaces to our guests from the northern kingdom, and even unto a poor fool. Very well, my lord, my ladies, forgive this poor jest and I will be off to find the maid that fits the gown to see if she indeed fits me." With that Jackie bounded from the room dragging the dress behind him, the green fabric shimmering and swirling about his feet.

At the high table Elizabeth sat cold and still. The message Jackie had been conveying was for her. There was only one person in all of Englene whose boyish hips and bosom would have fit that gown and who would have dared to wear it without the knowledge of the court. She looked at Lady Anne in cold disdain and decided the time had come to reclaim her cousin's attention. "What thought you, Cousin John, of our fool, Jackie? After the banquet is over he will no doubt entertain us with more clever mummings and masques. He's very good at that sort of thing."

"We have fools aplenty in Gaeland," observed John, reaching for a bowl of sugared violet petals. "We even have some that are professional jesters. As for the rest of my people, they're simply fools. Of course, they are looking forward to my being their king," he continued with sleek satisfaction, totally unaware of the incongruous nature of his remark. "I wish your father would hurry up and make me king. Mother of course tried to make it up to me by having me knighted, but still that's not the same thing as being king, is it?"

Elizabeth's eyes widened in surprise. "But that is my father's right! By what right did she command the ceremony of knighthood for *you?*"

"As I said, she wanted me to have some consolation for not being king yet, and she felt knighthood was a fair honor. And she did it by right of being Queen of Gaeland. You will never be a knight, no matter how good a fighter you are. But now I have that honor, and can march in processions on holy days wearing my spurs and my cloak of knighthood and my people honor me as they should. If you should come to Gaeland you'd be made to march behind me because you are but a princess and no knight."

"Your mother is queen-dowager of Gaeland," Elizabeth said. "She had no right to make you a knight. Only King Richard, your liege lord, has that privilege. And I think it wise that you ask him to repeat the ceremony so that it will be honorable and true. *If* he so wishes, that is—and if he heard your remarks, he would marvel at your idea of chivalry."

John spoke up so that his uncle might hear him. "My lord

uncle, my Cousin Elizabeth has said that the knighthood I
received at the hands of my mother Queen Renee is not right
in the sight of chivalry. Therefore I request that you make good
my mother's error and forthwith knight me."

Richard, who had heard the entire exchange, could feel the
blood pounding in his body. He could hear it singing in his
ears and he was fearful that it might burst from its appointed
course and kill him by stroke of apoplexy. How dare this foolish
woman knight her son without consulting her liege lord, the
King of Englene—and how dare that son twit his daughter
with the fact that she could never attain knighthood—and how
dare these two sit at his table smugly convinced that Englene
would be theirs? The moon would thrice turn blue before he
gave knighthood, his kingdom, or his daughter to John!

Taking a deep breath the king stood, pushing his chair backwards so sharply that it tumbled to the floor. At the sound of
the reverberating crash, silence fell over the room.

The king spoke. "My lords and ladies of Englene, hear the
pronouncement of King Richard. As is my right as King of
Englene, I hereby declare that this night there shall be the high
and holy ceremony of knighthood, and I will make my right
beloved and only daughter Elizabeth a knight of the Order of
the Silver Chalice. This is my will and my pronouncement. So
mote it be."

There was silence in the hall. No woman in the history of
Englene, if not the history of the world, had ever been knighted.
The courtiers looked at their king; his word was indeed law
and his was the power of life and death over them. And as if
pulled upwards by strings like marionettes, they rose to their
feet, rank upon rank of the nobility of Englene, and with one
voice shouted forth, "Health, health, to the new knight, Elizabeth. So mote it be!"

Chapter 9

The morning sun beat down uncomfortably on the head of the Princess Elizabeth as she rode forth from the Tower of BrynGwyn in procession toward the river Theames. She was surrounded by her father's courtiers, the twenty-four aldermen of Lundene, and the gorgeously caparisoned outriders of the royal procession. There was music of trumpets and drums as the princess, now Sir Elizabeth, rode through the streets of her father's capital.

Elizabeth's cheerful face belied the way she was really feeling. The sunlight beat on her head like hammers on a smith's anvil. Her eyes burned from lack of sleep, and her stomach rumbled fearfully from the excessive ale she'd had at breakfast. Breakfast had been a mistake. She had assumed, wrongly, that a quantity of ale and good beef would help awaken her after her long night of vigil in the chapel of BrynGwyn and the elaborate ceremony she had gone through at dawn that had made her a knight. Her skin still glowed pink from the scrubbing of the ritual bath in the dungeon she had received from her father and the other knights of the order, and the oil could still be seen on her forehead where Aleicester had blessed her and bid her be a good knight. All in all, Elizabeth was feeling tired, queasy, and more than a little drunk. But she had done her duty for the people by appearing before them cheerful and exuberant.

Unfortunately it was not yet the end of her duties. She must now hand over White Surrey to an attendant and descend into the royal barge, then travel downriver accompanied by the barges of her father's court to the landing at the Palace of Witchdame. There she would again mount a horse and repeat the triumphant procession, this time to the tiltyards at the palace, where she would change into armor and proceed to joust with any and all comers. She was not looking forward to the day's events; as she moved down the stone steps of the quay, acknowledging the cheers of her father's people, she found herself hoping that the river would not be running too high, and that there would be very little jostling of the royal barge. Seasickness would be absolutely the last straw.

The barge rocked under her feet and her squire, young Tom Seymour, reached out to take her hand and steady her. He led her to her place in the center of the barge and gave the signal to cast off from the quay.

"Bring me some wine, Tom," Elizabeth said in a weary voice as she passed a white silk handkerchief across the drops of cold sweat on her forehead. "Make it good strong Rhenish. I am in need of something to settle my innards."

She watched as the handsome blond young man brought her the wine in a gilt cup and presented it properly, kneeling before her. She took the proffered cup and reached out to ruffle his golden curls. Young Tom Seymour, the younger son of the Duke of Somerset, grinned at his patroness. "What say you, Tom, do you think there will be good tilting this afternoon? For me, I would wish myself safely in my bed—but this masque must continue, though I could think of better, more quiet ways of celebrating my birthday."

"When last I saw your challenge shield on the Arthur tree, it was quite covered with challenges. You *will* have quite a day of tilting. So it's good that the sun will not go down before eight or nine o'clock, otherwise you would not manage to get all the challenges taken care of. Buckingham has challenged you to swordplay at the barriers and Strafford has challenged you to no less than twenty courses with as many lances to break. The Earl of Oxford has challenged you to the *geschiftartscherennen* joust. I'm looking forward to that, Your Grace. I've not yet seen a clockwork shield fly apart when struck, and I must say it is an interesting innovation. Then too, you've been asked to fight the baston course with Henry Fitzroy, Duke of Richmond. The royal bastard has promised to wear one more plume than you do in your helm, no matter were you to cover yourself with all the ostrich feathers of Araby!"

Elizabeth laughed at the monumental egotism of her bastard uncle and nodded her approval of the program. "What say you to my challenging my Cousin John to a passage of arms? I remember when we were little I used to send him spinning like a top across the tourney field, and I doubt he's improved. Or do you think such a challenge would be unchivalrous of me?"

Thomas considered the question of chivalry and then said, "It would be expected of you. He is, after all, your cousin and there are many at court who would see him as your husband as well. Methinks a passage of arms that he loses might prove his unworthiness. Indeed it may be unchivalrous, but it would be politic, my lady. Shall I devise something for you?"

"Yes, do that. And make sure whatever it is shows me off to my best advantage and John at his worst. Ha! I've taken my vows not three hours ago and already I'm seeking ways to circumvent them! How shocked my mother would be at me."

"Thy mother was a politic animal, my lady, and I think she would approve."

A cloaked figure at one corner of the barge uncovered, revealing the copper colored hair and plump cheeks of the wizard Menadel. "Methinks young Seymour is right. There are too many at this court who favor John as a future king of Englene. Chivalry consists in part of doing well for one's people, and I do not think letting John be king of Englene is doing well for yours. I don't, in fact, think it is doing well for anyone but John."

There was the sound of laughter from various courtiers on the barge at the wizard's witticism. John, in his short stay in Englene, had managed to make himself unpopular, and there was more than one courtier who was seriously reconsidering the idea of the young king-to-be of Gaeland also being the king-to-be of Englene.

"Also on the shield, Your Grace, is a grand melee where no less than thirty knights have offered to face you in massed combat." Thomas laughed and said, "Knowing your father, he will probably have arranged for it to be rigged. It's a marvelous way for you to show off your prowess, but it really wouldn't do you or the knights any good if you should lose."

Elizabeth pulled her lower lip with two fingers and considered the possibility of the melee being indeed fixed. Such displays were customary for birthday tourneys, and it was a way to show off one's horsemanship, abilities with sword and mace, and was also a rather charming sort of mock combat. But the idea of it being won unfairly disturbed Elizabeth. Here was yet another occasion for breaking her vows of chivalry so soon after taking them.

"Tom, tell my father the melee is *not* to be rigged. I want to face those knights in honest combat. Have it known to the knights that I will reward any man who fights justly and with all his strength. Any man who holds back merely because I am a princess or a woman I will mark as lacking in true courtesy and I will brand him a coward."

Elizabeth leaned back against the cushioned chair and closed her eyes, trying to get a few minutes of rest on the way to Witchdame Palace. The tide had not yet turned and the Theames was relatively calm. Elizabeth was grateful for that. The wine sat easy on her stomach, and she came to realize that she was hungry—but knew that to try eating while on the royal barge might be courting disaster. There could be nothing worse for her reputation this day than if her courtiers in the surrounding barges saw her heaving and spewing over the side.

As they approached the palace, she saw that a large crowd was waiting at the watersteps. Her father and Archbishop Aleicester came forward to greet her as she ascended from the barge. The king took her by the hand and led her toward two grooms who held between them a mettlesome black horse ready for the princess.

To the cheering approval of the townspeople, it was her father who linked hands together to offer her a leg up onto her horse's back. She bowed deeply to her sire and then, placing one green leather-clad foot in his hands, she sprang onto the back of her horse. She then proceeded to show off the horse's paces while the king and other courtiers mounted and made ready for the procession to the tourney field.

There was, over the whole tiltyard, the scent of sweet fruit cooking in syrup, fresh baked bread, and chickens roasting over open fires. Off to one end of the field was a cluster of cooking pavilions and several ox carcasses were being busily turned by spit boys. There was the scent of woodsmoke and dust, musk and horses' dung. There was the cry of chickens and the wailing of small children, the whinney of horses and the sounds of armor being assembled. There were the birdlike cries of pleasure from the women and the deeper voices of the lesser nobility taking bets on one fighter or another. All of this made up a tourney; the sweat, the pageantry, the dirt, the bright brocades, the horses' dung, and the roasting oxen.

Elizabeth rode to her pavilion, which had been set up near the tiltyard. Its green and gold striped sides billowed in the breeze, her personal banner of her father's and mother's arms quartered snapped and thrashed on its pole. Tom Seymour and the assistant pages had laid out her armor of black and gold damascene work. With their aid she removed her riding habit and stripped down to a shirt of fine cambric and knitted linen tights. The pages scurried to bring her a quilted gipon which would protect her skin from the hard edges of her plate armor. Then piece by piece—greaves, tasset, breastplate, gorget, and tilting shoulder—the tilting garniture was bolted into place. The ostrich plumes were adjusted on her close-helmet and then, with reverence, Tom fastened around her the red and blue surcoat bearing the arms of Englene. He belted it into place with a heavy gold link belt and then knelt to place her gold spurs, badge of knighthood, upon the heels of her sabatons. Holding her round tilting shield in one hand, she was now ready for the lists.

She stepped forth out of her pavilion where her grooms were waiting with her barded destrier. The sorrel was calm. He knew what this day would bring; there had been many like it before. Giving the animal a pat on the small area of its neck which was exposed beneath its crinet, she mounted her horse with the aid of her groom and a step-block.

A trumpet sounded and slowly, from behind the stands,

came a dozen pages bearing overhead the large traveling pavilion which would cover her as she was escorted onto the lists.
Elizabeth took her place at one end of the field and waited
while Thomas Devereux, Earl of Essex and High Marshall for
the Birthday Lists, announced the first event. It was to be the
breaking of twenty lances, with the princess matched against
Robert Talbot, Duke of Strafford. There was much applause
from the stands as Elizabeth and the duke rode out from their
respective pavilions. Her queasy stomach and lack of sleep
forgotten, Elizabeth, with high good humor, adjusted her helm
and took from Tom her first lance. This was going to be fun!

It was still fun some hours later. Elizabeth had proved herself
a worthy opponent, and worthy of knighthood, in spite of her
queasy stomach and earlier misgivings. The day was wearing
to a close. There was already a hint of twilight in the air. There
would be but one or two more events and then off to the palace
for more feasting, celebration, dancing, masquing, and jests.
All in all it had been a good birthday. Elizabeth felt very pleased
with herself.

There were two events still left undone: a combat with Prince
John, and the melee. Well, it was time to declare the nature
of the combat with John. This part would not be fun. It was
being done for cold, spiteful reasons and Elizabeth still felt
unease at this breaking of her knightly vow.

Mounting her horse, she rode forward and saluted Lady
Anne of Pemberly, who sat surrounded by ladies-in-waiting in
her position as the Queen of Love and Beauty.

She nodded to Lady Pemberly and then made her horse bow
gracefully. "If it please you, my lady, I should like some
passage of arms with Prince John of Gaeland. Will you so
honor me by allowing it?"

Anne gave her gracious assent, saying, "With all good will
I do allow it, Your Grace. But I would ask what are the courses
of chivalry that you would ask of your cousin and fellow prince?
What would you have him do and what will you do for him?"

"I will, on my oath as a knight, give to him a splendid ruby
ring should he be able to unhorse me." There was a sharp
intake of breath from the ladies-in-waiting around Anne. It was
very unusual to challenge someone at the jousts to an unhorsing.
Generally the splintering of lances was considered quite enough

for a pleasant holiday sort of joust like this one. Bones could be broken in such a fall. Bones and, yes, necks. "I would also," the princess continued smoothly, "give unto him a fine destrier, a full set of armor, a shield, and an enchanted woodwitch blade should he be able to unhorse me." The gift was unusually generous; it matched well the nature of the challenge.

"And what," Anne asked, "would you require of him should you be able to unhorse His Grace, the Prince?"

"Why, my lady, I would ask no more of him than a sprig of heather for my pillow."

There was a loud spatter of applause from the stands as the princess's words were conveyed by heralds to the assembled populace. It was indeed a very chivalrous offer. All applauded and approved it except Prince John.

John had not entered any of the day's events. He sat beside his mother in the stands, eating comfits, drinking a great quantity of wine and fondling an obliging wench who had sat on his knee. He was not partial to the hustle and bustle of the tiltyard, and vigorous exercise had little appeal.

He smiled in sudden cunning. He'd not brought his armor with him, or a destrier; therefore, how could she challenge him? He rose to his feet and made this pronouncement aloud to the assembled crowd.

But King Richard had a simple answer. "We are surrounded by no less than a dozen pavilions, all of them richly supplied with armor, horses, and all the accouterments of jousting. Surely you can find somewhere in all of this host the armor and horse and equipment you need. If after diligent search you have not been able to do so, I am sure the Princess Elizabeth will be quite gracious and accept your forfeiture."

Put that way, John could not very readily refuse the challenge and he went off grumbling to accouter himself for a joust.

While Prince John was conducting his search for armor and a horse, trumpeters entered the tiltyard and blew a signal for a great and majestical challenge. A herald clad entirely in gold came forward and opened a silk-covered document of challenge.

It transpired, as the herald proclaimed, that six knights had procured, at great expense and danger, a large and ferocious dragon—and this dragon had offered to fight the Princess Elizabeth for the honor of Englene. Should Elizabeth be able to defeat the mighty dragon, she would be presented with a dragon's egg as a token of the esteem the dragon would hold for so valorous a knight. The trumpeters again blew challenge and, realizing this was but one more bit of royal pageantry, Elizabeth made a pretty speech of acceptance.

The crowd's cheers and applause turned to cries of pleasure as a stately bronze colored dragon composed of wood and cloth and manned by those same six knights entered the tiltyard with much growling and snorting of fire. Elizabeth adjusted her helm and gave her horse signal to proceed.

The dragon padded most realistically around the tiltyard and Elizabeth was put to some effort pursuing it. It was apparent that to slay the beast would require striking it very firmly upon a decorative shield hung around its neck. Elizabeth made two passes at the dragon to ascertain how best to kill it without damaging the knights who had provided so entertaining a spectacle. Finally she was ready for the tilt with the "fearsome beast." She couched her lance expertly, kissed her gloved hand to her father and then, lowering her visor, proceeded to attack.

Her horse cantered down the tiltyard, his hooves casting up great clouds of dust, his breathing as loud as the snorting of the artificial dragon. He bunched his muscles, ready for the impact of the lance; Elizabeth, feeling her mount's readiness, crouched low in the saddle and shattered her lance exactly in the center of the dragon's shield.

The crowd applauded and threw flowers as the dragon "died" quite dramatically, with its great tail lashing the dust as the final ringlets of smoke trickled out of its nostrils.

Two grooms rushed forward to assist Elizabeth as she dismounted and then, with a broadsword handed to her on bended knee by Thomas Seymour, she beheaded the mock dragon and presented the head, all gilt and satin, to the amused Lady Anne of Pemberly. She then stood and awaited the presentation of the dragon's egg.

Out of a side pavilion came the six knights, freed of their burden of the fake dragon skin. They carried between them a brocade sheet and, resting upon it, a large gilt egg. They placed it with reverence at Elizabeth's feet, handed her a wooden broadsword and directed her to tap upon the egg.

When Elizabeth did so the egg split in two, and there revealed in the shattered bits of the false egg was a real dragon.

The creature was perhaps a foot and a half long, one of those mysterious firelizards that were said to dwell deep in woodwitch country. With a cry of delight Elizabeth bent and took the dainty green animal upon her wrist like a falcon.

Elizabeth lovingly stroked the creature's back with one ungloved hand and then sighed. She knew what she must do with so rare a treasure. She drew herself up to her full height and marched with great dignity to her father's box. She bowed gracefully upon one knee and, lifting her arm, presented the animal to her father.

"My lord," Elizabeth said, "receive from me this token of my esteem for you, and accept this royal beast from my hands as a gift in symbol of your own greatness."

"You have honored me greatly, my daughter. I accept from you this gift, and I say now in the presence of all that are here, ask of me what thou wilt. I vow to give you what you would ask of me, even unto the half of my kingdom."

Elizabeth knew full well not to ask for half of her father's kingdom. It was, of course, a symbolic statement. But she could ask for almost anything else, and she knew what it was she wanted for a birthday gift. "My lord, I ask of you but the littlest and the least, and perhaps the ugliest object in your kingdom. I request that the fool, Jackie Somers, be given unto me as my liege man for as long as either of us lives."

King Richard gave his assent. It was, he decided, an excellent choice. "Jackie, Jackie, did you hear that?" the king asked, looking about to find where the jester had gotten himself to. "Somers, come out wherever you are, I have orders for you."

There was a wobbling and bobbing of the king's throne and then, out from under the chair and through Richard's legs, Jackie wiggled like a small parti-colored demon fresh from the mouth of the Nether Regions, to bounce to his feet before the king and kneel in obeisance.

"Jackie," the king said, "my daughter Elizabeth has asked that you be given to her as her liege man. I have accepted her request and I hereby give you unto my daughter for as long as either of you shall live. What say you?"

"My lord, most gracious King Richard," Jackie replied, "I do leave your service with tears, for I have been in it a goodly while. But with much pleasure do I go to the service of your

daughter, the Princess Elizabeth, and to her and her heirs for
as long as I may live I will be their liege man." By adding
Elizabeth's heirs to the vow, Jackie had increased it and shown
his own regard for the princess. He bowed deeply to the king,
now his former master, kissed his own hand, and offered it to
the princess, who took it between her own two hands and
accepted his oath of fealty.

"Jackie Somers, you are now my liege man," the princess
said. "You will wear from this day forth the green and gold
of the princess of Englene."

The crowd applauded the words of the king, the princess,
and the jester, couched as they were in the high chivalric manner. It had been a very pretty play of honor between the three,
and such shows were greatly appreciated by all.

The trumpeters again sounded and the heralds announced
the tilt between the Princess Elizabeth of Englene and Prince
John of Gaeland. The tilt had been freshly decorated in the
banners and coats of arms of the two combatants. This was to
be in many ways the highlight of the tourney.

Elizabeth and John came out of their pavilions and prepared
to do battle, but the crowd observed that there was something
strange in John's accouterments. His borrowed armor fit well
enough, his tilting lance was of the accepted size and shape,
and all appeared to be as it should—except for his saddle.

From some corner of one of the tack rooms of the Palace
of Witchdame Prince John had equipped himself with an old
teaching saddle used for the training of children. Pommel and
cantle were both tightly fitted to his body; indeed, the saddle
fit so snugly around his armor that John was as secure in his
saddle as a cork in the mouth of a wine jug. It would be
impossible to pry him from his seat. While it was true there
was no rule against such a saddle, for no rule had been thought
necessary, it was nonetheless a serious breach of chivalry.

Elizabeth at the other end of the field had not noticed her
cousin's equipment, being busy exchanging one of her gauntlets
that had seemed a bit faulty and readjusting her right vambrace.
It was Tom Seymour who quickly pointed out the anomaly.

Elizabeth's head swiveled, and her eyes narrowed like a
peregrine falcon that had seen its prey. Her mouth was a tight
straight line. How dare John? Not only had he made fun of the
tilt, he had made fun of her. He would have to be dealt with,

or Elizabeth would emerge from this tourney as a laughing-stock. If not in the eyes of her people, then in her own eyes she would be branded a fool.

She set her weight deep into the saddle, flexed her knees and brought them in closely to her horse's side. She adjusted the heavy lance carefully in the lance rest, and then reached up and brought the visor of her close-helmet into position over her face. She was ready to joust.

The two horses lumbered down the list toward each other. Elizabeth kept her lance point aimed straight at the bam-plate on her Cousin John's lance, next to his right hand. This would be the first place that would show some indication of his preparing to unhorse her.

The two horses came closer. The fighters both brought their lances into position, ready to strike each other, and then Elizabeth moved her lance to one side more than it would normally be placed, in line with John's left armpit.

John swung his horse savagely into the tilt to bring himself closer to Elizabeth and to give his horse something to balance against when he struck. But Elizabeth was the swifter of the two. She struck and her lance caught him expertly under the arm. With a mighty heave of her own battle-strong right arm, she lifted him bodily out of his saddle like a fly lifted in the hand of a schoolboy. She swung her arm about, and John was flung to the tiltyard ground with a sickening crunch of body, plate armor, and hard-packed dirt all meeting at once.

Elizabeth couched her lance and backed her horse away from his prostrate form, waiting while the heralds ran forward to ascertain the prince's damages. A physician was swiftly sent for, and John was assisted off the tourney field.

Elizabeth waited for the prince to be carried off. There was silence from the stands. She had not managed to break John's neck, but perhaps she had broken a rib or two. Elizabeth made her horse bow first to the silent stand on the right, then to the left, then to her father, and finally to the Lady Pemberly. Then she turned and rode off the tiltyard.

In the pavilion as she changed her armor for the melee, Elizabeth found that she was bone weary. There had been no joy in that last passage of arms. While she knew in her own heart that she first had considered the unchivalrousness of her challenge, what John had done far outweighed it. It was a stain upon her honor and somehow she had to remove it.

Tom Seymour brought her a cup of wine and a loaf of fine white manchet. "My lady, the wizard Menadel wishes to speak to you before the melee. Shall I admit him?"

"Yes, show him in."

Menadel slipped into the pavilion and stood waiting while Tom refilled Elizabeth's wine cup and brought a chalice for the wizard. Menadel accepted the proffered cup of Rhenish wine and then signaled the boy to be gone.

"Your Grace," Menadel said, "do you remember what we spoke of? The journey that you needs take. Are you still willing to make it?"

"More willing than ever." Elizabeth wiped her sweaty face on a linen towel. "I was going to ask my father after the melee if I might go on a quest, for his honor and my own. I feel besmirched by what happened between John and me."

"I think you're being rather silly about this whole question of your honor. No one really pays that much attention to chivalry anymore. Oh, well, perhaps on our journey you'll learn that your powers are to be used for more important things than breaking a lance with some courtly sprig of nobility. Tonight after the feasting, dress yourself in clothes of the common people and come to me at the north gate, and we will leave on our journey. So mote it be."

"So mote it be." Elizabeth extended her hand to the wizard, who took it between his own in token of their bargain.

"My lady," Tom's voice sounded from outside the pavilion. "They're almost ready for the melee and I have your gridiron basinet helmet here."

"Go, Menadel. You must not linger here or people will think that I dabble in magic to win the melee—and by my oath, I'll not do that ever. Not for this fight, or any other piddling joust. I'll save my magic for bigger things." She waved the wizard away and then called out for Thomas to enter. Menadel bowed his way out of the princess's presence.

Thomas adjusted the heavy globe-shaped helmet over his mistress's head and adjusted the iron grid over her face. He checked the finger plate on her blued steel locking gauntlet to make sure all was well and then assisted her out of the pavilion to where a fresh destrier was waiting.

"My lady," Tom said, "there's been a change in the plans. You were to fight the Duke Charles out on the melee field, but the Lady Anne has requested that your father lead the opposing force against you. It's obvious the Lady Pemberly wants to crown *him* her champion. For harmony's sake, my lady, it might be better to let him win."

Elizabeth frowned. That was all she needed to cap a very awkward day. Lady Pemberly had certainly been busy. Well, she'd be damned if she'd give Anne the pleasure. King or no king, she, Elizabeth, was the better fighter—and if her father went down to defeat before her, so be it. With Tom's assistance, and that of two of her grooms, she mounted her horse and accepted her blunted battle ax. She was ready for the melee. More than ready. It was interesting how annoyance added a sharp edge of anticipation to a mock battle.

The tilt had been removed from the field and in the large space behind two ropes facing each other were two mock armies of thirty knights to a side. With a blare of trumpets and a flourish of kettledrums, king and princess came forward into the cleared center space between their respective armies and there clasped hands and swore that the melee would be in the spirit of chivalry. No false blows would be allowed nor magic employed.

Elizabeth used the few moments alone with her father as a chance to murmur to him, "I intend to win, sire, even though I know Lady Anne wishes otherwise. This is *my* day and unless you command me otherwise, I will fight to win."

Richard, his head hidden behind the visor of his helm, merely nodded assent. He had felt uneasy at his would-be-mistress's request that he take the field of battle. It had been some time since he'd been so active. "The only thing I ask of you, daughter, is don't make me look too big a fool."

Elizabeth clasped her father's hand, and then moved back into position with her little army of knights.

The melee was as fixed and formal as any other event that day. Blows were carefully counted and weighed. Horsemanship was watched with great care. Marshals rode ceaselessly around the raging group watching for blows that might be dangerous, or not in the best interest of chivalry.

The melee was all in good fun. Carefully leashed blows were dealt and received. There was laughter and merriment in the stands. There were cries of delight when a good blow was struck or a difficult one parried. The nobility of Englene were watching an art form in the twilight of a summer day, and there was the feeling that perhaps they would never again see it quite so fresh or so beautiful as it was before them. There was a breath of change in the air. A shift of power from a middle-aged man to a young woman. And all who were present watching the princess at her skilled passage of arms knew that she would be the eventual victor.

On her reviewing stand, Lady Pemberly watched the dust and chaos of the melee, and knew full well Richard would not win it. Most of his knights were symbolically dead and Elizabeth and her knights were sure of victory. Anne's hands clenched on her mock throne. There had been very little in the princess's birthday celebrations to make her rejoice. Unless Anne could counter with a prince, Elizabeth would be queen—and there would be no place at her court for Lady Anne Heywood of Pemberly.

With a shout from the marshals, the last knight on the king's side had been declared dead. Elizabeth signaled her knights to back away so that there was only her father and herself facing each other. The two riders circled each other warily and their use of shield and battle ax was a beautiful thing to behold. The king, even though out of condition, had been a mighty athlete in his day and, from somewhere, he drew on some waning supplies of energy to give his daughter a rousing fight. The marshals circled in closer to watch each blow. But the king was tiring. His shield work was a trifle slower, his parrying a little less perfect.

Elizabeth fought as though she were fresh as a new morning. Her arm worked tirelessly with the heavy blunted ax, her shield work was crisp and sharp, her defenses were perfect. The blow she struck under her father's shield, clanging on his armor, had been as swift as a striking serpent. It had been a true and fair blow. The king acknowledged it as such. The marshals cried victory to the heralds, who proclaimed it loudly to the crowd. The Princess of Englene had won the melee.

Richard beckoned to his daughter to accompany him down the field toward the pavilion of the Queen of Love and Beauty. Anne rose at their approach.

"My lady," the king said, "I present to you your champion,

unbeaten, unbowed. Give to her the token of championship."

Elizabeth dismounted and her horse was led away by grooms. She removed her heavy basinet and gave it to Tom Seymour. She knelt before the furious Lady Pemberly, who placed upon her head the chaplet of gilded laurel leaves and fastened about her neck the gold and ruby chain of the champion.

It was now time for a boon to be begged by the new champion. Generally it was of a frivolous nature, a request for a lady's sleeve or a flower or some such token. But instead of asking her boon of Lady Pemberly, Elizabeth rose and went to where her father, still on horseback, watched.

She placed one hand on the bridle of his mount and, looking up at him, she said, "My lord the king, I beg of you a boon. Let me honor this tourney, this championship, and the battle so bravely fought by going on a quest. I would go to each of the four corners of your kingdom and there do some passage of arms or goodly task, that my honor and yours should resound through all such places where chivalry is observed. I ask this of you not only as a champion, but as your loving daughter."

Richard looked puzzled and perplexed. This was not something he had expected and for a moment he was unsure how to answer it. Elizabeth had put him at a loss, something he did not care for—yet what she had asked, while terribly old-fashioned, was not unusual. Had she been simply some duke's son he would have immediately agreed to it. But she was his only heir, and should he lose her there would be no one to reign on the throne of Englene after him save John, Prince of Gaeland—and that was an unpleasant possibility. While he considered how he should reply, Anne decided to step in and gain some advantage from her machinations.

"My lord the king," Anne said, "As Queen of Love and Beauty, I too request that you honor the princess's desire. Such a quest is a goodly thing and would aid the princess to get over her mourning of her mother." Anne smiled sweetly, her face a mask of concern for Elizabeth.

"With two such beautiful ladies requesting something of me, I cannot refuse it," the king replied. "Very well, daughter, go on your quest to the four corners of my kingdom. But bring back for me a gift from each of those quadrants, some small token of the peace and prosperity of my land.

"Now, my people, good people," he cried aloud to the

stands, "the joust has ended. Let us be away to the palace to revel, feast, and dance in honor of my daughter, and in honor of Lady Anne of Pemberly, Queen of Love and Beauty."

Chapter 10

The Palace of Witchdame was lit up to the brightness of midday with cresseted torches on the walls and a massive corona of candles suspended from the ceiling of the main hall. The feast was over and the dancing and revelry were drawing to a close. Elizabeth found herself wishing for her bed. Through it all she'd remained tall and proud and smiling, even though she ached and was so tired she could hardly keep her eyes open.

She managed to snatch a few minutes to slip behind a tapestry into an alcove with the wizard Menadel. "What are we going to do for horses and food, Menadel?" Elizabeth asked quietly. "You're quite right about Father. He's already giving orders to get together an immense train of pack ponies, soldiers, and all that sort of fa-la. But I don't know how I can get horses for us without being noticed."

"Have no fear, Your Grace. I will take care of all provisions," the wizard said confidently. "At midnight meet me at the north gate. We will go from there. Tell no one but your father that you are leaving with me, and you'd best do that only in a note. Your poor father is at times far too trusting of those he cares for, and the Pemberly has already shown a great deal of interest in your plans for the journey. I fear there may be mischief afoot." Menadel peeked round the arras to see who might be near their alcove. "Now go before we're noticed, Your Grace. Remember, midnight!" The wizard gave another nervous look back and forth, and then waddled out of the alcove into the crowded main hall, and vanished in between several courtiers.

Elizabeth stood catching her breath in the alcove and considered what she must do to get out of the palace and meet the wizard at midnight. His saying that he would provide horses and provisions made things simpler. All she had to do was get some sort of clothing for herself. Peasant's clothing, Menadel had said. She remembered the gypsy rags that the young courtiers had worn at the Pemberly's birthday ball and wondered if perhaps any of them were still in the room of the Master of Revels. It was entirely possible. Already dancers were slipping into the hall dressed in a fantastic assortment of costumery: gypsies, Moors, pirates, and milkmaids. Elizabeth nodded to herself and moved out of the alcove under the cover of the noise the masquers were making. She did not notice that behind her, in the deep shadows of the alcove, two figures lurked. The light from the hall glimmered on the jewels of the lady's dress; and of the other, small and shadowed, only alert blue eyes gave away the watcher's presence.

The north gate of the Palace of Witchdame faced out onto empty plowed fields. There was a cold breeze blowing off the river and Elizabeth found herself glad of the heavy brown cloak she'd borrowed from the Master of Revels's cupboards. She was rather pleased with her costume selection. She'd chosen a pair of high dark brown boots and a very full-cut red brocade kirtle that would allow her to ride astride. That, with a yellow silk shift, a red velvet coif, and a coin-hung jubon, completed her outfit. She felt free and very much the raggle-taggle gypsy—having, of course, no way of knowing what a real gypsy's life might be like.

She heard someone approaching the gate, so she melted back into the shadows until she could be sure it was Menadel. She heard the scrape of the bars being removed from the gate and then a figure slipped through. It was hard to tell with the robes the figure was wearing, but the bulk did seem to be that of Menadel. She waited, though, for one further bit of evidence. The figure turned, faced the gate, and began a locking spell. There was a flash of blue light, a puff of smoke, and some voluble curses from the figure. The spell hadn't worked. It was Menadel.

Elizabeth chuckled and stepped out of the shadows. "My lord wizard, if I may assist you?" Without waiting for an answer she turned to the gate and delivered a perfect locking spell. The gate responded and, with a sigh of its heavy bars, sealed itself again for the night.

"Very good, Your Grace, you do that well. It appears I've been a better teacher than I thought." Menadel scratched at the gate with his fingernails until he managed to dislodge two thick splinters. He gave one to Elizabeth, then tucked the other into his sleeve. "There, that's done. Are you ready for our journey?"

"Yes indeed. But I seem to recall you said you would supply provisions, horses, and pack animals, and I see nothing of that sort. What are you planning, Menadel, to produce them by magic?"

"Have no fear, Your Grace. I spent the past several hours studying the spells for producing horses, food, and pack equipment, and I assure you I have them down perfectly. You needn't worry. This is something that is going to work very well." Menadel moved out into the clear space in front of the gate and began to sketch runes, sigils, and symbols into the soil while muttering busily to himself. Elizabeth frowned. She made sure she was well out of range for whatever Menadel might produce.

There was a hissing sound and a sighing; an odd scent in the air like jasmine and pigeon dung; and then a blue cloud formed where Menadel had written his runes. When the cloud parted there stood four enormous hairy animals, golden brown in color, with long necks and two humps on their backs. Two of them were saddled. The other two bore rolled Moorish carpets upon their backs.

"Very interesting, Menadel, but what are they?" the princess asked, trying hard not to laugh. Whatever they were, they weren't horses.

Menadel sighed and looked at his handiwork. "Well, they are fit to ride. The Moors ride them all the time. They can cover a great deal more distance than a horse. But I'm afraid they're a little too noticeable. They won't do. No, they won't do at all. I'll have to try again." Menadel started another spell.

"Yes, but what are they?"

"Camels, I think. Just a moment. I've almost got this rune right. Don't confuse me."

Menadel's voice faded off into a pattern of eldritch mumbling. When the blue cloud again parted there were four rather large, damp beasts with big mouths and teeth, and little piggy eyes. They looked entirely too wide to ride, so no saddles had been provided, but two of them did bear on their backs enormous baskets of cabbage, endive, lettuce, and watercress. Unfortunately these beasts appeared to be fond of greens, and all four of them were trying busily to get their mouths into the baskets.

"Oh dear, oh dear, oh dear!" Menadel said to himself. "I know hippopotami are called river horses, but it wasn't what I had in mind." He bent again to go on with his runes. Elizabeth moved a little closer so that she might hear the spell and observe the runes. It was possible that if she got some idea of the concept behind the spell she might be able to make it work properly. Therefore she was almost nose to nose with one of the beasts that appeared when Menadel's cloud parted, and the beast was not at all happy about it. This time the animals were as large as the hippopotami but had skin like armor and horns on their noses—almost like a unicorn's horn, only shorter and squat. One of them had on his back a large, vividly colored red, orange, and gold pavilion. The animal was infuriated by the strange burden and did its best to buck it off.

Menadel grabbed her by one arm and pulled her back. "Watch out! They're fierce. I've done the spell requesting tame animals, but you never know. The ancient ones said you could never trust a rhinoceros."

Elizabeth wondered just how many other animals Menadel might manufacture before he managed to produce horses or she managed to learn the spell. She had a feeling this was going to be a long night.

"And what do you think you're producing out here, poppet? A new zoo for your father? I doubt BrynGwyn's fortress will hold all these strange animals." It was a very recognizable, cheerful voice that came out of the shadows and Elizabeth greeted it with joy.

"Jackie! What are you doing here? I thought we'd snuck out of the palace very carefully!"

"You must remember what arrases and alcoves are for. There I was, busy with the bodice laces of a very naive lady-in-waiting, and who should come bungling into my love nest but you and old Menadel! When I heard of your plans I lost all interest in bodices or ladies-in-waiting, and here I am. Your father has given me to you. Where you go, I go." Jackie came close enough to the blue flares of magic to be clearly seen. He had removed his motley and was clad in a buff jerkin, blue trunk hose, and russet buskins. A dark blue cloak hung from his shoulders and his curls were covered by a brown woolen cap. He screwed up his face in an expression of woe as he looked at Menadel's latest assortment of beasts to appear out of the blue cloud. "Lackaday, lackaday, *that's* going to alarm the farm folk! Wizard, you're being a fool as usual, and foolery is my job."

"Be silent, Jackie," Menadel said. "I think I have it right this time." There was again the flare of blue, and again four animals that weren't horses. Menadel swore, Elizabeth sighed, and Jackie laughed.

"Tell me," he said to the princess, "can't you do the spell this old idiot's trying? If he produces very many more creatures like that, there's not going to be a blade of wheat for the farmers to eat between here and Lundene. Call him off. I have a solution to the problem."

Menadel was producing, at a very rapid rate, runes, clouds of blue, and animals. A lot of animals, and as yet no horses. Elizabeth, realizing that the whole thing was getting rather out of hand, reached out and grabbed the muttering wizard by his arm. "Stop it! Stop it, Menadel. This isn't getting us anywhere. Jackie says he has a solution. Now come away from your animal making and let's see what can be done."

"He wasn't invited to go on this trip, he's not meant to go on this trip, nor shall he go on this trip," Menadel said, continuing the cadence of his spell. "Your Grace, we cannot take a human along on this journey. There is too much of magic he might learn, and that would endanger him."

"Don't be silly," Jackie said. "I wouldn't care to learn magic from you, Menadel. You make entirely too many mistakes—and besides, why should I want to make magic? I'm quite secure in what I do, and what I do is follow my lady. If she's going off on a journey to the four corners of her father's kingdom, it's going to be dangerous and unpleasant and take a great deal of time. My lady, take me with you. Let me guard you on the road from such dangers there may be, and most of all, let me guard you from an inept wizard." He looked beseechingly at her and added, "Elizabeth, you need me."

It was true. For a journey, Menadel's organizing wasn't the best. If Jackie had a better plan he should be rewarded for it by being allowed to go along on the journey. "You mentioned a plan, Jackie," Elizabeth said. "Tell me what it is, and if it's any good you will journey with us. You have my word as a princess."

"In that copse over there I have three sturdy horses and a pack pony loaded with food and clothing. Now, that will get us fairly well upon our way. But there are a couple of things I could not take care of. First of all, have you any weapons?"

"I need no other weapons but my own magic," Menadel said pompously. Jackie simply laughed.

Elizabeth said, "I have brought the woodwitch dagger my mother gave me last Year End. I think that should do."

Jackie nodded. He would have preferred a brace of broadswords but in a close fight a woodwitch dagger was better than nothing, and far better than most. "Very good; that takes care of weaponry. Now, what about money? This trip may be costly."

"We have no need of money," Menadel said. "I can make gold from lead any time. Admittedly gold from straw is a little harder, but it can be done if you—"

"No, no," Elizabeth said. "We don't need any more magic! I have these raggle-taggle gypsy clothes that I took from the revel master's stores. They're covered with coins. Won't that do?"

Jackie burst into raucous laughter. "Oh dear, oh dear, what

babes in the woods you two are. You'd be robbed and murdered at the first inn you stopped at. High court gypsy rags!" He went off into another gurgle of laughter. "Do you really think people dress like that, poppet? With those coins alone you've got the earnings of several peasants on your back. Come along, take that ridiculous bodice off and let me cut the coins from it."

Elizabeth handed over the jubon and Jackie set to with a will and a sharp dagger, cutting off the coins and jewels.

Menadel went to the palace gate and removed a large sharp splinter. "Here, Somers," he said, "put this in your cap. If you are to travel with me, you must travel protected."

"What in the name of the Three Regions is that?" Jackie asked. "I have no need of bits of dirty wood in my hair."

"It's a spell, Jackie," Elizabeth explained. "All witchlord pilgrims do it. It gives safety on the road."

"Not precisely; they use other buildings and gates as well as this one," Menadel said in his pedagogue tone. "The splinter represents the safety of the Palace of Witchdame. It is part of the magical theory of contagion—that which has once had contact with an object *is* the object. So with that bit of the palace in your cap, you have the palace with you on the road. Do you understand?"

"Now who's teaching magic to humans?" Jackie said in a silky voice. "Are you trying to get me burned, old man?" He laughed and went back to his task of ridding Elizabeth's jubon of its wealth while Menadel sputtered and groped for some kind of retort, but found none.

"There we are, poppet. I don't think the bodice is worth much now, and as for the other clothing you're wearing— well, the cloak's all right but the rest of it is quite unsuitable. Satin, brocade, and silk will not do where we're going. It's a good thing I managed to get a simple gown and a coarse linen shift from Lord Terrell's mistress. She's a witchlord's bastard, so she's about your size—and if it doesn't fit, a little hitching about and tying will no doubt make it work."

Jackie bundled the coins into his purse, and then led the wizard and the princess to where the horses were tied. He had indeed made excellent provision. The horses were sturdy Gaeland ponies that he had stolen from Prince John. They had good strong legs and firm backs, and could carry the weight of the

Princess Elizabeth. Jackie had found old saddles and such tack as would not be readily missed. The pack pony had a sturdy load of food, cooking utensils, and blankets.

Jackie swung himself onto the smallest of the three horses and grabbed the reins of the pack pony. Whistling at his own horse and digging in his heels, he directed it off away from the Palace of Witchdame.

"There," he said, pointing back at the palace. "We're on our way, and nothing more to worry about."

"Damnation!" Menadel said. "I think my horse just kicked the walrus. I hope it isn't dead."

"We needn't worry too much if it is," Elizabeth said. "There's at least three more of them. Now Menadel, which way do we go?"

Menadel pondered a moment and then said, "In a spell of this sort, my lady, we start with the west." He dampened a finger and lifted it up to test which way the wind was blowing and ascertain which way the west was. By the time he figured it out, Elizabeth and Jackie were already a quarter of a mile ahead of him, due west. Menadel could just barely hear her shouting out the words of the traveler's spell: "Water cannot drown me, earth cannot bury me, air cannot freeze me, fire cannot burn me. In the name of Sulis and Diona, so mote it be!"

WEST

Salve Gabriel cuius nomine tremunt nymphae
subter undas ludentes.

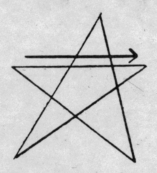

I pray to the Sea-serpent, ruler of the deeps,
Guardian of the bitter sea, great prince of
    the element of water!
Be with me, I pray thee. Guard me and
    mine
From all perils approaching from the West!

Chapter 11

The early morning sun cast long shadows across the floor of the deserted barn. The small outbuilding smelled of cow dung, mold, rat droppings, and old straw, of smoke and of a tragedy long past. The farm buildings not far from the barn had burned to the ground the previous winter, leaving only the shaggy roofed, half-timbered barn as any indication that there had once been humans dwelling in the midst of overgrown fields and empty pastures.

The morning sun reached farther into the barn and touched the faces of the three figures huddled together on the moldy straw.

Elizabeth stretched in her unfamiliar bed and realized that she ached all over. She was still bruised and tired from the joust, and the midnight escape and long ride into the early hours of the morning had done her little good. She was young, she would recover quickly from her bruises, but at the moment she felt herself a rheumatic old crone.

She rose with a groan, knelt by the side of the jester and shook him roughly. "Jackie, Jackie, wake up. I know you're not really sleeping, you're shamming it! Wake up, I say." She shook him again and watched as he stretched his twisted little body into some semblance of a waking posture. His eyelids fluttered and his large blue eyes focused on his princess.

"Aye, I'm awake and small comfort to you. Couldn't you let me sleep just a little longer? We were riding all night and I think that entitles me to sleep all day." He knuckled his eyes and looked at her again, taking in the full glory of her reveler's gypsy costume. "Oh, am I glad I brought other clothes for you, my lady! Even without the coins on your bodice that outfit is still rich enough to get your throat cut by any one of a number of people around here. I'd best have you change before we go much farther."

He got to his feet, went over to where his packs had been left the night before, and began rummaging in them for the shift, kirtle, and simple blue gown he had obtained from the Lord High Chamberlain's mistress.

"Now don't be asking me, poppet, how I got these because I'd rather not speak of it. All I can tell you is that my love of you does lead me into many a strange place. Now here, put these on. Then I suppose we had better wake that old buffoon Menadel and be on our way. We're still close enough to Witch-dame Palace that your father could easily overtake us." He handed the garments to Elizabeth, and waited while she stood staring first down at the clothing and then at him. "Well, if you're going to be excessively modest about it," Jackie said, "you can dress down in the loose box at the end of the barn, although I've seen you naked more times than I can count."

"I—I—I don't know how to put this on," she admitted in a faltering voice. "I've never had to dress myself before. I don't know how to do the laces properly."

Jackie stared at her, incredulous. The idea that someone could actually be eighteen years old and not know how to dress herself was astonishing. But then he reconsidered. Why would a princess of Englene have to learn to dress herself? She'd been surrounded since infancy by servants, ladies-in-waiting, bondwomen, and more than enough willing hands to do what she had not needed to know. His bewilderment exploded in a trill of laughter. "Then tell me, poppet, how did you get into that ridiculous thing you're wearing?" he asked, once he could draw a breath after his fit of giggles.

"I had a lady-in-waiting do it up, of course," she answered, her face flaming red. "I brought the clothing up to my bedroom and told young Nan that I was going a-masquing, so she naturally helped me out of my gown and into this. How else could I have done it?"

"Oh aye, I hadn't considered that. She did it completely without question. All right, I'll be your lady-in-waiting this time. Come with me."

He led her to the loose box and helped her out of the false gypsy rags, and then with a great deal of banter he began to instruct her in the art of dressing herself. The banter won out over more serious instruction, and soon both he and Elizabeth were reduced to giggling incoherence.

Their laughter woke Menadel. The wizard rolled over and sat up facing the loose box. "Children, children," he called out, "if you've finished whatever silly games you're playing I think we ought seriously to give some consideration to our mode of travel in the future. A hayloft, or barn as the case may be," he glanced around him and shook bits of hay off his mouse-colored robe in a fastidious gesture—"is not fit for folk such as us. I know we wish to do nothing to attract the attention of the populace, or of any assassins sent after us, but I do think this is sinking to a level that is quite unnecessarily crude. So if you two will join me, we will give some thought to our housing in the future. The sooner we get it done, the sooner we can go in quest of breakfast. Unless, of course," he eyed the heap of supplies that Jackie had brought, "Jackie has made some provision—"

"Aye, and that I have." Jackie came out of the loose box, leading Elizabeth by one hand. "Look here, Father Menadel, what I've found. Isn't this a fine buxom village wench?" He thrust the princess forward and she stood revealed in an ill-fitting blue gown, linen shift, and brown kirtle.

Menadel nodded his approval. He had already realized that this situation was perhaps more than a little beyond him and felt some comfort in handing it over to Jackie. He said nothing of this to the jester but again repeated his request for breakfast.

Jackie bounced across the floor, clicking up his heels in

sheer enjoyment of the morning and the situation. "Don't worry, I've provided more than enough for breakfast. The cooks at Witchdame Palace will find themselves several loaves of fine manchet and a ham short this morning, plus a jug of good brown ale. But we three will breakfast like kings."

The next hour was devoted exclusively to the bread, ham, and ale. But finally, as the last crumbs were eaten, the conversation turned to the subject of their future.

Jackie wrapped the remains of breakfast very carefully and repacked what was left of the ham and the ale. "I think we ought to avoid the major villages along our route," he said, pulling a linen cap for Elizabeth's hair out of the pack. "There are lesser inns and small cottages where we might find shelter and not be recognized by greater folk. I quite agree that roughing it in this fashion is perhaps abusing ourselves far more than we need to." He showed the princess how to tie the cap in place.

"But that's one thing I'm not quite sure of," Elizabeth said. "Where exactly in the west are we going, Menadel? We've never really discussed that. You simply said to go west."

Menadel nodded. "I've given the subject much consideration and I think the shrine of Mage Dumus in Pembrokeshire should be our first goal. We must be careful not to fall afoul of the Archbishop of Cymru, for he has his ecclesiastical palace there. He's a king's man, and should we need his help I think he will freely give it. But it will be far better not to require his assistance if we are going to complete our journey successfully."

"But I know Archibishop Tysilio! I can't see what's wrong with asking his help," Elizabeth said. "As you yourself pointed out, he's a king's man. Should we need him, why not take advantage of it?"

Menadel stroked his scraggly red beard and seemed lost in thought for a moment or two. "There are many temptations in this world, my princess," he said at last, "and the greatest of these is inertia. I tell you now, in many ways it would be far easier for you to return to the Palace of Witchdame than to continue this journey. As we go from this place it will become more and more difficult. It may even reach a point where you will look back on this cold night in a deserted barn with some affection because it will have seemed the height of comfort to you. And what I fear is that, should we seek the archbishop's assistance, he will seduce you back to your father's palace with offers of comfort and a return to your proper station."

Elizabeth sat on the floor of the barn and considered Menadel's comments. It was true that this first night away from the palace had been extremely uncomfortable, and Menadel was promising her worse. Yet the memory of the man in the Circle and the tremendous joy she had felt with him spurred her on. "Menadel, if I complete this journey of yours will my wish be mine?" She looked at the wizard searchingly.

"If you go to each of the four corners of the kingdom and there show forth your powers as heir to Englene, you will get what you want. That and more; but you must truly want it, Elizabeth. And you will learn on this journey to want other things as well. I hope in time you will gain *all* your desires. But this is the first step of the journey, and if you are going to turn back, you'd best do it now."

"I intend to go on," Elizabeth said. "This journey takes me away from all I have known and toward something I only sense. I know that whatever lies at the end of this, I must have it! No one, not my father, nor the Archbishop of Cymru, nor anyone else will stop me. So lead onward to Mage Dumus!"

The village of Burford was a welcome sight after days of traveling through unkept woodlands. The town was all alight and festive, since it was market day in the village square. The village was choked with wagons and wains, flocks of sheep, geese, cattle, and haggling goodwives. Elizabeth, Menadel, and Jackie threaded their horses carefully between noisy mobs of men, women, and animals, and searched diligently for an inn. Unfortunately the two respectable-looking inns of the village were filled to capacity. So were the three unrespectable ones. They were forced to journey out of the village until they came to a small inn that rested almost in the shadows of the encompassing forest.

The inn looked reasonably well kept, and the innkeeper had hung a garland of green leaves from his sign to indicate that fresh ale was available. Menadel, particularly, found this sign heartening. Much of the ale they had encountered along the way was the sour end of summer's barrels, and this indication of fresh brewing was indeed a pleasurable sight. With very little persuasion, Elizabeth and Jackie accepted the idea of staying the night in this small wooden building, hardly larger than a cottage.

The interior was equally clean and well swept, but it was also quite empty. This emptiness caused a creeping unease, for surely on the major market day it should be filled to brimming.

The man who came bustling out of the kitchen at their cries for ale and food was as tidy and pleasing as the inn, and he seemed quite eager to care for their wants. The ale was indeed good and the cheate bread and the cheese that accompanied it were some of the best they'd encountered along their journey. But still they could not help a growling feeling of uncertainty about remaining alone in the inn.

After having eaten, Jackie asked the innkeeper for the use of his loft and three straw mattresses for the night. The price the man wanted was reasonable, and Jackie did not haggle. He paid the shot and came back to the table shaking his head. "I'll not believe it. This man either has some clacky-handed scheme up his sleeve or else he's a true lover of his fellow man. To ask but tuppence for bread, a penny for ale, two groats for cheese, a penny for fuel and a candle, another penny for beds, and five pence for the horses's shelter and food! His prices are half what I would expect to pay. I'm quite puzzled."

"Do you think we ought to stay?" Elizabeth asked in a worried tone of voice. The fire on the hearth was dying down, and long shadows formed in the corners of the timber and thatch building. "Do you think it's safe, Menadel?"

"But we have the splinters," Jackie said. "I thought they were supposed to protect us."

"Yes-s-s," Menadel said, "but that charm will not protect against *everything*. I for one would like one charm too many rather than one too few. I would suggest, my lady, that we put out the watch-and-wards tonight, to assure our safety. Otherwise—I should not like to awaken in the morning with my throat cut."

"If you had your throat cut," Jackie said, "You'd not be likely to wake, and that's precisely what we're worried about!"

"You might not wake, my fine human," Menadel bragged, drawing himself up, "but I would, cut throat or no. It takes more than a mere slitting of a vein or artery to kill Menadel the wizard."

The jester said nothing in reply.

The innkeeper appeared and led them upstairs to the sleeping loft. The room, seen by the light of the flickering torch, seemed well enough. The straw ticks were clean, there was no sign of bedbugs or rodents, and all seemed to be safe and secure—but they decided to be very sure of their safety.

"I'll set the watch-and-wards," Elizabeth said as soon as the innkeeper had left them.

At the wizard's assent she paced slowly around the room, gazing for a second or two at each of the four quadrant points; then she moved to the center of the room, drew her woodwitch dagger, held it aloft, and in a loud voice said, "All right, Lords of the Watchtowers, on your guard. I need you!" She returned the dagger to its sheath and then threw herself on one of the straw ticks. "There, that ought to hold us," she said in a voice of quiet satisfaction as she arranged her cape around her to serve as a blanket.

"That—that—" Menadel sputtered. "That wasn't the way you do it! You bow, you genuflect, you trace pentacles, you draw a circle. You address the Watchtowers with prayer and reverence, not in so abrupt a fashion, Elizabeth! Who taught you to do a circle in that fashion?"

Elizabeth unrolled herself from her cape and sat up. "My father taught me to do it that way," she said. "It's very effective. If you don't believe me, watch." Elizabeth spread her hands and closed her eyes in quiet concentration. She traced a pentacle in the air with one finger, leaving a tracing of blue on the empty air. She muttered a spell under her breath so it was barely audible. Suddenly in the four quadrants of the room, blue flares appeared, and a circle of blue fire formed upon the floor. The Watchtowers and the circle were as complete as if she had spent a half-hour setting them.

"You see, you really don't have to go through all of that nonsense if you don't want to. Oh, it's very nice to do it when you've got the time and when you're feeling like a little ceremony. It can be restful, and put you in the proper mood. But when you need magic, you need it, and it doesn't do you any good if you need it in two seconds and it's going to take you half an hour to produce it. Father said that magic in many cases is nothing but symbol. A spell merely opens the right doors in your mind."

Elizabeth curled up into her cloak, and Menadel could hear the quick repetitious rhythms of the princess saying her evening prayers. The wizard shook his head.

The night was quiet, but in the morning when they unbolted the door a strange sight greeted their eyes. For there was the landlord stretched across the threshold of their room, dead. Or at least they assumed it was the landlord. They saw a shaggy, feral-eyed, long-legged thing wearing the landlord's clothing. In its hand was the sharp bladed carving knife they had seen the landlord use the night before on their cheese and bread. But this thing was not human. It was something long-fanged and sharp-clawed, and smelled of sulfur from the Nether Regions.

They rolled the body over and found that it had been stabbed through the heart with a splintery stake. "A night demon!" Menadel exclaimed.

"Well," Jackie said, "you're to be congratulated. A spell of yours finally worked."

"Not *my* spell, but the power of the Palace of Witchdame did this. I only had the idea to use the spell." Menadel was all modest pride. "We mustn't forget to thank the archangels for a good watch-and-ward. The palace provided the weapon and the angels did the rest. This thing would have killed us all in the night; instead they have killed it."

"Aye," said Jackie, kicking the body sharply. "It stuffed us with good ale, cheese, and bread, and was going to serve us forth. All we lacked was an apple in our teeth."

"I wonder," Elizabeth said, "how long this inn has been here. I like it not that such darkness could exist in my father's land, and that a demon such as this could openly go about his evil intentions. I don't like it, I don't like it one bit."

The three travelers gathered their gear together and left the inn. Elizabeth looked back at the inn and said, "I think we'd best make sure that this no longer will serve as a temptation for unwary travelers or for demons. I left the watch-and-wards standing in our room. I think now I will extend them over the entire inn and thereby safeguard it. And if it is more or less than an inn, my spell will cleanse this place of all evil."

Elizabeth stood a little ways from Jackie and Menadel and drew again her woodwitch dagger. She turned to each of the four quadrants, genuflected, and murmured a prayer of greeting to the Lords of the Watchtowers. She drew their appropriate pentacles and then, with a circling motion over her head, indicated that the circle upstairs was to widen. It did, and soon the entire inn was bathed in the pale blue light of wood-witch/witchlord magic. The building trembled as the evil enchantment left it; then, with a clap of thunder, it vanished away to dust and cold ashes.

The blue of the circle faded into the earth, leaving a slight sparkle in the shadows to indicate that this place was clean of all evil. Elizabeth nodded in satisfaction of her work and said, "There, that ought to do it. It wasn't an inn after all, but simply some door to the Nether Regions. I think we can now go safely on our way."

The three travelers mounted their horses and, leading their two pack ponies, they traveled onward toward the land called Cymru.

Chapter 12

Elizabeth took care as they passed from Hereforde into Brecknock and Carmarthen to get the permission of the local tree spirits and naiads that ruled the areas through which they traveled. These water and tree spirits were neither witchlord nor woodwitch; they were something far older. They dated back to the very beginning of the time of the Elf Kings, before the woodwitches or humans came to Englene.

Occasionally Elizabeth would talk to one of those slow-voiced, elderly rock spirits, and more than once she had left part of her lunch out on the rock to serve as an offering. Earth spirits could be dangerous, and in some ways less trustworthy than those of the trees. Yet it would not do to ignore the crotchety spirits that dwelt in the rocks, for they were also very wise. In this fashion they passed safely into the marches that were the gateway to Cymru.

As they rode, Princess Elizabeth found herself considering

seriously the problems they'd had upon the road. There had to be some form of protection for her and her friends, and the one person who could provide it was the Archbishop of Cymru. Then too, with the archbishop's aid she could send a message back to her father to reassure him that she was well and that her journey was going as it should.

As the travelers journeyed deeper into Cymru, the people of the area appeared to be of an entirely different sort than the fair-complected, light-haired, blue-eyed humans and witchlords of Englene. It was Elizabeth who noted a strong resemblance to the woodwitches in the short, dark people. She had met few woodwitches in her life other than her mother; they were rarely, if ever, seen at court and ventured into cities only when seeking needed supplies or to redress some grievance. When she asked Menadel if Cymru was indeed a land of the woodwitches, he replied in the negative.

"Your Grace, it's true that these Cymru people are like unto woodwitches. In fact, back before the time of the great wood-witch war, before King James Woodwitchbane, may his name be cursed, these people were indeed woodwitches. They were a particularly warlike tribe living in the mountains of Englene. But it was the Woodwitchbane that took away their magic. He drove them out of the woods and the hills and forced them to live in this place. He made them to live like humans and punished them for practicing the old arts. So gradually they left off being woodwitches and did not deal with their brothers and sisters of Englene.

"And as you can see, Your Grace, they have descended into being a most unhappy people. They are stunted and poor. Their lands give little to them. They live a hard and short life. This could be a land of great plenty with the help of the witchlords and the woodwitches together.

"But I fear that never will those two proud peoples come together for the good of Cymru. There is too much enmity, too much hatred, and too many old memories that go back so many centuries. The war was over in 1193, but the fear and the destruction goes on even now. When you are queen, think on what you see this day. Think on the people, and what you, who are both woodwitch and witchlord, might do for them."

"But did not my father express some concern for these people? Surely Cymru is his land, he would have some concern for these woodwitches even though they have no power he must fear."

"Power and fear are the only things the woodwitches have to keep from being like unto these, their poor cousins," said Menadel. "Cymru, since it is quiet and peaceful—and there are no more wars or battles anymore—Cymru is forgotten. It is merely a land far to the west, and nothing more to your father."

They rode on deeper into the land of Cymru's southern county, the land called Pembrokeshire. They crossed over the great river Tewy by ferry at one of the fords and spent several days journeying in the mighty forest of Erechfa. This section of Cymru was a flat, terraced land that moved in easy increments to the sea and the white cliffs of Mage Dumus. It was a land of farm cottages, charcoal burners's huts, small villages, mighty forests, and astonishing greenness. It might have been a very beautiful land save for the perpetually overcast sky, the darkness, and the rain.

"The people of Cymru," Menadel explained one night while trying to keep a fire going in a rainstorm, "have at least three dozen ways of describing rain. Any land that puts that much emphasis on a subject in their language must have a great deal of whatever it is they're talking about."

"And you must have no words for magic, old man," Jackie said. "Use a fire spell and get a good hot bonfire, for I am soaked to the skin."

Menadel blushed sadly and admitted that he lacked power to do fire spells. Elizabeth, as his pupil, had not been taught the proper spells, nor had she until now needed them.

"But Jackie," she said, "you've always built the fire before—"

"Yes, with dry wood and no rain! I can't keep fire going in the rain, but you two should be able to do it. Damnation, there's no place to shelter anywhere near here, and we're all likely to die of lung-rot if *you* don't do something, poppet, and do it quickly. Use your woodwitch dagger or something."

Elizabeth sighed and constructed a cone of power over the pitiful blaze—but it was not entirely satisfactory, since the cone would not let any of the smoke out of its configuration. They could have heat with smoke, not one or the other.

Elizabeth stared into the fire which even by magic they were barely able to keep alight. "Tell me, Menadel, does it ever not rain in Cymru?"

Menadel laughed and said, "I was told that in the reign of your great uncle, Henry the Hopeless, at midsummer day, between two of the clock and dusk some six hours later, it was said not to have rained in the town of Millford Haven. But of course, Your Grace, Millford Haven is to the south of us, and it's possible that some local disturbance or spell gone awry banished the rain for some short time. I do not know. But 'tis true that this land is very damp."

"Not nearly so damp as Faerie," Jackie observed, turning to keep his body in the blue cone and his head out in the rain so he could breathe. "I am told that if you stand at the very point of land that is at Mage Dumus you may look northward and see Faerie, that green boggy armpit of the universe. Isn't that true, Menadel?"

"Yes, 'tis very true. If the winds are clear and the weather's good, you can indeed see Faerie. But I'm not sure why anyone would want to. They say the Goddess created Faerie—if so, it was on a bad day, for a more unpleasant, boggy, dire place cannot be found upon this world! Its inhabitants are all were-folk, Boggies, or Things of great evil. No, I think we must consider Faerie as a land the Goddess forgot. We had best forget it, too. It's not part of your father's kingdom and we have no need to go there." Menadel wiped the smoke tears out of his eyes and sneezed violently several times.

"I'm sorry it's not a better spell," Elizabeth apologized. "It's the best I could do. Anyway, Faerie has been a very unlucky place for my family. My great-uncle, King William, was killed in Faerie when he tried to conquer it." She shuddered. "And my Uncle Robert was eaten in Faerie by a Thing. Anyplace that was evil enough to destroy my Uncle Robert and leave my Cousin John in charge of Gaeland is no place for the likes of me." Elizabeth, overcome by the smoke, poked her head out of the cone and took several gasping breaths.

"Well, we'll not have to worry about it," Menadel said. "You need go no farther than Mage Dumus itself. There's no need to go out to the headland unless you want to see the seacoast. Mage Dumus is west enough for what you need to do."

"And what is that?" Elizabeth leaned back into the cone and waved her dagger over the fire, watching the blue flames leap a little higher to sizzle as the rain touched them. "I hope whatever it is I do in that city will be of benefit to these people. Of course, right now I'm more interested in getting some proper shelter. I'm tired of these damp forests, this fire spell, and we've not seen so much as a hair of an inhabitant of these lands for two days running. How far are we from Mage Dumus?"

Menadel drew a large parchment scroll from out of his sleeve, unrolled it and studied its markings. "According to my calculations we should be in Mage Dumus by the night after next. There we'll worship in the shrine of the God. As to what deed or event must occur in that town, we will leave that to the God and Goddess to decide. Do not anticipate, Your grace, that is a grievous sin. Simply accept what the Gods might send."

Menadel could not be tempted by either Jackie or Elizabeth to enlarge on his comments. He simply shook his head, rolled up the scroll, and pushed it back into his sleeve, where it promplty seemed to collapse in upon itself and vanish into the folds of the heavily woven fabric.

Elizabeth, having no other choice, curbed her curiosity and waited for what Mage Dumus might bring.

Although it was referred to as a city, Mage Dumus was really hardly more than a good-sized village. It was the presence of the shrine of the Mage Dumus that made the village so important. In truth it was divided into two parts. There was the Shrine Close, and Mage Dumus Without-The-Walls.

The first abbot of the Mage Dumus shrine, one Dewi Sant, had stated that this valley had been created by the mighty Mage Dumus as a place where peace and tranquility could always be found, where the people would be especially blessed by the Goddess so they would always have beauty, wisdom, and the gift of song. No harm would come to these people as long as the shrine should stand. But Dumas had been dead since the sixth century BWE (Before Witchlord Era), and even so mighty a man of magic and power as he, must expect, after so long a time, that his power would gradually fade away.

The travelers clattered down the High Street and climbed the steep path to the gatehouse.

"Ho there, ho in the name of the Archbishop Tysilio," called one of the sentries. "What do you here in this land, and who do you seek?"

"We are but three gentle pilgrims," Elizabeth said, "come to make our vows and worship at the shrine. We ask nothing of you but to be allowed to worship in peace. And, if it be his will, I would seek audience of His Grace the Archbishop."

"What name shall I give to the Archbishop, that he might know you?" the sentry asked, staring in curiosity at the witch-lord woman and her two strange attendants.

"Tell him that Elizabeth, daughter to Richard, wishes to speak with him. That name should be enough."

"I'll relay your message to His Grace, the Archbishop. Go you now to the shrine, worship and fulfill your vows. May the blessings of the great God Owain be with you. May Freyja the Goddess bless you also."

Elizabeth replied with the proper formula of "Blessed be ye in the name of the God and the Goddess," and then beckoned Menadel and Jackie to ride through the gate toward the shrine.

Elizabeth, Menadel, and Jackie had prostrated themselves before the great altar and had murmured their prayers to the God Sulis-Owain. They knew their prayers were heard, for it was known to all that it did not matter by what name one worshipped the God or Goddess, as long as one believed that the God and Goddess were there.

They then made their way to the ladychapel, and Elizabeth presented herself to the Goddess and pronounced prayers to her in the name of Freyja. Taking the small handful of the sacred poppies from an attendant priestess, she kissed the blossoms and placed them at the feet of the Goddess's statue. She then moved closer to the altar and reached out her hand to touch the blue painted fold of the Goddess's cloak.

"Grant me my wish, gentle Goddess," she murmured in a low voice. "Let me be a good ruler over these that will be my people. Give me the man in the Great Circle at Avebury. Do not do this merely because I ask it, but because it is thy will as well. If it be yea or nay, I will accept, great Mother."

Elizabeth stepped backward from the lady altar, genuflected and left the chapel. Behind her on the face of the carved wooden figure there appeared a smile; then again, it may have only been a stray shaft of sunlight which had managed to find its way past the heavy sky of Cymru.

The highlight of the shrine, the place of awe and veneration, was the throne of Cymru. It was in the choir loft, off to the side, almost hidden under the large satin banners of the mage, the God, and the Goddess. The throne was not of ivory or gold or any precious stone. It was simple wood, carved with loving hands by a master craftsman. On the throne was a purple velvet cushion, embroidered in gold with the legend "Upon this throne sits the true ruler of Cymru." But no one sat on the throne. In all the history of this western land, back to the time of Dewi Sant himself, no one had ever successfully sat in the throne of the ruler of Cymru. Some said the throne had been built for Gabriel himself, or to Gabriel's orders.

Folk tales and legends had grown up around the throne. It was said that when the true, glorious ruler of Cymru sat on the throne, that Cymru would come into its own. There would be peace, prosperity, and good living for all the people of the land. It was murmured very quietly beside the fireplace, late at night when it was hoped no one was listening, that if this true ruler came, the woodwitch powers would be restored to the people of this land and they too would take their places as mighty mages and magicians of skill.

Over the years, one truth emerged: The throne was dangerous for any who tried to sit there without the right to do so, for sudden death visited any unworthy who sat on this, the sacred throne. A warning notice had been put up at the order of King Richard III, after the archbishop he had sent to this area had mistaken the throne for his cathedral chair and died.

Elizabeth, Jackie, and Menadel found their way to the choir stalls and stood before the legendary throne of Cymru. Elizabeth carefully read the notice placed there by orders of King Richard III, then looked at the simple throne and its velvet cushion and shook her head in wonderment.

"Menadel, it says here the death is a particularly nasty one. The very blood boils away in your brain and your body twitches with great agony. You fall down upon the ground foaming and cry out. You remain in that fashion until the sun goes down, and then your heart itself bursts in your chest and you die like a dog." She shuddered. "I like it not. Why is such a thing allowed by the God?"

Menadel shook his head and said, "But Your Grace, the throne is a thing of great mystery and power. It is neither good nor evil. Like any power it can be used for good or ill—but since it is of such tremendous power, it protects itself from any who would do evil by sitting in it. Only that one who is a true prince of Cymru may sit there. I wonder how long the people of Cymru will have to wait for their prince. They've waited for many a century—"

"And they will wait no more!"

It was a high childish voice, but a voice of great power; and when it spoke the wooden angels on the mighty hammer-beam roof above cried out, "Hosanna! Hosanna! Hosanna! The prince is come! The prince is with us!"

Bathed in a radiance of light which seemed to flow in all directions around the shrine and filled the choir, stood a young Cymru girl of some fourteen years, with the cropped hair and simple white robe of a novice priestess. She was, as most of her people were, short and darkhaired. Her eyes were the black of a woodwitch, large and knowing. She moved forward to kneel at Elizabeth's feet, and the light narrowed and centered in a cone around the princess herself.

"Hail, mighty prince," the girl said. "Hail, prince of Cymru. Hail, heir to the throne of the archangels." The wooden angels hosannaed again and again, while motes of golden light fell from their wooden hands and faces.

Elizabeth stood dazed and perplexed. She reached down, embarrassed, and lifted the child to her feet. When she looked into those dark, far-seeing eyes, she realized with a shock that this child had the *seeing* powers of her woodwitch ancestors— and prophesied true.

Elizabeth placed her hands on the child's head and murmured a blessing over her. Then, turning, she mounted the three shallow steps to the throne of Cymru—and sat on it. The organ cried out great peals of triumphant melody and the priests and priestesses gathered from the far corners of the shrine to bow before the throne. Overhead the grey sky of Duyfed parted, the clouds melted away, and the unhampered light of the sun shone on the shrine. Birds in the graveyard took up the cry. Soon bells all over the village began ringing by themselves, crying out the message that the prince of Cymru had come.

* * *

In the Archbishop's Palace, David Tysilio listened to the bells ring. He cried for his deacons and arrayed himself in the purple and scarlet and gold robes of high holiday. Seizing his crosier, he ran in a most undignified way toward the shrine, to see that miracle which had finally come upon his land.

The archbishop prostrated himself before the throne and intoned with the priests, the priestesses, and the angels on the roof, "Hosanna, hosanna, hosanna, the prince has come!"

Then he rose to his knees and faced Elizabeth. He placed his palms together in an attitude of prayer. "By my miter and crosier, I do hereby swear, lady, that I will not rise from this place until you accept my oath of fealty to you as the true ruler of Cymru."

Elizabeth considered this request. It might possibly be judged as treason to her father to accept such fealty. "I say to you, Archbishop, I will accept your fealty on this understanding: That no harm be done to the king by this oath, nor must there be any diminution of the honors due him. Will you so swear fealty?" She leaned forward and clasped her own hands around those of the archbishop.

Tysilio looked up into her eyes, bowed his head over their clasped hands, and murmured, "I do hereby vow and swear to be your liege man from this day forward, but in no wise negating my oath to His Majesty, King Richard of Englene. I do hereby pledge myself sworn unto the Princess Elizabeth of Englene to be her man forever. Whatever she may ask of me, so mote it be."

Elizabeth nodded gravely. "So mote it be," she said, removing her hands from those of the archbishop. "Now arise, my lord, and escort me to your palace, for I am weary and would rest and talk with you this day. But first let me know who is this young maid that did cry out my right as prince."

The archbishop saw the young girl standing beside the choir stall. "Ah, Guenhwyvar. I should have known that if our prince was come it would be you who would know it first." He beckoned to the child and when she came to his side he encircled her shoulders with one arm, pushing her downward into a kneeling position before the princess. "Your Royal Highness, may I present the child Guenhwyvar. She is my seer, possessor of that eldritch art, the second sight. She *sees* the future, my lady—not always when one would wish, or as clearly, but nothing but truth. She has been a rare and precious gift to us at Mage Dumus, but I present her to you to do with as you see fit."

Elizabeth leaned forward in the chair to look searchingly at the girl's upturned face. "Tell me, maiden," she said, "will you put that gift of the sight at my command? My life and safety may well rest in your hands."

The child nodded shyly, and glanced at the archbishop for reassurance. Then she said, "I'll be where you be, my lady, and if you go far off into strange places, I go with you. I am yours to command for all of my life."

Elizabeth accepted this simple oath. She then rose from the throne and stepped down to the level of the archbishop and the maiden. She reached out one hand to Tysilio and the other to Guenhwyvar and said, "Take me to your palace then, for I am sore weary, and all this glory is more than I can bear."

Chapter 13

The archbishop's solar was warm from the heat of blazing logs in the massive fireplace. The room, just off the chapel, was cozy and comfortable, but not ostentatious. Tysilio obviously used the room as a combination of library and study. His papers were scattered about, and there was a stack of beautifully bound books on the top of a massive table he was using for a desk.

The archbishop showed his guests into the room and bid them to take comfort there. He sent for a servant and ordered ale and oatcakes to be brought. Then, taking his place in the chair behind his improvised desk, he asked Elizabeth what she might wish of him.

"You must understand that I am uncertain how to deal with this situation. . . . I'm not sure my father will be any too pleased with these events. And as for the Lady Pemberly—oh my! What a fine kettle of treason she could make of that."

"Well, it might be best—that is—I mean, Your Royal Highness, depending of course on your will—" Archbishop Tysilio lost the thread of his conversation in a welter of twittering. "There are several possibilities, you see, and they must all be considered. Perhaps you should return to your father's palace and discuss this situation with him. But, on the other hand, if you have some important task to complete in this part of Cymru, I of course cannot prevent you from doing it—"

"I am on a pilgrimage," Elizabeth said. "I must visit the four quadrants of my father's kingdom. I have my father's permission for this, and I intend to continue my journey.

"I will need the following things from you: fresh horses, food, and changes of clothing for me and my companions. This last month on the road has been frought with difficulty. I think from this point on in the pilgrimage we had best change our tactics somewhat." She turned and looked at Menadel and Jackie. "I think you'll both agree with me. It's time I changed my identity. I will take on one of the positions which is mine by right, that of minstrel. As one of those lesser priestesses I will be protected by law from many of the dangers of travel, and my tabard will guarantee us shelter."

"A minstrel—but you can't—Your Royal Highness!" The archbishop was off and twittering again. "To send you forth in such a guise, a princess of Englene! How shall I justify myself to your father? You cannot ask that I tender such poor hospitality to *you*, the heir to the throne."

"That's exactly what she's asking for," Menadel said in measured tones. "She travels this way not as the princess of Englene, but as a woman fulfilling a holy vow. I bid you, do not hinder us, for it would be a grievous sin indeed."

"In that case—I suppose we'd best do it the way you wish. But what about your father?" Tysilio said.

"Send good King Richard a message that his daughter is bonny and buxom and that you sent her on her way with your blessings," Jackie explained. "It's simple enough. We've had nothing less from many a goodwife and innkeeper along the way. Surely the great Archbishop of Cymru can equal a lowly innkeeper's hospitality."

"Very well," the archbishop said, giving up completely. "I will do your will and provide you with what you want. Lord Menadel, speak to my steward as to what supplies and clothing you need. But I would request that you be my guests for a small feast this evening, and that you lodge overnight within the walls of my palace. In the morning I will see you on your way with all my blessings."

Tysilio was already mentally composing a letter to King Richard which would report that Elizabeth was in good health and continuing her pilgrimage. But Tysilio did not deem it politic to tell King Richard about the event that had taken place in the shrine. It would not be wise to let him know that after the miracle there, all of Cymru would consider Elizabeth, and Elizabeth alone, to be their rightful ruler.

Just how much Cymru wanted the Princess Elizabeth was demonstrated that night. The archbishop had sent messages hastily to some of the local nobility to attend their true prince that evening. Of course, by nobility it was not meant that he sent for witchlords. There were indeed some half-dozen witchlord overseers scattered in castles across Cymru—but like the question of not notifying Richard of his daughter's new position, it was unwise to let any other witchlord know of it either. Instead, the archbishop had sent for the chieftains of various Cymru Tribes.

For the entertainment of the company, an elderly druid had been persuaded to come out of his isolated retreat and sing songs of old Cymru, and even a woodwitch hymn or two. The songs were sad and gentle. They told of a time when all of the woodwitches had been one, united in power and strength, and the Goddess's blessing had been on them all. More than one face was marked with tears by the time the druid finished singing.

The dark blue clad old man put down his Cymru harp at the completion of his songs and came forward to stand in front of the table facing the princess. He said, "All of Duyfed is yours. All Gwynedd is yours. All of the lands and territories of Cymru are yours. You are that true prince and ruler we have waited for since the great Archangel Gabriel first made the throne. Now that you have come, it is time for you to lead Cymru to its glory. All the men, women, and children of this land will rise and follow you. They will gather up their pruning hooks, their plowshares, their reaping tools and their eating daggers, and they will follow you—yea, even into the very heart of Englene, and they will place you on the throne of

Englene as Queen Regina of all these great lands. You have
but to say the word, almighty prince, and an army such as the
world has not known before will rise up behind you, and fight
to the last small infant in your name. What say you, men of
Cymru?"

The druid turned and raised his arms to the chieftains and
their people. A great cry went up of "Elizabeth, Elizabeth,
ruler and prince forever. Elizabeth, we fight in your name."
The shouting filled the rafters and echoed in the far corners of
the Great Hall.

Elizabeth's hands gripped the arms of her chair until her
knuckles threatened to burst through her skin. She could not,
and would not, commit treason against her father.

She rose slowly to her feet and stood there, quietly looking
at each of them, one after the other, and then at last she stared
into the brown eyes of the old druid—eyes as brown as her
own. But his were old and wise and far-seeing, albeit in her
sight what they saw was an untruth and an impossibility.

"Great leaders of Cymru, Archbishop, and you, oh reverend
sir, I must say unto you that I have listened to what you have
said this night, and I know you have spoken a truth. All of
Cymru *would* follow me should I ask it. But I do *not* ask it.

"I will be your prince and I will carry the memory of your
love forever in my heart. I will do all in my power to increase
the benefits to Cymru. But do not ask me to come into my
own one day, one hour, or one minute sooner than the Goddess
has declared. Pray to the Goddess and to the God to make me
queen of Englene in their good time. But I say unto you as
your prince, do not ask that my father be cut off untimely. For
if I find that the hand of even one child in the land of Cymru
has been raised against my father, all of Cymru will be as
nothing to me. Hear me as your prince and *obey!*"

Elizabeth's words carried unmistakeable tones of majesty.
She spoke words of power to them and they bowed their heads
and accepted what she said. They would not commit treason
against King Richard. At least not now.

After the archbishop's guests had left, the archbishop, Elizabeth, Jackie, Menadel, and the young maiden Guenhwyvar
retired to the small room lying behind the dais of the Great
Hall.

"Oh dear, oh dear, oh dear," Archbishop Tysilio said. "We do seem to have an unfortunate strain of treason here in Cymru. These people, being of old woodwitch blood, chafe under your father's rule. I've done my best to make them a loyal people. You cannot blame me, Your Royal Highness. Nor can your father think ill of me for what has occurred this evening. I am deeply ashamed that my teachings have gone for naught, and I have not managed to make these people loyal to my king."

"Stubble it," Jackie said. "King Richard would not send a tyrant to these parts, nor would he send someone totally useless to him. I tell you, O *great* Archbishop-Yea-and-Nay, you are probably just the sort of willow-spined courtier the king needs in these wild parts. For if you had opened your budget out there in the Great Hall and screamed 'Treason, treason,' you'd have gotten your skull cloven open with an axe for your pains. There is no treason here. These men have merely declared their loyalty to their lady, Elizabeth, who in turn has declared her loyalty to the king. You have naught to worry about, so spare me your 'oh dears, oh dears.' I for one grow weary of your scuttling back and forth like some sort of timorous mouse."

"Tell me, Somers," Menadel said, "where did you learn so much of King Richard's policies? I am truly amazed. I did not know that our king had made a jester his chief counsellor."

"And you stubble it too, my fine fat tunny!" Jackie snapped. "We have no need to hear the opinion of an inept wizard at a time like this. I'll tell you where I learned politics, I learned at King Richard's knee. I am the one person in all of the kingdom who has access to the king at all times, in and out of any chamber, including the jakes. So do not point the finger at me and say, 'Where did *you* learn politics?' I was born and bred in the politics of the court, and I know how Richard picks his counsellors. I know this too, that while I am not of witchlord blood, I am human and I know what it is like to live under an overlord that is not of my people. These great chiefs you saw this night will go away praising our princess and her loyalty, and they will for a time obey her. But when the winter winds blow cold off the mountains and their children cry for bread and there is little or nothing to give them, they will remember this night and they will wonder if Elizabeth is indeed their prince. Then they will look eastward toward Englene and contemplate the sharpened edges of their plowshares.

"I say to you it must be one of two things: Either King Richard must improve the conditions here in Cymru, or he must prepare for war. I kept my ears open and my tongue still as we traveled through this land, and my young ears heard a great deal. There is a darkness here, a darkness of want and hunger. There is a spirit in this land that bodes evil for Richard and Englene. You, my lady princess, may manage to stave it off for some small time, but not forever—unfortunately, not for even as long as Richard might live."

"Guenhwyvar," Elizabeth said, turning to the young maid, "tell me, on your oath, is what my jester says true? Is there indeed such a spirit of darkness in this land?"

"Aye, my lady," the maiden said, coming to stand in front of Elizabeth. "Aye, it comes out of the sea until it covers all of Cymru. It's a mortal big darkness, it is. It comes in, dark and cowled, like a breath of the grave itself, and there's many of us with power that fear it. It is no good thing for Cymru or Englene. For I did *see* these twelve nights past in a sleeping condrim the face of Cymru scorched and broken. The men had gone and all the mothers were weeping for their dead children. When I dream, it can be so or not. What I *see* in the daylight hours is a truth that nothing can change, but what I condrim at night, that is what *might* be." The maiden took a deep breath, panting a little, as if such a long speech was not customary for her.

Elizabeth reached out and brushed the child's black hair off her face. "What you have told me is most disturbing. Archbishop"—she turned to Tysilio—"I wish parchment and a goosequill and ink, for I must write to my father that there is a darkness in the land that may indeed be some breath from the Nether Regions. After I have written my letter, I wish me and mine to be shown to your guest apartments so that we might sleep. With the morning sun I would be gone from this place, lest your chiefs come back and attempt to make me their general by force. If they should come to you after I am gone, you will not tell them where I am. That will not be a lie, for I shall not tell you where I go."

The archbishop bowed his head in submission and went to fetch the required writing things.

"Whatever persuasion he uses," Elizabeth said, "I will not remain here more than the night. You're right, Jackie, he is a bend-every-which-a-way courtier. My father *would* choose such a one for this unhappy land. But I do not entirely trust him. For while we night travel away from this place, he must stay and dwell at peace with the chiefs. The lords of Cymru are closer than my father, and I am sure the archbishop fears them far more than he fears King Richard. Tonight I will set the wards, and we will be watchful. As soon as there is the first sliver of Sulis's smile on the horizon, we will be gone."

True to her word, Elizabeth woke Jackie and Menadel in the last dark of the early morning. They dressed quickly in the clothing that had been provided by the archbishop's servants. Menadel now wore a black hooded robe, its heavy cowl large enough to pull over his face as far down as his chin.

Jackie had been given the second-best suit possessed by the archbishop's jester. It was a close enough fit and Jackie capered about the room to show off the glories of the vivid black, red, and yellow motley. The outfit was completed with high red boots, ass's ears, and a jester's bauble.

Elizabeth felt pride in what she wore. Like most of the royalty of Englene she had a talent for music. Her voice was clear and pure as a mountain spring, and she had been trained since infancy by the choirmaster of Westmonasterium. At her father's request she had applied for membership in the Minstrels's Guild when she was twelve and had been accepted. She was rightly entitled to the blue tabard of the minstrel.

The lady-minstrel's outfit consisted of a white linen shift and a fine red woolen kirtle, high blue knitted stockings, and stout red leather boots. Over all went a deep midnight blue tabard with a gold harp embroidered over the left breast and a light blue woolen cloak lined with red.

When they came out of the guest chamber into the Great Hall, they found that the archbishop had ordered a breakfast for them of oatcakes, porridge, cold mutton, fried herring, cheese, cider, and ale. The ale was fresh and potent, being that sort the common folk called "Father Whoresonne," and Menadel, Jackie, and Elizabeth all pronounced themselves quite pleased.

"I'm glad you appreciate such simple hospitality," Tysilio said. "The more I live in Cymru, the more I come to appreciate the simple ways of these folk. It is a part of understanding them. You, Your Royal Highness, must come to understand these people who you will someday rule over. I have a suggestion to make, if it please you. The cold months will soon be upon us and it would be better far were you to stay here with me in the palace until spring be come. Then you can go forth again wherever it is you wish to complete your vows. You'd find great comfort here and we would make good cheer together. I bid you give the suggestion some thought."

Elizabeth crumbled a piece of oatcake in her fingers. It was as she had thought; the archbishop was going to attempt to keep them there in Cymru. "My lord Tysilio," she said. "I am honored by your suggestion, and most grateful for it. But I cannot accept. My vow requires speed."

The archbishop bowed his head. "So be it," he said. "I will give you my blessing and then speed you on your way."

A strange sight met their eyes as Elizabeth, Menadel, Jackie, and Tysilio came down the great steps of the palace. There in the central courtyard, several of the archbishop's grooms were attempting to capture a magnificent white horse. In the early morning light the animal appeared to be carved from a single pearl, so luminescent was its coat. Its mane and tail flowed like silk, the tail so long that it brushed the ground. Its dainty feet and well-shaped head, flared nostrils, and dark eyes proclaimed it a Moorish horse, and Elizabeth gave a cry of joy at the sight of so beautiful an animal.

The archbishop's grooms were having a great deal of difficulty catching the horse. They ran after it with ropes, bridles, pieces of carrot, and handfuls of fresh grass, but the horse shied and danced and trotted out of their reach. They'd stop and wait for it to come closer, and then it would begin its game again. Elizabeth laughed to see the horse play so cleverly with the grooms. "Stay, stay, villeins," she cried to the grooms. "You'll not catch such a clever creature that way. Let me see what I might do with it."

At her command the grooms moved away from the horse, leaving it alone in the middle of the courtyard. Elizabeth walked slowly toward it, making pleasant chirping sounds and snapping her fingers at the animal. "Come, come, my beauty. Come, come, my lovely one," she called softly to it.

The horse stood still watching her, its nostrils wide to catch her scent, then gave a joyful whinny and trotted toward her. With a polished gracefulness, it bowed its forelegs deeply to her and rested its muzzle on the ground at her feet. She bent to caress its long narrow head and stroke its cheek. Its skin was as soft as swansdown, and the scent of it like new mown hay. The horse raised its head and pushed gently at her chest with its nose.

It nickered in recognition of her and allowed the princess to climb upon its back. She rode the horse bareback once, twice around the courtyard, and then brought it to a stop in front of the steps where the astonished archbishop and the others had watched her performance.

"Tell me, my lord archbishop," cried Elizabeth from the horse's back, "where did you find an animal of such rare beauty? If you can bear to part with it I will gladly purchase it from you."

The archbishop shook his head in bewilderment. "Alas, Your Royal Highness, before this day I have not set eyes on this horse—and as you say, it is a creature of great beauty. It is a horse fit only for a king and a ruler, and it is my thought that this horse was sent for you."

"Sent by whom?" the princess asked. "Are the chiefs attempting to bribe me into doing battle for them? Almost this horse tempts me, but I cannot accept such a gift if the price of it is war with my father."

The archbishop signaled to his head groom to come forth. He then questioned the man as to where the horse had come from. All he could say was that with the first flicker of dawn upon the far mountains the white horse had appeared in the streets of Mage Dumus Without-The-Walls. It had come straight to the archbishop's palace and had trotted into the courtyard as if it had lived there all its life. But any attempt on the part of the grooms to catch it or ride it had met with failure. Therefore the animal obviously did belong to the Princess Elizabeth, and it was the head groom's opinion that the horse was a creature of great magic.

"Good Archbishop," Elizabeth said, "I wish I could take this horse with me upon my journey, but the way I go is straight and narrow, and not for such an animal as this. Please, would you see this horse safely to my father's court? Give it into the hand of one Thomas Seymour, my squire. And if you love me,

Archbishop, you will give it to none other. Not to my father, not to the Lady Anne of Pemberly, nor to aught *but* Thomas Seymour! Will you so vow, David Tysilio?"

The archbishop bowed deeply to his princess. "I do so vow, and I will go with this horse to your father's court and be sure that your squire receives it. For should some lesser man go, the king or his lady might dissuade the messenger from his task."

Elizabeth slid off the horse's back and patted its shoulder in appreciation. "Well, my fond beauty. Will you go with the archbishop to my father's court and will you let Tom look after you and ride you?" The horse stretched its neck and tossed its mane, and Elizabeth took that for acceptance. "Very well, my lord, see you to it and give my blessings to young Tom, for I do sorely miss him."

"We had best be on our journey, Your Grace," Menadel said sharply, looking at the rising sun with some apprehension. There was far away on the distant hills a cloud of dust that well might be horsemen.

"You're quite right, Menadel. Now, we are all together except for the child Guenhwyvar. Where is she?"

"She slept last night in the maidens' dorter. I have asked her to present herself here and I confess to some surprise that she is tardy."

"I am sorry, my princess," Guenhwyvar said in a breathless voice as she ran out the door and down the steps to join the group in the courtyard. "Pray forgive me and do take me to foreign parts with you even though I am late. Old Madge the cook was exchanging my old kirtle and apern for this bit-o-best to make my journey in. Is it not mortal fine?" The young girl spun round so Elizabeth and her companions might see the handsome wine red gown she wore. She lifted the hem to show off the blue kirtle and dainty shoes. "Never fear that I'll not be able to ride in it. I shall, and be with you wherever you are going, but it is such a good thing to do it in new clothes."

Elizabeth laughed at the young girl's joy and realized that new clothing was not something a person in her position as a novice received very often. "Very well, child, mount that bay pony there and let us be gone."

Guenhwyvar looked to where the grooms were collecting the group of sturdy horses for the journey. "And will you be riding Jibriel? The Archangel Gabriel sent him for you, my lady. He came and told me so this morning while I was at my prayers."

"Ah, so it *is* your horse, my lady Elizabeth," Tysilio said. "I see that you are truly in the care of the Gods, and so I will say unto your father."

Menadel had started at the horse's name, and he went closer to the animal to get a better look at it. "Jibriel?" he asked dubiously, and as the horse winked at him he said, so softly that the others could not hear, "Forgive me, my lord, I did not recognize you!"

But the horse said nothing in return.

With an invoking of the Gods for safety on the journey, much formality and salutations on both sides, the travelers took leave of the archbishop and his palace. They rode out of Mage Dumus Without-The-Walls and traveled west toward the sea. It was best not to let anyone in the village see precisely what direction they were going to travel next. Menadel kept watching the cloud of dust in the distance. He was sure it was the warrior chiefs of Cymru riding out of the east.

"I would hide myself somewhere this day, Your Grace," he said. "I think the archbishop will send spies after us, so he will know which way we travel. Jackie, do you know of any hiding place in this wretched land?"

Before Jackie could answer, Guenhwyvar spoke up. "If you don't mind that it's naught but a farm, my father and mother live but half a league from this place. They would be glad to give you shelter there. Then too," she said, "I could bid them farewell and ask a daughter's blessing of them, for I may not see them again. Three days past when I came to visit them they were feeling so common. My father complained of agonies in his chest and head, and my mother sat by the fire and stared at the flame, saying she saw demons in it. I worry for them. There is a she-demon of blackness that gets into the lungs and lodges her eggs there, and they grow until no air can get in. What little life there is left to a body oozes away until one is cold and dead with it. It is an evil thing. So if it be your pleasure and by your leave, I would see to their comfort before going foreign."

"It is by my pleasure," Elizabeth said, smiling at the maiden.

"I know how dear my parents were to me, and I would not ask of anyone that they leave their country and land without parents's blessing. Lead the way, child, and we will follow." But to Menadel she said, "I like it not that such a thing could be in my father's land. We must do what we can to aid Guenhwyvar's folk and end this demon's deadly reign. How could my father let such a thing be?"

Menadel had no answer to the princess's question.

Guenhwyvar's father's farm was large and prosperous looking. There were many sheep and fine cattle in the fields, and the stone and timber buildings were strong and well built. But when Guenhwyvar called out to her parents and the servants, no one answered.

The maiden slid off her small pony and ran to knock at the farmhouse door, but there was still no answer. "They are shy of strange folk," she said in explanation. "Perhaps a fever rests upon the servants too, and they cannot take themselves from their beds."

There was an undercurrent of fear in the young woman's voice. In silence Elizabeth got off her horse and put her arm round Guenhwyvar's shoulders, holding the child to her as Menadel and Jackie forced the door of the house and entered it. They returned in but a moment, both of them grave.

It was Jackie who, with great pity in his eyes, said to young Guenhwyvar, "I fear, my little lass, that your parents have gone into the Western Lands and have not stayed long enough to give you their blessing. As for the servants, they have fled."

Guenhwyvar burst into tears, and buried her face in the princess's tabard.

"There, there, my sweetling. There, there, my little one. Hush, hush, hush." Elizabeth held the maiden and rocked her against her body. She then looked at Menadel and Jackie and there was quiet command in her eyes as she said, "Kill the demon's young and deal with what remains as should be done. I will take the child some little pace away. When you've finished, and naught but mounds of earth remain to show her parents's resting place, call out and I will bring her back so she might say some words of farewell."

Elizabeth took the weeping child away from the house toward the carp pond. She gently persuaded the maiden to tell her about the ducks on the water and whether they had names or not, and what were their individual characteristics: which was mean, which was cross, and which laid the most eggs. In this fashion she distracted Guenhwyvar from the sound of shovels and the fall of crumbling earth.

It was well on to noon when Jackie found them by the pond. Taking Guenhwyvar by one hand, he led her to the spot where he and Menadel had buried her parents. She stood silent at the foot of the larger of the two mounds. Jackie had put flat stones at their heads and scattered flowers over the raw dirt.

"It is a fine burying you've done for my folk and I am glad of it. She turned to look at Elizabeth, pleading with the princess with her eyes. "Would it be fitting for me to be left alone here for some moments to mourn them properly? I would say goodbye in my own way. If I were to break down and throw myself into the dirt and mewk like a motherless kitten, I would at least not shame myself in front of such grand folk as you."

Elizabeth, Jackie, and Menadel moved away, and the maiden did what she deemed necessary to aid her parents safely into the Western Lands of Avalon.

Compassionately, Elizabeth helped Guenhwyvar mount her pony. Then, mounting her own horse and taking the reins of one of the pack animals, she turned to Menadel and said, "We'll leave word for the servants and the archbishop at the next farm over, so that this place shall be cared for in my name. But what shall I do about the night hag? Is it my duty to deal with the demon, or should I tell the archbishop or my father to destroy it?"

"My lady, the demon is gone. It has lost its young and now looks for other victims. You will have more than your share of demons to deal with in the future. Leave this one to the archbishop."

After a moment's consideration, Elizabeth nodded.

"What will you take from this land to give as a gift to your father?" Menadel asked. "Remember, he did ask that you bring him some sign of the peace in his land."

"I think I will have Guenhwyvar tell him of the demon who killed her folk," Elizabeth muttered, half to herself. "That should give him some idea of *his* peace in this place."

Menadel shook his head in wonderment at the bitterness in

Elizabeth's voice, and Jackie whistled sharply at her clear wish to do insult to King Richard. But one look at her face and the jester decided it would be far better to say nothing.

Menadel agreed. He asked in a very mild voice, "Where would you lead us next, Your Grace?"

Elizabeth turned her horse's head toward the distant hills of the north of Cymru. "North!" she said in a ringing voice. "We travel north in the name of Archangel Uriel, and my vow."

NORTH

Salve Uriel, nam tellus et omnia
viva regno tuo pergaudent.

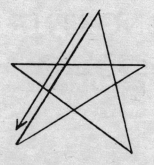

I pray to the Black Bull, master of the earth,
Dark ruler of the mountains and all that lies
Beneath them. Great prince of the element of earth!
Be with me, I pray thee. Guard me and mine
From all perils approaching from the North!

Chapter 14

Elizabeth and her companions journeyed northward through Dewisland toward the mountains of Meirionydd, those great northern hills they would have to climb in their journey to the northernmost point in the kingdom of Englene.

Elizabeth noted the changes in the turn of the seasons as they journeyed northward. The land changed from the golden green of the harvest season to the reds and yellows of the autumn of the year. A cold wind blew off the bay and there was the hint of the snow to come—and the rain.

The miracle in the shrine did not stop the rain from falling every night. Guenhwyvar attempted to lighten the journey by teaching Jackie each of the twenty-eight ways her people had of describing the rain. While such expressions as "the sky is emptying" and "the rain, 'tis main hinderable," and such delights as "it's mizzling fair to make the ground sappy" were interesting additions to the jester's vocabulary, their humor faded after a time—particularly the wetter the jester got.

Guenhwyvar seemed to suffer the most from the rain. A cough had settled in her chest, and the cold only served to make it worse. As if rain and cold were not enough, there was the constant fear of being overtaken by an army sent by the chiefs of Cymru, or perhaps the king's men sent by word of the Archbishop David Tysilio.

It was with a certain amount of relief that the travelers sighted a band of pilgrims along the Ceredigion road. And with Menadel's approval they joined the band of woodwitches, humans, and sprigs of witchlord nobility who were on their way to the festival of Owain Glyn Dwr, who was known in these lands as Glyn Dwr the Mage, although his title was not recognized in Englene.

This Glyn Dwr had been a great hero of the lands of Cymru. It was said that he had been a mighty woodwitch warrior who had battled King James Woodwitchbane, that accursed king who had caused the great civil war with the woodwitches and had exiled them to the forests, the hills, and the far lands of Cymru. There were those among the pilgrims who spoke of the coming of the prince, a new Glyn Dwr who would lead them to freedom and to their former powers.

Elizabeth found this talk of the prince fascinating. Even in the few short days since she had left Mage Dumus and its shrine, the tale of the miracle had spread throughout Cymru. It was with great amusement she heard herself described as seven feet tall, carrying a fiery sword, speaking perfectly the tongue of Cymru, and, most amusing, being undoubtedly male. After some laughter at this change of gender, she realized that in that fact lay her chief safety. If all Cymru was seeking a mighty warrior prince, they were not likely to look too closely at a witchdame minstrel woman.

The journey to the shrine city of Aberystwyth was lightened by the presence of the pilgrims, and many a merry tale and song were shared among them. Two young witchlords of Cymru, Robert of Carmarthen and David, Lord Beaumaris, journeyed as pilgrims and Elizabeth found comfort in these young witchlords's company, reminding her of an earlier part of her life, a part that now seemed far away. For even though Elizabeth was on the pilgrimage to find the man of the Avebury Circle, she was still a lusty young woman. While at night she might dream of her mysterious hero in the gold mask, during the day her interests were on a much less lofty plane. Robert and David were as alike as two eggs from the same hen, with their blond handsomeness, cheerful gossip, and quick wit, yet she felt no physical interest in either man, and she found herself seeking instead the company of another pilgrim, a human named Thomas the Cordwainer. Thomas was, by any standards, an extremely handsome man. His skin was the color of a ripe peach, and his hair was a deep tawny gold with red highlights. Elizabeth was sure that she, or any other woman, could drown in the deep violet blue of his eyes. He sat a horse well, and his singing voice was by far the best of any of the pilgrims; it blended with Elizabeth's like a nightingale with a lark. The pain and travail of travel became insignificant as long as she could share the difficulties with Tom.

A day or two out of Aberystwyth, Jackie found himself riding at the back of the train of pilgrims with Menadel, who was trying to deal with a balky pack horse.

"Jackie," Menadel said, "I think when we get to Aberystwyth I shall have to do something about these horses. What we really need are sturdy northern ponies that can deal with these hills. I'm afraid the archbishop's horses are entirely too dainty about where they put their feet."

"Well, young Cordwainer says there's an excellent horse fair to be seen at Aberystwyth. You might do well to trade them off. You can, I assume, trade horses, or are you as bad at that as you are at magic?"

Menadel turned in the saddle to look at the jester. "You needn't worry, fool. I will do very well by the horse fair. But what of you? Are you going to visit the fair and buy some trinket or fairing for the Lady Elizabeth?"

Jackie looked glum at the mention of Elizabeth. "I'd buy the poppet a fairing if I thought she could appreciate its coming from me. I think I'd best take young Guenhwyvar to the fair. I doubt she's ever seen one. She might be more appreciative of it. As for Elizabeth—" Jackie sighed and scratched his chin. "As for Elizabeth, I think she'll probably want to see the fair with young Thomas, more's the pity. What think you of her caring for him?"

"I see no harm in it," Menadel said. "He's simply a human, and his presence in her bed won't make any difference one way or another. I know in her heart she wants a proper consort, and she is going through a great deal of travail to get one. An escapade along the way, like the cordwainer, troubles me not."

"Is that all it is to you and to her, one more human in her bed? Did you ever think of what it might be to him?" Jackie asked bitterly. "Or for that matter, to any human? She can bestow her favors where she wishes, and when she has gotten what she wants, on to some witchlord and forget that she ever even noticed a human existed."

Menadel looked at Jackie searchingly, and then shook his head sadly at what he saw so plainly on the fool's face. "Jackie Somers, I say to you, do not involve your heart too much in the romantic affairs of a princess. While there is no harm in Thomas the Cordwainer being in the princess's bed, there may be a great deal of harm with someone she cares for more deeply. I give you this as a word of caution, for I will not see the Lady Elizabeth hurt by you or any other."

"I would rather have myself pulled apart by horses, or chopped in two by the king's executioner than harm the Lady Elizabeth! I promise you, old man, I will not hurt her. But I hope Thomas the Cordwainer can say the same."

And Jackie began to sing a lament for his lady. In hopes that Elizabeth might hear, he sang it quite loud:

> *What dreamed I this night?*
> *Methought the world was turned upside down*
> *The sun, the moon had lost their force and light;*
> *The sea also drown tower and town*
> *Yet more marvel how that I heard the sound*
> *Of one's own voice saying, "Bear in they mind,*
> *Thy lady hath forgotten to be kind."*

But Elizabeth had ears for only the cordwainer's voice.

Had Jackie or Menadel been able to read young Thomas's mind they would have both been greatly relieved, for Thomas had no interest whatsoever in a tall, gawky witchdame. Indeed, he was betrothed to a fair and buxom young lass who lived in Aberystwyth, and was looking forward to being reunited with his beloved Megan. Elizabeth's languishing looks had been at first highly amusing, but now they had begun to grate. He worried about the woman's interest, for he knew full well that a witchdame's anger could be a frightful thing.

Aberystwyth was in full fete for the Glyn Dwr fair. There were cookstalls, tinkers, gypsies, and sellers of trinkets. There were handwoven fabrics, pots, pans, toys, and perfumes from Araby; cakes, suckets, gingerbread, huffcap ale and Longbow cider, comfits, sweetmeats, and strongly scented fruit wines. A young man could buy rings and necklaces, chains, charms, and bits of lace for his lady. There were sports, games, and tests of skill, a maypole, a greased pig, and even an archery contest. All of Aberystwyth was a riot of color and noise and savory scents. It was enough to quicken the blood and warm the heart of any lusty young lad or wench.

Over dinner, Menadel announced his intention of going to the horse fair the next day and exchanging their high-bred animals for sturdy northern ponies. Elizabeth, having dealt with her own recalcitrant horse, was quite in agreement with his plan.

Jackie asked her if she wished to accompany him and savor the joys of the fair. With a stammer and a blush Elizabeth refused Jackie's offer. It was clear to everyone at the table that while Thomas had not yet asked her, she had high hopes of asking him.

To cover the embarrassment, Guenhwyvar piped up and said, "Oh Jackie, Jackie, do take me! You know I've not been to a fair before. I want to see the horses and the gypsies's booths, and perhaps have a bit of gingerbread."

"Of course, little lass. I'll buy you gingerbread to fill your belly, and even get you fair mazed on strong ale. We'll look at all the animals you wish. Then, like any farm lad with his fair lass, I'll buy you a fairing. How does that sound to you?"

Guenhwyvar bounced up and down on the bench like a child and clapped her hands. "Oh Jackie, that would be a marvel! I'd love being about with a wee handsome lad like you. It would be a beauty to see a fair, all-a-both with you and my lord Menadel."

Elizabeth smiled at the young maid's enthusiasm. She sat back against the wall and listened to Jackie and Menadel outlining their plans for what to see first at the fair and what would most please young Guenhwyvar. Her own thoughts were on what a splendid opportunity it was to get Thomas the Cord-wainer alone. Perhaps they would wander the fair together and eat gingerbread, and then come back to the inn for something far more interesting. She drifted into a pleasant daydream of how lovely a day she would be able to spend in the company of Thomas, and found she could hardly wait until the morrow.

In the morning Elizabeth saw Menadel, Jackie, and Guenhwyvar off to the fair, and sat waiting in the taproom for Thomas to appear. He came down from the dormer after all the other pilgrims had left for the shrine. He was so late that Elizabeth had begun to fear she had somehow missed him in the rush. But just as she had almost given up hope, he came down the stairs, a scrubbed and brushed vision of human hand-someness.

He had put on a new white shirt, blue trunk hose, and a buff leather jerkin that Elizabeth had never seen before. His high boots had been brushed to perfection. He had even man-aged to acquire a velvet cape that, while much the worse for wear, still had more than a touch of courtly dash to it.

Elizabeth's breathing speeded up and she smiled at the thought that Thomas had dressed so enchantingly for her.

"You look fair as the day, Thomas," she said sweetly. "Would you be going to the Glyn Dwr fair? If so I would be glad of your company—for the fair and aught else we might consider."

"My lady," Thomas answered, "I am going to the Glyn Dwr fair, but I am not going alone. For in this town lives my betrothed, Megan the blacksmith's daughter. I would rather spend the day with her than with any great lady born."

Elizabeth saw this as only a slight impediment; it did not occur to her that this human could be refusing her request. "Thomas," she said in a peremptory voice, "I will only be in Aberystwyth this day and then we travel on. You will have many days to spend with your betrothed. I *ask* this day of you. This day and anything else I might wish of you." Without realizing it, her voice had taken on a royal tone of command.

Thomas shook his head, prepared to argue with a witchdame minstrel. "I am sorry, my lady. I cannot honor your request. It's wrong for the likes of you to ask it of the likes of me. If you want someone to take you 'round the fair, and into whatever forest glen you fancy, there were two young witchlords with us. I suggest you ask them.

"But as for me and mine, I am a human and I ask nothing more than a bonny human lass to share my bed. This day is for Megan. This day, tomorrow, and as long as she may live. I will not freely give my body or my love to another."

Elizabeth felt her face go red with shock and embarrassment. She had never been refused anything she might ask of witchlord or human male. Many a young man at court had vied for even the honor of touching her hand. And to have this grubby little human stand up to her and say "no" tempted her sorely to turn him into a frog. But she wasn't at all sure she knew the proper spell, and anyway, it did work best on Royalty!

"Oh, very well! Go your way and see the fair with your little mopsy. I don't know why I even troubled myself with the likes of you."

Thomas bowed low to Elizabeth, then turned and walked out of the inn without even so much as a glance backward. And in later years, when he realized what and who he had turned down, he felt no regret. What an interesting tale it made to tell around the fire of a cold winter evening—how he refused the favors of the princess of Englene!

It was full dark when Jackie returned alone to the inn. Menadel had taken Guenhwyvar off to buy herbs to cure her cough, and then to see a puppet play that was being presented in the forecourt of the Glyn Dwr shrine. The old man and the young girl had taken to each other well. Jackie had found himself more and more an outsider in the conversations the two had. He had wandered forlornly around the fair, looking first at this great amazement and then at another. He saw the tooth-puller, the two-headed fish, and the woodwitch who swallowed fire, and could not even think of one good jape to make. He ate gingerbread, but it was as sawdust in his mouth. Even Guenhwyvar's excited laughter when he presented her with a wooden jumping jack did not appease the gloom that filled his soul. At last he wandered away to see the fair on his own.

On the very outer fringe of the fairground, where gathered gypsies, woodwitches, and those who might have some dishonest deal in mind—a daughter's virtue to sell, a pocket to pick, or a purse to cut—he found even these slight touches of depravity had no amusement for him. So he turned his way back towards the inn and met an old woodwitch woman who was selling flowers beside the roadway.

"Aye, there's a likely young lad!" the old woman cried out. "There's a fair bonny boy who wants to take something pleasant to his lass. Buy my violets, buy roses, buy marigolds, buy something sweet for you lass, pretty-faced one!"

Jackie stopped to look at the flowers in the old crone's basket. Much to his surprise, they represented flowers from all seasons of the year. There were daffodils, daisies, holly, and chrysanthemums. There were fair spring roses and a pure white midwinter rose all mixed together, and it was a rare sight to see. The magic of it reminded him of Elizabeth and he felt in his purse for a copper or two.

"Tell me, old woman, what of all the marvels in your basket is the most marvelous? For I would take a fairing to my lady, even though she disdains me."

"Ah, something special for a cold-hearted lass. I have just the thing, my boy. Just the thing to make her buxom and bonny and bouncing in bed." The old crone laughed and, to Jackie's surprise, it was not a cackle but a clear high trill like the cry of a blackbird at dawn. She rummaged in her basket and took out a small bit of coarse cloth, which, when she unwrapped it, revealed a small ring. At first Jackie thought the ring was made of flowers, little blue forget-me-nots in a circle, with a drop or two of dew still upon them. Then with a closer inspection he realized the ring was silverwork, and there were small moonstone crystals caught on the delicate turquoise petals. It was a pretty piece, a simple fairing of nothing more than silver and semiprecious stones. But it pleased him well, and he knew it would also please Elizabeth.

The old woman pointed out the inscription engraved on the inside: "When this you see, remember me"—and gave him the ring in return for his coppers. Then she said, "I tell you, little one, there is an enchantment upon this ring. Catch your lady's tears in it, and she will be yours forever. No matter who she may marry or where she may go, she will remember you with great tenderness. How can *you* ask for more than that of *your* lady?"

Jackie slipped the ring onto his hand, made his fairwell to

the old woman, and walked away. The woodwitch sat watching him with tears in her eyes for a lovesick fool.

Jackie hoped that Elizabeth would have sent the cordwainer on his way, so perhaps she might have some time for him. Just a little time, to talk and laugh together. Then he would give her the fairing to let her know that no matter what may have been between her and Thomas, she was still his poppet and his lady.

Elizabeth was not in the taproom, so with a heavy heart he went upstairs to the chamber that she and Guenhwyvar shared. He stood outside the door, with his ear against the wood, listening for any activity within. But there was no sound of bed sporting from the room.

He lifted the latch quietly, and with the skill of long practice eased the door open slightly. The room was dim, lit only by one candle. Elizabeth was alone in the big bed that she shared with Guenhwyvar. She was dressed in a nightshift, and her hair was unbound and flowed about her shoulders like a copper spider's web.

As Jackie stood by the door, marveling at how fair she was, he realized she was crying. He heard sniffling and snorting sounds that made it clear she'd reached that point in her weeping where her nose had become stuffy, red and uncomfortable, and that she was in need of a handkerchief.

Walking toward the bed, Jackie pulled from the bosom of his shirt a fine white linen handkerchief, one that the Queen Dianne had embroidered for his last birthday. Mutely he offered it to the princess, and then turned his head while she proceeded with a great honking and snorting to work the stuffiness out of her nose.

"Thank you, Jackie," she said wetly. "it was very kind of you. Far kinder than I deserved. I know I've been ignoring you shamefully lately. I didn't mean to. . . ."

She burst out in fresh weeping, so Jackie climbed onto the bed beside her, to pat her shoulder and comfort her. "There, there, there, poppet, there, there. Don't be aweeping like that. You've got your eyes all pink and your nose shines like a red coal on the hearthplace. Come, come. Leave the crying for those who do it prettily, like the Pemberly. You and I can't manage to do anything but become sodden wretches when we cry. I learned early on that if I could not do it well, not to do it at all."

Elizabeth mopped her face with the now soggy handkerchief. "I can't help it!" she wailed. "I feel perfectly miserable. I want to go home. I'm tired of this traveling and I'm tired of being cold and wet and uncomfortable. I'm tired of sleeping on the ground, and I'm tired of humans!"

"Ah," Jackie said. "Now we reach the meat of it. Tired of humans, are you? A queen who is tired of half her population will not remain queen long."

"But they hate me!" Elizabeth sobbed afresh. "They don't know their place. They don't know what they're good for, and he didn't want me!" Elizabeth went off into a fresh crying jag.

"Indeed, we have come to the meat of it. So your fair Thomas turned you down. Take heart, poppet, there'll be more like him, and you'll soon forget."

"It's not just him, Jackie. This is the first time anyone has ever turned me down. I'm the Princess Elizabeth! *That* makes me desirable. But to Tom, I was simply a witchdame, and if he didn't want me, then perhaps others have felt the same, too. I know I'm not beautiful, I haven't a slender waist or a little high bosom, nor are my hips as slender as a snake's, and my face goes too pink in the sun."

With much wailing, Elizabeth enumerated her shortcomings as she saw them. She did not realize that in Jackie's eyes they were not shortcomings, but merely aspects of his dear Elizabeth, his lady.

"What if no one had ever really wanted me? Here I am, going through this wretched journey to get my consort and what if he doesn't really want me, the great gawk? What if he only wants Elizabeth the princess, heir of Englene? I would die of shame."

"No one dies of shame. It's obvious that though you might have wanted Tom, he did not want you. But he is but one man among many. You are a fine, buxom, bonny woman. And in my eyes there is no fairer in all Englene, or even the lands over the sea."

"What would *you* know of rejection?" Elizabeth said. "You're in and out of any bed you want. But I wanted this human and he did not want me, or anyone like me. I did not know I could be despised in that manner."

"Elizabeth," Jackie said softly, "you act as though, because one human has rejected you, all have rejected you. But this is not true. Believe me, you are beloved in the hearts of your people. More than one human male has said to me that he thought you were a fine figure of a woman, and in case you have not noticed, my dear—"

Jackie bent close to the princess, and placed one hand gently upon her cheek to wipe away her tears. And as he watched, he saw her tears flow over the little forget-me-not ring he wore. He looked at it and remembered the old woman's words.

"In case you have forgotten, poppet, I am human, and I have wanted you for many a long and lonely night." Jackie gathered the weeping princess in his arms, and with a gentleness that was born of both love and pity, he kissed away the tears. First the ones on her cheeks, then on her neck. He even chased the one or two errant drops that had managed to fall on her soft white bosom.

The morning sun found its way through chinks in the shutters of the dormer room of the inn at Aberystwyth. The sun striped its way across the bedcovers and the sleeping mound that was the Princess Elizabeth. Menadel opened the door to the princess's room and stood waiting by the bed, uncertain whether to awaken his lady or not. The sun was well up, though it was still before noon. But Menadel had done well in the horse trading and his six chosen mountain ponies were all eager and anxious for the journey.

He reached out and gently shook the sleeping woman by the shoulder. Elizabeth stretched and turned over, reaching out with one arm toward the empty side of the bed. Her eyes opened, she yawned and turned over, smiling into Menadel's face. The pleased expression on her face changed to one of startled surprise.

"Where's Jackie?" she asked, sitting up in bed.

Menadel frowned. He now understood why the jester had not come to the men's dormer that past night, and young Guenhwyvar had insisted on sleeping in the maid's dorter. "The fool is out saddling our horses. I thought it wise to be on our way north. It's a long way to Berewic and I fear with so many people in the city your identity might be known."

"All right. It's probably a good idea to get on the way,

although I should have liked an hour or two more sleep."
Yawning, Elizabeth slid from the bed and walked across the
room to open the window. She leaned on the rough wooden
sill and looked down into the inn courtyard where she could
see Jackie and Guenhwyvar readying the horses. She waved
to them, completely oblivious of the fact that she was clad only
in a sheer linen nightshift. But on her left hand she wore Jackie's
little ring.

"My lady! Come away from there until you're dressed. Did
not the Lady Jane teach you it was an improper thing to be
hanging out of windows with half your body exposed?" said
Menadel, shocked to the core. "I cannot understand how your
mother could have come to raise such a hoyden." There was
a tone to Menadel's voice that Elizabeth had never heard before,
a biting asperity.

She turned and faced the wizard. "Shall I dress in front of
you, Uncle? Or do you want to wait beyond the door? You are
not yourself this day. Are you angry with me, or did last night's
dinner disagree with you?"

"As to the latter, I ate well; and the former, yes, I am angry
with you. And as to that other question that figured in there
somewhere or another, get yourself dressed, child. At my age
and position in life the sight of a young maid clothing herself
will not do anything to my humors. Besides, knowing your
usual skill with clothing, you will probably need me to lace
you up and fasten what furbelows you insist on wearing."

"You *are* in an irritated mood. I thought you said the trading
went well," she said as she bundled herself into her minstrel's
gown and tabard. "Can you help me lace this kirtle, please?"

The wizard grabbed the lacing cords in his strong hands and
gave them a solid yank, causing Elizabeth to squeal in dismay.
"Either tell me why you're irritated or leave off. I am in a
perfectly lovely mood, and will not have it ruined by you
blackdogging about me."

"I tell you this, my lady." Menadel was redfaced and puffing
with rage like a toad. "I had no fear of you spending the night
with young Cordwainer. But I did not know you would be
inviting the fool to your bed. It is not wise! Were I in your
father's place, I would have young Somers's head removed
from his shoulders for so daring a deed as seducing his princess!"

Elizabeth laughed and said, "Execute Jackie for climbing into my bed? He's been in *every* lady's bed at court—including, so he claims, Aunt Marguerite's. About the only citadel he's not been able to conquer is the Pemberly. So why all this fuss about Jackie and me? It's a perfectly natural thing for a man and a maid. Frankly, I preferred him to that milky faced boy, Thomas the Cordwainer."

Menadel sighed. He had seen Thomas the Cordwainer with his buxom young maid when he had walked about the fairgrounds with Jackie and Guenhwyvar. He had a good idea what had happened between Elizabeth and the young man.

"Do you remember why we are going on this journey? Do you remember the man in the Circle at Avebury? Will you give up your quest so quickly for a tumble with a lewd jester? Does his twisted little body pleasure you so much that you've forgotten that golden demigod that was given to you?"

"I've not forgotten," Elizabeth said in a sulky tone. "And I say to you, that man will be my consort if *he* wishes to be. For I have learned that I cannot automatically assume that any man I might wish will be mine."

Menadel bowed his head in submission. The pattern of Elizabeth's life was in far greater hands than his.

Chapter 15

"I thought we'd *never* reach the sea before full dark." Elizabeth stood in her stirrups, the better to get a glimpse of the rocky coast below. Jackie, Menadel, and Guenhwyvar were but silhouettes against the setting sun. "Jackie, where in the name of the Nether Regions *are* we?" she asked. "I can see a town and a castle beyond, but the fog is coming in too fast for details." She could hear a gull cry out and the sound of a merman answering from the waves below, but the cold wind on the hillside tore at her own voice, reducing it to a whisper. "I don't like the look of it," she added. "I don't like it at all. Too dark, by half—"

"According to our map, that should be Bamborow Castle and the village of Bamborow-lea," Jackie said. "Do you know who the local lord is?"

"It should belong to one of the Percys, Your Grace," Menadel spoke from deep within his cowl. "Young Thomas Percy, I think, but he's nigh fifty if he's a day. Not young, but still a Percy, for all that. . . ."

"Bamborow, Bamborow," Elizabeth mused. "That means we're not far from the border of Gaeland. This is as north as I go. The king said I was to see the land I would rule, but I don't think Father meant I should be paying calls on my Cousin John. I'm not passing over Grandfather's border, and if you look there to the north you can see the reflection of it on the clouds. Do you see that blue Aurora Borealis? That's King Edward's work."

"What? Is that still there?" Menadel stretched in his saddle to see the line that Edward the Just had marked with his sword, dividing his kingdom into two parts for his twin sons.

"Of course it's still there," Elizabeth said impatiently. "When my grandfather did something, he did it stay. That dividing line will last until the ruler of Englene decides to destroy it, and Father's not likely to do that."

"It's all very interesting," said Jackie, "but it buys us no bed for the night. Where do you intend to sleep? I smell snow in the air. Should we push on, or do you think the Percys will give us shelter?"

Elizabeth glanced at the castle out of the corner of her eye. "I don't like the look of that castle. I can see a blackness there that no Percy would have made. What do you think, Guenhwyvar? Can you *see* anything?"

"I don't like it either." The maiden coughed and settled back in her saddle. "I *see* the blackness there and it doesn't look a healthy place for us. Isn't there a bit of a ride, though, between here and any other castle? I wouldn't want to be out in the dark. I can *see* that there are too many things in this north country we can't control. I think we should risk your right as a minstrel to shelter. But I am afeared."

"Your Grace," Menadel said, "I too fear this place, and wish we could find other shelter this night, for it will be dreadfully cold this far north."

"If you continue to call me 'Your Grace,' your fears will be quite justified. I've caught you in it enough times already. How can I be a minstrel if someone is 'Your Gracing' me right, left, and forward?"

"I'm sorry." Menadel pulled the cowl of his robe down over

his face, bent his head in an attitude of prayer, and then in a voice like a royal herald he pronounced, "Her Royal Highness, the right high, right noble, and right excellent Princess Elizabeth, Princess of Englene, Princess of Cymru, Princess of Pleasance, Chief Witchdame of Englene, Duchess of Avalon, Duchess of Atlantium, Countess of Firenza, Maiden of the Holy Circle, Knight of the Silver Chalice, and Defender of the Honor of King Richard of Englene." When he had finished, the wizard pushed his hood back around his neck and breathed a sigh of relief. "That ought to do it."

"Ought to do what?" Jackie said. "I'm the fool around here, in case you've forgotten it. Shall I loan you my bauble and ass's ears?" He shook his head at the wizard.

"If you loan me your ass's ears and bauble," Menadel retorted, "I would place the ears on you permanently and your bauble between your legs in a position that would no doubt send any maiden you tried to bed into gales of laughter. What I did was a silencing spell. I am now no longer able to pronounce any of Lady Elizabeth's titles, and I think that will make us safe. *Now* who needs ears and bauble?"

"Both of you," Elizabeth said with a sigh. "I quite understand what you've done, Menadel, and I agree with it, but you left out the offending term which, as I recall, was 'Your Grace.' I suggest you rectify your error before we come to Bamborow Castle."

She watched while the wizard pulled his hood back over his face and intoned in a deep voice, "Your Grace." She then turned to Jackie, who was still grinning at the wizard.

"I don't think you have much to laugh at," Elizabeth said. "Arguments about ass's ears and fools gain us no shelter, either. That castle yonder reeks of dark magic, and we may all be found with donkey ears if we shelter there. It is my right to ask it, but I wish it were not my need as well. Come on!" She dug her heels into her pony's side. "To Bamborow, to Bamborow, in King Richard's name, and death and destruction to all who darken the king's land." Her cry was carried away by the wind and the darkness.

It was now full dark, and the fog had thickened to a wet cloud that blocked the moon, the phosphorescent sea, and King Edward's border light. Darkness had taken over Bamborow-lea. The town was tightly closed and there was no sign of any inhabitants. Even the light from window chinks was swallowed by the fog.

The travelers clattered over empty wet cobblestones on their way toward the castle. It sat upon a jut of rock, facing out to the sea away from the land, its dark bulk disdaining either one.

As Elizabeth reached the edge of the moat, she could see that the fog was not coming off the ocean, but from the castle itself. It rolled off the highest tower, thick and oily, settling down on the lower ramparts and then oozing out over the sea. As her pony's feet struck the hard wood of the drawbridge, all sounds ceased. She could not even hear her own breathing, and had to turn in the saddle to be sure that Jackie, Guenhwyvar, and Menadel were following her.

The silence was unnerving to their ponies. Elizabeth's tried to whinny, but no sound came from its mouth. The air was dead and still; even the sea was abashed by the fog. Elizabeth drew a breath of cold air and began to sing.

> *I'll sing a song, O,*
> *Sing I a song, O.*
> *I come a minstrel, O.*
> *Take this my song, O.*

Elizabeth could barely hear her own voice as she sang the traditional greeting of the minstrel seeking shelter. She sang again, this time with the rune spell for power as a first verse. The resulting noise had all the power of a new-hatched chick, and Elizabeth felt fear rise with the fog.

The castle was huge, its towers and buttresses lost in the fog. The portcullis gleamed damply, its bars white and sharp as a sea monster's teeth. Two guards in full armor stood beside the gatehouse, their faces dead skulls. There were no eyes in their sockets, no lips over their teeth—but even Jackie, with no gift for magic, could hear them breathing.

"I don't like this," he tried to say, but only the guards's heavy breaths could be heard in the stillness.

There was a clinking sound from the battlements above, the sound of a door being opened, its hinges protesting. Elizabeth, Jackie, Guenhwyvar, and Menadel looked up in surprise at the unexpected sound.

"Who goes there, and what is your errand at Bamborow Castle?" It was a woman's voice, deep and rich as old wine. It came from the tallest tower along with the fog, and did not sound welcoming.

"I am Elizabeth, minstrel of Englene, with my entourage: Jackie Somers the jester, Guenhwyvar the seer, and Menadel the wizard. It is my right to ask shelter here. I have sung the greeting, but you have not answered it, nor have you opened your gate."

"You sing like a dead owl! Get you gone from my gates. You'll get no shelter here." The fog parted around the tower, and the woman appeared, garbed in black robes, her long white hair billowing in the breeze. "Get you gone," she commanded, "or it will be the worse for you."

"But my lady, I have the right—"

Elizabeth's words were lost in the soggy splash of dishwater drenching her and the others. Laughter, hoarse as a crow, sounded from the battlements. "Go to, go to, scum. I have no need for such as you at Bamborow."

Elizabeth shook the dirty, greasy water out of her eyes. "Good woman, I am a minstrel and as such I've a right to shelter if naught else. I bid thee welcome me." Elizabeth's voice had an edge of steel, but she was wasting her anger. There was no one on the ramparts. The woman had gone.

Elizabeth sat on her pony, her back straight and quivering with the anger she felt. "With my powers, I could probably destroy this castle to the ground," she muttered. "I might curse this family's seed forever, but I shall not. There may be a reason why minstrels are not welcome here, and I will not judge this woman harshly until I know if she has some such reason. Come, I think I saw a tavern when we passed through Bamborow-lea. Perhaps it will give us a welcome." She turned her horse and cantered back over the drawbridge, with her companions in close pursuit.

The village of Bamborow-lea was small: thatched cottages, a fisherman's hut or two, and not much else. But there was, as Elizabeth had said, a tavern—small, crumbling, disreputable, not at all a fit habitation for the heir to Englene. But at the moment the heir to Englene looked like a sodden mermaid and smelled of old cabbage. Her major concern was clean clothes, a bed free of fleas, and information. The clean clothes she had with her in her saddlebag; the bed and the information the tavern would supply—and perhaps dinner, too. Her stomach rumbled at the thought of dinner, and she bade it to subside. It was entirely possible that whatever dinner this tavern might offer would be as disreputable and as disgusting as its exterior.

The tavern's interior was dirty and smoky, with an ill-cleaned fireplace. It reeked of piss, sweat, and stale beer. The air was filled with the raucous sound of drunken singing and clanking of ale mugs. Elizabeth paused on the threshold to listen to the song.

> *We never eat piggie, for it makes us all bores,*
> *But ale, ale, bring us good ale.*
> *We never eat oysters, 'twill drive us to whores,*
> *But ale, ale, bring us good ale.*

On the chorus, ale cups were slammed together and slammed again on the tabletop. It was not a good song. It was not even a bad song. It was a raucous din.

> *We never eat white swan, the king gets that dish,*
> *But ale, ale, bring us good ale.*
> *We never eat sea snake, for it's not a fish,*
> *But ale, ale, bring us good ale.*

> *We never eat sweetcake, for it makes us fat,*
> *But ale, ale, bring us good ale.*
> *We never eat porridge, that's fit for the cat,*
> *But ale, ale, bring us good ale.*

> *We never eat garlic, it makes our breath reek,*
> *But ale, ale, bring us good ale.*
> *We never eat dormouse, because it will squeak,*
> *But ale, ale, bring us good ale.*

"How long does this go on?" Elizabeth asked, turning to Jackie. "Do they keep this up all night, or do they stop long enough to answer questions?"

"Oh, they stop when they're either too drunk to continue or have finished up all the ale. The song gets worse, poppet. Some of the verses can get very questionable. If you want to increase your vocabulary of the human tongue, listen to about twenty verses of this and you'll learn things you never heard about at your father's court."

"Twenty verses of this will drive me either to lunacy or to cutting throats, one or the other. I hope they end it soon."

Elizabeth chose an empty table in a darkened corner and motioned her friends to sit down. The inhabitants of the tavern observed the entrance of the strangers and gradually the song died away until there was only one voice, drunken and determined, continuing its way through the next verse.

> *For we'll never breed malt worms as long as we sing,*
> *Ale, ale, bring us good ale.*
> *And we'll never stop drinking, for that's a fine thing,*
> *Ale, ale, bring us good ale.*

On the last "ale," the singer fell face forward into the slopped beverage on the table in front of him, and his bubbling snores filled the silent room.

No serving wench appeared, no landlord to ask what his guests might require. The humans sat like carved wooden statues, staring at the travelers.

Finally one stout yeoman, perhaps a bit drunker or a bit braver than his companions, pulled himself to this feet and staggered toward their table. He leaned his hands on the rough wooden surface and brought his face close to that of the Princess Elizabeth. He stared at her, blinking the dregs of drunkenness clear from his eyes.

"Be 'ee witchlord get?" he asked. His breath stank of onions, salted fish, and a great quantity of ale. "'Ee look to be witchlord get. 'Ee got the red hair, the height, and the breadth, but 'ee no got the blue eyes. May be byblow or that sort o' parti-color kind of witch—" He scratched his greasy hair and peered closely at her.

"I have witchlord blood, but it's no business of yours," Elizabeth retorted. "I want the innkeeper, and unless you are he, I suggest you go back to your singing and ale." She stared down the yeoman, causing him to back away from the table in awkward hopping steps. He caught his balance with his back against a table.

Staggering, he shook his head to clear his thoughts. "Innkeeper, aye, 'ee be needin' Old Tom." He turned his head in the direction of the back room of the inn and let out a bellow like a drunken bull. "Tom, Tom! Get they big belly out here and don't be botherin' the wenches no more. There's a witch-lord customer, witchlord get! An' she be wantin' somethin' o' 'ee."

"Hush they bellering, Black Will. B'ain't I be comin'?" The innkeeper appeared suddenly like a jack-in-the-box. He was big-bellied and red of face and nose, indicating he had sampled a great deal of his own good ale. His eyes were small as black currants, and it took him a moment or two to spot Elizabeth and her party. His eyes narrowed and almost vanished in the suety lumps of his cheeks. He came slowly and reluctantly toward the table.

"What would you wish here, lady? I see by they sodden clouts that you'm be a minstrel. You'm be used to better than this inn. What do 'ee want with me and mine?" The man was clearly uneasy at the presence of a witchlord in his inn, and glanced at Black Will for some kind of explanation.

"Nay worrit, Tom," Black Will said. "'Er will 'elp us with our black luck. I seed she was witchlord get."

"If it's any comfort, innkeeper," Elizabeth said, "I am but half witchlord, and my tastes of late are not that dainty. I'll accept whatever bed you can find for me and mine, and I'll pay for our food and lodging with good coin of the realm. The chatelaine of Bamborow Castle refused me entrance, so I have no choice but to grace your humble hall."

"Aye, that she would," Old Tom said. "The black lady b'ain't abide the code of minstrels. She gives no comfort to no one, not to us her bound folk, nor to strangers, nor witchlord get. Was it 'er wot dumped ditchwater on 'ee? I smell it from here. Stinks of cabbage and old mutton. 'Twouldn't surprise me; seems like 'er kind o' trick." The innkeeper heaved an enormous sigh and started to turn away.

"But what of the room and the food?" Jackie asked. "We're cold and we're wet and we're hungry. Would you turn us out into the dark like the lady of Bamborow?"

The landlord turned back again with a sigh so big his entire belly quivered with it. "I'll not have it said that I be the same as the black lady of Bamborow for all that. I'll give you wel-

come, shelter, food, ale, and a place to change. And then,"
he waved his hand in the direction of the other inhabitants of
the inn, "these has something to ask o' 'ee. But first change
they clothes, eat, and drink. Their problem, 'twill keep, it's
kept long enough."

The travelers were shown an attic room hardly as big as a
clothespress, and there was a great deal of bumping of bodies
and complaints as the four of them changed their garments.
But the feel of clean clothes and the washing of faces made
for a somewhat better temper, and when they returned to the
tavern the landlord had, as promised, brought tankards of that
ale called "Dragon's Milke" and a plate of an unidentifiable
stew which smelled surprisingly savory. Elizabeth ate four plates
of the stuff before she pronounced herself full; Jackie, Guenhwyvar, and Menadel kept close count behind her. She had
abstained from more than one tankard of ale, but Menadel had
matched his consumption of ale to that of the stew and was
now leaning against Guenhwyvar's shoulder, snoring gently.

Jackie had drunk but half the ale in his tankard. "'Tis a
strong brew," he remarked. "And in case the landlord took it
into his mind to add an extra ingredient I thought that one of
us should have a clear head." He glanced at Menadel. "Wondrous good he's going to do us if we're in trouble."

With a large snort, Menadel announced, "I heard every
word of that, fool. I sleep, but I don't sleep that deeply." He
subsided again against Guenhwyvar and the snores continued.

With the meal done, the villagers began to edge closer to
the table until they ringed it, and Elizabeth found herself looking up at a group of dangerous-looking men. They were all
dark-complected, grizzled, not very clean of person or clothing.
Their wide, splayed hands, weathered skin, and heavily muscled shoulders identified them as the peasants they were. It was
also possible that they were thieves, cutthroats, highwaymen,
and half a dozen other less savory trades. It was clear that they
wanted something from Elizabeth.

"Well," she said, "I have eaten, I have changed my raiment,
and I have drunk. The landlord said you wish something of
me. I think the time has come for you to tell me what it is."

The men mumbled among themselves, pushing first one,
then another toward the front, unsure of who should be spokes-

man. Finally Black Will moved to the front of the group and again placed his hands on the tabletop, his face within inches of Elizabeth's.

"We have a dragon, 'ee see. 'Tis a proud and ferocious dragon, big as Bamborow Castle. It's burnt the woods, eaten our sheep, drunk all our milk, and it's not been above eatin' a villager or two. Only the magic can slay a dragon. 'Ee be witchlord, even as a byblow, and 'ee be magic, and 'ee be minstrel which makes 'ee that more the magic, so 'ee will slay the dragon for us." He stood up, his piece obviously said.

"Wait," Elizabeth said. "A dragon? Are you sure it's a dragon? Why, the last time I saw a dragon. . . ."

Elizabeth was about to reveal that the last dragon she'd seen was the charming little thing riding on her father's wrist at her birthday tourney, and nothing particularly fearsome, although it did stink of sulfur. It would have been an unwise comment.

"In the south, where I'm from," she explained, "dragons are little beasts of only slight danger. The biggest one I've ever seen in my life was no bigger than a greyhound. And besides, I think you have your magic mixed. It's knights, lords, princes, and a minstrel or two that go after dragons. A minstrel who's a man. I'm a maid, peasant—or has the drink clouded your eyes so badly that you cannot tell that? I say to you that, as I am a maid, I don't slay dragons."

"Aye, we seed 'ee be a maid, fair pretty duggys 'ee got." Black Will grinned, and the villagers laughed and nudged each other in the ribs at the sally.

"No, lady," Old Tom explained. "This be no piddlin' southron dragon; 'tis the great worm o' the north country. 'Tis big as Bamborow Castle with a temper to match the black lady. 'Tis right that a man slays dragons, but more important it is that *magic* slays the beast. Bamborow be out of the main way, and none o' the court cooms here. Ever since Lord Percy died we be plagued with this dragon, and noon o' the castle will aid us. 'Ee be magic because o' the witchlord blood in 'ee. It hap a woman like 'ee can slay the dragon. We canna go on havin' our milk drunk up, our sheep gobbled down and our folk, too."

"Aye, aye, Tom, wasna that wot I was to say?" Black Will grumbled. "I was to arst 'er to kill the beast fer us an' you go and mubble it out afore me." Black Will scratched his hair again, and this time came up with a flea, which he promptly cracked between his teeth. "Well, we 'ere, we no be nobles, nor magic, an' we have need o' 'ee. I takes leave to arst you to slay the dragon, or"—his eyes narrowed a little in cunning—"or maybe we leave 'ee trussed like a chicken for the black lady o' Bamborow. 'Er not be happy to find 'ee at 'er gates again, an' you'm get more than the dish slops thrown on 'ee then." He laughed, showing the stumps of his black, rotting teeth.

Elizabeth drew her dagger and placed it on the table. At a word from her it flamed and flickered with blue light.

The crowd moved back, awed. They knew the penalty for owning such a blade without the permission of the legendary woodwitches, and they knew that they were dealing with a person of very high magic indeed. It was not often that the woodwitches granted their favor to one of witchlord get.

"You and who else, Black Will?" Elizabeth said softly. "I don't like being threatened. I've half a mind to tie you up and leave you out for dragon food—or would *you* prefer the dark lady of Bamborow?"

"No, now, lady. Be kind to Black Will," Old Tom said. "He didn't mean no harm. We are fair mazed by the dragon, an' that's the right truth. His wits 'ave gone wanderin', that's all."

Elizabeth grunted, and put up her dagger. "Very well, I'll not leave him for the dragon—or the dark lady. But I don't want to be bothered again by the likes of him. And if I am, innkeeper, it's your hide I'll cure on your own front door. Do you understand me?"

"Yes, lady. But if you'm not be for slayin' the dragon, who will we get? It may be years before another such as 'ee comes to Bamborow-lea, an' we'll have to tell him, after 'ee goes, that 'ee did not abide by minstrel's code to aid such as us. That makes 'ee and the dark lady breakers o' the code." Tom rubbed his chin and watched Elizabeth react to his words exactly as he'd hoped.

"I make no promises tonight," she said, "but I will keep what you've said about the code in mind. I want no comparisons made twixt me and the dark lady, innkeeper. I'll talk this thing over with my companions, and in the morning I'll give you my decision. Not before then. And"—her eyes swept the crowd—"I'm not doing anything for the likes of you. If I kill this dragon of yours, it will be for my own honor and glory alone. If I decide not to kill the beast, and word of this comes to the ears of the witchlords, I will defend myself by telling of the threats made against one who has witchlord blood, and this town will be reduced to the rubble from which it sprang." Elizabeth rose to her feet and beckoned Jackie, Guenhwyvar, and Menadel to follow her upstairs to the stuffy little room they had been assigned for the night.

The floor of the room had been covered with a straw tick and was just big enough for the four of them to stretch out in very close proximity. The room was airless and hot, but the straw and the tick was fresh, and there didn't seem to be any indication of fleas, so Elizabeth pronounced herself content.

"What about the dragon?" Jackie asked. "Are we going to see some fancy tilting tomorrow, poppet? I've never seen you take on a real dragon. It might be rather fun."

"Fun for whom?" Elizabeth asked. "The dragon or me? I've never killed a real dragon in my life! I'm not even sure how you do it. I wonder if this thing *is* as big as Bamborow Castle. Why don't I send Menadel back to court and have Father send an army of knights to the area, or maybe ask him to simply destroy the dragon himself. The ring Raziel is enough to kill any dragon within the range of thought. I'm the only child he's got, Jackie; even if I am half woodwitch, I'm the only child he will have. If I die fighting some stupid monster, who inherits the throne? My idiot Cousin John? Fine king he'd make!

"From what I've heard, dragons have poisonous breath and breathe fire, and they've got claws and teeth. My mother never raised me to be dragonbait. No, I can't see doing it. It's pointless. I've never heard of a woman taking on a dragon. It could be a serious error. And the error could likely be one I won't live to regret."

"I saw a sea serpent once," Guenhwyvar said. "It was besporting itself off the coast below Dewi Sant's chair. It and a silkie were doing the old dance of bounce and tickle. It was a fine sight to see."

"But do you *see* any chance of my being eaten by a dragon?" Elizabeth asked. "I wish your gift was a bit more certain. Menadel, you've got to teach this child how to *see* when we need it. Otherwise, the information is too little and too late."

Guenhwyvar's face puckered with unshed tears, and she began to cough hollowly. Elizabeth hastened to reassure the maiden that she was indeed of use on their journey.

"I promise to tell you all that I might *see* in the night," the maiden said. "but for now all I know is that a great gift will come to you from the towers of Bamborow Castle. Uryan will be yours."

"What, or who, is Uryan?" Jackie asked.

"I don't know!" And Guenhwyvar began to sob in good earnest.

Menadel comforted her, making sugar rabbits appear from out of his sleeve. When the maiden's sobs changed to giggles, he said, "Then too, there's the problem of weapons. It's not as if you'd be well-armed, Elizabeth, and our pack ponies aren't sturdy enough to go against a dragon. What you need is a destrier or something similar. You've got no armor, no sword, and these louts can't provide it. Besides, if any of them does have a sword, he's not likely to make the information public. And if you think you're going to walk up to a dragon with that little blue toad sticker of yours and kill it, well, it doesn't work that way. The dragon would have you in cinders before you could get within thirty feet of it."

"*If* it's that big a dragon," Jackie added. "You know what dragons are like at home. Why even the big one at BrynGwyn's Tower, it's so small I rode it at the last Beltane Masque. I admit I had to throw my motley away afterwards—stank of sulfur and brimstone—but dragons just aren't that dangerous. And if these foolish villagers think they've got some kind of a monster out there, well, go out and dispatch it. May be a bit exciting. And besides—think of how your father would feel if you brought a dragon's head home from the north. Even a small dragon's head is still a dragon's head."

"That's part of the problem. I'm afraid it will be a small dragon," Elizabeth said. "Do you have any idea what a fool I'd feel going out into the woods looking for some stupid lizard? I'm the heir to Englene—not some salamander hunter. You know how villagers exaggerate. Big as Bamborow Castle, Gods's teeth! I'm going to feel six times the fool if there's nothing out there but their imaginations."

"But what if there is a dragon?" Menadel asked. "They're a rude lot, but they're right. If there is a dragon, it is your obligation to kill it. The fact that you *are* heir to Englene means that you cannot pass up this battle. You don't have a choice. Remember that you must do some deed of greatness in this place, and killing a dragon will be a thing of great power and magic."

Elizabeth yawned, stretching, and, in the process, bashing both Jackie and Menadel soundly alongside their heads.

"Sorry, I didn't mean to do that. It's a bit cramped in here. But dragons . . . I'm a princess. Princesses don't go after dragons . . . I guess I'll have to do it, though. Father would hate having everyone laughing at me because I refused to fight some silly little dragon. . . ."

She yawned and turned over, hitting Jackie with her arm, and was soon snoring softly, dreaming of dragons.

Chapter 16

The next morning when Elizabeth stumbled soreboned down-stairs, she saw that the collection of drunken louts from the night before had been augmented by a variety of villagers, most of them a bit cleaner and a somewhat better class than Black Will and his crew. There was even one portly little gentleman in a dove-gray robe with a chain around his neck, who was obviously the local mayor. At the sight of Elizabeth he huffed and puffed his way through the crowd toward her.

"My lady minstrel. We've been informed by sundry inhab-itants of this village that you intend to kill our dragon. I, as mayor of Bamborow-lea, am here to offer my warm thanks and great appreciation for this deed. We have been sorely troubled by this dragon and we are honored by your presence. And should you return successfully from the woods, we will of course have a feast in your honor."

"I notice, my lord mayor, that you use the word if. You

don't sound very sure that I will return."

The mayor fidgeted from foot to foot, looked down at the toes of his shoes, and then up at Elizabeth, who stood at least a head and a half taller than himself.

"Well, you see, you are a maid—but you are of the magic, so we do have to assume that will work . . . but I've never heard of a woman slaying a dragon. Usually dragons take them prisoner or eat them. You've taken a large task on yourself, lady, and a grave one. And I am proud that you have come to my village and I will tell my grandchildren in years to come how the minstrel maid came to Bamborow-lea and was willing to sacrifice herself for the benefit of these small, unimportant people."

"Yes, yes, I'm aware of all that," Elizabeth cut the mayor's speech short. "But you see, I do have a problem. If I'm going to go out after a dragon, I'll need some armor. I don't have a sword. I haven't even a proper horse. My little pony would probably run like a rabbit at the sight of the beast that's been described to me."

"Oh, we've looked to that," said Black Will from the crowd. "we found a horse and we made 'ee a dragonstick, and even got 'ee a shield. John Hightop up at Oakfarm, he was plowin' last spring and his plow hit this bit o' brass right there in the field. Turned out to be a shield maybe fifty, sixty year' old. Still be a bit good. That is, the metal b'ain't too bad. I takes leave to say, 'ee got everythin' 'ee need."

Elizabeth tried not to smile or cry. The thought of the sort of horse a village like Bamborow-lea would come up with was appallingly obvious; the idea of a corroded old shield dug out of a field was ludicrous; and what in the name of the Three Regions was a dragonstick? "Ah, thank you very much. I think I'd like to have a look at my accouterments before I set forth to battle the monster."

Elizabeth found herself swiftly surrounded by villagers who gently pushed her toward the door of the inn and out onto the street. And there, standing on the cobblestones, was indeed a horse. A plow-horse. A large plow-horse. A large, old plow-horse. A large, old, dirty plow-horse. There was a piece of sacking tied around its middle in some semblance of a saddle, and the plowing reins had been shortened and made into something that could be used to guide the horse's head—but on the whole the animal looked more fit for catmeat than fighting dragons. Beside it on the cobbles was the shield—green with decay, sagging, bent, its leatherwork cracked and broken. It was useless as any sort of defensive weapon. The dragonstick proved to be a long ashwood pole, perhaps seven feet in length. One end of it was wrapped in rags, pitch, and bits of oddments that Elizabeth could not identify. Its purpose eluded her.

"What's that?" she said, pointing to the stick.

"'Tis a dragonstick, lady," Black Will said. "Have 'ee no got them in the south? We teach all our young aboot dragonsticks, so's they b'ain't fools when aidin' a knight to slay dragons. Even our lasses are told aboot proper ways to kill dragons. Our womenfolk make the sticks o' winters—sore troubled by dragons we be 'ere in the northlands, 'ee see. Why, every lad in this village can tell 'ee what a dragonstick is for."

"Then find a lad from this village to tell me, because I have never in my life seen anything like that nor have I any idea how one uses it on a dragon."

"'Tis obvious, poppet," Jackie said, bounding out of the inn in time to study the object of contention. "Judging by its shape and size, you either ram it up one end or the other of a dragon. I suspect it depends on which part of the dragon you come up on."

The crowd laughed at the witticism. Elizabeth refrained. "Tell me, Somers, my little fool, how would *you* like to face the dragon—either end?" Elizabeth did not feel in a mood for jests. It was obvious the decision of killing the dragon had been taken quite out of her hands. She was surrounded by villagers who confidently assumed she was going to take the job, and here was Jackie making obscene comments about which end of a dragon one should stick a piece of wood in. It was all a little more than could be taken, especially on an empty stomach.

"Lady Elizabeth, is anyone going to fix breakfast?" Menadel's plaintive voice could be heard inside the inn. "Guenhwyvar is hungry as a hawk, and is threatening to take a bite out of me. I too would like breakfast before watching a dragonkilling. However, since I've never seen it done, there's always the possibility that eating breakfast might not be a good idea. Is there any chance that I'll lose it—the breakfast, that is?" Menadel and Guenhwyvar had appeared in the doorway, and the wizard addressed his last question to the crowd. This remark, too, was taken as a witticism and received a round of applause and a great deal of laughter.

Elizabeth walked to the head of the dragonstick and kicked the ragged pitch ball with one foot. "What do I do with it?" she asked. "And don't give me any more nonsense about how every boy in the village knows how it's done. I don't, and unless you tell me you can deal with your dragon yourself."

"Well, you see, lady," Black Will obligingly explained, "'ee takes this here stick and with flint and steel 'ee set fire to they ball of rags and pitch on the end. Best to do it once 'ee on they horse; gettin' on a horse wot seed a flamin' dragonstick b'ain't easy. Wal then, 'ee got they dragonstick alight. 'Ee best not light the dragonstick until 'ee see they dragon. No point havin' it go out before 'ee coom wot be near the beast. So, there you'm be on they horse with they dragonstick and they dragon. Then 'ee rides down on the beastie, fast. The dragon'll see 'ee coomin'. An' that dragon will open 'is mouth— he'll open it big, 'cuz he's goin' to spew fire and poison at 'ee. But 'ee takes they stick and 'ee rams it down 'is throat, quick as 'ee can before he breathes fire, an' he chokes to death on they stick. An' then when he finishes flappin' aboot, 'ee cuts 'his head off. 'Tis simple."

"If it's so simple, why hasn't anyone in this village done it?" Elizabeth asked.

"There be no un in this pur village wot's of the magic," Black Will explained, as if to a slowminded child. "An' the penalty for usin the magic if not magic born is burnin' 'ee at stake in the middle of the square, were 'ee to slay a dragon and not be magic. No, lady, there be no un in this village can slay a dragon, savin' 'ee or the black lady—but 'er no be willin', neither."

Elizabeth sighed.

The village goodwives brought out tankards of huffcap ale, collops of home-cured bacon and fresh oat scones with honey, and Elizabeth found herself making a very good breakfast indeed. And considering that it might be her last one, it was right that it was hearty and pleasant. But she couldn't help wondering how she would taste to the dragon, nicely stuffed with ale, home-cured bacon, and fresh-made scones. The dragon might find it very hearty, too.

Finally the last morsel of food was gone, and there could be no further delays. The villagers directed her to the forest where they said the dragon was, and Elizabeth mounted her own mountain pony. Accompanied by Menadel, Guenhwyvar, and Jackie and leading the plow-horse, she set out to find the dragon. Elizabeth had handed the dragonstick to Jackie, begged Guenhwyvar to try and *see* something, and turned the shield over to Menadel in hopes that on their journey to the dragonwood he might be able to do some minor spell on the shield to put it in better condition.

The dragonwood was surprisingly easy to find. Too easy. It was obvious from the destruction that there was a very large dragon in the area. They had been traveling for over two miles in heavily wooded forest land and suddenly, as if a forest fire had raged through the area, there was scorched earth, burned trees, emptiness, and the smell of sulfur in the air. In the distance Elizabeth could see a jumble of rocks that contained the dragon's cave. Dragons were known to frequent caves and, judging from the size of the massive slabs of rock, it was a good-sized cave with a good-sized dragon.

Elizabeth sighed and got off her pony. She tied its reins to the nearest tree and, drawing her dagger, she held it before her eyes and prayed to Sulis and Diona to protect her. It was the least that could be done and, should either the God or the Goddess be awake at that hour of the morning, perhaps they'd be willing to lend a little aid to the heir of Englene.

She returned the dagger to its sheath and reached for the shield, which Menadel had been working on. It had been somewhat improved; the leather straps now looked brand new, the shield was not as dented, and the corrosion had vanished. She was about to congratulate Menadel on an impressive job when she realized that the heft of the shield was wrong. She shifted it from arm to arm, testing its lift and balance. She knocked on its surface experimentally with her knuckles and instead of the dull boom of metal there was a crystalline chime. The shield was repaired and beautiful . . . and glass.

"Menadel . . . ?"

"I know, I know. It was a mistake. A *slight* one." The magician wrinkled his forehead, his round cheeks turning pink with embarrassment. "I thought I had drawn the rune for *brass,* but with my pony bobbing the way it was—well, the rune got a little misshapen, you see, and—"

Elizabeth looked at the surface of the shield and realized that while it appeared metallic, it had a very high gloss that would never have been possible on a proper shield. It reflected sunlight very well. There was the possibility of distracting the dragon with it, using it almost as a mirror. She remembered vaguely some legend or another of an ancient hero slaying a monster while looking in a mirror—or was the monster looking in the mirror? She couldn't quite remember, but she knew it did involve a mirror. So there was a possibility that tradition was being upheld, and she accepted the shield as it was.

She handed it back to Menadel while she attempted to mount the plow-horse. The horse did not appreciate the idea. It was obvious he had never in his life been ridden. She spent several minutes turning him in circles, and was surprised at how much energy there was in such a bag of bones. Finally getting the animal under control, she reached for the shield and then took from Jackie the dragonstick.

"Will you be needing flint and steel?" Jackie asked sweetly. He knew the answer, but he felt it necessary to come up with some sort of witticism, seeing how glum Elizabeth looked.

"I'll flint-and-steel you to the Nether Regions," Elizabeth muttered. "Flint and steel, indeed! That's a human trick. I at least can do *one* fire spell, so when the day comes that I need flint and steel to *start* a fire, that's the day I'll renounce my titles, go live in a sea cave, and communicate with lobsters. Flint and steel!"

Jackie's remark had had the desired result. Elizabeth was irritated and ready to take on the dragon. Jackie recognized only too well Elizabeth's stubborn tone of voice, and he found himself almost pitying the beast.

Elizabeth kicked the horse sharply in the ribs and got it to move into a shambling sort of gallop that was very uncomfortable to her backside and spine. She kicked it again, hoping for a little more speed, but the horse only shook its head and continued its awkward, loping gallop.

As they came closer to the rocks, the stench of sulfur and brimstone was enough to gag a maggot. There was a smell of old bones and rotting flesh, and underneath it all the green metallic odor of dragon. Elizabeth found herself coughing violently. Her eyes were watery and she wondered if she would be able to see well enough to deal properly with the dragon, should it present itself.

The dragon appeared from behind a slab of rock beside the entrance to its cave. The rocks were huge, and the dragon that stood beside them was equally gigantic. Elizabeth was not positive that it was the size of Bamborow Castle. It might only have been *half* the size of Bamborow Castle, but it was not a point she cared to argue with either the villagers or the dragon.

The creature's large reptilian head swung from side to side, its nostrils flaring as it caught the scent of horse and woman. Its eyes, red and hot, turned to look at her. It snorted, and a jet of yellow steam escaped from its mouth, followed by a tiny flicker of flame. This was no little lizard to carry on one's wrist. This was a proper dragon.

The horse reared suddenly, almost throwing Elizabeth from her perch on its back. Only her quick reflexes and the good firm grip of her knees kept her in place. She brought the animal down and tried to calm it, but it stood shaking at the sight of the giant reptile. There was no way Elizabeth was going to get this animal to run toward the dragon. There was, of course, the possibility that the dragon might take it into its head to run toward Elizabeth—in which case, whether it was the horse running or the dragon running, the dragonstick would be equally effective.

The dragon snorted again. The clouds of yellow smoke almost hid its face; then it took two steps, three, four, toward her—slow, cautious steps, but definitely in her direction. Elizabeth decided the time had come to light the dragonstick.

Unsure of what would work against a dragon, she muttered a few basic protection spells, drew her dagger and touched it to the shaft of the dragonstick. Instantly the ball of rag and pitch burst into flame. The dragon, whether alarmed by the dagger and its glow or by the flame at the end of the dragonstick, retreated a step or two, and then—much to Elizabeth's surprise—it sat down on its haunches, looked at her, and began to weep.

Elizabeth sat on her plow-horse, feeling like a total fool, watching her dragonstick flame spectacularly while at the same time the dragon's tears, each one the equivalent of a bucket of water, fell sizzling to the scorched earth below. And then, to make matters worse, the dragon opened its mouth and sobbed.

This was definitely a development none of the books on zoology had ever covered. Dragons did not, as a rule, cry.

Elizabeth couched the flaming lance against her ribs and, giving the horse a sharp kick, managed to make it move forward a step or two in the direction of the dragon before it came to a halt, head down between its forelegs. The horse was not going to be cooperative about getting any closer to the dragon.

The dragon was making a rather loud noise, which caused the rocks around it to vibrate like a minor earthquake, and its tears were threatening to produce a goodsized swamp on the spot. It was a very bewildering situation. And true to Elizabeth's luck with fire spells, the dragonstick sputtered, flared one last flash of pitch, and became simply a smoldering remnant of its former glory.

Elizabeth uttered a vulgar oath under her breath and contemplated the stick with disdain. She hadn't thought anything quite that ridiculous would work, but the villagers—down to the youngest lad, supposedly—all believed this was the way to kill a dragon. There might, Elizabeth considered, be better ways.

"Dragon! Dragon!" she called. "Would you stop that infernal racket and tell me why you're weeping? Dragons aren't supposed to do that, you know."

The dragon stopped its caterwauling, but still continued to weep. "But you see," it said in a highpitched, whining voice, surprisingly slight for so large a beast, "you're going to kill me. I expected a prince, of course. I really was hoping for a prince, but it's quite clear that you do have the magic and you're going to kill me, and I'd really rather you didn't. I'll give you something of great value if you let me live. You see, I'm not a dragon at all, I'm Lady Katheryne Percy, but I'm under an enchantment. That's why I was hoping for a prince!" The dragon took up its boo-hoo-hooing again.

Elizabeth sighed in resignation. This was not going to be a good day. First a plow-horse instead of a proper destrier like her own White Surrey, then that foolish dragonstick going out on her, and the memory of her own magnificent broadsword with at least sixteen very good spells on it (which, unfortunately, was at home in the Palace of Witchdame), and now a dragon that claimed to be a maiden under enchantment. Elizabeth found she had a headache, probably due to all the sulfur in the air. But there was the possibility that the dragon was telling the truth.

Elizabeth tried to remember what she could of her classes on dragons. Admittedly they'd been relatively slight; the BrynGwyn Tower zookeeper hadn't been very concerned with dragons, and had covered the material in a remarkably short time. He'd been fascinated by unicorns, and had droned on for days on that subject until Elizabeth was bored to tears, but he had had very little to say about dragons—particularly about their truthfulness.

"Dragon! Tell me why I should believe you are a maiden under enchantment. You look very much like a dragon to me."

"Have you ever been to Bamborow Castle? Have you seen the black sorceress, my stepmother? She made me into this, and she told me no one would ever be able to turn me back because they'd kill me first. I've tried to be a *good* dragon; I only ate sheep that were small and scraggly and not likely to survive the winter, and I *am* sorry about burning the wheat field, I didn't mean to. And the villagers *would* keep filling the troughs with milk for me and I wasn't going to let it go to waste. And the people I ate . . . well, they weren't very nice people. I've tried to be as honorable as I could while being a dragon. I would very much like to be a maiden again. Of course, my stepmother will probably think of something worse to do to me than this." The dragon began crying again.

The lachrymose behavior of the dragon was one thing that gave Elizabeth some slight inkling that the story might be true—and she had encountered the black lady of Bamborow and could well believe she would change her stepdaughter into a dragon. "All right, dragon. Every spell has a counterspell. I'm sure yours does. Would you mind telling me what it is?"

This only seemed to make the dragon sob even more. "But I wanted a prince, " it blubbered. "It was at least something that would make being a dragon worthwhile, because with the counterspell and all, at least I would end up with something, and you're not even a man!"

"Yes, yes, I know I'm not a man. I've known that since the day of my birth, and I know what a problem it's been to everyone, including my parents. Now would you hush up about the subject and tell me what the counterspell is? I'm getting very tired of all this, and in a couple of moments I'm going to turn this horse around, go back to the village, and tell them that you're some twit of a Percy and not a dragon at all, and to stop bothering with you. So there!"

"Oh clip they sword and bend they bow, and give me kisses three," the dragon crooned, off key. "For though I be a poisonous worm, no hurt I'll do to thee."

Elizabeth found the dragon's singing even worse than its copious tears. "Oh dear. Kiss a dragon," she muttered. "I don't even kiss my pet dog, let alone a dragon. Are you sure you're a maiden and not just lying to me? Because if I get close enough to kiss you, you're likely to make lunch of me."

The dragon nodded sadly. "I didn't think you'd believe me. It is such a silly counterspell. But it is true, and besides, you have a woodwitch blade; if you're close enough to kiss me, you'd be close enough to cut my throat if I was lying. So you see, you haven't too much to risk."

"I've got my hide, hair, and soul to risk," Elizabeth snapped. "I suppose it all comes down to trusting you, and also trusting in the fact that my reflexes might be faster than yours, and my blade a little more deadly than you expect. All right, I suppose we'll have to try it."

Elizabeth dismounted from her horse, which promptly turned tail and ran back in the direction of the clump of trees where Jackie, Guenhwyvar, and Menadel waited. She turned to watch the horse go, an expression of disgust on her face. "Well, now I haven't much choice but kissing you, I suppose. But oh, if this is a trick, am I going to look foolish. If I live long enough."

Elizabeth stomped across the soggy ground, wet with dragontears, toward the dragon. Up close, it was even bigger than she had imagined. Its head towered so high into the sky Elizabeth could barely make out the scales on its head. She could, however, see its very sharp, long teeth and the little gusts of sulfurous breath.

"Well, bend down here," she yelled up to the animal. "I can't kiss you with your head up there." She was standing in the shadow of the beast, within reaching distance of its large, heavily scaled body. She was up to her ankles in wet mud; it was hot and sticky, and she was sure her boots would never be the same again. The dragon obediently lowered its head until it was eye to eye with Elizabeth. The sight was not reassuring.

Its eyes were as large as the platters used to serve boar's

head on her father's table, and its teeth as long as her dagger. They reflected the blue glow of the blade as she held it under the dragon's chin. "Remember," she said, "this blade at my command can slit you open like a trapped hare. Don't try anything silly. Now let's see, where am I supposed to kiss you?"

The dragon, holding its breath so Elizabeth would not be poisoned by the stench, murmured, "Anywhere. I don't think it matters." She brought her enormous, scaled head as close to Elizabeth's face as possible—far closer than Elizabeth would have liked.

Holding the dagger firmly in one hand, she reached out with the other hand to clasp the side of the dragon's head to hold it steady. It was a surprisingly pleasant feeling. The scales were sleek and had the feel of a good silver chalice in her hand; they were warmed by the sun and she had an urge to reach up and scratch the beast behind one enormous ear. Its eyes seen close up were not nearly so fearsome. They were large and sad, and more than a little hopeful. Elizabeth found herself patting the dragon gently and saying, "There, there. There, there. It's going to be all right." Then, taking a deep breath, she leaned forward and kissed the dragon three times on the nose.

There was a shattering earthquake and the rocks of the cave split apart. Elizabeth found that she was being kissed back by a pair of very warm, very feminine lips. And in her arms, with the dagger firmly under her chin, was the Lady Katheryne Percy. Her hair was witchlord blonde, eyes wide and blue, and her face had the sort of simple prettiness that would have found great favor at the court. The dragon hadn't lied; she was indeed a maiden.

Elizabeth lowered her dagger and stepped back from the young woman for a better look. Lady Katheryne was stark naked, a fact that didn't seem to embarrass her. After all, having been a dragon for several months, very little embarrassed her.

"Oh good, a mirror," Lady Katheryne said, grabbing at the enchanted shield. "I was so worried my complexion would suffer from all that time out in the sun, but it still looks perfect! I'm so glad you rescued me, even if you aren't a prince. My father, Lord Percy, wanted me to marry well, you see." She blew a kiss at her reflection in the shield. "And marrying well does take beauty!"

Elizabeth sighed with exasperation. The girl was obviously

a silly twit who might well have been better off as a dragon.

"It's clear you're of witchlord blood. Why did you allow your stepmother to put this spell on you?" Elizabeth asked. "She may be a black sorceress, but you should have at least been able to hold her at bay."

Lady Katheryne nodded sadly. "You see, my father died last year, and my stepmother took over the castle. I'm not eighteen yet, and I haven't been initiated in a circle, so there was nothing I could do. I was helpless. Father should never have married her. She came down out of the north—at least, that's what she said. I think she was from someplace a lot more evil, the Nether Regions perhaps. My father looked at her and forgot all else—the village, his hunting, his good greyhounds, and me. And within a year of marrying her he was dead and I was heir to Bamborow Castle. My stepmother didn't like that, so—" The girl spread her arms. "She made me a dragon. She assumed someone would come along eventually and go out dragonkilling, and naturally wouldn't be inclined to kiss a dragon, and would kill me, and there would be no one to challenge her for ownership of Bamborow Castle. You saw the darkness there. It creeps farther and farther every night. Eventually it will cover Bamborow-lea, and then it will move north to Berewic and then south toward Eboric. She's a very strong black sorceress, my stepmother is."

Elizabeth slipped off her minstrel's tabard and handed it to Lady Katheryne to cover herself with. The lady accepted it gratefully, and belted it around her body. And then, following Elizabeth, the two of them made their way back toward the pack ponies. Menadel and Jackie both gawked at the sight of a half-clad maiden where once had been a fearsome dragon. Jackie even commented he'd go looking for more dragons if that was the result of finding them. Elizabeth told him to hush and listen to what Lady Katheryne might say about her stepmother, and the possible ways of destroying her.

"Oh, but you can't," the maiden exclaimed. "She's very powerful. She'll know that I've been turned back into a maiden and that the spell has been broken, and she'll be there at the castle surrounding herself with every protection spell against death and destruction that she knows. You won't be able to touch her with lance or spear or sword, or any weapon known. Even that dagger of yours will be useless. She'll simply stand

and laugh at it. And then, perhaps she'll turn you into something awful like a dragon."

"I find that highly unlikely," Elizabeth said. "Your stepmother may find that, in me, she's met her match. So she'll have protection spells against most weapons? That's interesting. I'll have to think about it. There's an old spell—now if I can just remember how it goes . . ."

Elizabeth helped Lady Katheryne onto the back of her pony and then climbed into the saddle herself.

"Put your arms around my waist and hang on," she commanded. "I'm going to do some hard riding. Jackie? Guenhwyvar? Menadel? We've got a castle to visit. Let's do it. But on the way I want to stop in the village and get a weapon." Elizabeth kicked her pony sharply and the animal leaped into a faster gallop than Elizabeth had expected. It was a definite relief from the behavior of plow-horses.

Their appearance back in the village was quite unexpected, but joyous. Lady Katheryne was recognized by the villagers and greeted with a great deal of rejoicing.

Elizabeth asked the villagers to assemble what possible weapons they had, and was amazed at the assortment of clubs, sticks, hoes, and rusty old pikestaffs they brought her. None of them was what she now knew she wanted. And then a farmer handed her exactly the thing she'd been looking for. Mounted on a long pole, almost as tall as Elizabeth herself, was a very sharp-edged sickle used for pruning trees in the north country. Elizabeth tested its sharpness against the edge of her thumb, and was rewarded by a line of red and a drop of her own blood on the sharp steel. She watched the blood foam and become a part of the metal. She smiled in quiet satisfaction as the steel turned coldly blue.

"There's an appropriate spell for the dark lady!" she muttered to herself. "May she have joy of it for eternity."

"I think I have what I want," she said aloud. And mounting her pony, she set off alone for the Castle of Bamborow.

The air around the castle was black and thick like fog. Elizabeth thought that she would have to beat her way through it. But she drew her dagger and, holding it aloft like a lantern, she moved through the darkness, her horse's hooves thumping soundlessly on the drawbridge. The two sentries were still there, one on each side of the enormous wooden gate. They did not appear to have moved in the slightest from the position they had held the day before.

Elizabeth sheathed her dagger and dismounted from her horse. She dropped its reins, looked into its eyes, and commanded it to stay where it was. The horse had no choice but to obey.

Elizabeth knew that tradition called for her to stand and bargain with the chatelaine of Bamborow Castle. She should issue challenge and brag of her own prowess as a sorceress. There were spells to cast and insults to be phrased prettily. But Elizabeth was in no mood for tradition today. She had already defied one tradition by going after a dragon; now she was coldly angry, and tradition be hanged.

Holding the sickle in one hand, she walked up to the massive gate and, calling on the power within her, she struck it three times with one tightly balled fist. The gate thrummed to the rhythm of her pounding, and on the third blow crashed inward.

"I didn't mean to hit it quite that hard," Elizabeth murmured as she stepped over the shattered wood to face the sorceress in the center of the courtyard.

The air in the courtyard shimmered with the blacks, reds, oranges, purples, and blues of at least a dozen spells. The sorceress stood, her proud, beautiful head high, and the smile on her face cold and evil.

"Have you no respect for anything, minstrel maid? You issued no chall—"

That was as much as Elizabeth allowed the sorceress to say. Moving forward with the swiftness that had earned her many a prize in the tiltyard, she swung the sickle around her head once and struck. The sorceress's head parted company from her body and bounced across the courtyard. Elizabeth watched the sorceress's body dissolve into a pool of black, bubbling tar. The old spell had worked.

"Every spell she could think of. Every spell but for a farmer's enchanted blade," Elizabeth laughed in triumph.

A croaking sound from one side of the courtyard caught her attention. She turned to see that the sorceress's head had come to rest by the lip of a siegewell, and there, caught in the white hair of the Black Chatelaine of Bamborow Castle, was a large green frog. Elizabeth put down the sickle and walked over to the frog. Kneeling, she scooped it up in her hands and looked at it. Its eyes glistened balefully. It was quite clearly the spirit and soul of the sorceress.

"You see, my lady," Elizabeth said lightly, "tradition doesn't really matter to me anymore. I'm a princess, and I've gone out and taken care of a dragon. Princesses don't do that. And you used all the wrong spells because you thought I'd follow the traditional course. If you'd realized that a maid could slay a dragon, you would have been clever enough to figure that such a maiden wouldn't give a snap for other traditions, either."

Elizabeth glanced over the lip of the siegewell and could see far below her the glitter of water. She looked at the frog that was now puffing itself up with indignation in her hands; the look on its face was one of pure spite. Elizabeth smiled back at it and patted it lightly on the head, then dropped it over the edge of the well.

"You see," Elizabeth said, "I don't kiss frogs, either!"

Menadel and Jackie pushed their way through the shattered gate, with Guenhwyvar and the Lady Katheryne Percy following close behind. "Guenhwyvar did not *see* the sorceress die, but all her evil is gone," Menadel said. "How did you do that?"

"I've turned her into a frog," Elizabeth said with glee. "I didn't know I could do it. I'm a better sorceress than I thought, Menadel! But I suppose it's only fair that she's been turned into a reptile after what she did to Lady Katheryne. I think—" Elizabeth kicked her heels against the coping of the siegewell in amusement at the thought, "I think I'll be mean about it, and once every hundred years I'll let her come back as a woman. But only for one night, *and* she cannot go anywhere but the battlements of this castle. I'll let her spend all that time shrieking her folly to the stars, and they will not listen."

Elizabeth began drawing pentacles and runes and eldritch words along the wall of the siegewell. She muttered under her breath in Latin and blue fire followed the line of the fingers along the marks. She completely covered the lip of the siegewell going deosil; when she came back to her original starting point she made a line connecting the circle and then stood back to watch as a blue fire raced over her words around the well and rose to form a cone over the siegewell, then collapse back into nothing, leaving only the runes carved deeply into the lip of the well.

"There!" Elizabeth said. "That ought to hold her. All the books say you should let an enchanted beast be human once in a while. It adds to the annoyance, you know. I think by the time a hundred years have passed the black sorceress of Bamborow will be very annoyed indeed."

She gazed at the runes in satisfaction, then said, "I'm still not entirely sure how I turned her into a frog, but I was very angry—"

"That is sometimes all it takes, my lady," Menadel said. "And I must say I am very proud of you. There has been a fair bit of magic done here this day and you have placed your foot one step farther on the path to acquiring your power. I am very pleased with you, Elizabeth. Now if you could only learn to master a fire spell. . . ."

"Thank you very much for your help, both of you," Lady Katheryne said after Elizabeth and the wizard cleaned the castle of all traces of black sorcery. "But remember, when I was a dragon I did promise you a treasure for rescuing me. It's a sword, a very special one. My father told me that it was brought to him by a mysterious man dressed all in brown and green. He had the countenance and behavior of an angel; he told Father that the sword was called Uryan and that it was the most magical weapon in all of the Three Regions. Indeed, Father said that he was told it was made from the Tree of Life that stood in the Garden of Beginnings. Now I, in gracious token of the great deed you have done for me, do present this sword to you. Wait here a moment and I'll bring it to you—that is, if I can find it. *She* may have hidden it somewhere."

"She did indeed hide it," said Menadel. "But if you look up at the north tower overlooking the sea you will note that the sword has revealed itself to one that is the true owner."

' They looked upward toward the tower where Menadel was pointing and saw that it was alight with a vivid green fire touched with an amber brown. There was a sound in the air of a deep, clear note like that of a shrine bell. Then a scent wafted down from that high tower—a scent of trees and green things: pine and birch, apple and apricot.

With the Lady Katheryne leading the way, they formed a procession that traveled with reverence through the Castle of

Bamborow and into that high tower room where the black sorceress had hidden the great sword of the Archangel Uriel.

The sword was wrapped in green brocade and tied with brown silk cord. Katheryne presented it still wrapped to Princess Elizabeth. But when the princess unwrapped the sword and took it from its wooden sheath, she found that the blade of the sword was also wood. A fine grained, aromatic wood from some eastern land, but nonetheless wood.

"What can you do with a wooden sword?" Elizabeth asked, looking at it.

Menadel studied the wooden blade in the princess's hands and then said, "You never know, my lady. Sometimes the oddest things can be very effective weapons. This sword, simple as it is, may be no less powerful a weapon. I suggest you keep that in mind, and when the time comes for you to use it in its rightful purpose you will know it—just as you know that the deed you must perform in the northern lands has been done."

"I would feel safer if we had a few good steel broadswords to back us up," Elizabeth observed. "This may indeed be a weapon of power, but still—"

"Oh, if you want swords," Lady Katheryne said, "I can give you my father's. There are two of them, one for war and the other to threaten the Gael with. They're called Peacebond and Gaelbane. If you have need of them, please take them with my blessings."

"I for one would be glad of a good bit of steel," said Menadel. "Thank you, my lady. The fool and I will no doubt bring glory to your father's blades. If so, we will return them to you with a minstrel to tell you tales of power and courage. I promise that the tales *will* be true."

Menadel watched as Lady Katheryne left the room, and when he was sure she was out of earshot he said, "Now tell me, my lady Elizabeth, what will you take to your father as his gift from the north?"

Elizabeth sheathed the sword and rewrapped it in its brocade case. "I have been giving that a great deal of thought. I should give him, along with Gwen's tale of the blackness in Cymru, something to show him the blackness of the North Country. Jackie," she said to the fool, "see if you can find me somewhere in this place a small bottle or jar. I would fill it with that black, sticky tar that was left of the body of the black sorceress. I'll take it to my father and show him what evil he has allowed to exist in *our* land."

Jackie nodded assent and turned to hurry from the room. But as he reached the door they could hear him muttering, "The king isn't going to like this. He isn't going to like it one *bit*. These aren't the sort of fairings he expected to be brought back to him. I hope my lady knows what she does. . . ."

Elizabeth stood listening to Jackie's words as they faded away down the staircase. She shrugged and murmured, "My father's gifts are my father's weaknesses. So mote it be. Now," she said, turning to Menadel, "where do we go from here, oh wise sage?"

"East, my lady. We go east. In great Raphael's name we journey from this place even unto Great Yermouth, and may his blessings be upon us."

EAST

Salve Raphael cuius spiritus est aura e montibus
orta et vestis aurata sicus solis lumina.

I pray to the Eagle, the ruler of tempests,
Storm and whirlwind. He who is master of the
Ethereal vault. Great prince of the element of air!
Be with me, I pray thee. Guard me and mine
From all perils approaching from the East!

Chapter 17

Elizabeth and her companions traveled south from Bamborow toward the great capital of the north, the walled city of Eboric. They traveled with the wind at their back and snow flurries in their hair. Menadel had suggested that they spend the heel of the winter in Eboric, and it proved to be a very good idea. Elizabeth asked for and was granted shelter by her aunt Catheryne and her husband, Andrew the Mage, Archbishop of Eboric.

Not only was their stay pleasant, but it was profitable as well. Elizabeth and Jackie performed mummings and expert minstrelcy for both the archbishop's guests and the common folk during the twelve days of Solstice and Year End. This was a time of merriment and festivity and the generous giving of coins to mountebanks, and so Jackie found himself with a fat purse indeed.

At the turn of the year, the first tiny leaves big as a mouse's ear did not appear on the trees, nor did the birds return. Spring

was oddly late. Guenhwyvar's cough had not improved, even
with all Lady Catheryne's prayers, and the priestess said that
perhaps only the sea air of Raphael's quadrant would heal the
child. She hung on Guenhwyvar's neck a lead charm engraved,
"Optimus egrorm madicus fit Raphael bonorm." Which was to
say, in the common tongue, "Those good people that are sick,
Raphael is the best of physicians."

Guenhwyvar kissed Lady Catheryne and thanked her for
both the medal and her healing prayers. But the dry cough
continued.

Menadel declared it time to be on their way, spring or no
spring. "The village of Great Yermouth is our goal, my lady,"
he said to Elizabeth, "and we have many a mile to go and
many an adventure to seek before we reach that easternmost
point. I would suggest to my lord archbishop that fresh horses
be provided and fresh changes of clothing and foodstuffs, and
with the dawn we must be away."

The next morning found the travelers well on their way
down the great road toward Lincoln. The traveling was a bit
easier than it had been in the north country due to the excellence
of the old Elvish roads, which were still, after centuries, in
excellent repair. They forded the little rivers that were deep,
swift, and very beautiful, and the water spirits greeted them
and bore them safe to the other side of the waters.

They rode along right merrily and Menadel ceased to cast
stern looks at Jackie and Elizabeth when they sported together,
for there was every sign that Menadel and Guenhwyvar had
come to an arrangement of their own. In the village of Goole,
Menadel took Guenhwyvar off to see a very wise wood sprite
who was said to confer blessings on woodwitch virgins. Menadel insisted that Guenhwyvar speak with the sprite and perhaps
gain some knowledge that would be helpful in attaining full
woodwitch power.

Jackie and Elizabeth were amused by Menadel's cheerful
attitude toward leaving them kicking their heels in a small, not
too impressive village.

"Look you," Jackie said, "that old wizard of yours lectured
us on our behavior and here he is going soft in the head over
a young woodwitch girl. He ought to be ashamed of himself,
at his age."

"Don't be so hard on him, Jackie," Elizabeth answered. "Uncle Menadel really hasn't seemed to get much pleasure out of life at court, and I for one am glad to see that Guenhwyvar has brought him some joy. He is not *so* old, after all, and she is not *so* young. Were she to decide to marry him, I would give them my blessing and take their part against the court. I know how my father and the court will feel about another woodwitch in their presence now that they've gotten rid of my mother."

Elizabeth sighed thinking of her dead mother. "I am in the depths of homesick melancholy, and I think I shall go and walk among the tombstones in the shrineyard and think gloomy thoughts."

Jackie pulled his face into an expression of dismay. "What, going out to the garden to eat worms? What's the matter, poppet? Are you feeling that it's been entirely too long since Avebury and your strapping Sun-God? Is he perhaps becoming less and less real? I for one hope so, and I will not let you wander alone through some shrineyard thinking gloomy thoughts. Yes, to the shrineyard! But I'll go with you and devise some amusing bit of verse on death and dying, and perhaps before the day is out I will have you laughing fit enough to split your stay strings."

Accepting Jackie's promise of mirth to come, Elizabeth allowed him to accompany her to the small stone shrine in one corner of the village of Goole. It was an attractive building, warm and glistening in the sunlight, and the contrast between the sunny gold of its walls and the gray-blue of the lead roof tiles was very pleasant. But as they drew close to the shrine they realized that there was a great peculiarity in it. The spire of the tall bell tower was as crooked and twisted as Jackie's spine. The handsome leads of the spire roof danced up and down in a drunken pattern round the strange corkscrew twists and turns. Even before they reached the shrineyard Elizabeth was moved to fits of laughter at the sight of such a peculiar spire.

"You see, poppet," Jackie said, joining into the laughter. "I've managed to make you laugh without even half trying. I wonder what caused that spire to be such an odd shape. They must have used green timber when they built it and perhaps the heat of the sun split and twisted the supports so that it corkscrewed and bulged so. I can think of no better explanation than that."

"That may be true, but come. Let's walk among the stones and look at that strange spire from different angles and see what we might make of it. And when we tire of that, we can read the inscriptions on the tombstones."

Elizabeth opened the little wrought iron gate that led to the shrineyard. Soon she and Jackie had circled the shrine deosil, twice, and had studied the oddly twisted spire from all angles. They then began to walk up and down the rows of graves in the shrineyard, reading the inscriptions. Some of them were terse, nothing more than the name and the birth and death date; others exhorted the viewer to think on his or her own mortality; others had messages of cheer and pleasantness, and devout wishes that the grave's owner was now with the Gods.

Jackie and Elizabeth had been so absorbed by their literary pursuits that they had failed to notice that in one corner of the graveyard a sexton was busy preparing a new grave. When they reached that far corner, the man called a cheerful greeting to them and they saw he was a brother of the order of Bram the Pious, an ancient and revered witchlord mage who had been devoted to the care and proper laying out of the dead and the efforts that were required to keep graveyards in good repair. His was a contemplative order, and considering the dour nature of their calling, the brothers of Bram the Pious were to the last man a cheerful and good-natured lot.

"Blessings upon you, my children!" the monk said. "Is it not a fine and pleasant day, and did you see the snowdrops, how they bloom there in the corner that gets the sun?"

"Whose grave do you dig, reverend sir?" Elizabeth asked. "Was it one carried off by the cold and the winds? If so, I hope he was of a goodly age."

"Aye, a goodly age. It was old mother Elinora, she who was called Elinora the Mage, a wise woman who had seen a hundred and fifty years. Perhaps she might have said she would have wished for a few more, but for those of us who have not attained it, it is a goodly number indeed. I bury her here by the dragonstone, for I feel she was magical enough to share space with that mighty beast, and wise enough to commune with him should there be any communion between mage and dragon when they are dead and buried."

"What do you mean by the 'dragonstone'?" Jackie asked, walking over to the edge of the grave where, just beyond, he could see a large flat circular stone big as Arthur's Round Table. It was as sleek and polished as a steel mirror.

"That is the dragonstone," the sexton said, pointing to it with his spade. "A great and fearsome dragon is buried there and it was his lady wife who bent the shrine spire into that strange shape you see. Ah yes, he was a monstrous dragon with wings large enough to blot out the sun. But then I speak only from hearsay, for it was many, many years before my time and even many, many years before the time of Elinora, whose grave I dig."

"Good sir," Elizabeth said, "I would think that has the makings of a goodly tale, and if we sit here quietly and do not disturb your office, would you perhaps tell it to us?"

The sexton pulled a handkerchief from the sleeve of his robe and mopped his sweaty forehead. He looked at Elizabeth and Jackie and then nodded twice.

"I can see that it would be a good tale for you, for by the witchlord blood that is in me I can see that you two are lovers. Not yet handfast, but your bodies cleave one to the other. I see it in your shadows, how they reach out to touch even when the two of you are apart. I say to you, child," he looked at Elizabeth, "I can see that you are of mixed blood, that you bear the strains of woodwitch mixed with witchlord, and that is not a good thing. But you stand in danger of damnation, for you would mix *that* blood with the blood of a human and the results of such a union should never be seen upon the earth of Englene. It is a sin. I do not think the God Sulis would approve."

"And what of the Goddess?" Jackie said in a belligerent tone of voice. "She is the one who takes more interest in we poor humans than Sulis, and I for one have sworn my allegiance to her."

The monk nodded. He leaped back into the half-dug grave. He said nothing while several shovelsful of earth came flying out of the hole, and then his head popped up to ground level. "That may be as that may be. I have no say of it. My allegiance is to the God. What the Goddess wishes none can forestall. But I do say such a union is not a good thing, and I cannot give my blessing to it for whatever my blessing is worth. Since I promised you a tale, I will give it to you—but there is an ending to it that you may not care for, because it will open vistas to you of great temptation and the possibility of thwarting the will of the God."

He then began to tell the tale of the faithful dragon wife.

Once upon a time (the monk said), there was a mayor in this village called Shoebuckle, and he was as foolish as his name, for he was naught but a tailor with ambition and jumped-up pride who had gotten himself made mayor by his bosom companions and what ale-knights he was able to bribe in the taverns.

And it came to pass during the time of this mayor that a great dragon scoured the land and did gobble down sheep and virgins, and drank milk from all the cows till the children wept that there was nothing to put on their porridge nor was there butter to put on their bread.

And the people of Goole and the surrounding countryside, being sorely distressed, did come to Mayor Shoebuckle and say, "Send to Lundene for a mighty knight or prince, that this dragon would be taken from us."

But the mayor was prideful and said, "There is no need to send to Lundene for a knight. I, Thomas Shoebuckle, will deal with the dragon." And true to his word, he took from a hiding place a great sword which he had no right to own. It had been stolen from the corpse of a dead knight who had the misfortune of being thrown by his horse on the great highway that entered into Goole; and Mayor Shoebuckle, being the sort of man he was, kept the sword knowing that a time would come when it would be useful.

He went out to face the dragon with, I must admit, great courage for so puffed up a man. And he did slay it, with much trial and tribulation. He marched back into Goole triumphantly carrying the dargon's head, which he placed on the high altar here at our little shrine.

Now, the man who was priest in that day, Simon the Mage, he who was of the order of Bram the Pious, was greatly grieved at what the mayor had done, and said that no good would come upon the town for the fact that such a deed had been done by a human rather than a witchlord. So Simon gathered together all the people of Goole to pray to the God and Goddess to save them from the wrath of the king and his knights.

But the days went by and there was no sign of the king, or the king's men, and it seemed that all was safe in the village of Goole. So Shoebuckle waxed prouder and prouder, and would strut about the town telling all and sundry about his mighty deed of slaying the dragon.

Of course, when the wind blew from the north, the stench of the decaying dragon in the high meadow was very strong, and flies descended on Goole and bit the people, but this was considered a small curse in return for getting rid of a ferocious dragon. So it was that all were content in the village of Goole. Until one morning, early, before even the cock had crowed, everyone in the town and the surrounding countryside awoke to a horrendous bellowing cry. It echoed through the trees, and made the bells clang together with the reverberation of it. It blew away the parsonage gate (I will admit, the gate hung on but one hinge and was not the most stable). The cry was repeated and the shutters banged together, and the people leaped from their beds in terror of such a horrible sound.

And there in the first light of the morning sun they saw perched upon the tall shrine spire a monstrous dragon. A dragon so big as to make the former look as small as a child's toy. While the wings of the dead dragon had blotted out the sun, this dragon's wings were so tremendous they blotted out the universe. Its hide was of a brilliant gold touched with jewels— sapphires, emeralds, pearls, and rubies. It was indeed the very queen of all dragons, and she wore upon her narrow sleek head a golden crown that signified her rulership of those great beasts.

The noise was very loud and teeth-jarring in its intensity, and when the people of Goole looked closely at the dragon on their shrine spire they saw that she was weeping great tears which splashed into the shrineyard and watered the graves that were there. For it seems that this dragon was wife to the dragon that was dead, and she had come to mourn her consort and lord. She cried day-and-night, day-and-night, day-and-night for forty days and forty nights, and nothing caused her to cease her weeping.

The villagers shot arrows at the dragon. They threw rocks and brickbats. They offered her milk and freshly killed sheep, and even the virgin daughter of the village blacksmith. But the dragon would have none of it. She ignored the arrows, rocks, and brickbats, and she stated, in between sobs, that she was not hungry and had no wish for sheep, milk, or a virgin. She wanted nothing. Her lord was dead.

Now in all this forty days and forty nights of dragon's tears there had been little sleep in the village of Goole. Not even all the pillows of finest goosedown put carefully over the head could blot out the sound of a weeping dragon. The people were haggard, their eyes ringed with black, and they knew they could not continue with such a visitation. They went to Mayor Shoebuckle and demanded that he do something about the dragon. After all, by killing one dragon he had shown that he was some sort of an expert on dragons! So with great reluctance, Mayor Shoebuckle went to speak to the Dragon Queen.

"My lady dragon!" Mayor Shoebuckle shouted up at the great beast. He may have shouted, but he was being as polite as he could be. This dragon was so large that one sweep of her tail would have mashed Mayor Shoebuckle into blood pudding, as well he knew. "My good lady dragon, Your Majesty, Queen of Dragons! I beg you to cease this visitation to my town, and this dreadful noise, lest my people be forced to leave their ancestral village."

"I care not for you or for your ancestral village. I weep for my lord and I will continue to weep until his bones be naught but pearlescent ivory in yonder field. There is none who has given my lord burial, and he is entitled to good and proper burial, for he is a magical beast, sacred to both the God and Goddess. It was not right that he be killed, especially since there is no stink of magic about his corpse, so he was not slain by anyone with the magic to do the deed. It was treason, treason, treason, against my consort and against me!"

"My lady dragon, Your Majesty, Your Grace—Your Royal Highness—" Mayor Shoebuckle's knees were beginning to knock together very loudly, almost drowning out his voice. For he knew that the dragonwife did not know who had slain her husband, and should she find that it was he she might decide that she was hungry after all and gobble him down, thereby assuaging her hunger and avenging her husband at one and the same time. This was a fate Mayor Shoebuckle would as life avoid. So with all humbleness—and it was a very great humbleness for so proud a man—he abased himself before the dragonwife.

"O great favored child of the Goddess," Mayor Shoebuckle said, searching for any other honorable title he might give the Dragon Queen. "Is there naught that we can do to assuage your mourning? Is there nothing I and my poor people can do to make you cease your grieving?"

The dragon considered the mayor's request and even ceased to weep while she thought of all the possibilities involved. Had she been a wicked dragon she could have demanded of them tribute of many hundreds of sheep or the most succulent of their sons and daughters, but she did not do so.

Instead she said, "I will ask but one thing of this miserable village. If you grant it, you will never see hide, jewel, nor scale of me again. My wish is this, that you give my lord and husband honorable burial here in this shrineyard. Every year on the anniversary of his death you will place flowers on his grave and you will weep for him. If you do these things, I will keep my promise and leave. But should you at any time in the future—from now until the Goddess swallows up the entire universe and holds it in her belly and gives it birth again—if at any time in that great cycle of birth and rebirth, you cease to weep yearly for my husband, I shall return and I will decimate this village. I will eat every inhabitant of it and reduce every house and building to splinters and pebbles. This is my word. I, the Queen of Dragons, have said it."

The mayor groveled even deeper. "Very well, Your Majesty," he said. "We will indeed bury this great dragon in yonder empty corner of our shrineyard. We will put upon his grave a tombstone greater than any man, woodwitch, or witchlord has ever had. We will say for him every year a solemn funeral service. We will weep greatly for him, and for the sin which our village has committed."

"Very well. But I will not leave this place until the task is done," she said with great cunning, not entirely trusting Mayor Shoebuckle, and in this she was wise.

So all the village labored together day and night to dig the dragon's grave. Then they brought the dragon's bones to the shrineyard, buried him, and said for him the requiem prayers for the dead. They had their maidens and their young men sing

and scatter flowers on his grave. They beggared themselves
gathering together all of their coins, valuables, and whatever
bits of jewelry they had, to take to a witchlord magician that
lived in the village of Howden. Then the wizard came forth
and made the great tombstone for the dragon lord.

And so it was done, all as the Dragon Queen had required.
And she kept her promise, ceased her weeping, and after carefully inspecting the grave and all its arrangements she spoke
thusly. "Verily I say unto you, village of Goole, I will place
a spell upon this tombstone, a spell so powerful that it will last
through all eternity. And this is my spell: That any man and
maid who come here and, with all good intention one to the
other, sleep upon this stone under the light of the Goddess's
sky on the night of the full moon, that man and that maid shall
love each other faithfully all the days of their lives. They will
never again so much as look at another man or woman with
the slightest thought of lechery. For their hearts, minds, and
bodies will turn only to that one which they loved enough to
sleep upon the dragonstone with. For I have loved my consort
and lord so much that I, in all my thousands of years, have
looked at no other dragon with the slightest thought of lust.
Neither did he look at any young lusty female dragon with any
hunger in his eyes or body. This is my blessing upon this stone
and perhaps also my curse. Think it through wisely. Do not
sleep upon the stone casually or in jest. For to be forever bound
to one person without love is a painful thing indeed. So mote
it be!"

And with that, the Dragon Queen—she who was a faithful
dragonwife all the days of her life and took never again another
consort—spread her mighty wings that stretched wide over all
Englene, and rising on the tips of her claws, flew away from
the village of Goole. But so great had been her weight and so
mighty her body that her many days of sitting upon the spire
twisted and bent it into such a shape as you see this day. And
we of the village of Goole have left it such in token of our
pledge to the faithful dragonwife and her consort. Even now,
year by year, we come on the anniversary of the dragon lord's
death and we say prayers for him and we weep at his grave.

"But does the grave really have that power?" Elizabeth asked.
"Is it true that a couple who sleep on that stone are forever
faithful?"

The sexton nodded. "Aye, it's so and you see what I meant when I said what a great temptation I put before you. For should you two, sinful couple as you are, sleep upon the stone this night, you are bound to one another for the rest of your lives and no one, not even the God, the Goddess, or all the holy archangels will be able to pull you apart, for such is the power of the dragon's spell."

The sexton jumped out of the now-completed grave and looked at it. "I must go and change my raiment," he said, "and prepare for the funeral of the Lady Elinora, which is to be this night at midnight. But should I come upon you two here in the moonlight—for it will be full moon tonight on the dragon's grave—I will be sore tempted to break my vow of peace and destroy you myself, for I think my sin would be the lesser." With that he picked up his spade, turned his back on them and walked away.

"Ooh!" Elizabeth said with a shiver. "I wanted gloomy thoughts, but that's a little gloomier than I was hoping for. What think you of the monk's words? Do you want to sleep on the stone after Elinora the Mage is safely buried?"

Jackie skirted the open grave and went to stand on the large granite slab of the dragonstone. He looked down at his fore-shortened shadow which lay across the stone and saw that even though the sun was not in that direction his shadow had turned and was reaching toward that of the Princess Elizabeth. He observed the phenomenon in silence and then spoke, but his words were filled with a deep sadness. "My lady princess, the monk was right. It would be a sin to link you and me together for all eternity. I know that your duty both to your father and to your kingdom lies in marrying the great golden demigod who was in the Circle of Avebury. I have known that for some time, though I have tried to bar that knowledge from my mind. For I do love you beyond the love of ordinary mortal man. Because I love you and only want what is best for both of us, I will not sleep with you on the stone, this night or any other."

Jackie faced the open grave, and then somersaulted into it. His voice rose hollow and distant out of the grave. "It's not that I fear your father, or even that I fear the Goddess. But in time you may come to hate me for binding you to me too closely and I would not do that."

He jumped up out of the grave again and stood on the edge of it, looking down. "Now your gloomy thoughts have made

me gloomy. I've almost forgotten I'm a jester." He shrugged
his motley into place and said with a mocking grin, "Besides,
everyone knows that Jackie Somers, king of jesters and jester
to kings, has never been faithful to any woman, nor is he likely
to be!"

And with that, Jackie ran away, laughing, through the grave-
stones, leaping over them faster and faster. His laughter echoed
loudly through the trees to hide the sound of his tears falling.

Elizabeth watched the jester's flight and understood it full
well. She walked to the small sun-touched corner of the shrine,
picked the snowdrops that grew there and put them on the
dragon's grave. She stood and watched them wither in the
sunlight and realized with a terrible clarity that any love between Jackie and herself was as fragile as the first flowers of
spring. Frost or the touch of the sun could wither and eventually
kill it.

Chapter 18

Elizabeth was to remember for the next few weeks the image of that green and white clump of little snowdrops that had grown in the shrineyard of Goole, for it was the last green thing they were to see in their journey southward. The snow of winter shrank away until it became only dirty gray patches in the lee of buildings and under thick branched trees. The dark earth of Englene was revealed, rich and black and ready for the mystery of spring's fertility.

But that mystery did not come. The earth remained black. There were no brave little green shoots, neither of grass, wheat, or even the green herbs. Only the woodwitch places deep in the woods seemed to know that spring had come to Englene.

The travelers paused for a week's time in Lincoln and joined with all of the priests, priestesses, townsmen, farmers, and peasants in the great shrine to raise their prayers to the God Sulis and to the Mother Goddess Diona so that the green magic would soon appear on the land. But the Goddess did not hear and the God did nothing.

As they journeyed southward, the air became a constant thick wet mist that shadowed everything with the colors of death and dying. Then the travelers appeared already shrouded in their burial garments. It was the same the further south they went. No sunlight, no good green earth, nothing but the stink of impotence upon the land.

They journeyed eastward through Kings Lynn and Dereham in Nordfule—and this rich farmland, a place of fat sheep and acres of thick wheat, was barren. The sheep died in the fields, their feet rotten and decayed from standing in the thick, black, fruitless mud.

Through village after village it was the same. The people were thin and gray from the long winter, their teeth loose and their gums bloody, but there were no green scurvy-herbs to cure the sickness. The salt meat and the flour were low in their barrels and there was no new provision.

As the travelers came into the east border of Englene, the lands that were close to the sea and the great channel, they expected to see wagons of fish being brought to the townsfolk, but there were no fish. The harvest of the sea was as empty as the fields. There was little in the way of foodstuffs, and the people grew hungry.

Elizabeth looked at the land of her forefathers there in the quadrant of Englene sacred to the great Archangel Raphael, and knew the depths of her father's lack of caring and loss of power. For with the great ring Raziel upon his hand he should have been able to remedy this evil. Yet he had not. The impotence of his member had spread to his body and spirit. The land cried out and King Richard did nothing. But the Princess Elizabeth looked at her inheritance and, like the sky above her, wept for it.

The little ale-slake in the red brick and whitewashed town of Yermouth was depressingly like so many of the inns Elizabeth and her party had frequented in their travels. It was small, grubby, and filled with the disgruntled subjects of King Richard of Englene. The ale was as dark and sour as the conversations the princess overheard at the other tables. The room smelled of wet wood, damp woolen clothing, unwashed bodies, and treason against the anointed king.

"'E is not able to do it no more, I tell ye, Perry. That 'igh and mighty witchlord King o' ours b'ain't be able to get his member to come to attention. And because 'e can't do it, neither can our fields and your bloody great ram. We've got ourselves a king who b'ain't bein' a proper king!"

The speaker was a little nutcracker of a man who by his clothing was a local farmer. Elizabeth listened in on the conversation with great interest and very little surprise.

"'E be comin' up on a double seven, 'e be. I'm not for one think' that we or the Goddess should accept any sort of substitute. The time's come for the king to see where 'is duty be and let somebody with a proper vigor take care of our fields, our animals, and our women's wombs."

Elizabeth sighed and leaned back in the settle. It was a very odd thing to be, on one hand, the princess and heir to the throne of Englene and, on the other, merely a scruffy witchlord minstrel to whom the inhabitants of the inn paid little or no attention. She had spent her entire life surrounded by servants and had spoken quite freely in front of them, and they in turn now spoke quite freely in front of her, their future ruler.

"Ah, but what about the fire on all the hills when our fair princess became a woman?" The serving maid had stopped to speak to the farmers. She entered their conversation with the ease of long acquaintanceship. "I tell you, 'twas said that even in La Bonne Terre the light of our lady losing her maidenhead was known."

A couple of the farmers laughed and made rude noises with their lips, and one of them, a broad-shouldered, red-cheeked rustic, said, "No lass, there was no loss of our princess's maidenhead that night. 'Twas nothin' more than a witchlord trick. Those flames on the hill were no more than bonfires. 'Tis said that the king was unmanned there in the Circle and our beauty of a princess is a maiden still. Would that I had the unmaidening of such a fair lass, for I'd see it was done right and proper!"

The farmer's companions laughed, dug each other in the ribs and made rude gestures. The general consensus was that whatever had taken place at the Great Circle of Avebury, it hadn't been the king that had done it.

Elizabeth turned away, blushing fiercely. "How do they know that?" she asked of Menadel. "It's supposed to be a secret.

I thought only Aunt Catheryne, Thomas, and Aleicester knew there was going to be a substitute. Yet these rude humans, who have never been more than five miles from their homes, know of my father's shame. How is it?"

It was Jackie who answered her. "Poppet, don't you understand that a mouse can't squeak in any of King Richard's palaces without the lowest apprentice hearing the sound and knowing what its potent is? There is no secret *you* can keep from anyone in Englene. Oh, I vow that you witchlords manage to keep secrets one from the other—but from a human, never!"

Elizabeth turned and stared at the jester. "Do you mean to say my every action and deed is the bibble babble of the tavern? Look you, these rustics can't even get their facts straight. They speak of me as a great beauty, yet not one of them would recognize me were he to pass by this table this minute. How can they know truth of me and mine when they do not even know the truth of appearance?"

"Ah, but you see," said Jackie, "every princess is a beauty simply by being a princess. One goes with the other. Were you to come into this rude abode clad in silk, velvet, and your jewels, every man jack of them would swear you were the most beauteous princess in all the Three Regions. As for these poor knaves and their not recognizing a princess in their midst, most of them wouldn't recognize their own mothers or be recogized by those same mothers. But do remember this. They know a truth when they hear it. And all Englene knows the truth of King Richard's manhood and his lack thereof. Those farmers have only to look at their empty fields, barren wives, and dying livestock to know that the king is less than a man. For the king must be more than human, more even than witchlord. He must be the health and the well-being and the vitality of a nation. Your father has fallen far short of these people's needs or desires. Unless he finds some way to revive *his* desires, I doubt not that we will be in for a very bad harvest and an unhealthy year."

"For once, Somers has managed to say something both truthful and sensible," Menadel said. "I'm amazed. The fool has put on wisdom. This journey has done a great deal for all of us. My lady, you must face the fact that until your father's manhood is restored, the kingdom will suffer, and I for one do not think it will be restored during his lifetime. Think on that and consider your own position."

Elizabeth shook her head, then signaled the slatternly serving maid for another round of ale. "I never thought I would find a time when I would not have the wish or the will to defend my father. What he has done to this land is a grievous sin against the Gods. But I do not know *what* to do about it. My heart tells me one thing, my mind another, and it grieves me, Uncle. It grieves me very much."

Menadel, his face as full of sourness as the ale in his tankard, could find very little to say of comfort to his princess.

Guenhwyvar snuggled closer to the wizard, her face white and drawn. The cough had made her pale, a shadow of her former self. She looked up at Menadel's normally cheerful face and, sighing, looked away. "What does this mean, my lady Elizabeth? Will you take arms against your father? You could have done it months ago in Cymru and saved much grief. Will you do it now?"

"Of course she won't!" Jackie slammed his tankard hard down on the tabletop, slopping ale across the battered wood. "And I'll not hear anything like that said against my lady! I'll have you know, little woodwitch, that were every man, woman and child in Englene to swear an oath of disloyalty to King Richard, my lady would stand by him even against all these people. On the day she changes, or becomes less than my loyal lady, I will open my poor fool's veins and let my blood run into the earth and die, glad to be out of such a world."

Elizabeth placed one hand over Jackie's and said, "There, there. You needn't worry, Somers, your blood will stay in your veins for many a long year. I will not raise my arm against my father. But when I return to the palace and face him, I will demand a reckoning! For it is my right as his heir. I will have to do something to aid this country. But it will not be by usurping the throne.

"But how can I get him to understand what is happening? I *must* make him see what the country has become! He should know that this is happening. Perhaps I should end this quest and return to court to stop the blackness from going any further on the land. What think you?" Each of her companions paused to consider their answer.

It was Jackie who spoke first. "Tell me, poppet, compared to what you have seen this spring, how important to you is that randy buck you coupled with at Avebury? Do you still think pleasuring in his bed is more important than the welfare of your country?"

Menadel shook his head. "No, fool. You have it wrong. It's not simply one or the other. It is in many ways a matter of both. I say we should continue on our journey—for, you see, you will have need of such a man of power by your side when you become queen, Elizabeth. Your heart is hasty and quick to make you think that you can hide your father's flaws from this world with your powers. I say to you, your powers are not yet *that* great. You must see *all* the land, west, east, north, and south. You must come into your own as the heir to this kingdom and you cannot do it without completing the spell."

"But—" Elizabeth was torn between her sense of obligation to her father and her understanding of Menadel's words. There was some comfort to be taken from the fact that Menadel was saying that the spell was for more than just a man in bed, and perhaps it was a larger and more important quest she was on. She struggled to articulate her thoughts and then noticed young Guenhwyvar had gone still and pale. She was looking past the princess's shoulder at nothing at all.

And then the girl spoke in a voice full and mature, and not that of a Pembrokeshire girl at all. "Elizabeth, you must complete the spell. And then you must come to me, the Mother-of-All, so that I might fulfill your destiny and send you forth a warrior maid ready to be queen. I, the Great Mother of Englene, say this to you."

Guenhwyvar stopped speaking, closed her eyes momentarily and then opened them, and on her face was a look of pure terror. She brought her hands together in a gesture of prayer and in her own soft voice said, "Please, please continue the journey. For my sake, go on, for I have *seen*—I have illseen endings and beginnings. I have *seen* blood upon the ground, blood that can be mine or yours. I have *seen* your death and I have *seen* mine, and yet I know—they need not be—that you alone can prevent them. You must go on. To give up now means my death and yours. Please, my lady, please. Think of Englene, think of the child you will someday bear—"

"A child?" Jackie was all attention. Bedding with a princess of Englene might not send him to the block—but if he'd gotten her pregnant, that was another matter."

"When the princess is fertile," Guenhwyvar said slowly, "and has a belly big with child, the land would reflect that fact. For she is the lady wife of Englene and her fertility would counteract that of her father's lack."

Menadel nodded and stroked his fuzzy red beard. "Aye, and the princess's belly and all the other parts of her body are what this trip was about. When we find the man that she seeks at journey's end I swear on my beard and *my* belly that a fair prince will be the result of this search—and I do not need Geunhwyvar's ability to prophecy. I simply know this as a truth, even as I knew it before we left on this journey."

Elizabeth leaned forward, an expression of rapt interest on her face. "Then I will find him!" she said with some excitement. "Thank you, Menadel. Thank you for reassuring me that this is all worth it. I am going to find that man and—a prince. What would my mother have said to that? I am going to give Englene a prince!"

Her voice brought sunshine and light to the dimly lit room. The happiness in her was an echo of generations of royal women who had but one prayer: "Give me, o Mother Goddess, a prince." It was the cry heard throughout time by those women whose bellies were wombs of history. Many of those ladies had gone to their graves in sorrow for failure to gain a prince.

"Tell me, Menadel," she demanded of the wizard, "will my prince, my son, be good for Englene?"

But the question was not one destined to be answered, for before Menadel could open his mouth the door of the tavern crashed open and a breathless excited fisherman ran into the room shouting, "A witch, a witch! They're going to burn a witch in the sea square. The priests caught a human that dared to do the Great Rite with his daughter in his own field."

The ale-slake erupted with sound and action. Tankards were knocked over, benches fell crashing to the floor, shouted questions, exclamations, and rude remarks filled the air. The building emptied rapidly as the ale-knights hurried away so as not to miss this latest bit of drama. Elizabeth, Jackie, Menadel, and Guenhwyvar, caught up in the surge of excitement, fell in with the crowd and found themselves being hurried down narrow lanes and through alleyways, down steep cobbled paths toward the sea.

And there, coming suddenly out of a fetid alley, they found themselves in a wide cobbled stone square, three sides thick with timber and brick buildings and the fourth side open facing east toward the sea. There was already a considerable crowd forming and more people streaming from their houses, alleyways, and byways. Even the fishermen ran up from the beach to see what the commotion was about.

But no matter how crowded the square became, still a wide large space was left open in the center. For there was the large stone ring surrounding a tall iron post. This was the traditional place of death for a murderer, a highwayman, a brigand—or a human who dared to practice witchcraft. In Englene only the woodwitch and witchlord were allowed the knowledge of magic. Should any human venture to perform even the smallest spell and be caught at it by the witchlords, the penalty was burning at the stake for the great sin of heresy.

Elizabeth bullied a path through the crowd to the front and made sure her companions had an excellent view. They did not have to wait long for the spectacle. Slowly into the square filed, rank by rank, twenty of the king's archers. They formed a square around the burning post, facing outward into the crowd lest some foolhardy human attempt to rescue the condemned man. Then into the square came a double line of priests and priestesses of the God Sulis. They chanted dolefully the hymn of the dying heretic, and while their words wished the condemned man well in his journey through the western gate, there was a strong element of hypocrisy in the fact that they were so eager to send him there post-haste.

Last of all came the condemned man. He was dressed in a long yellow robe, and upon his head was a tall pointed yellow cap. There was a long moaning sigh in the crowd as they watched the man who had been their neighbor being chained to the stake with tinder, brush, and faggots of wood heaped about his feet and up his legs, even to his thighs.

It was clear from the attitude of the priests that no mercy would be shown this man. He did not have a bag of gunpowder hung about his neck, so that when the first flames rose the gunpowder would explode and take his life quickly and mercifully and leave naught but a dead body for the flames.

A priest of Sulis came forward and pronounced a benediction

upon the witch, and asked him if he had aught to say before dying.

The farmer raised his face to the dark overcast sky and in a voice loud enough for Sulis himself to hear it, he shouted, "I am guilty of what I have been accused of. Hear me, O God and Goddess. Hear me, O King Richard. I took my virgin daughter into my stinking, rotting fields and there I entered her and performed the Great Rite so that my fields might flourish. I ask nothing but that the Goddess herself will accept my death as a sacrifice for the king. But if the fields lie barren, the sheep die, and our children starve, then I curse you, Sulis! I curse you, O Great Mother! Most of all, I curse thee, O King Richard of the lost power. Yes, I curse thee, King Richard Lackseed!"

The cry from the crowd was ominous and fearful. It was not directed at the man condemned to die, but rather at the Gods and the king.

With tears in her eyes, Elizabeth turned and fought her way out of the mob. She ran away from the square, down toward the beach and out across the sand until she stood ankle deep in the sea. She stood alone on the cold wrack and raised her hands aloft, fingers spread. She cried aloud, "Raphael, Raphael, ye who art the Archangel of the East! Hear my voice. Listen unto me, Elizabeth, Princess of Englene, and heed me. Take my word as vow and take my life if I do not fulfill it. I ask of thee the power that shall someday be mine, the power of the ring Raziel. I ask it in the name of these suffering people. Take from me what thou wilt, Raphael, but give me a storm, that I might rescue this man. I will not have him die cursing my father's name. Aid me, O Great Raphael, that I might bless thy name forever!"

There was a great silence, as if, for some moment of eternity, the very waves themselves halted, considering her words. But the silence was for only a moment. The leaden sky was split from Ethereal Regions to Earth by a bolt of lightning which touched the sea at the horizon and caused it to boil.

Winds gathered and roared down through the clouds, brushing the tops of the sea and moving inland toward Yermouth. Lightning danced on the waters and the foam gathered and coalesced into the shape of great white destriers, sea-horses of the Archangel Raphael. The horses came pounding up through the surf towards the beach; hundreds of them, rank on rank, their hides the color of foam and their eyes green as the sea. Their manes and tails were lightning and their hooves struck blue fire when they touched the sand.

The horses divided around the princess, their hot breath touching her as they passed close enough for their flanks to rub like silk across her skin. As the last rank thundered up the beach she turned and, grasping the lightning mane with her bare hands, she vaulted onto the back of the largest and most fiery of these mighty warhorses. With an eldritch cry of power, she rode forward until she led the thundering heard toward the witchburning square.

The priests, priestesses, and villagers scattered at the fury of the slashing rain and the angel horses. They ran screaming out of the square and sought shelter in the narrow alleys where the horses did not follow.

Elizabeth circled the square deosil and shouted aloud her triumph and her thanks to Raphael. Then, reigning in the horse, she rode up to the burning stake and, with one sweep of her dagger, cut the heavy iron links in twain. She shouted to the farmer, "Give me some of the faggots that lie at your feet and then take my hand!"

Startled, the farmer did as she asked and passed up to her a small bundle of the fuel that had been meant for his execution. Elizabeth tucked it securely into her tabard and then, grasping the man firmly around his wrist, she swung him up onto the horse in back of her. "Hold on," she shouted. "Hold on, we ride for *your* life."

Elizabeth thundered out of the deserted square as if all the darkness in Englene was after her. She rode back again toward the beach, and down the wet sand for some two or three miles, until she was well clear of Yermouth and saw that there was no pursuit.

She pulled the great sea-horse to a stop and turned to face the man riding behind her. "You are safe now," she said to him. "But I would advise you not to return to your farm or your family, and definitely not to Yermouth, for to do so would be your death. I can only stop what they would do this day."

The man nodded his acceptance. "Aye. I feared it was so. But then, I was dead when I took my wee Joan out to the field and did what I did unto her. My life was forfeit then and it's forfeit now. I'll do what every forfeit man does and take to the woods as an outlaw. Should my family choose to come with me, so be it. But as for me, the woodwitches be a great deal kinder to those who use magic illegally. They'll not burn me, but will shelter me from those who will."

"You're right, an outlaw's life is the only choice. I rescued you for one reason only, and that was because I feared your curse on the king. I will not argue the right or wrong of what you did, but the reward I ask of you for your life is that you curse no more the name of King Richard."

The farmer slid down off the back of the mighty sea-horse and patted its enormous white flanks in appreciation for the ride. "I think the Goddess sent you and you saved my life for her purpose. Therefore I will heed your words and will no more curse the king's name."

Elizabeth leaned forward to give the man what few coins she had with her. "Take this. It will ease your way to the forest. I will pray for your safety."

The farmer tucked the money into his tunic and gave her thanks for it. He took her hand and kissed it; and then with a wave of his hand he turned and walked up the sand dunes and away over the black bare fields toward the dark green shadow of a forest that stood against the hills.

Elizabeth kicked the sea-horse lightly in the ribs and, leaning forward, found herself encircled by the sparkling lightning mane. "Come, Gift of Raphael. Take me to my companions, in the archangel's name."

The horse, at her words, began to gallop along the sand back toward Yermouth. But before reaching the town the horse swerved inland and began climbing the great sand dunes. Elizabeth clung tightly to the animal's back as its great legs sent sprays of sand flying into the air to meet the still falling rain. She looked northward at Yermouth and saw that the storm was still sweeping through the town.

She pulled the horse to a stop and, turning the animal to face the sea, she again raised her arms and said, "O mighty Raphael, angel of the air, I give you my thanks and my blessings, and I acknowledge my debt to you. Now I ask that you take back your storm and when you return me to the company of my companions I will return this, your steed, to you."

Even as she spoke the air lightened and the clouds began to roll away. She sat on Raphael's horse and watched the storm die away to wisps of cloud and light gusts of gentle rain. Elizabeth gave the horse its head, knowing that, with the aid of the angel, the horse would lead her straight to her companions.

She found Menadel, Jackie, and Guenhwyvar, with the horses, hiding in a small copse outside of Yermouth, on the road south. They did not seem overly surprised to see her still riding the great sea-horse. After exchanging greetings with them, she slipped from the animal's back, thanked it, and, giving it a light slap upon its shoulders, sent it running back toward the sea, the sky, and its master.

Menadel's face was alight with pride as he said to Elizabeth, "That was a magnificent storm you raised, my lady. I am pleased by such display of your power, knowledge, and the strength of it."

Elizabeth tightened the cinch on the saddle of her horse and then mounted the animal. "I did what I had to do, Menadel, though I thank you for your praise. I bargained with the Archangel Raphael, and asked of him a loan of power that would eventually be mine as queen, and he granted it to me. Of course"—she laughed—"I promised him he could have anything he wanted in return, so I suppose that even an archangel considers that a good bargain."

"Oh dear, oh dear!" Menadel's face clouded over. "I wish you hadn't done that. The spell required the use of your *own* power, not another's. I hope you have not lost this Watchtower with too much haste and too little thought. Your hold on the Archangel Raphael is slight, for your mother did not complete the four Towers that were to give your family control over the archangels. And of all the towers, Raphael's is slightest, being only one-quarter finished. He will take full advantage of your offer. I fear what he might ask of you. Perhaps he will not give you his protection! Oh dear, oh dear!"

"I've always been taught that he was benevolent and kindly," Elizabeth said. "I trust him to ask no more of me than I can properly give, and what he asks I will give cheerfully. That farmer did more for this country by his actions than my father has done. I hope the Goddess understands that and allows the fields to grow green."

"Poppet, they may grow green in this place," Jackie said. "When we came across the field, fleeing your storm, I noticed green leaves appearing upon some of the trees. There was even a faint haze of wheat in one of the fields. But I doubt the power of one human and his virgin daughter will be enough to affect more than a county or two. If this spring is as bleak as it seems, all Englene will suffer from it."

Elizabeth frowned and reached into her tabard and pulled out the bundle of twigs.

"This," she said, "is my gift to my father from the east part of his kingdom. The wood that should have burned a witch! I will tell him why it did not, and speak of that man's deed which was believed worthy of burning, and what I did at Yermouth. I hope he *fears* what I have to say, and takes every word of it to heart."

"Menadel," said Jackie, "what do you think will be the result of the gifts our princess brings to her father? With the exception of young Guenhwyvar, not one of them is very attractive or pleasing."

Menadel stroked his beard and considered for a moment, then said, "I don't think our lady princess means them to be pleasant—and if our lord the king heeds the gifts and the warnings, he may yet be saved. But if he does not . . ."

Elizabeth tucked the twigs back into her tabard, and kicked her horse into a gallop. "Southward, southward," she cried. "We go south into the land of Michael. May he give us shelter and comfort and perhaps present us with some better things than the despair of Cymru, Bamborow's sorceress, and Yermouth's witch."

SOUTH

Salve Michael, quanto splendidior quam ignes sempiterni est tua majestas.

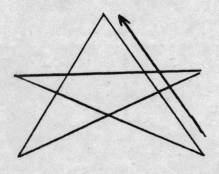

I pray to the Lion, the lord of lightnings, master of
The solar orb. Great prince of the element of fire!
Be with me, I pray thee. Guard me and mine
From all perils approaching from the South!

Chapter 19

Menadel spent a great deal of his time studying his maps for their journey southward. He pointed out to Elizabeth the necessity of journeying through Lundene. "You can see, from the map my lady, there are no suitable fords east of the city. The unnatural spring rains have made the tides too strong to allow for crossing the Theames farther down. We must go back through the city. I for one am not pleased by that, for until you have completed your journey there is great danger to you should the Lady Pemberly and others know where you are. I have studied the skies, and the configuration of your stars is not good. The sign we're entering indicates grave danger for you. I do not like it, my lady. I feel, even from my map, an emanation of evil. Take care, be sure that you pray to the Gods. I will do what *I* can to keep you safe."

Elizabeth heard and accepted Menadel's words. Ever since she had bargained with Raphael she had felt a strong sense of unease and incompletion, as though something had not yet been finished.

Guenhwyvar seemed also to be aware of things to be. She spent most of her time wrapped in her cloak murmuring prayers, and her eyes had a *seeing* look. She traveled more in vision than in the real realm.

The season had not improved as they journeyed southward. They saw no more green upon the fields, and it was clear that the farmer's spell had not extended very far beyond Yermouth. The fields were black and muddy and stank of rotting seed. The sheep slipped their young and did not carry to fruition. The land was dying and all around them was the Goddess's charnel house.

The journey through Lundene was accomplished with great difficulty. They found that the city, even at night, was ablaze with light. Men and women danced frantically in the streets. In every alleyway there was the clicking of dice, the susurrus of cards, the thunk, thunk of ale barrels being opened, and wine jugs gurgling dry. It was clear from the smell of the city that the culverts had run for days with wine and ale; the king was attempting to keep his people content. But the city was not protected from the darkness of evil. It seemed to camp like a siege army about Englene and it had successfully breached the walls.

Elizabeth, Menadel, Jackie, and Guenhwyvar, leading their horses, slinked through the alleyways. They traveled constantly vigilant against thieves and murderers. This was not the city they had known. An evil had sprung up in it which had nothing to do with the darkness outside it. It was as though Lundene was rotting from the center, and that center was the king's member.

When they reached the Great Bridge, they mounted their horses hurriedly and clattered across the cobblestones as though demons pursued. Menadel removed the splinter from his hat and threw it violently into the Theames. The shadows of the houses and shops cast weird, twisting shapes on their faces and there were cold icy fingers of wind coming off the river.

When they reached Southwarke they did not pause, but rode out into the countryside. To her sorrow Elizabeth found herself consoled by entering the ranks of darkness. For she had traveled many months with the darkness and knew it. It would take much effort and a great deal of power and magic to clear the capital city of the cancer that had grown in it like some forbidden fruit.

Their journey continued southward, and as they traveled they saw the same desolation and emptiness they had seen in the east quandrant. The sky continued to sullenly spit rain and the roads were naught but muck and mire. They had to stop frequently to clean the cumbersome black mud from the frogs of the horses's hooves. The trip south was slow and sad.

Elizabeth had a great deal of time to think. She wrapped herself securely in her cloak and said little to her companions. All that she had seen in her father's lands had impressed itself deeply into her mind. Something had to be done. Her father could not continue to allow the land to fall apart. At the same time she, Elizabeth, could not attack him. With much sighing, she commended the matter to the Gods, content that it was not her shoulders alone that bore it.

Some days out of Lundene, at an ale-slake in a small town called East Grinfielde, she met again with the witch-farmer of Great Yermouth. He seemed less surprised to see her than she him.

"Well, my lady minstrel," the farmer said, looking up at her from his scanty lunch. "We meet again! As you see, my circumstances are somewhat changed. I travel alone, for my wife and children have deserted me." He fingered the long green gown he wore and the penitence collar about his neck. "'Twas the woodwitches in Yermouth Forest that gave me this. They told me to go south to the great Ashdowne Forest, and I would be given sanctuary. They gave me a new name to carry southward. They called me Jack-in-the-Green, a name of great power. But this meeting of ours is not by chance. For I did hope, ever since I left Lundene, to see you, gentle lady. Now I know who and what you are, and I say that my life is thine forever, and my allegiance as well. If I may do a small service for you, there is a piece of news you *must* hear."

Elizabeth leaned forward with an abrupt gesture and lowered her voice. "Speak not of what I am, or who I am, in this place. Swear on your life and mine that you will say nothing!"

Jack quickly swore his oath, one hand on his heart and the other on the hilt of Elizabeth's dagger. He said, "My lady who cannot be named, I have heard that there is a great troop of warriors come after you. It's said they wear no badge nor coat-of-arms. But when alone they speak of the Black Lady of the Circle who drives them onward; She-who-would-be-queen. The king has made her High Priestess of Englene, and she did use the powers he gave her to find you. There are those who say that the darkness and the lack of spring are due to that blasphemy.

"I tell you this, both by my knowledge as a human and that knowledge I have gained from the woodwitches. She will do you a great harm if given a chance. So I would suggest that you bide with me. Together you, your companions, and I will go into the forest and there be protected by the woodwitches."

"It is said," Menadel commented, "that woodwitches do indeed inhabit the Ashdowne Forest, and those woodwitches are Pikeys. They have Elvish blood, and are like unto the Cornish woodwitches. Their magic is very old, older even than almost any clan of woodwitches in all of Englene, saving those that dwell in the Heartwoods and serve the Goddess herself. There is a clearing deep in the forest and the grave mound of a long dead Elvish queen. We could seek safety and protection there. If the woodwitches will aid us, they will do it in that spot, for it is sacred. Come, Guenhwyvar, *seek* for some sign of this troop that Jack-in-the-Green speaks of."

Guenhwyvar obediently closed her eyes and reached deep within herself to tap the power of her gift. But there was nothing there save a great darkness. "I fear my lack of *seeing*, my lady," she said after several minutes of intense concentration. "It may mean there is no future for me to *see*. The time of death may well be upon us, and I will commend my spirit to the Great Mother. So should we all."

"Nonsense!" Elizabeth said. "I refuse to give up before doing battle. If this day means my death, so be it. Let us be gone from this place quickly. I'll put my trust in the wood-witches and their dead Elf-Queen!"

They hurried out of the inn, saddled up their horses and rode off toward the Ashdowne Forest. The road ended abruptly at the edge of the forest. There seemed to be naught but paths made by deer, leading deep into the tangled dark green woods. This was no pleasant hunting preserve, but a stretch of raw forest with tangled undergrowth and large shadowing trees.

Menadel got off his horse, put his ear to the ground, and listened. Raising his head, he said to Elizabeth, "It's true. There is a troop of at least twenty horsemen heading this way. We must hurry into the forest and try to reach Elf-Queen's Clearing before they are upon us. Quickly, quickly, away!"

With a great crashing of underbrush and snapping of branches and twigs, Menadel led a furious ride deep into the forest. His voice cried aloud like that of Hern the Hunter as he cajoled and pleaded with them for speed.

They reached the clearing at a time that lacked but an hour of sunset. There in the thickening twilight they saw the place which might mean their deaths by the Lady Pemberly's assassins or their deliverance by the woodwitches.

The clearing was not large, hardly bigger than Elizabeth's own bedchamber. The great mound in the center of it was higher than her head. It rose gently, curved and rounded as a woman's breast, and was covered over with green grass and little yellow daisies. The calamities that had overtaken the land of Englene had not touched this place. The great Ashdowne Forest was green and growing and fertile. The woodwitches had their own magic to preserve the fertility of their land and had had little concern for the impotence of kings. Jack remounted his fat cob and then, bidding farewell to Elizabeth, Jackie, Menadel, and Guenhwyvar, he set off into the forest in search of the woodwitches.

Elizabeth and her companions did not wait with meek acceptance for the troop of assassins. Menadel cut a stout ash pole and helped Elizabeth to bind her dagger to the end of it, making a very effective killing spear. He and Jackie took from their scabbards the swords they had received from Bamborow Castle. The weapons jumped into their hands, sharp and ready, their edges flamed with blue, and the runes of many an old spell glowed, waiting for the blades to taste blood. Jackie and Menadel had had but little need of the blades since they had left that great castle in the north, so the spells did not need renewing nor the edges sharpening.

Guenhwyvar assisted by collecting a large supply of sticks and stones and sharpening ash poles so that she might use them as a weapon. She refused a dagger, saying she had no knowledge of how to use it save for eating. It was better, she said, to deal with weapons she was familiar with—a stone and a stick—the weapons that of old had been used by the peasants, the disenfranchised, and the desperate.

They did not need Menadel's keen ear to hear the horsemen now, for the troop had followed closely on their trail. It was only the thickness of the forest undergrowth which had slowed their pursuit, straight as an arrow, to the clearing. Birds rose from trees, screaming at the sound of the horsemen's passage. A crowd of ravens came flying in their wake. It was well known that these birds could smell a battle from miles away, and would come quickly at the sound of horses's hooves and clashing steel so that they might feast upon the losers of the battle.

It was not only ravens that the battle had brought, but another witness. There in the shadow of a great oak stood the Angel of Death, her pale face alight with the possibilities of the battlefield to be. She too had come to carry off the losers.

It was Guenhwyvar who saw her first and, with a shriek of dismay, she pointed at the angel, saying, "Look, look, our doom is upon us. Our Lady of Darkness is here already! Since I see her my death must be nigh upon me."

"Where, where?" Jackie said, looking in the direction that Guenhwyvar had pointed. "What are you talking about? What lady? I see nothing and no one. What do you mean by such bibble babble at a time like this?"

"I see her," Elizabeth said, "and I smell the apple trees of Avalon. That must mean my death is upon me, too. Very well, if it be the Gods's will that I die here, I will do so. But 'tis an unfair trick to serve on Englene."

Elizabeth glanced at the Angle of Death and saw the woman smile as if in recognition. *Well, my Lady of Darkness,* Elizabeth thought, *if it be my time I will go. But I warn you, I will go west fighting, and if necessary I will fight even you....*

The Dark Lady of Death nodded her head as though she had heard Elizabeth's thoughts. She spread her hands in a gesture of acceptance. Then, furling her wings closely about her, the angel leaned back against the oak tree to watch as the first of the horsemen burst through the encircling trees into the clearing.

In later years, and after many battles, Elizabeth would find that it was no more possible to describe this first battle than the others she had led. It was a confused tangle of horses, sword thrusts, blood, sweat, and dirt. It was screams of agony and the thud of bodies. It was the feel of a sword nipping into her own arm and the surprise that the pain was so little, only a sharp sting. The blow had been slight, merely the glancing edge of a blade as it fell from the hand of a man Elizabeth had speared with her dagger. His body fell heavily almost at her feet and she had a small moment, like unto the eye of a storm, to look down and with great dispassion watch as his entrails spilled out upon the ground. She found that the sight neither disgusted nor pleased her. She looked up then at the sound of horse's hooves and braced herself for the next assassin.

He towered above her on a blood bay destrier. His sword sang as he circled it above his head and brought it down for a killing blow. But the blow never landed. The sword flew from his hands as blood came pouring out of his mouth, and he fell down between his horse's legs. Elizabeth could see a wood-witch arrow protruding from his back.

The air sang with arrows, but none of them came near Elizabeth, Menadel, Jackie, or Guenhwyvar. The arrows homed in on the assassins as if sent by the hand of the Goddess, but where the arrows came from was a matter of mystery. There was no one to be seen in the encircling forest. There was no sound of a bowstring, no shout of command. There was only a deep silence and the hiss of a passing arrow seeking out its chosen target. Elizabeth stood with her back to the Angel of Death and watched as one by one the assassins died.

She did not know when the angel left and it was only later that she realized that the Dark Lady had not come for her, but for these others. Yet the battle had been so close and the likelihood of her death so apparent that the angel had let Elizabeth see her doom before it had come.

When the last assassin was dead and the clearing spattered with red daisies of blood, Elizabeth danced among the bodies whooping a witchdame cry of triumph. The battle had been won, and she knew she owed it to the people of her mother far more than to any skill in warfare she herself had. When she had completely circled the clearing, dancing always deosil, she stopped to face the south. She raised her arms and lifted her voice in the sound of power.

"Hear me, O people of the woods. I, Elizabeth, say unto you this day that in token of what you have done here I will

bring you again into your own when I am queen. You will not
find me ungrateful for this day's work!"

Menadel, blood spattered and leaning on his sword with
exhaustion, came up behind her and reached out one foully
grimed hand to touch her sleeve. "Come, my lady, we have
now a deed to do which is unpleasant but necessary. We must
bury these men by the grave of this Elvish queen so that she
may have their escort in whatever western world she has gone
to. For I would leave no man as food for ravens and wolves.
I am not sure that the woodwitches will give these men decent
burial, so it remains to you and me to do it."

But when they turned to deal with the burying, they found
that the mound in the center of the clearing had shifted and
changed. There was now a large opening in one side of the
grassy knoll. The opening faced west and there arose from that
opening the dank, sour-sweet smell of the mouth of the grave.

There had been no sound or any indication that the dead
Elf-Queen or the woodwitches had done the deed; it was simply
there. It was as though the spirit that protected the clearing had
said, "See, here is my altar, here is the place for your offerings.
Bring them unto me."

And it was so.

Chapter 20

They journeyed southward from the Ashdowne Forest to Lewes and then down toward the sea. They hurried, for Guenhwyvar was sickening. The dry harsh cough she had first experienced on the way north had gotten worse, and since seeing the Angel of Death in the forest she seemed to have given up the fight.

Her face was small and pinched, and her eyes bright with fever. She bent over her horse's neck and coughed rackingly, trying to clear her congested lungs.

In Lewes they were told that the seawater at Brighthemstone would be good for the girl. The wise women said that bathing in the seawater of the southern shore would bring the blessing of the Archangel Michael upon the unwell or feeble.

They rode quickly from Lewes to Brighthemstone, but it was clear when they saw the rocky shore that the water would be of little good to the woodwitch maiden. There was a thick, black, tarry substance in the water that turned the very stones

of the beach black as coal. It smelled vile, and the sea roiled
and threw up upon the shore the carcasses of fish and sea
monsters and dead mermaids and mermen.

Elizabeth looked upon the waters and saw that the black
filth and decay was a fit gift for her father. And as she gathered
the darkness, Jackie made no protest.

Menadel and Jackie found a small cottage that was available
for rent and they moved the badly stricken woodwitch there.
The cottage was hardly bigger than Elizabeth's garderobe at
Witchdame Palace, but there was clean straw for a bed and a
large fireplace for the working of magic. The men took room
for themselves at a local inn so as not to be in Elizabeth's way
as she did her magical workings.

Elizabeth went to the witchlord at Arondele Castle and obtained from him the materials she would need for the white
fast. This fast was a healing spell of great power, and was used
only rarely by witchlords, for it was very draining to the energies of a healer.

The fast was in this manner: For three days nothing was
eaten save milk and a little white cheese. Elizabeth abstained
from all meat, sugar, and spices, all ale and wine. Then three
days of naught but a little water and, at the end of that three
days, nothing for three days more.

Elizabeth was waiting for the taste that would come into
her mouth, that strange flavor of flowers and decay that would
indicate her body had begun to feed upon itself to find power.
When that time came she took a quantity of foxglove, powdered
it well, mixed it with water, and drank it as a purge. She spent
a night outside in the rain as she alternately voided and vomited
all that was left in her body. At dawn she arose clean, clear,
and lightheaded with the lack of food, to begin the ritual that
would free Guenhwyvar from her illness.

Elizabeth took four lighted candles of virgin wax and placed
them at the quadrant points of the room. She sprinkled fine
incense of frankincense, myrrh, and dragonsblood upon the
fire. She inscribed on the floor of the cottage a great triple
Circle of nines. Then blessing it, she conjured up the four
Watchtowers and asked their aid and mercy.

She put the fragile, naked body of Guenhwyvar into the
middle of the Circle. The girl's chest rose and fell with in-
credible effort to continue to breathe. Then Elizabeth bowed

to the north, to the east, to the south, and to the west, and, raising her hands aloft, she conjured up the blue fire until the three Circles were hidden in rank after rank of waist-high flame. The Watchtowers sang with her power and all was ready.

She spoke in the words of magic. "Great fire, my lord and defender, son of the greater sun, he who cleanses the earth of all foulness. Deliver Guenhwyvar this day from sickness. Deliver her from what torments her at night and day."

Elizabeth paused and then, arranging Guenhwyvar's shivering body in the position of the evening star, she kissed her on the forehead and said, "Earth will protect thee." Then she kissed the maiden's lips and said, "Air will heal thee." She kissed the soft tendrils of Guenhwyvar's pubic mound and said, "Fire will warm thee." Then she kissed each of her feet and said, "Water will cleanse thee."

The princess wrapped the maiden again in a warm cloak and placed her on a north-south axis with her head to the north and her feet to the south. She stood over the girl, left leg to the west, right leg to the east. She raised her hands high above her head, clasping them tightly in a gesture of prayer, and began the chant that must bring healing. It was a chant of descent, letter by letter, taking away from the name of the great demon of illness:

> *OCHNOTINOS!*
> *CHNOTINOS!*
> *HNOTINOS!*
> *NOTINOS!*
> *OTINOS!*
> *TINOS!*
> *INOS!*
> *NOS!*
> *OS!*
> *O!*

When Elizabeth finished this chant she was shrieking the words aloud in a voice that thundered like the ocean waves, like the wind upon mountains, like a forest in flame, and like the shifting soil in an earthquake.

Then there was silence.

Elizabeth knelt beside Guenhwyvar and saw that the maiden's breathing was a bit easier, but her pulse was rapid and fluttering, and the fever was not diminished.

The princess knelt naked and powerless, and wept. As the Maiden of the Circle, as the chief witchdame of Englene, she could do nothing.

She dismissed the blue fire and thanked the Watchtowers. Then pulling her clothing roughly around herself, she went in search of Jackie and Menadel, who had been staying at a small inn in the area while Elizabeth did her magic.

The moment Elizabeth walked into the inn both Menadel and Jackie could tell from her face that she had failed. Jackie shook his head and Menadel brushed a tear from his eyes. Then, as if gathering power unto himself, the wizard stood and brought himself up to his full height and said, "The time has come, my lady. It is time to do what you *must* do. It is now that you must realize that you are two systems of magic in one. You have tried the magic of your father and it has availed you nothing. I know your mother has tried to teach you, and I know you have not listened well to her teaching. But surely you remember some of it! It is the night of a full moon. I have borrowed a basket of the innkeeper's wife. Go out into the woods, gather what you know you must gather and do what you know you must do to save Guenhwyvar's life."

Elizabeth sighed and rubbed at her sleeplessly sore eyes and said, "It's of little value. A few green leaves, roots; what would it avail when the great powers of the triple Circle did not work? She's going to die. Guenhwyvar knew that when she saw the angel and there is nothing in the Three Regions that can change facts."

"Don't be a fool, Elizabeth!" Jackie jumped to his feet and faced her, his hands on his twisted hips. "I've never known you to back off from a fight. Surely your lady mother taught you healing spells when you were still at her knee? Don't sneer at what might indeed be slight power, but go and do as Menadel says. If you fail, you fail. But if she dies, you will go to your grave cursing yourself that you did not do the one thing that *might* have saved her."

Without a word, Elizabeth took the basket from Menadel and walked out of the small smoky room to go in search of woodwitch herbs to save a woodwitch's life. For like calls to like; such is the way of the wood magic.

* * *

All night under the light of the full moon, Elizabeth gathered the herbs that would be needed; they were picked carefully in combinations of three, seven, or nine, as her mother had taught her. She found some on the banks of streams, others hidden in small dark corners of the forest. But they were all there. In this small secluded forest there was springtime. She knew herself to be in a woodwitch place, for in traveling southward she had seen that green existed only where there were woodwitches.

Elizabeth had grown up with a magic that was made of promises, extravagant vows, and prayers uttered in the high language of ritual and ceremony. But there was no ritual to wood magic beyond the gathering of the herbs and preparing them properly. She was uncomfortable with this, and felt the need of a vow or prayer. Elizabeth stopped her gathering and, glancing about at the trees that had their spring leaves clear upon them in the moonlight, she said, "I vow to you, O woodwitch place, that should your magic heal Guenhwyvar, I will heed my mother's words and go to the Heartwoods to learn of the old woman who lives there. I, Elizabeth, heir to Englene, do vow this."

Feeling somewhat more at ease with what she was doing, Elizabeth finished her task and with the dawning returned for another day of ceremony and effort to aid Guenhwyvar.

She found the woodwitch much as she had left her. The maiden was somewhat more easy in her breathing but the fever still raged and her body was hot and dry. Menadel and Jackie had taken turns bathing her with cold water and had forced milk between her lips, but it had done little good.

Left alone with Guenhwyvar, Elizabeth gathered together pots, pans, and little bottles, and began preparing the various herbs. Some were to be scattered over the fire. Others were to be made into possetts to be forced into Guenhwyvar. Still others would be wrapped in linen and place on her chest as a poultice.

The princess took coltsfoot and brewed it for the catarrh. She threw still more leaves of the coltsfoot upon the fire so that the smoke might be in the air, for that did aid the shortness of breath. Then she mixed elder flower and its leaves and woodsole, boiled them in milk, and gave the mixture to Guenhwyvar to drink.

The day continued and the sun shifted, and still Elizabeth

labored. Ground ivy in milk and water was administered hour
by hour, and more ground ivy cast upon the fire.

Guenhwyvar's fever began to abate and in the twilight of
the evening, as the sunset tinted the horn windows of the cottage
blood red, Guenhwyvar began to cough. Elizabeth held her,
pouring what strength of hers was left into the maid. With a
mighty wracking of her body, Guenhwyvar began to cough up
black globules and, with a final wrenching of her lungs, she
brought up that which had been troubling her.

There in the basin lay the twin black fetuses of the night
demon. They had come with the darkness that had covered
Cymru, and had been laid in Guenhwyvar's chest by their
mother, a demon of the dark winds and of disease. Like her
parents, Guenhwyvar had been chosen by the demon to hatch
out her young; for when Guenhwyvar's dead body was placed
in the ground, the demons would have fed upon it, hatched
and come forth to cause havoc, disease, plague, and despair
wherever they had been born.

Elizabeth looked at the two dead things and knew she would
take them to her father as the gift from the west, rather than
Guenhwyvar herself. For in a land where demons can lay their
young in the body of an innocent maiden, in that land the
witchlord king has lost his power.

Elizabeth knew why the witchlord magic had not worked.
For the demon mother had been of equal power to Elizabeth
herself and had no doubt found it amusing watching the witchdame's futile struggle. But a demon has no charms against the
herbs and the love of a woodwitch. So the demon had fled
with the smoke from the fire, deserting her young, and now
they lay dead in Elizabeth's hands.

Elizabeth sat beside the now peacefully sleeping Guenhwyvar, while the fire on the hearth faded away into nothing and
the room became dark.

Exhausted by her long fast and lack of sleep, Elizabeth had
no wish to move; her mind drifted in its own path without any
indication from her where she wished to travel.

She saw strange shadows, little sparks of light gleaming
like brief stars. She saw rainbows and drifting fog, and she
found herself floating higher and higher out of her body until
she realized that her spirit-self was floating up by the roofbeam,

looking down from the ceiling. Even though the cottage was dark, everything in it was clear. There was the sleeping maiden and the body of an exhausted woodwitch/witchdame.

Elizabeth observed the scene and approved of it. Its peace and tranquility had a strong appeal. So did the knowledge that there was more peace and more tranquility further out. The scent of apples was in the air, and she longed to stretch her wings and find that ultimate tranquility in the shade of the western gate.

The door to the cottage opened with a crash and Menadel strode into the room. He wasted no time, but threw a heap of logs onto the fire. With a snap of his fingers and a muttered word, the fire burst forth. He snatched up an ale bottle and grabbed Elizabeth's head, tilted it back and poured the ale down her throat.

With a thump, Elizabeth's spirit came back into its body. She gagged, choked and coughed; ale ran out of her mouth and nose, tears dripped from her eyes. "What do you think you're doing?" she sputtered. "I have ale all up into my head, and it hurts!"

"It might have hurt less had I been a few minutes later. Your spirit would have drifted away from you and gone on to the island of Avalon, where even I could not reach it. Here, finish the ale like a good child, and I will give you food." He hurried to bring milk, honey, and bread. Much as Elizabeth had fed Guenhwyvar, Menadel sat on the floor pushing food down his princess's throat like an anxious bird with but one chick.

"Enough, enough!" Elizabeth said, with honey and crumbs running down her chin. "I can eat little of such sweet stuff after a long fast. But I do feel as if I could eat a whole cow, drink a ton of ale, and afterwards sleep for a month round!"

"You were right, Menadel. I did shirk that power I had as a woodwitch, and now I see that I can no longer do that. I must honor both sides of my parentage. I made a vow out there in the woods, saying that if I cured Guenhwyvar I would go to the Heartwoods to learn of the woman my mother called Nerthus. I do not know which is best, to go to the Heartwoods now and fulfill my vow, or go to my father and assist him in curing the land. I am puzzled and have sought the answer within myself. But the only answer I found was the peace and serenity of the western door, a door that is no answer."

"He'll help you." Guenhwyvar's voice was slow and sleepy.
"He has to, you know. He's *your* angel."

"What?" Elizabeth turned to look into the herb-drugged eyes
of the young woodwitch.

Guenhwyvar yawned and knuckled her eyes with childlike
fingers. "I thought at first he was an archangel, perhaps even
Gabriel himself, but then I realized that he couldn't be Gabriel
because he came with you from the east. But I knew from the
very beginning he was an angel. I just wasn't sure which one."
She looked at Menadel and smiled sweetly. "You never did
tell me, my lord, and I would so like to know . . ."

Elizabeth looked at the man seated beside her; his shadow
stretched long across the room, and there was about it a sparkle
and shimmer as if little tiny stars were caught in his wake.

Menadel's face and hands were not as old as they had been,
the wrinkles were gone save for the faint smile lines around
his eyes. He was still plump and a bit thick about the waist,
but his red hair shimmered with fire, and his blue eyes danced
merrily.

"No, no, sweet one, I am not an archangel." He reached
out to pat Guenhwyvar lovingly on one shoulder. "I wish I
was, for your dear sake. While I am Elizabeth's angel by right,
I am yours out of love. I say to you, my little lady of the
Cymru woods, you are my lady and I am your lord. I was
wrong to tell you we must wait until you are older, for I never
wish to be parted from you again. Even though I cannot join
with you in earthly marriage, I can join with you in one in
which our bodies and spirits will be united as one. You and I
together will produce glorious children for the honor of Englene."
He continued patting Guenhwyvar's shoulder till the girl, soothed
by his touch, fell into a gentle, dreamless sleep.

Elizabeth sat there gnawing on the heel of the loaf and
thinking a great deal. She had known that Menadel was not a
witchlord, nor was he of woodwitch blood; yet she had been
taught to call him uncle. He had always been there, since her
very infancy, but now she realized the time had come for
explanations. As she started to speak, she heard the door open
and Jackie entered the room carrying a covered plate and a jug
of Gascon wine.

"Look what I found, poppet! Although I needed to search

every inn in this place to find it. Wine and a proper bit of meat for you." He uncovered the plate to reveal crudely cut up pieces of freshly cooked fowl, and the room was filled with a lovely scent of chicken, onions, and sage.

Hastily giving her thanks to both Jackie and the Gods, Elizabeth grabbed the meat and fell upon it like a ravening wolf. It was only some minutes later when she came up for air and another serving of the wine that she had time to ask of the jester, "Jackie, did you know that Menadel was an angel?"

Jackie sat back on his heels and roared with laughter. He fell over backwards on the floor, his feet kicking in the air as he bellowed his mirth. His cheeks turned bright pink and tears ran down his face; then, doing an awkward little flip, he pulled himself back into a seated position.

"An angel! *An angel!* Of all things in the Three Regions that Menadel may nor may not be, an angel is by far the oddest. Tell me, poppet, did your nine days of starvation teach you that? If so, I think it was a very untrue vision. An angel!" Jackie went off again into giggling fits which ended with a wheezing sound like a bellows with a hole in it.

"Now Jackie, stop that ridiculous noise. It seems Menadel is indeed an angel, so sit up properly and be respectful to him after this. If we're both very nice he may tell us about it."

Elizabeth suited her actions to her words by smacking Jackie upon the back until he stopped wheezing, and then she emptied what was left of the wine into a cup and helped Jackie to drink it.

"I needed that. In fact I think I will need a great more of it, if I am to believe that Menadel is an angel. After one jug of Gascon wine I would believe almost anything, and after three I will believe that I am an angel, but *Menadel*—an angel?"

Menadel nodded and spread his hands in a gesture of embarrassment. "Yes, I am indeed an angel, although very few members of your father's court know of my true identity. I was brought down to Englene by you, Elizabeth, on your naming day. For such is the tradition; all witchlord babes must prove their power by conjuring up their guardian angel before they can be named."

"Oh I know that," Elizabeth said. "But once the child conjures up the guardian angel and the angel pronounces that child's name, the angel goes back to the Ethereal Regions. If you are indeed an angel, Menadel, what are you doing here?"

"Well, you see, when your mother and father took you aside into the naming chapel and you conjured me up I was unfortunately one of the lesser angels." Menadel paused to blush rosily. "There are 496,000 myriads of angels in the Ethereal Regions. You managed to conjure up one from the fifty-ninth rank of angels, and the only rank lower than mine is filled with the little pink brats with wings who go around decking everything with blue banners. So as you can see, as a guardian angel I was a bit of a disappointment. I am only Menadel Mazal, and my particular position is Angel of the Exiles. While your mother and father were disappointed, they did admit that in your position as half woodwitch and half witchdame you might, indeed, be exiled from one part or another of your heritage.

"I of course found the whole thing quite fascinating, and decided I really didn't want to go back to the Ethreal Regions. So I decided to stay, and, quite frankly, I don't think anyone in the Ethereal Regions has even missed me."

Menadel paused to pour himself a cup of the ale, and then drained it. "Of course, your mother and I both realized that, given your blood lines, you would have a very troubled life and we knew that a fifty-ninth rank angel such as myself was not really adequate to serve you. With my help, your mother began the construction of the Towers of the Palace of Witchdame. It was to be a spell of great magnitude. It was the square within the circle; the four Towers making the square, the circle was the moat. Unfortunately it was not finished. This spell I've had you do was a way of finishing what your mother began, for in your journey form Lundene to Pembrokeshire, then up to Berewicshire, then east into Nordfuleshire, and then back to Lundene, you completed the Circle that I would have you do."

"But what about coming here to the south? Was that unnecessary?" Elizabeth asked.

"Oh no, not unnecessary at all! Because you see, you had formed the circle. But you needed the square outside the circle—that square formed by the four Watchtowers. By going first west to Gabriel, then north to Uriel, east to Raphael, and now south to Michael, and exhibiting powers at each place you have formed the square around the Circle. That is the reverse of the sigil your mother made with the Palace of Witchdame, and those two placed one upon the other will bring you far greater powers than any witchlord or witchdame has ever had.

"But I fear my plan went slightly awry. I did not count on what happened at Yermouth. When you went to the sea and conjured up the power of Raphael and made your bargain with him, I fear you lost his Watchtower. The spell will not be complete, and when we return to the Palace of Witchdame it will not have four towers as I had hoped.

"For with your power and those towers, you could have healed the land and brought spring to it simply by returning to the center of that pattern. By standing in the forecourt of the Palace in the center of the crossed shadows of the four towers, Englene would have been healed. So in answer to your question as to what you should do, you *must* go to the Heartwoods! You must plead with Nerthus to intercede with Raphael. Perhaps even without Raphael it will be enough, but I do not know. . . . " Menadel shook his head in sadness. "I did try, but even as an angel I'm afraid I'm a bit inept."

Elizabeth reached out to hug her angel to her, and as her hands crossed his back she felt the brush of stubby feathers against her fingers. "There, there, Menadel. I know you've always done what is best for me, and it is not your fault but mine. I was too hasty. And you are quite right. I will go to the Heartwoods and put myself in the hands of Nerthus. I hope for the sake of all of us that either she is able to give me power so I may do without Raphael, or she will show me some way to restore the archangel to me. So mote it be."

THE
HEARTWOODS

I, Elizabeth thy daughter, call upon thee, O Great Mother of All, she who is bringer of fruitfulness. By flower and fruit, by seed and root. By bud, stem, and all green things. By my love for these thy creations, do I ask thee to descend upon the body of this, thy servant and thy priestess.

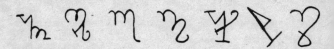

(the runes of the name Nerthus)

Chapter 21

Instead of coming back through Lundene—a route which Elizabeth quickly vetoed, having no wish to see again the decadence that the capital had fallen into—their path was instead that of the road to Windleshore. They caught a water ferry on the Theames just below the city of Windleshore which carried them across the river to the edge of the leafless forest of Windleshore Great Park.

"There is no green here, Menadel. Why is that? Is not my father even able to protect his own royal forest?" Elizabeth asked, as they rode through the echoing silence.

"My lady, it is as you can see. Between the loss of power your father has experienced and the rise of the Lady Pemberly, even the great forest of the king is being destroyed. We will see no green until we reach the Heartwoods. So come, let us quit this place and make quickly for that verdant shelter."

There was a small village on the edge of the Heartwoods

called the village of Hyghgate, for it was indeed the gateway to Lundene.

The forest was, as Menadel had said, green. Everywhere one looked it was the color of the Goddess as mother and wife. The edge of the wood was touched with the white, gold, and yellow of early primroses, daisies, and snowdrops. There was the hum of bees gathering nectar, and the song of every good and honest bird. Above them was the patter of squirrels in the treetops, and in the grass below the gentle swish-swish of a rabbit's passing. It was a beautiful place, touched by awe of what it contained.

As they moved deeper into the forest its character changed. The yew trees were taller here and the shadows deeper. A cool breeze flowed through the woods, bringing with it a scent of deep mystery.

There were little glades of sunlight untouched by the tree branches, and in those glades were altars to the Mother Goddess. By tradition the ruler of Englene must come here every seventh reign year and raise an altar to her, and then watch as the ivy vines and brambles would quickly swarm over the top of the altar and hide the offering from view. This was a sign that the great Mother Goddess had indeed accepted the offering.

But should no green come and the food, flowers, and fruit that had been offered remain untouched on the top of the altar until the sun's going down, then the Goddess had signaled that the ruler was no longer fruitful or desirable to her. Then in that place the Priestess of the Goddess would seize the unfortunate monarch and cut the holy one's throat, so that the sacred blood would fall upon the ground and refertilize it.

They went deeper into the forest. There were fewer sunlit glades. This was a place of pine trees and rowan, of thick thorny dells, the slow trickle of hidden springs, and owls in the treetops. The altars were older here, cracked and broken. Their stonework was crumbling away under the enveloping plants.

And then suddenly there was a clear place, large, empty, sere, and black. For the diameter of a triple nine Circle nothing grew save a tall pillar of ivy and bramble, tangled in a green column just a little over Elizabeth's height. Beside the column stood a black granite altar, innocent of even the slightest trace of lichen or moss.

The altar's black sides gleamed as if it had been freshly

built, and its sharp edges were not crumbled by weather or rain. The ground around it was as empty as if it had been sown with salt and there was no path of green leading from outside the circle to that tall pillar of ivy and bramble.

Elizabeth reigned her horse in to study the scene. She felt rising from the ground under her an icy current of doom. She turned to Menadel and asked, "What means this place, and why is such a thing of darkness in the middle of the Great Goddess's Heartwoods?"

Menadel did not answer, but merely dismounted from his horse and came to the edge of the circle. Kneeling, he asked the blessing of the Goddess that he might enter that place in peace and safety. He walked toward the pillar of green and stood beside it for a moment. Then, circling it deosil, he reached into the enveloping ivy and drew forth a shining white femur held tightly still in the grip of the ivy. Menadel let go of the bone, which sprang back into the ivy as if it could not, save by great magic, be removed.

"Come here, my lady. Come and look upon all that is left of one of your ancestors." Menadel reached up and brushed away some of the ivy so that Elizabeth might see the white, gleaming skull. She dismounted from her horse and came to stand beside him after making the proper ritual request of the Goddess to enter.

"What means it?" she asked again. "Which ancestor is this? Is it woodwitch or witchlord?" Elizabeth studied the skull which was obviously too large to be that of a woodwitch, and somehow the light and the shadow in that part gave it almost a look of still being clothed with skin. There was a look of surprise upon its countenance.

Menadel let go the ivy and watched it again envelop the skull. "This," he said, "is all that remains of Queen Isabele, that was called 'The She-Wolf,' wife unto William the Unlucky. She did steal the ring Raziel, murder her husband, and kill all of the king's children—which were her children also—save one small babe that was hidden away by his nursemaid. That brave woman substituted her own child for the royal one, and had to stand by and watch it slaughtered.

"The She-Wolf took the throne and took unto her bed great Mortimer, the Marcher lord of Cymru, and with him planned to conceive a new line of witchlord kings for Englene. But the Goddess did not give her a child until time came for her to approach the Heartwoods. Then, big with her unholy babe, she came to this place with fear and trembling, for she knew the wrath of the Goddess.

"Isabele did raise this black altar, and upon it she put the proper fruit, beautiful flowers, and flourcakes of astonishing whiteness, their thick dough studded with raisins and citron, sprinkled with sugar. She stood before the altar, glorious in her terrible beauty, and on her face a smile of sure power, for she was a witchdame of considerable ability.

"Since she knew the Goddess would not cover her altar, she ordered the bushes, brambles, and ivy to come at *her* command, usurping the right of the Great Mother. The bushes, brambles, and ivy did come, but not to the altar. In the blink of an eye or the falling of a dewdrop, she was covered completely by the plants to such a depth that none heard her dying shrieks as an ivy shoot strangled her.

"The priestesses and courtiers fled before the wrath of the Goddess and, as you see, the Goddess did smite this place so that nothing would ever touch the black queen's altar. This place stands as a memorial forever to the power of the Goddess. What evil you feel here is the resounding of the anger of the She-Wolf Isabele—but the power, the power, my lady, belongs to the Mother Goddess. Keep that well in mind."

Elizabeth bowed her head before the horror of Menadel's tale. Then she said softly, "And the babe?" She knew the answer before she asked, but some dreadful premonition required it.

Menadel pushed aside the ivy a little lower down the column and there it was, a small gleaming skull not much bigger than an owl's egg. Elizabeth cried out to let loose the ivy.

"Fear not, my lady. No child that you shall have will be so taken from you by the Goddess; nor is there evil in you like unto the She-Wolf. Come here in the time of *your* pregnancy and the Goddess will bless you. I, Menadel your guardian angel, say it is so."

Menadel came to the princess and took her hands to lead her out of the accursed Circle. In silence he helped her mount her horse and then, taking her cold hands in his, he kissed them and said, "Fear nothing. You are safe here. For you are a blessed child of the Goddess."

* * *

Elizabeth noticed that Jackie was no longer with them and, with some terror, began to search the wooded glades on each side of the path. She feared she might see her jester changed into a pillar of ivy and bramble for some insult to the Goddess.

Menadel calmly asked what she was doing and when she told him, it was Guenhwyvar who tried to calm her. "Oh, there's nothing to worry about, my lady. The High Priestess, an old woman called Nerthus, came and fetched him. She said they had much to talk of, and that he must go with her to the center of the Heartwoods. Jackie said to tell you he knew the old woman—he met her at the Aberystwyth fair in Cymru. In fact, your little ring was a gift from her. So, as you see, he is quite safe."

"Do you know that from your *seeing*, Guenhwyvar, or is it just something you feel?" Elizabeth asked.

"Oh no, I didn't need to *see* it. I trust Jackie's judgment." Guenhwyvar laughed and continued, "He really is far more cautious than you realize. Then, too, like many humans he holds the Goddess and her priestesses in much greater veneration than the God and his priests. He will be very careful not to offend Nerthus."

They rode on, but Elizabeth was only partly reassured. She knew Jackie had a certain native caution, but as a court jester he was entirely too used to offering up barbed jests to royalty; he might indeed say something to the High Priestess that could be mistaken for an insult.

Filled with concern, Elizabeth followed Menadel as he led her and Guenhwyvar toward the center of the great Heartwoods, where stood the mighty temple to the Goddess.

This temple was in the form of a double terraced ring sloping downhill. The outer ring had a large arched gothic gate cut in it with pillars and obelisks adorning the entrance. The inner perimeter was a series of low stone doors decorated like Egyptian temples. They ringed a great earth embankment which was shaded by an enormous cedar tree. It was said that this tree was as old as time, and that the giant serpent of eternity wrapped itself around its roots.

Their horses' hooves on the leaves underfoot made the only sound as they wended their way into the inner ring. All of the doors to the inner circle were alike. Their lintels were carved with a design of wings and moon orbs. Serpents twisted around the pillars that held each lintel in place. The wood doors with their heavy wrought iron hinges were quite prosaic in such a setting, but the door knockers, made of twisted brass serpents, were sufficiently exotic to make it known that no mere goodwife or village herbwoman lived therein.

"My lady," Menadel said, "you must go around this ring, deosil, thrice. Then you must knock at one of the doors. Nerthus—if such is her pleasure—will open to you."

"But—which door?" Elizabeth asked. "Does it make a difference?"

"It's said that your need and love of the Goddess will guide you." Menadel rubbed his beard until it was a fiery tangle on his chin. "At least that's the way the spell is supposed to work."

"Very well, and may the good Goddess be with me."

Elizabeth, Menadel, and Guenhwyvar dismounted, tied their horses to a convenient ring, and Elizabeth, with prodding from Menadel, went forward and walked thrice around the circle.

Then, as she stood trying to ascertain which door might lead to the High Priestess, Elizabeth felt something soft and wet patter onto the top of her head. She looked up to see Jackie sitting on the top of the great ring wall. He was cheerfully stuffing himself with brambleberries and tossing the overly ripe ones at her.

"Fool, what are you about? I hope you have been most respectful of Mother Nerthus's dignity. 'Tis said she does not take kindly to impudent knaves like you," Elizabeth said, smiling in relief at seeing him safe.

"Poppet, I am always in good odor with the priestesses of the Goddess. They treat me with great kindness and I do the same to them. Old Nerthus had much to say to me; I now know my place in the Goddess's scheme and I am content with it."

"And what place would that be?" Menadel asked.

"Lackaday, lackaday! We have an angel with us and he cannot unravel a simple fool's jest. If you know it not, old angel, it is because the Goddess has no wish for you to know. It is enough that *I* know." Jackie tumbled over backwards into a thicket of ivy and came up draped in green, giggling like the lord of misrule. "Ah, 'tis my riddle, and I alone know the answer!" he crowed.

"Well," Elizabeth said impatiently, "if you'll not tell me, either, at least have the good grace to tell me which door I must knock on—or is that an unknowable riddle, too?"

"Oh, that one." Jackie twisted his body about until he could toss a ripe berry neatly into the middle of the doorknocker on the door directly in front of Elizabeth. "Contrary to what you have been told, all paths lead to the Goddess, and all doors open to those who seek her. So knock and enter, my lady."

Elizabeth laughed and knocked upon the door thrice.

The door opened with a bang, as though the inhabitant had been merely waiting for the signal. There, framed by firelight from the torches illuminating the room, stood the woman known as Nerthus. She was clad in what appeared to be a moss green houpelande completely covered with a tracery of silver embroidery, with little silver flies caught at intervals in it. When Elizabeth looked closer she realized the houpelande was indeed of moss and its silver embroidery was the webs of carefully trained spiders. The edges of the houpelande sleeves were dagged with ivy, and the old woman wore atop her gray hair a horned hennin of hammered silver work; caught in the horn was a large silver moon disc. The veiling which fell from her headdress was of the same shimmering stuff as her embroidery, and it was clear that this indeed was a woman of great wood magic.

"So, you have finally decided to come, Princess Elizabeth! Your mother promised on her deathbed that she would send you to me. She died, as I recall, in the month of Ripening; here it is come round to Leaf month. I would have thought that even had you walked from the Palace of Witchdame, it would have taken you less time than this."

Elizabeth knelt at the woman's feet and said, "Forgive me, my lady. But tell me, before any more is between us, are you— are you by some chance my mother's mother?"

Nerthus laughed, a sound like the tinkling of little silver bells that goats wore when they fed upon the hills. "Mercy no, child! Did you think to find in me a comfortable granny who sits by the hearth stroking her familiars? Am I to be someone who would teach you to make the rats dance in the thatch or perhaps comfort you with comfits and fresh-made gingerbread? I am mother to all who are of woodwitch blood, for such was she and such are you.

"But as for Menadel—" She looked at the angel from under frowning brows and Menadel was seen to visibly shrink within his garments. "Yes, as for Menadel—must you always be so inept, my friend? I had thought you were to lead this child into completing the great sigil. Instead, according to what I have been told, she made an evil bargain with Raphael and has spoiled the pattern. I may help her mend it—but that depends upon her and her character."

"My lady . . ."

Menadel spread his hands to plead with the woman, but it was Guenhwyvar who stepped to the front, and said, "It was not for want of trying that this adventure went badly. I will not have you blame him when not even my lady does so."

"Ah ha! And what have we here?" Nerthus leaned forward to study the young woodwitch. "An untrained maid who claims to have the gift of sight. A gift she can't even control, nor call up when she wishes it. I suppose you take no blame either, mistress? For any woodwitch who is foolish enough to allow the very demon who killed her folk to lay eggs in her body is very inept. But then you woodwitches in Cymru always were of very little skill."

"Enough, enough, old mother!" There was a sudden showering of brambleberries from the top of the ringed embankment. Jackie dropped two or three more berries and with great satisfaction heard one of them tap upon the moon disc in the High Priestess's headdress. "Don't be picking at those with less power than yourself. It's rude, and the mark of a bully."

Nerthus leaned out to get a better view of the jester above her. She laughed and said, "Well, my little barbary ape, no one else but you could be so foolish or so brave. Have you taken up the defense of angels and woodwitches too, little one?"

"Aye, my lady, and anyone else you should choose to use the sharp side of your tongue on. For I say to you, mighty queen of the woodwitches, if you so abuse my lady Elizabeth, I'll take no part in the Mother Goddess's plan, and I *will* tell the king about you."

"And why should you think the king has any power over me? In fact, he must come here before the summer is out, and lay his offering upon the Goddess's altar. And I as High Priestess will cut his throat, for he has brought no strength and goodness to the land this year!"

"Nay, nay, good mother," Menadel hurried forward to place one hand on Nerthus's houpelande. "Please, speak not of the death of the king, for Elizabeth is a loving and loyal daughter, and I would not have her grieve at what might only possibly be."

Nerthus brushed his hand away as lightly as she would have removed a spider. She turned to look at the woman in front of her, six foot one in bedraggled red and blue minstrel's robes. "So, this is what the king calls his 'great gawk,' is it?" she said, abruptly changing her tone of voice to one less bullying. "I see before me no unfledged adolescent, but a woman. The journey round the land has forced her to grow, and has made of her a suitable clay for my kiln.

"Now as for you, pretty little woodwitch," she said to Guenhwyvar, "it's not entirely your fault that you were born in Cymru rather than here in Englene. I will leave your training to Menadel. I see that your shadows yearn toward each other. And as to your little monkey," she glanced up at the jester who was busy feeding berries to a trio of squirrels. "Pay attention, little ape, I'm talking to you," she said with her accustomed asperity. "I expect you to go with these, your fellow servants, and lodge in the inn at the village of Hyghgate. You will stay away from this place for one full month's turning. You *will* not return to Lundene, nor will you speak to any man, woman, or child of what your charge is, nor why you stay at the inn. Should you return to this place before the moon is round, I will turn you into frogs, salamanders, or some creeping thing.

"So heed my word, and get you gone. I want to see neither hide, hair, nor bent twig of any of the three of you or your horses within this forest by the time the sun goes down, or I will set my fox packs upon you. I tell you, there are times when the Goddess fancies other sacrifices than merely fruit, flowers, or raisin cakes. Now shoo, shoo, all of you.

"And as for you, my pretty," she turned to smile grudgingly at the princess, "come, enter my house and be received there with joy, and stay with me one month while I make of you a good woodwitch."

Without a further glance at Menadel, Guenhwyvar, or Jackie, she seized Elizabeth by one arm and bundled her into the dwelling, slamming the heavy oaken door shut behind her.

Chapter 22

The interior of Nerthus's home was far larger than Elizabeth had expected. The door stood in the center of the large curved side and the inner curve was covered by a tapestry depicting the Mother Goddess doing battle with a giant on Goddess Field. There were other tapestries on the walls depicting legends of the Mother Goddess, and the floor was covered with animal skins: wolf, griffin, fox, and bear. There was even the skin of some animal Elizabeth did not recognize; it was a peculiar yellow and black stripe, and its catlike head had very sharp teeth indeed.

On one side of the room was a large carved wooden bed, every inch of it covered with designs of flowers, fruit, and plants. The sheets were of green silk, and the swansdown coverlid was embroidered with forget-me-nots. The bed curtains were white, embroidered in yellow and green. There was no fireplace, but merely a fire ring in the middle of the room with a smoke hole out through the ceiling. A small white ferret slept beside the fire ring and giggled in its sleep. Elizabeth watched the smoke spiral upward and saw that the ceiling was composed of earth, held in place by interwoven roots of the cedar tree.

There were cupboards, chests, and tables, all of them covered with jars, bottles, packets of herbs and the implements of the old woman's craft. The room was lit by a lamp which hung from the ceiling and was in the shape of a large silver wyvern with a torch in its mouth.

There was a large iron kettle, simmering over the fire. Elizabeth approached it carefully, unsure of what might be cooking there.

"It's naught but soup for dinner, child," Nerthus said. "What did you expect, birth-strangled babe with eye of newt and toe of frog? I assure you that all those rumors you've heard about how woodwitches steal human babies and eat them are quite untrue; nor do we prepare our potions with human blood. Those are very old lies told against us, and I will teach you what lies they are. For in the next month you will learn from me everything that you should have learned in the last eighteen years, and it will not be easy. You will learn the use of all herbs, plants, and growing things, for good and for evil. You will learn how to speak to animals and understand them, how to play with salamanders without burning your fingers, how to prevent the bite of any serpent, and all of my recipes for curing the ills of mankind. You will learn to speak to the water, earth, wind, and fire. Then, when the time is right, I will initiate you in a woodwitch Circle so you may be one of us just as you are one of them.

"But come, sit down. We have but little time and a great deal to do." Nerthus beckoned to the princess and had her sit on a small wooden stool beside the fire, and then she gave her soup, bread, and fresh brewed ale.

Announcing that the meal was at an end, Nerthus carried away the empty dishes and commanded Elizabeth to stare into the fire. "Look at it deeply, child. Look beyond the fire to what it is composed of. Look at the element of fire. Watch it dance and flame. Think of all that is not fire and all that is and listen to my voice. . . ."

Elizabeth slipped easily into the fire spell that the witch,

Nerthus, had prepared. The trance state was an easy thing; she was as a salamander in Nerthus's fire and she saw all that was fire and all that was not.

"First you take vervain, add to it rue, then wormwood, and then the wild teasel. Take these herbs, pound them together, and add them to the freshly laid egg of a vulture. . . ."

Elizabeth came out of the fire and found herself sitting beside the now-empty fire ring. The door was open and sunlight streamed into the room, and she knew from her hunger and from the slant of the sunlight that many days had passed.

The witch Nerthus fed her well on baked pigeons, fresh bread, eggs, cheese, and good cider. Then she had Elizabeth look deep into a bowl of water and beyond it until Elizabeth slid easily into the water and became a naiad swimming freely, and she saw and knew all that was water and all that was not.

"The sea turtle is wise but says little, while the fox converses well but is prone to nonsense. I would not talk with the lion while he feeds, nor with the vole. . . ."

Elizabeth came out of the water and found herself sitting on a stool with an empty bowl in her hands, and she knew from the light through the door and from her hunger that many days had passed, but she had the gift of understanding all animals.

She found that the little white ferret, Nerthus's familiar, reminded her of Jackie. He had the same barbed wit, and when he danced on the hearthstones and laughed his snorfling little laugh, she found that she missed her jester. She caught up the little animal, kissed it, and smelled its musk upon her hands.

Nerthus fed Elizabeth on nuts, raisin cakes, fresh brook trout, and dainties of field and stream. Then Nerthus brought to the princess a lump of earth, placed it in her hands, and made her feel it between her fingers and watch the earthworm crawl around the root, pale and waxen, that was growing in it. Elizabeth found herself a mole burrowing deep through the earth and she slid into the spell easily. And she knew all that was earth and all that was not.

"Candied sea holly is an erotic sweetmeat that will bring any man to your side. Boil the root in clear water and fine sugar until it be tender. Then add to it more sugar until the

water will hold no more. Take it out and cool it, roll it in
powdered musk and ambergris. Cut it into small bits like
sugar lumps. Then heat again the water and sugar; dip the pieces
once, twice, and thrice. Repeat again until you have dipped
nine times. Boil the sugar until it is brittle, and dip again nine
times. Cool, store in an airtight crock, and when a man pleases
your fancy give him to eat of this sweet and he will be yours
forever. . . ."

Elizabeth came out of the earth, knowing all there was to
know of what was between a man and a maid, what might be
the ways of bringing babies and the ways of preventing them.
She knew how to avoid giving birth to monsters, and how to
bring forth twins, how to tell if a woman carried a boy child
or a girl, how to know when a woman's time was past and she
would not bear again. She saw the dry dirt and the dead earthworm in her hands, and knew that many days had passed.

Then Nerthus laid a fire of charcoal upon the hearth, and
put to it dragonsblood, rosemary, myrrh, and frankincense.
She made Elizabeth breathe deeply of the smoke, and the princess slipped into the spell easily, rose with it, like a bird, to
fly free. She learned all there was to know of air and all that
air was not.

"To dream of water is a journey; to dream of the sun is a
goodly thing. To dream of the hangman means not always
death, but can mean change. To dream of the shattered tower
bodes ill. The flight of the raven will tell of the deeds of men,
and the casting of the knuckle bones will tell of the deeds of
the Gods. . . ."

And Elizabeth came back into herself. The incense was no
more and she knew that a good part of the month had gone.

As Nerthus had promised, she now knew all that she must
know to be a woodwitch. She had learned of dreams and di-
vination, of herbs, and of the ways of all people, animals, and
things. She was now ready for the final test.

Nerthus fed her well, and had Elizabeth sleep in the large
bed and cosseted her for two days, morning and night. Then
the old woman said to her, "Now, child, the time has come
for thee to learn by far the most complicated subject thou must
know. Namely, thyself."

Nerthus went to the end of the room and removed the great tapestry of the Goddess and the giant, and there behind it was an oaken door. When she had opened the door, Elizabeth saw a stone corridor, rough hewn from the living earth, slanting downward.

Taking Elizabeth gently by the hand, Nerthus led the princess down it. The descending steps were nine hundred and ninety-nine, and they wound down into the very bowels of the earth until they came out on a flat stone platform. There was nothing but the stairs, the stone floor, and a wall of Flame.

And the Flame burned higher than Elizabeth could see, and wider than she could look in either direction.

"This, then, is the heart of all I would teach you," said Nerthus. "This is the place where you will learn all there is to know of you, Elizabeth. In this Flame you will know all your power completely. You will come to know the limits of your intelligence, and the far reaches of your soul. And—now, this is most important—you will learn your capacity for evil. You will know all the petty, ugly things of your heart and soul. You will know the harm you have done to other people and you will understand and accept every ugly thing that you have done in your life and know that they are part of you. I give you the cursed gift of honesty about your motives and your deeds. So, my child, walk through the Fire and know what thou art."

Elizabeth stood before the great wall of Fire and felt the heat turning her cheeks red and causing her hair to crisp at the ends. It was a heat that made clothing on her skin unbearable. One by one she shed her garments till she stood naked before it. And then she took a step toward the Fire, and then stepped back in fear of its power.

"Perfect love, perfect trust, child," Nerthus said. "Your mother gave it me, and I ask it of you. In return I will give unto you my love and trust, but only after you have given me yours."

Elizabeth turned back toward the Fire and, taking a deep breath like a swimmer about to plunge into water of unknown depth, she stepped forward into the Fire and was one with it and alone with herself.

And there were scenes of beauty in the fire and scenes of horror. There were crawling, creeping things and slime. There were flowers that pierced the heart with their ugly beauty. There were perfect crystal eggs that burst, showing the rottenness within. There were garlands of silks and satins, sackcloth and ashes. There was death and decay. There was strength and honor. There was the ability to kill and the ability to be killed in turn. She saw how much she was loved and how much she was hated. She knew how much *she* loved and how much *she* hated. She heard voices singing praise of the Goddess, and knew they were all her own. She heard weeping and knew it was hers, and she heard joyous laughter, and that was hers also. She saw with perfect clarity all that she was, and trembled at the horrible grandeur of it. She saw all that she was *not*, and wept at the things she would never do or be. She saw not only every evil deed she had done, but all the evil done by her *lack* of action, and that was most painful.

Elizabeth cried out in pain as the Flame bit deep into her heart.

Like a tired swimmer who had gone beyond her depth, she dragged herself out of the Fire and onto a narrow stone ledge. She lay there panting, catching her breath, feeling as if every bone and sinew had been burnt to ashes. She reached up to touch her hair, amazed that it was still there; then, exploring her body, she found that she had eyebrows, eyelashes, and pubic hair yet. The Flame had not touched her, at least not physically.

Elizabeth sat on the ledge and breathed deeply, calming her racing pulse. Then, when she had come again completely into herself, she looked about for a way to leave the ledge, and there was none. Above was only stone, below was stone, and all around was the Flame. She saw something white and gleaming at the back of the platform and when she reached for it, she realized that it was a skull—a skull of some unfortunate who had come through the Flame. And then as she held the skull in her hands it spoke.

"Now child," the skull said in Nerthus's voice. "You must come *back* again through the Fire and look deeply into all that you are now and re-form yourself into what you will be. This I tell you: Not only will you have full knowledge and complete power, but you will know me as I am."

Elizabeth bent her head and wept. Once through the Fire had been almost more than she could bear. The idea of going back through it again was terrifying. She looked down at the skull and knew why this person had not gone back through the Flames again.

But she remembered her duty to Englene, and to both her father's people and the woodwitches of her mother.

Elizabeth walked into the Fire and felt Flame on her soul. But she knew her power over it, and walked through Fire and saw no visions or dreams. She felt the Fire do her bidding at last, remolding her, shaping her into the queen she would be.

Elizabeth came out of the Fire a warrior maid. She would never again be the great gawk. Her body was firmly muscled and taut, rippling with the grace it had not had. Every move was fluid, perfect. She had the ease of a dancer, a warrior, a traveler in the Goddess's path. Her face had lost its baby fat and was fine-honed; her cheek bones had sharp edges to them and there were deep creases from her nose to her mouth. Her eyes were those of a haggard falcon come savagely to hand. Her hair, thick and lustrous, rippled like burnished bronze around her shoulders and down to her hips.

Elizabeth walked out of the Fire on feet light as Ariel, and saw there before her in all glory Nerthus, Mother Goddess, Great Mother of all. Standing behind the Goddess was the shadowy figure of the God Sulis. The God became as smoke, and the swirling substance of the God coalesced into the body of the Goddess and they were one.

"There is but one God!" Elizabeth said in terror, for she had been taught from childhood that there were two Gods, Sulis and Diona.

"Yes, my child," the Goddess/God answered. "We are but one; that which you call 'Sulis' and the woodwitches call 'Njord' is but another aspect of me. We were one and all tasks are done by only one—the Goddess."

Elizabeth knelt at the Mother Goddess's feet and kissed her/his hand and said, "Great Mother, matriarch, God of Gods, I am yours. I serve only you forever."

Nerthus drew Elizabeth, the hope of Englene, to her feet and gave her the five-fold kiss thusly: upon the feet, saying, "Blessed be they that brought you to me"; upon the knees, saying, "Blessed be they that kneel at my altar"; upon the mound of life, saying, "Blessed be this that brings forth hope"; upon the breasts, saying, "Blessed be they that are moved to love"; and upon the lips, saying, "Blessed be this that praises my Name!"

Then Nerthus did say, "Welcome, my child, greatest of my priestesses. You will go forth and do great things in my name. For you are mine and we are yours."

Chapter 23

It was a full month come round since Elizabeth had come to the Heartwoods, and now on the night of the full moon she stood naked save for a chaplet of roses and ivy in a forest copse deep in the Heartwoods. Through the leafy branches she could see the open glade where the sacred woodwitch Circle had been prepared. She found it to be less and yet more than any Circle of the witchlords. There had been no elaborate drawing out of the Circle's dimensions, nor calling down of Watchtowers or angels. It had been simply the slipping into the forest glade one by one of the woodwitches who would celebrate this night with her.

The great Mother Goddess Nerthus and her human lover, Jack-in-the-Green, had built a mighty bonfire in the middle of the Circle. Then, after partaking of blessed crescent cakes and raspberry wine, the woodwitches—both men, women, and small children—got up and stripped themselves down to their birth skins. Along with Mother Nerthus and Jack-in-the-Green, they did dance deosil, always deosil, round the burning fire and sang and cried aloud with joy. They shouted encouragement to the woodwitch musicians who played pan pipes and goatskin drums, that they should play louder and faster. The dancing continued and they danced in their Circle until even the moon and stars danced in their Circles overhead. The conies, foxes and the wee hedgehogs came out of their burrows and entered into the woodwitch Circle and danced. The field mice capered, the night crows sang, and all danced. The trees swayed their branches to the music, and the streams in the forest added their notes to the joyous celebration.

Soon Nerthus and Jack led the dancing up the hill and deosil round the copse where Elizabeth waited. And then taking the girl one by each hand, Jack and Nerthus led her into the Great Circle Dance of nature itself, and she did dance with them. And the moon rode higher and higher in the sky and a great silence fell upon the earth. A silence of waiting.

The dancers moved slowly about the Circle, their hands joined. They sang softly of the joys of the woods, the fields and streams. Then the Mother Goddess led Elizabeth into the center of the Circle near to the fire, and the circle of dancing figures was close about them.

Out of the fire stepped another dancer. His naked skin was ruddy gold in the firelight. The hairs of his body were gilt. Sweat ran over the hard muscles of his belly and his member was erect. When Elizabeth looked to see his face she saw only the great horned mask of the forest-king, he of the deer's head, the antlers, and rampant sexuality.

The man took her in his arms and danced swiftly with her about the Circle; then, breaking through it, he danced her away over hill and dale to a place that had been prepared for them. A bower filled with spring blossoms, soft silken covers, and sprinkled with sweet oil of roses.

And then the woodgod laid her down upon the silken green sheets and with his hands brought her to a readiness to receive him. When Elizabeth opened her body to the thrust of the forest-king, blue flames danced on the hills and she knew him, for he was the man who was with her at Avebury and, as at Avebury, he pleasured her well.

*   *   *

The faint light of dawn touched the glade and woke Elizabeth. She found to her surprise that the man still rested beside her. But when she went to lift away his deerhead mask, he reached out and gripped her wrists and said, "No, my sister, my love, you may *not* see my face. Had you obeyed the Angel Menadel and performed an act of magic of your own power at Yermouth, this would be as our wedding morning and I would be yours. But you have not completed the spell and we must remain apart. For until you have Raphael's agreement you cannot have me."

"But this is so unfair!" Elizabeth cried out. "I went through cold, wet, and misery to find you and now having found you I am told you will not be mine. Am I so undesirable, my woodprince?"

"I'd have thought our activities this night would convince you how desirable I find you, my sister, my love. I say to thee, I am thine and will be to the day of thy death." He laughed, and ran one finger down her belly to the copper curls clustered between her legs. "I do not find my slavery unwelcome. We must pray that Raphael be reasonable, and agree to join in the great spell that will give you power. But for now he gloats over your foolishness and dreams of what price he may require of you. They say he is a gentle archangel, but the power your mother would have given you over him was not complete at her death, and his tower was but a quarter done. It is not wise to slight an archangel; they are very sensitive about such things. The tower must be completed and it takes great power to do that.

"I give you a paradox: You must complete the tower to gain Raphael, but you cannot complete the tower without Raphael. Answer the paradox how you may—but not to me, to Raphael."

Elizabeth sighed. This foolery of spells, rituals, and towers was becoming very annoying. She had what she wanted, here within her grasp. This man *must* be her consort. "Look you," she said. "As heir to Englene I could order you to return with me to the Palace of Witchdame and, with my father's blessings, you would become my lord. What say you to that?"

The man in the deer mask laughed. "I think, my sister, my love, we waste a good morning. For when old Nerthus returns I must be gone, and you must away to your father and the court. So let us not dally anymore with talk."

He reached for Elizabeth, drawing her body close against his. "Also, my princess, I am not your subject. I am a prince of a great and far place, and you have no command over me. But I will be with you when you return to court. In fact, you will find me there awaiting you. Your actions may convince great Raphael to ask no more of you than you asked of your cousin John when you fought him in tourney on your birthday. Perhaps Raphael would be content with a sprig of heather for his pillow."

"Archangels, as far as I know, do not have pillows!" Elizabeth said with some annoyance.

The man laughed and began the touching, tickling, and patting that would bring her ready to him. "Come, all will be well. I swear it."

And so in that place and that time, for some little while, it was well between Elizabeth and her forest lord.

It was past midday and Jackie, Menadel, and Guenhwyvar were beginning to worry. They had waited at the entrance to the Heartwoods since dawn but there had been no sign of either the Princess Elizabeth or the woodwitch priestess Nerthus. They were starting to despair of their lady's safety when they heard coming from the forest the sound of a procession.

First came the woodwitch Nerthus, then came many woodwitches, men and women together, and they played on flutes and goatskin drums. Young maids danced with bronze cymbals upon their fingers and young men played upon pan pipes.

Preceded by banners of green silk, the Princess Elizabeth rode out of the woods. She was mounted upon a magnificent barbary bay. Her saddle armor and bridle hangings were of brass and she was clad all in armor of bronze. From her shoulders hung a cloak of richly embroidered green silk, and in her helm green ostrich feathers twisted in the breeze.

The procession came to a halt before the companions, and Nerthus said to them, "Behold, I have brought you again the Princess Elizabeth. I think she will prove a surprise to you." Nerthus laughed and then waited while the princess rode forward to greet her friends.

There was a stillness about that mighty figure seated on the horse, and Menadel, Jackie, and Guenhwyvar felt a great awe in her presence. It was as if the armor hid some blinding light from their eyes, and when the princess removed her helm they saw that it was so. The sun gleamed about her head like fire, her long hair was a molten banner that blew in the breeze, and they saw that she was indeed changed.

Jackie looked up at her, his jaw agape in surprise. He started to call her by that fond cradle name he had used all her life, but the word "poppet" stuck in his throat. This was no poppet. This was a warrior maid come forth out of the heart of Englene to do battle with darkness. Jackie felt a tear slide down his cheek, for he knew that never again would he call the great and mighty Princess Elizabeth "poppet." He knelt before her in the dust and waited until she bid him rise.

"Come," she said in a voice as cold as her bronze armor. "We must be away to the Palace of Witchdame and my father's court, for there is a great and terrible evil there and I must deal with it."

In silence, Menadel, Jackie, and Guenhwyvar mounted their horses and gathered the reins of the pack animals. In silence, they rode behind the Princess Elizabeth to the Palace of Witchdame.

THE TOWERS
OF WITCHDAME

Chapter 24

Elizabeth had been warned that there might be changes at court which she would not find pleasant. There were new courtiers whose shadows cast weird reflections of the Nether Regions upon the walls. The darkness had conquered Richard's court.

Elizabeth and her companions went swiftly to the king without staying to wash or change from their travel-stained garments; when Richard looked up from his throne he saw coming down the room toward him a strange and marvelous apparition. There was a knight clad all in bronze armor carrying a soiled traveler's pack, a wizard who shimmered with power, a wood-witch, and, bringing up the rear of the procession, Jackie Somers the fool.

The knight was a fearsome thing, gleaming in the torchlight of the Throne Room, and it was only when the person knelt at the king's feet and spoke that he realized it was his daughter Elizabeth—much changed. There was a cold anger upon her face when she looked at him and no sign of love in her eyes.

Elizabeth was startled by her father's appearance as well. When she had left the Palace of Witchdame she had carried with her memories of a vigorous man in the summer of his years. That pink and gold gleaming giant was no more. In his place was a frail, aging man. The rich blond hair was now streaked with white, and the once rosy cheeks were pale and sagging. Richard's blue eyes were rheumy and watered. His hands trembled on the arms of his throne, and his body was shrunken within his glittering robes. Richard's loss of power had affected all of him. With its passing had gone his midyears and the last traces of his youth.

Elizabeth opened the pack and said, "Sire, I have brought to you the *gifts* you requested. Those tokens of the peace and prosperity of the four corners of your kingdom." And she poured out onto the floor in front of him the thick black tar of the witch of Bamborow Castle, and the wood from a witch's pyre. She brought forth the stinking wrack of the shores of the southern sea, and then placed upon this disgusting heap the rotting remains of the two dead demon fetuses taken from Guenhwyvar's lungs.

There were exclamations of outrage from the courtiers about the king's throne, and Richard waved a scented handkerchief in front of his face in protest at the stench. "What mean you with these gifts, my daughter? I hope you have an excellent explanation. If not, I shall be very angry with you, for you have come here into my Throne Room with no word of greeting for me, nor kiss of love, nor any token of your respect for me. You have stood before me cold and distant as a stranger, and I *would* know why!" A little of Richard's old power crept into his voice, and as she spoke he gestured with his right hand, causing the ring Raziel to dance with fire and light.

Elizabeth rose from her knees and stood before her father. "There *is* no peace and plenty in Englene," she said coldly. "I found rottenness on the land. I found demons living freely in your country. There are children dying of starvation, and cattle losing their young before time. I found blasted wheat, and falcon eggs that rotted before they could hatch. I found black muddy fields and long rains, storm, Fire and Flame, but I found no peace in Englene. The land has farmers who curse your name, and women whose wombs are empty; they cry of a night for your aid and you have not given it. I have brought this proof back to you.

"High Summer approaches, my lord, and you must away to the Heartwoods. I tell you, the Goddess is most angry. You have not come to her asking her aid, nor have you been penitent and willing to admit your lack of power, but you have let Englene suffer for your sins."

"These words are treason!" The statement came not from Richard, but from Lady Anne of Pemberly. She pushed her way out of the crowd to stand before Elizabeth in a periwinkle blue court gown hung with queen's sleeves. In her ears she wore the diamond and pearl earrings of the dead Queen Dianne. "Treason, I say, and were I king I would have you taken to the dungeons of BrynGwyn, there to cool your heels and think on the dishonor you have heaped on your own father."

"Now, now, my lady," Richard said, reaching out a feeble hand to the woman. To his sorrow, she ignored it. "I am still king here," he continued. "While I *am* king, I decide who goes to the tower of BrynGwyn and who does not. My daughter's words are harsh, but she has been on a harsh journey and I would speak more of it to her—but in private, not in front of my court." He looked up at the courtiers standing around, and said, "Get you gone, all of you! I would speak with my daughter alone. I would have *none* of you stay save only the physician Michael Mittron, so he might attend me."

The courtiers, with much bowing and scraping and no little smirking behind their hands, got themselves quickly gone from the Throne Room, leaving only a handsome blond man clad in simple saffron robes marking him as a physician. He came to the king's side and, holding Richard's right wrist, he gently took his pulse, then placed a hand upon the king's forehead and felt for fever. The king meanwhile stared the Lady Anne down, until she too turned and left the Throne Room.

Elizabeth, with Menadel, Jackie, and Guenhwyvar, stood watching the doctor and waiting while he fussed about the king. Then, his examination complete, he stepped to one side. He smiled at Elizabeth, a smile of singular sweetness.

"My lord, who is this new physician that attends you? I do not remember him being at court."

"I am Michael Mittron, physician from the city of Firenza. I came because I heard of the king's troubles and thought I might aid him. But I am afraid, my lady, I have been of very little service."

"No, no, Mittron," the king said, "the fault is not yours. You have eased what discomforts of my body you could. But my greater affliction is that of the spirit and you cannot touch that. For what my daughter has said, even though she spoke it rudely, is true. I am feeble and have lost my power, and because of that the land suffers. I know that I should have gone to the Heartwoods at midwinter as an early sacrifice, and there laid my neck outstretched for the High Priestess's blade; but I have a love of life and would cling to it for as long as I can. It is not yet the anniversary of my reign and of my birthday, and I have until that time." He turned back to face his daughter. "Now tell me of your travels, daughter, and of this change that has come upon you."

Elizabeth said, "I will tell you the tales of my travels and what these vile things before your throne mean, and these my companions will tell their tales. But the stories will not be pleasant, and I think many a salt tear will fall from your eyes to mingle with this waste."

"Thomas," said Elizabeth to the mage, "I sent for you in the hopes that you might have some explanation for what it is that ails my father. Is it the sickness upon the land that has affected him, or is it more? I heard many rumors upon my journey as to how the king had lost potency and power. If so, can we by our magic return it to him?"

Thomas was silent as he paced the princess's privy chamber. He picked up a seashell full of potpourri and ran his fingers through the dried petals. He replaced the shell and remarked, "'Tis your mother's mixture. I recognize it, and it is of this and your father we must speak. For when your mother died such potpourri was found scattered in her room. It was thought that she had done some sort of containing spell upon King Richard, but when we tested the dried flower petals we found them nothing more than what is here in this shell. Aleicester and Lady Anne thought at first that your father's infirmity was temporary, that he was grieving for his lost wife. Then at Avebury there was such power and flame they thought him cured, but soon they came to know that he was not cured, and that it was unlikely that he was the man in the Circle at Avebury."

"He wasn't. I don't know who was there, but it wasn't Father," Elizabeth said.

Thomas nodded in agreement. "Yes, I've heard you've had reason to know that. But it was your lady mother we were speaking of. It was the Lady Marguerite who told me of your mother's last deed. For she did curse your father with a grievous woodwitch curse that took all the power of his manhood from him. She told Marguerite she had done it for you, to protect the throne, so that no child born of another woman would take it from you. She said she would not let your father, the king, feel any grief at his loss of manhood since he would see it as his body's tribute to her, and that was so. It was that fact that kept Richard from admitting there was anything wrong or that there might be a curse on him. Even after Marguerite told him what had happened to him he refused to believe. Now he is as you see him. For he and the Lady Anne have tried many things to remove the curse. He has dined on lust sallet made of orchid, mandrake, periwinkle, and mountain lizard. He has ingested many noxious substances and bathed himself in herbs. He has gone to Circles, and prayed to many blasphemous aspects of the God and Goddess at their strange and devious shrines. He has damaged his health through much seeking after potency, and I fear that he will lose his life because of it."

"Damn her! May my mother's name be damned in Englene! May she be no more to me than one who has caused a great harm to my land," Elizabeth said with cold savagery.

Elizabeth had blamed her father for the problems of Englene, and taken some comfort in the thought that her mother had been a good and wise queen. Now she knew that this was not so, and that the guilt must be shared equally between Richard and Dianne. So Elizabeth's love for her mother faded away until it was as little as her present love for her father, and that was but a small drop in an ocean of anger.

"I know, my lady," Thomas said. "I know you have every reason to feel anger and hatred, but do not allow it to turn inward and fester. There is much darkness already at your father's court. And there are vultures who have come to pick the bones. Your cousin John and his mother had barely returned unto their lands when, hearing of your father's impotence, they returned post haste to feast on Englene's disaster. John pays large bribes to your father's courtiers, in hopes that they will make him king in your place."

"And has he any chance of that?" Elizabeth asked.

"Not now. There is a man with greater charm and skill in winning courtiers to his side. He is—" Thomas struggled for accuracy while barely managing to overcome his distaste. "He is of a . . . pleasing countenance, and is openhanded and generous. He speaks well and is a knowledgeable man. Eblis is the prince of a mighty country and people, and there are those who think he would do well ruling Englene. Do not let me color your opinion of him. Go and view him with an open mind, Elizabeth. For you may find him of more value than I did. He dines with us tonight. He and his . . . retinue. I hope you find it amusing, even though I shall not."

Chapter 25

For dinner Elizabeth wore a gown of dark green brocade in a color like the shade of the forest Heartwoods. Her kirtle and foresleeves were of gold tuft-taffeta and the girdle she wore was of pearls the size of hazel nuts combined with gold roses; it fell to the hem of her kirtle and ended in an onyx and gold jewel. The dress's queen's sleeves brushed the floor at the back, and Elizabeth wore on her head a dark green velvet cap trimmed with an ostrich feather. With her head high she sailed forth like a galleon to the feast.

The Great Hall was arranged for dinner with its high table hung with damask. Elizabeth passed through the tapestry behind the high table and stood for a moment looking at the court.

Much was as she remembered and yet much was changed. There was her father glorious in ermine and purple velvet, but he was no longer the blond giant of her childhood. There was the Lady Pemberly beside him, but she wore queen's sleeves

and Queen Dianne's earrings. The king and the lady stood
talking to the Archbishop Aleicester, Lady Mary, and their son,
Duke Charles. That family group, too, was the same, but yet
when Elizabeth looked at the handsome young duke she found
herself wondering how on earth she could have found such a
callow youth interesting or sexually exciting. He was simply
one more young courtier, and not even a shadow of the man
she had known in the Circle. The courtiers were more and less
than they had been: noisy as jackdaws, greedy, and eager for
whatever morsel of gossip they might overhear. Jackie, who
stood beside her chair, was also the same and yet changed. He
was still the mischievous, misshaped little man she had always
known, but her months on the road had taught her his depths
of love and devotion.

The only person in the court who seemed entirely unchanged
was Aunt Marguerite. She sat at her place at the table busily
reading. She ignored the courtiers, and it was as if none of the
changes mattered to her. Elizabeth suspected that if Marguerite
were some merchant's wife or even a farmer's good dame, she
would be exactly the same as she was, and that thought was
oddly comforting.

There was a blare of trumpets from the minstrel's gallery
and the king and his relatives took their places at the table.
Elizabeth could see that there was an empty chair between the
king and the Lady Pemberly, and she wondered for whom the
chair might be.

There was another blare of trumpets and into the room strode
a magnificent man. He was golden blond and clad all in cloth
of gold and scarlet. His manner was strikingly authoritative,
and from the way the courtiers reacted to him it was clear he
was a high favorite of all. He came into the Hall accompanied
by page boys and priests, courtiers wearing his scarlet and
black livery, and their shadows were those of demons dancing
in triumph.

There was a flurry of confusion as these attendants found
places and the king welcomed his guest, Prince Eblis of the
Bene Elim. He introduced the prince to his daughter and Eblis
lingered a little too long over Elizabeth's hand, his lips cold
against her skin.

She looked up into his eyes and saw in their bright blueness
a little flame dancing in the place of his pupils. When he turned

to take his place and his coat flew out about him she *saw* the red and gold flames of the Nether Regions enveloping his hard muscled body. She trembled, for this man was a demon.

But when Elizabeth looked about the Hall she could see that no one else was concerned; it was quite clear that no one had seen what she had seen. King Richard, who should have been the most observant man in Englene, saw nothing. But after what she had seen of the darkness in her father's lands that fact did not surprise Elizabeth. She turned away from watching Eblis and sat staring straight ahead, while the various dishes were brought into the Hall.

The serving boys had been fantastically dressed in costumes representing various beasts. They were dragons, unicorns, griffins, and cockatrices, and as each one brought the dishes to the table there was fanfare of music from the gallery above. There were plates of oysters and jellied broth of mutton, there were marrow bones, a grand sallet, and several partridges on a plate all gilded with saffron. There was a roast swan in plumage and an enormous pigeon pie. But Elizabeth noticed that while these dishes were in great supply, other dishes were being brought, and they were being placed in front of the king, Prince Eblis, and the Lady Anne Pemberly. These she quickly realized were of a strange and worrisome character, for each and every one of them had been designed to fan the fever of lust.

There was a great sallet of periwinkle, mandrake, and rocket, dressed with oil, sugar, and ginger. There were the tongues of virgin harts and cucumbers stuffed with oyster pudding. There were stewed sparrow brains, and roosters's stones mixed with bacon and artichokes. There was a fearsome pike, fat with roe, and a large dish of snails in ewe's milk. On a presentation platter there was a cockatrice of pig and chicken sewed together, cunningly wrought.

Elizabeth watched while her father ate only of those dishes. Beside her, Jackie murmured, "Be careful, my lady, that you serve none of that messed about stuff to me! For if you do, I cannot swear to restrain myself, and you might find yourself violated here in front of this great company."

Elizabeth laughed and served herself and the jester from those foods she knew to be safe from an erotic influence. As she ate, she felt a great disquiet, for she saw that her cup—

that great carved piece of solid turquoise held aloft in a silver
merman's arms—was missing. True, the cup before her carved
of rock crystal and held in the grasp of a golden titan was
indeed beautiful, but it was not *her* cup. Wondering, she looked
about and saw the goblet in front of the Lady Anne of Pemberly.

And a great rage filled Elizabeth, and she said to the lady,
"Madam, I see that the pages who set the table have made an
error. The cup before you is *mine.* I wish it back."

Startled, the Lady Anne looked up at the princess and then
at the king. It was obvious to all that Richard had allowed the
lady to usurp not only queen's sleeves and the queen's earrings,
but a princess's cup as well. "But my lady princess—"

"I want it back *now!"* Elizabeth's voice was cold and hard
as a woodwitch's blade.

The king looked up from his discussion with Eblis and turned
to face his daughter. He saw something there that made him
shrink away; turning back to the Lady Anne, he said in a dead,
empty voice, "Give my daughter her cup. It is hers, just as all
in my kingdom is hers as my heir."

With poor grace the Lady Pemberly passed the cup down
the table and the crystal and gold one was given to her in return.

Elizabeth had her table page wash the cup carefully and
then fill it with Rhenish. She could not demand the earrings
nor the removal of the queen's sleeves, but this one small
victory was, for now, sufficient. The meal continued.

The serving boys brought in the banquet course with many
a pie and pudding and plate of cakes and wafers. There were
bowls of fruit, peaches and apricots and grapes from Queen
Dianne's greenhouses in the Palace of Witchdame. There were
sugared nuts, candied flower petals, and many an elegant and
pleasant dish—but it was her father's food that Elizabeth
watched.

Those dishes were like unto the feast food in effect, for
there were sea holly suckets, rose petal jelly, and candied leaves
of dogs-tooth violet. He had bowls of dried figs, olives, and
caviare, and wine flavored with mandragora, grains of paradise
and musk. Then a little serving maid slipped into the room and
placed a small silver charger beside the king. On it were strange,
thin, paperlike wafers and Elizabeth knew with cold certainty
that they were the end product of a powerful love spell. The
wafers were made of bull's sperm and fine white flour baked

by body heat on the breast of a ready and willing woman. Her father's quest for virility had indeed become desperate.

Then, with the sound of sackbut and drum, the subtleties were brought in. First was a mighty black dragon made of marchpane, its scales coated with blood boiled black. This was in honor of Prince Eblis, for a black dragon on a scarlet field was his coat of arms.

There was silence in the court as the other subtlety was brought to the table. The courtiers busied themselves with the food on their plates or in conversation with each other, and tried to ignore the sight of that overly emphatic *thing* which was placed before Richard. At first Elizabeth thought it was merely a marzipan representation of the Sun God Sulis, for there was the gilded sun mask of the God and the glorious red and gold flaming robes. But she could not help noticing the robes were parted, and the God's member clearly exposed: crimson, engorged, and erect. The subtlety stood before the king, and Richard, with great deliberateness, ignored it.

He turned to Eblis and suggested that the dragon be observed closely, for it had been said by Henry Terrell that there was many a cunning surprise to the dragon.

When Terrell stepped forward with a lighted taper and applied it to the mouth of the dragon, smoke billowed forth; then the dragon belched flame and roared out as the gunpowder within it was fired off. The dragon split neatly in two, and revealed to all a treasure of suckets and bonbons, flower petals, gilded walnuts, and small jeweled treasures.

Those at the high table reached eagerly for the contents of the dragon, and none but Elizabeth noted that the figure of the god-king had been knocked from its plum cake base by the explosion and now lay flat on its back, its member askew and drooping. As she watched, drops of white wine flowed from the mangled organ onto the damask cloth in a large wet stain. It was not a pleasant thing to watch.

The rest of the banquet was not something that Elizabeth found enjoyable, for she noticed that the aphrodisiac foods were having their effect—but not on her father. Lady Pemberly and Prince Eblis were growing more and more friendly. His hand strayed often to her bare shoulder or lower to the curve of her bosom. Her hands were often to be seen twined in his silver gilt curls, or feeding him suckets and maids-of-honor tarts.

The entertainment began, and Elizabeth had to listen to Jackie's dark muttering from behind her as he discussed viciously the quality of the revels that were being performed without him. The king had gotten himself a new jester, an extremely ugly little dwarf named Jeremy. The dwarf's wit was limited, and he made up for it by performing none too skilled acts of acrobatics. The page boys brought into the room an enormous custard pie, far bigger than any Elizabeth had ever seen, and they placed it on the righthand table.

Then Jeremy danced upon the tabletop and, with a whoop, ran the length of the table and dove full length into the custard pie, splattering the unfortunate courtiers nearby with the thick, gooey mess. Those of the court who had not been splattered found it good fun and applauded, calling for an encore. Elizabeth found it nauseating, and wondered how things had come to such a pass that this would be taken for wit. Even Jackie's rather poor taste in parading around in the cast-off green gown of the Pemberly was of better humor than this.

"Look at that!" Jackie said virtuously. "I'd never do anything *that* stupid. If I couldn't manage to get the laughter of the court through my skills, without making a total ass of myself, I would have resigned from being a jester and taken up the job of gargoyle upon the roof of Westmonasterium. Alas, alack, what has your father's court come to?"

"Hush, Jackie, keep your professional opinions to yourself. If you want to make yourself useful, you'll find that page of mine and see if he can procure more Rhenish for me. I have a bad taste in my mouth and would like it cleared."

Jackie vanished and returned shortly with the young page who, from his demeanor, had obviously been sampling more than a little Rhenish himself. He took Elizabeth's cup and staggered off to the sideboard to fill it. When he returned and placed the cup before her, Elizabeth saw that it had undergone a mysterious change.

The great chalice that Queen Dianne had given Elizabeth had been a gift to her from the Archangel Gabriel on the occasion of her wedding to King Richard. It was a known fact that turquoise would detect poison, and no doubt Gabriel, knowing of the problems Dianne would face with the king's court, had felt that such a stone would be useful for the wine cup of the queen.

But Dianne had never used it, saying, "If I, a woodwitch, cannot detect poison in my food I deserve to die." She had put the cup aside, and when her daughter had gained sufficient age, presented the cup to Elizabeth, both because of its beauty and because of the potency of the stone. It had never, in all her years, indicated poison.

But now the brilliant robin's egg blue of the cup had been stained an irridescent black by the Rhenish wine within it. Elizabeth stared at the cup in anger. Someone at this court had tried to kill her.

With a cry of rage, Elizabeth stood and looked past her father at Anne. The woman, startled by the princess's outburst, looked to where the young woman's hand was pointing and saw the goblet. Lady Pemberly's cheeks went pale with fear. She knew the whole court would think that since the cup had been in her possession it was she who had attempted to poison the princess.

She looked to Richard to see what he would say, but the king did nothing. He merely drank of his herbed wine, and it was clear that the mandragora had reduced him to a state of stupification.

The court, silenced by the princess's outburst, waited to see what she would do. Prince Eblis leaned forward on one elbow, watching her face, his eyes brightly afire with malice.

Elizabeth picked up the full chalice in one hand, and said in a voice of power, "My lord Gabriel, take back unto thyself what is thine and leave what is evil behind. I thank thee for saving my life this day." Holding the chalice aloft, she threw it the length of the Great Hall.

It sailed cup over bottom, revolving in the air, but not one drop of the fluid spilled from it. With a mighty crash it struck the kitchen screens at the end of the room and fell with a clatter to the floor. The fluid within burst into flames, blue-black and stinking. That portion of the Hall smelled of sulfur, henbane, and aconite.

The fire burned pure blue, reducing the turquoise to dust and the silver to a pool of molten slag which spread across the floor and seeped into the cracks between the golden brown glazed tiles. Then the fire died away, and the silver began to hiss and steam as if touched by cold water.

All was still and silent in the Great Hall. The silver had

become a blackened metallic pool over some dozen of the tiles. It was obvious to the courtiers that the remains of the princess's cup would be there on the floor of the Great Hall as long as the Hall might stand, a reminder to all who might raise their hand against the princess of Englene.

"Look you at it. Look you, all the witchlords and witch-dames that are here in this Hall," Elizabeth said in the voice of power. "Let any who would raise their hand against me be as this cup. Let them become as wind-blown ash, scattered to the four corners of the universe!"

There was silence in the room as the courtiers watched to see if anyone would be touched with blue flame and fall sizzling and melting to the floor. But it did not happen. At the high table by the side of King Richard, Prince Eblis smiled. His red lips parted to show even white teeth that were a bit too sharp. Gabriel's Flame did not touch him, for he was already a creature of Flame.

And the princess knew this, and was greatly afraid.

Michael Mittron and Prince Eblis met after the banquet in the alcove behind the arras. It was a meeting that Doctor Mittron had asked for. The prince lounged against the stone wall of the alcove, picking his sharp teeth with a gold toothpick, and waited for what the court physician might say.

"I would not advise you to try anything of that sort again," Doctor Mittron said in a soft voice. "For if you do, I do not think you will survive it."

"If I had meant for her to die, she would have died." Prince Eblis had no doubt of what the doctor was referring to. "But tell me, my good *physician*, will you prevent me were I to decide next time that she *was* to die?"

Michael Mittron grinned. His smile was as sharply fanged as Eblis's. "Yes, I would prevent it. Remember, I saw you fall screaming, my prince. I saw you fall first of the host after that bright lord you followed. And if necessary I *will* see you fall again. I think it is time you left this court. There is no place for you in it."

"Will you *make* me leave? Or will you need help from others? It would be very interesting to try my strength against yours."

"No, I will not be the one to make you leave; the Princess

Elizabeth, heir to Englene, will see to that."

Prince Eblis laughed. "What! The great gawk? That is too amusing for words. No, I think I will stay and offer the lady my hand in marriage so that she and I will rule this land together. It would amuse me and amuse my lord."

"It would not amuse me or the Lady Nerthus. Do not call Elizabeth the 'great gawk' *ever* again. When the day comes that you face her in battle, you will find what she is truly made of and you will know fear."

As an answer, Prince Eblis pushed aside the arras and started to step out into the darkness of the Great Hall. "Tell me," he said over his shoulder, "how fares my lord Raphael? Is he content, and does he sit at ease in his pavilions?"

There was the sound of laughter filling the Great Hall as Prince Eblis crossed the empty room. But as he walked through the door, his shadow fell across the metallic puddle that remained of Elizabeth's cup. His shadow touched the metal, and it scorched, sizzled, and shrank away toward his body. Prince Eblis did not see, but in the alcove with the arras edge in his hand, Michael Mittron saw it and was pleased.

Chapter 26

The days passed swiftly and the time of the Midsummer Festival had come. It was a god-king summer, a time of celebration, a recognition of the joys that the Goddess might bring and a remembrance that the witchlords owed their power over Englene to the Goddess.

Elizabeth had searched the court for her woodgod, but could not find him, even though he had promised he would be at the Palace of Witchdame with her. Menadel counseled leaving all in the hands of the Goddess. With much sighing, Elizabeth did so, and waited for her lord to reveal himself.

But her greatest grief was that, with all the power she had from the Goddess, it was not enough to help her father or heal the land of Englene.

Richard called Thomas the Mage unto him and sought some escape from the fate that was his.

"Thomas," the king said, "in three days's time is Midsummer Day and I must go to the Heartwoods. What think you of my chances of returning from that place alive?"

The question was rhetorical. The king was aware that Thomas knew the answer as well as he did. But he had to ask it, in hopes that Thomas had seen in the oracles some other fate.

Thomas looked at his king with pity. "My king, would that you could live forever. But the signs and the portents are such that there is no chance of the Goddess being merciful; a great dragon comet has come, the kingworms stir, and the scent of apples fills the air—"

"All my loved ones have fallen away!" the king cried out. "The Lady Anne, whom I loved as myself, has denied me and has found another to give her comfort. Prince Eblis will console her, and he, at least, will be a whole man in her bed."

"I am sorry, my king," Thomas said. "I know of no way for you to regain your former vigor and be able to save the land from famine."

"So mote it be," the king said with a sigh. "If the Goddess wishes my life, she may take it, but not in *that* way. To go to the Heartwoods, be killed, and have my dead body flung across a horse and my member mutilated is more than I can bear."

Thomas bowed deeply to his king, abasing himself before his lord. It was the least he could do to honor the man who had been his ruler for so many years, and he found in his heart he agreed with his king, that to die in honor and in one's own time was indeed a better thing.

And on the morrow, in the great shrine of Westmonasterium, on the high altar of the Mother Goddess was found the body of King Richard of Englene. He was laid out in robes of green, gold and white and had upon his head the crown of Englene, and in his hand, the scepter. Beside him on the altar was the body of his wife, Queen Dianne, and they were one in death as they had not been in life.

There was no mark of violence or bloodshed upon the king's body. The Mother Goddess Nerthus had granted one final gift to Englene's king and that was to take his spirit gently from him in the place of his choosing. For though he had been a weak man, he had fulfilled her plans for Englene and had been the father of her beloved daughter, Elizabeth.

Those who came sorrowing to bear away the king's body to be prepared for burial found that the great ring of power, which had been given to the witchlord king by the Archangel Raphael, was missing. For Raphael had taken it back unto himself.

Chapter 27

Elizabeth was dressed in full dewle. Her black velvet gown was trimmed with bands of jet and ivory around the neckline and on the long hanging sleeves. Her kirtle was black brocade and the collar of her shift was high and edged with black work. On her head was a black velvet cap trimmed with black ostrich feathers. She looked elegant, tall, and stately—every inch a queen.

She stood beside the empty altar in the chapel of the Goddess at the shrine of Westmonasterium. Her fingers caressed the gold and marble surface as if seeking some last trace of warmth left by her father's body. Queen Dianne had been returned to her glass-topped casket in the family crypt and Richard's body was now in the hands of the mages, who would embalm it and make it ready for burial.

"I would have my mother's coffin removed from the niche it is in, Aleicester. I want it placed beside his. I know the place he has chosen for his burial; his choice of a deathbed has shown it. Directly beneath this altar, there shall be built a crypt for my father. There in such splendor as befits a king, he and my mother will be placed for all eternity. See to it."

Aleicester bowed deeply to the Princess Elizabeth. "It shall be done as you wish," he said. "I can have the workmen open a wall into the crypt of the kings so that there will be an arched opening between the room for your father and the place of his ancestors. But, my lady, I am troubled as to when we should bury your father. I have declared six months of full mourning, and no celebrations of Midsummer shall take place. We should not wait until the crypt is finished, for that may take many a month. Nor should we bury him too quickly. The mages will have his body ready tonight, but I would not recommend it, for we cannot give your father honorable burial without his successor being named."

Elizabeth turned away from the altar to face the Archbishop of Avebury, Bathford, and Wells. "But my lord, what problem is there? I am Queen of Englene now that my father is dead, so there is naught for you to do but proclaim it."

"It is not that simple, my lady. Indeed you are the heir apparent to the throne, and were it not for the absence of your father's ring I would have declared you the moment his body was discovered. But the law and custom of Englene dating back even unto the time of King William the Lucky has been that only he or she who wears the ring of the Archangel Raphael is true ruler of Englene. The ring is gone, and I am sore troubled in my heart as to how we may get around this problem. Since you lack the ring of power there will be those who will dispute your title. Your cousin John has already declared himself King of Gaeland, and now he looks to add Englene to his titles. Prince Eblis feels that he has some claim to your throne, since you are not a male descendent. Then too, your woodwitch blood troubles him."

"His concern for my throne troubles me. Do *you* doubt, Aleicester, that I am the true ruler of Englene? Declare me and I will keep the throne! I have the backing of the Mother Goddess herself. With her aid, I will complete Queen Dianne's plan and have the power of all four of the archangels behind me. What more would you wish?"

Aleicester wrung his hands nervously and looked upward

at the hammerbeam roof of the chapel, and then to one side and the other. Finally his eyes focused on the high altar. He did everything but look directly into his princess's eyes.

"My lady, what you speak of is indeed great power, but much of it remains to be fulfilled in the future," he said slowly. "There *is* the law—the law states that he who has the ring of Raphael rules in Englene. I cannot take the risk of the God Aquaesulis giving the ring unto another. I would be struck down by the Gods were I to place a claimant on the throne that they did not approve of. . . ."

"I have heard, my lord Archbishop, a great deal about what you do not recommend that we do," Elizabeth said with some impatience. "Pray tell me what you *do* recommend."

"I have a solution that I think will work, my lady," Aleicester said. Elizabeth could tell from the slight tremor in his voice that what he was about to suggest was probably not going to meet with her approval. She was right.

"You see, one of the problems is that you are a woman," Aleicester continued. "Were you to have a strong consort by your side, that fact would help cement your hold over your kingdom. So what I would suggest—"

"I will not marry John *or* Prince Eblis! Englene is mine. I will not share it with a foreigner."

"No, no, my lady. I was not going to suggest either man as a candidate." Aleicester hurried to placate the angry princess. "No, I had something in mind that I think will be far more to your pleasure. You might marry my son, Duke Charles." Aleicester patted her hand and smirked. He was positive Elizabeth would find the idea acceptable. "He is your own cousin by blood, born and bred in Englene. The people would approve of such a match and would welcome Charles as king. . . ."

Elizabeth smiled coldly. Here it was, the unholy bargain she'd been expecting and she had to admit it was less unholy than she had feared. She had been sure when Aleicester started speaking of marriages that he would choose Prince Eblis as his candidate. But the Duke Charles—ah, that was a pretty choice. Charles was handsome, intelligent after a fashion, well versed in the politics of the court, and not unpleasing. But when compared with the majestical man of Avebury and the Heart-woods, Charles was but a firefly compared to a forest fire.

"So, Archbishop, that is your bargain. I marry your son and

you will crown me queen, ring or no ring. Of course, at the same time you will crown Charles king. How very interesting. I think I smell the stink of treason here! For if you would crown me queen without the ring but married to your son, by the same token you should be able to crown me queen without the ring and without marriage to *your* son. I wonder how a stay in the tower will sharpen your sense of logic?"

"Unfortunately, Your Grace, you have not the power to do that, much as I wish you did." Thomas the Mage came into the chapel, his face set in lines of controlled anger. "What do you here, my brother Aleicester? The princess is indeed right when she says she smells the stink of treason. I smell ambition, pride, and no love for Englene. And I say to you as High Chancellor of Englene, I will not allow so wicked a bargain to be. For even should you persuade the princess of its rightness, I will go before the Great Coveyne and denounce you for what you would attempt this day. I will not see Englene become but a maiden's dower for the son of an ambitious archbishop."

Aleicester turned in rage to face Thomas. "Then do you declare war on me, Thomas? Remember, no matter what power you may have as Chancellor, I alone crown the next ruler of Englene! I swear to you, by the Goddess, her altar, and by my devotion to the God Aquaesulis, I will not crown *anyone* ruler of Englene until that person wears upon their right hand the ring of Raphael! I will go to the block on Tower Hill before I will break my vow. So mote it be!" And with a furious rustle of his black taffeta robes, the Archbishop Aleicester bustled his way out of the shrine of the Goddess.

"Well! My lord Thomas, you have either made or marred my chances of becoming queen. But like the Archbishop Aleicester, all I can say is, so mote it be."

Thomas laughed and said, "Fear not, my lady. For I have consulted the oracles and prayed unto the Goddess, and she has answered me. You will be Queen of Englene by Midsummer Day. I swear it. *So mote it be.*"

True to his words, the Archbishop Aleicester announced to the court and the Great Coveyne that he could not crown the Princess Elizabeth or anyone else until the ring Raziel was found. He explained at great length the historical reasons for this, and made a great deal of fuss about how Elizabeth was indeed the true heir, but the ring and the ring alone verified the claim. There was a certain amount of muttering and mumbling from the Great Coveyne. The court received the news first with silence, then a buzz of speculation, and finally an explosion of activity.

There was a mad scramble throughout the palaces of Englene. Courtiers searched in every nook and cranny for the ring Raziel. They combed the White Tower of the Palace of BrynGwyn. They raced to the mighty fortress Castle of Windleshore to go through even that old dwelling, though Richard had not been there in many a month. But most of their efforts were concentrated on the Palace of Witchdame. There was a mighty turning out of coffers, clothespresses, and chests. Clothing was rummaged through, tapestries were torn from the walls to see if there was some hiding place behind them, and rush mats were thrown askew in frantic speed to find the ring first. Everyone from the lowliest page boy even unto the Earl Marshall himself searched for the ring Raziel, for with the finding a king or queen would be declared.

John of Gaeland and his mother had set their wild Gaels to the task, and they had all but dismantled some of the state rooms of the palace. It was necessary for Thomas the Mage to order them restrained lest they destroy the palace down to the foundation blocks. There had even been a bloody battle between two of John's men and a man-at-arms belonging to the Princess Elizabeth, because the Gaels had seen the man with a ring in his hands. It was merely one he had found in the rushes of a disused dining parlor—nothing more than a trumpery thing of silver and glass—but it was enough to cause the Gaels to savagely attack the man, and he barely escaped with his life. He complained to Thomas and the mage felt it necessary to set certain ground rules.

Aleicester might be the one who would put the crown on the head of the new ruler, but Thomas was the one who must approve the crowning. He said that he would give no such approval to one who had the blood of the innocent on his hands.

That made the quest a little less dangerous but no less fevered. The Lady Anne of Pemberly kept her ladies-in-waiting at the task both night and day. Not only did she search her own rooms and the king's chambers, but she even dared to attempt a search in the rooms of the Princess Elizabeth herself. Lady Anne and her ladies received short shrift from Guenhwyvar, who had been made Elizabeth's chief lady-in-waiting, and were sent packing.

Through all the turmoil Prince Eblis walked through the court with a smirk of satisfaction on his face. There were those who thought that he already possessed the ring and would reveal his ownership in good time. So, while searching feverishly for the ring, many a courtier made sure to be as courteous as possible to this smiling prince for fear he might turn out to be the true king.

Tempers were frayed and feuds broke out between some of the oldest families in Englene. Elizabeth said unto Thomas the Mage that if the ring was not found soon, all her palaces would be naught but a shambles and no government would get itself conducted in all of Englene. Thomas reassured her to have patience and trust in the Goddess, for she would be queen by Midsummer.

"But Thomas," Elizabeth said in some exasperation, "I take leave to remind you that Midsummer Day is tomorrow, and there is no sign of the ring!"

Elizabeth and Thomas had gathered with several other members of the court to search the Throne Room of the Palace of Witchdame. Jackie had commandeered a ladder and swarmed up the wall to check each and every one of the elk and deer heads which decorated the wall, but there had been no ring.

"Fear not, my lady," Thomas said. "I have great faith in the Angel Raphael. He will see that the ring, of necessity, belongs to you." The mage held the ladder steady so that Jackie need not fear falling.

There was a clot of courtiers at the door, and the Lady Marguerite had to push her way into the Throne Room; not even for a princess would any give way in the search for Raziel. Marguerite looked at the chaos in the room and shook her head. "I do not know what my brother Richard would have made of this mess. It is a shame that such a thing is being done in his name, and all for naught."

Marguerite held out her hand. On her palm shimmered a brass ring set with an enormous emerald. The light from the windows caught the stone and sent green light flashing about the room. "I have Richard's ring here, and—"

Marguerite did not manage to finish the sentence. For every courtier in the room had turned and as one knelt to her, and even one or two cried out, "The Gods save Queen Marguerite!"

Standing by the raised dais of the Throne Room of Englene, Elizabeth did not kneel. She stood looking at her aunt and the great glowing emerald in the woman's hand, and she felt her universe shatter around her. There was a roaring in Elizabeth's ears like the roaring of the sea at Great Yermouth. The floor felt as unsteady under her feet as the sands on that beach. She felt sickness rise in her throat, the taste of defeat and bile. Raphael's ring in Marguerite's hand!

The room was filling rapidly. Courtiers had run from the Throne Room with the news that Marguerite had the ring, and from all points of the Palace of Witchdame people were coming to pack the Throne Room and bow to Marguerite.

It had been but the space of a minute or two since the elderly princess had entered the room, but now all time seemed tangled. Marguerite still stood in that same position, a few feet from the door, where she had stood when first she had revealed the ring. There was no attempt on the part of the courtiers to bring her forward to the dais nor to touch her. It was like a scene on a tapestry. There were the courtiers and the vivid colors of their gowns, there was a beautiful Throne Room, and the woman they were now ready to acknowledge as queen.

"Where? Where did you get the ring, Aunt Marguerite?" Elizabeth asked, her voice a harsh croak.

Marguerite started at the sound of Elizabeth's voice. She looked at her niece, and it was as if there was no one else in the room but the two of them. Slowly Marguerite came forward to stand before Elizabeth. The older woman looked dazed, puzzled and frightened. Trembling she held out her hand to Elizabeth to show her the ring, that copper and emerald jewel that Elizabeth had seen flash in her hand.

"I—I—I—" Marguerite struggled for words. "It's—it's the paste ring for his funeral," she managed to get out. "The court jeweler gave it to me so that it could be placed upon his hand for burial. I brought it—to Thomas the Mage so that he might have the care of it," she said with a rush of breath.

Elizabeth sagged with relief. She reached out to take the ring from Marguerite, but before she could touch it a shriek rent the air of the great hall. Elizabeth looked up to see the

Lady Anne, with unaccustomed haste, running the length of the room. The woman came to a halt breathing hard from her effort.

"It can't be! It can't be that an old hag like this would have found Raphael's ring!" Lady Anne managed to shout when she could draw a breath. "It was to be mine or Prince Eblis's. The demon of the Black Circle promised me it would be so. It was to go to neither of *you!*"

Elizabeth looked coldly at her father's leman. "So, you have been busy with black spells and circles, have you? And a demon has been your aid. I do not find that unusual for you. I know you worked many a spell and circle to kill my mother and gain favor with my father. Indeed, you were the instrument of my mother's death! Now I find that you have aided in the chaos since my father's death. I tell you I will not have it!"

Elizabeth's voice rose to a shriek worthy of the lowest fishwife. She found herself raging at the Lady Pemberly in a way she had never before dared to do. But the relief at finding that Marguerite had only that glass jewel which was to go with Richard to his tomb had so affected her that she had to get rid of the tensions within her.

She found herself calling the Lady Anne of Pemberly "mopsy," "jade," and "infamous harlot" to her face, and took great pleasure in it. For many years she had kept silent for her father's sake, and now there was no need of such restraint. In her haste to abuse the Lady Anne, the lesson of Great Yermouth was forgotten.

The court was silent around them. Prince Eblis had come forward to stand next to the Lady Pemberly. He said nothing as Elizabeth raged at the woman, but merely observed the contrast between Elizabeth's scarlet cheeks and the pale face of the Lady Pemberly. Eblis watched and waited.

"I say to you," Elizabeth said in a loud, angry voice, "as soon as I come into my own, and I am queen, I will have you in the Tower. Given the chance, I would bring you to Tower Hill and there separate your head from your body! You have been a source of pain to me and mine for too long, and while I cannot harm you yet, I can promise that I *will!*" Elizabeth lashed out at the Pemberly as if to strike her, but instead fastened her fingers upon one of the large pearl and diamond drops that hung on the lady's ear. With a savage yank the princess ripped the earring from the woman's lobe, tearing her delicate skin.

There was a cry of dismay from the courtiers as they saw the blood running freely from Lady Anne's torn ear down onto her gown. But even though tears ran down her cheeks, Lady Anne said nothing. She realized full well the danger she was in, for Elizabeth was most likely to be queen—and the day she *was* made queen was the day Anne of Pemberly might lose her life. There was a great deal of dignity in the lady as she stood there, saying nothing. She merely reached up and took from her undamaged ear the other earring and wordlessly handed it to Elizabeth.

Elizabeth clutched her mother's jewels and said bitterly, "My father the king gave these to my mother on the morning after their wedding night. You, the greatest harlot in Englene, had the gall to wear them! Now they are free from your contamination, madam."

"Nay. I say that you have done a great wrong, Your Grace." Eblis's voice was soft and silken. He had decided the time had come to strike. "I know that your father, King Richard, gave those earrings to the Lady Pemberly to honor her as a lady who had been most kind to him in the time of his infirmity. You had no right to mistreat a lady in this manner. I, as a knight, do protest your lack of chivalry and I challenge you for those earrings." Eblis looked about the room and saw the courties approved of what he had done. So he said in a louder voice, "I, Prince Eblis of the Bene Elim, do on this day issue challenge to you, Princess Elizabeth of Englene, that tomorrow at Midsummer you will meet me on the tourney field and we will fight for a lady's honor and a queen's earrings."

Elizabeth cursed herself for losing her temper and being so hasty. She had forgotten her upbringing and training as a princess, and had behaved very badly. Eblis had used her own weakness against her by challenging her to a tourney. She looked at the man and realized that, unlike Prince John, he was probably a very good fighter indeed. Were he to unhorse her and cause her disgrace on the tiltyard, it might destroy what little repute she had left.

The princess could see that her courtiers did not approve of what she had done to the Lady Anne. She had made a martyr of the woman; her threats and her cursing had done nothing but ennoble the king's leman. There were many in that room who remembered how much King Richard had loved the Lady Pemberly, and what joy he had found in her.

Elizabeth realized she would have to put the best face that she could on it. But when she looked at Eblis and saw the flames dancing in his eyes, she knew that the man who had challenged her was no ordinary mortal, and that she stood in grave danger of her life. To accept his challenge might mean her destruction—but to refuse might mean the loss of the throne.

Offering up a silent prayer to the Goddess for aid, she said, "Very well, I accept your challenge, O mighty prince. But since the challenge was from you to me, I will pick the place and the style of the tourney. We will fight in the center court of the Palace of Witchdame, and we will run three courses, by lance, mace, and sword. And whoever of us unseats the other, that one will be victor. So mote it be."

Eblis smiled, the smile of a hungry dragon. The flames danced higher in his eyes, and Elizabeth could smell sulfur and brimstone. He nodded his head in acceptance, and in a voice of gloating triumph said, "So mote it be."

Chapter 28

"But why did she do it, Menadel? Why did Aunt Marguerite let the courtiers bow to her? Why didn't she say right away that it wasn't Father's real ring? I don't understand." Elizabeth paced the floor of her privy chamber, wringing her hands in deep distress.

"I, at least, *do* understand," Menadel said. "Have you ever stopped to think of what it must be like to be your Aunt Marguerite? She's of no consequence to the court, of no political importance, and she does not have a husband and children to console her. Hers is a lonely life. Her only relief is her books. I don't think she meant any harm when first she spoke of having the ring, but the reaction of the courtiers was a surprise. I have no doubt that for a moment or two the thought of what it might be like to be Queen of Englene did cross her mind. You have known since childhood that you might be queen, but dear Marguerite has had nothing. Do not begrudge her that moment or two of glory.

"Now it is over and she again has nothing. Marguerite has enough power that she might well have managed to fool the entire court and convince them that it was indeed the ring Raziel. She might even, had she been a wicked woman, have managed to be crowned queen. But I do not think Marguerite would have allowed the situation to go *that* far. The very fact that she came and gave you the ring was enough to show her innocence."

Menadel sighed and then said, "Of course, your behavior with the Pemberly over her earrings hasn't helped anything. I don't like the idea of this challenge. Even I can tell that Prince Eblis is a demon. He means your destruction and you have placed yourself directly in his power. I hope you have enough strength and ability to defeat him."

"I'm worried about that too," Elizabeth admitted. "Of course, I've got Nerthus behind me and three of the archangels, but if *only* I had Raphael! Can't anything be done?"

Menadel went to the window of the chamber and looked out onto the courtyard below. Even at night the bands of shadow from the four Towers were very apparent. They were a darker black than the surrounding air and any light that was reflected from doorways or windows caused little stars to glimmer within them.

There was the one long shadow which was that of the Tower to the South—the finished Tower that was Michael. To the West, Gabriel's Tower, three-quarters finished, the shadow three-quarters long. To the North, Uriel, the shadow but half the length of the courtyard. Then there the short stumpy shadow of the East Tower, the Tower to Raphael.

"There's where it will have to be done," Menadel said. "I've talked to him, and he won't listen to anyone as unimportant as I am. Michael, Gabriel, and Uriel have reasoned with him, reminding him of his hatred of demons. Even Nerthus herself has spoken to him, but he stopped his ears with his fingers and would not listen. I think he's waiting for you to come to him. So this night at his hour, you *must* do so. Go into the unfinished top of the East Tower and there, with circle and spell, give supplication to Raphael, and perhaps he will listen to you."

"I was told if I had all four of the archangels behind me the

Towers would be completed and their shadows would be one and the sigil would be one," Elizabeth said. "But having Raphael behind me would not change the fact that the other Towers are not complete either."

"But having all four of them does complete the pattern and the Towers will be completed by the power that is yours. Get Raphael to back you! Get him to give you the ring and you *will* have all."

Elizabeth joined Menadel at the window. She leaned her elbows on the sill and looked out at the Tower pattern. "I suppose," she said, "that having four archangels and the Mother Goddess behind me should be enough to defeat that demon, but why must I have the ring? What's so important about the ring?"

"You must understand how the ring came into your family, so I will tell you now the story of it. There was a king called William the Lucky. He was the son of Geoffery the First and his wife Katherine, and from his early infancy William was a man of extraordinary ability. He was brave and pious. He was a goodly man who gave the Gods their due. Had it not been for his name of 'the Lucky' he might well have been called 'William the Pious.' For no matter how often he won at tourneys, at dicing, or at cards, he always gave thanks unto the Gods.

"And so it was as William grew to manhood, the Gods favored him and he found he could not lose at any game of chance. When he raced his horses with the other young princes, he won. When he placed bets on the bearbaiting, he won. Every game of chess fell victorious to him. And so it was that he became king and his luck rubbed off on the kingdom of Englene. The land was prosperous and did well. William accumulated much wealth, but he was no spendthrift, nor was he a miser. All his monies were used for the benefit of his people and they were used wisely. He took a wife and she was the fairest princess in all the lands, for she was called 'Anne the Fair.' She was a good and virtuous wife and gave him many children and strong sons.

"William continued to be lucky. And there came a time when this luck gave him discontent. For when you are able to always win at games the savor goes out of it. If there is no risk there is no thrill. William found that, much as he loved games of chance and gambling, he grew weary of them.

"So he spoke unto a wizard of his court, telling him to solve the king's problem even as you do now. That wizard said, 'Sire, it is well known that the Archangel Raphael loves games of chance, casting of lots, and gambling, for he is the angel of the gambler. It is said that Raphael loves nothing more than dicing and he even will leave off his healing for a chance to dice with the other angels. I say to you, if you wish to return some sense of sport to your games, dice with the archangel, for there is none higher in all the universe.'

"William considered his wizard's words. At the appropriate season, month, and hour he did the triple eight Circle and, putting on the purple of Raphael, he summoned the archangel to him and they diced together. William put up as his stake the land of Englene, his fair wife, his children, and all that was within his power. The Archangel Raphael put up as his stake his ring of power, the copper and emerald ring Raziel. They agreed to dice from night until morning, and from morning unto the following night. At the end of their dicing, when the lots were toted up, it was found that King William had beaten the Archangel Raphael. And Raphael, with much lamentation, gave the king the ring Raziel and promised him that all his powers should be given to the king and his descendents as long as they had the ring Raziel, and that the good of Englene rested in that ring. Then the Archangel Raphael left King William.

"Now William found that he had a ring that gave him power over all things. That he could heal the sick, and level a country at a thought. He was the most powerful witchlord king that had ever been, because he had the archangel behind him. But he found that there was no more pleasure to be had from games of chance or sport than he had had before he'd diced with the archangel. Once he had diced with the greatest he had no interest in dicing with the lesser. So, with great sorrow, William left off his horse racing, his dicing, his cards, and his other sports and pastimes and devoted the rest of his life to his wife, his children, and his kingdom. Never again did he gamble, and so it was until the day of his death."

Elizabeth considered the story for a moment and then raised an objection. "But he could have asked Nerthus to gamble with him. She outranks the Archangel Raphael."

Menadel laughed softly and said, "If he had challenged the Goddess, he would have lost. Nerthus does not always play fair."

"But how will this story aid me, Menadel?" Elizabeth asked. "Should I dice with the archangel to get the ring back? I am aware it was my folly at Great Yermouth that has cost me the ring, but might it be a greater folly to expect him to give up that ring so easily again?"

Menadel turned his back on the East Tower and considered. "Raphael admired the hubris of King William, and he loves to gamble. Perhaps he will also admire your courage and find the wager too tempting to pass up. He does *love* to dice! We can but see what this night may bring."

Elizabeth looked out at the shadow of the East Tower and said, "So mote it be."

It was cold and dark at the top of the East Tower. The room which Elizabeth had chosen as her place for working magic had no roof and was open to the stars. It was one of the clock on Wednesday, the hour and day of Raphael. It was the first hour of Midsummer Day, and the heavens blazed with stars, all of them watching the princess as she made a circle of three eights. She stripped naked, then she put on the purple and gray tabard of the Archangel Raphael, embroidered in copper with the sigil of Mercury, the planet under the control of Raphael. She cried aloud the name Raphael eight times, eight being Raphael's number. And then she prepared the white wine for Raphael, and she smote the ground with the wand that was the implement of Raphael. Around the Circle braziers burned with the incense of Raphael, for she had taken fennel, thyme, rue, pennyroyal, chamomile, and geranium and mixed them well, and burned them with charcoal in his name.

Then she bowed to the ground, and said, "O eternal and omnipotent Goddess who has ordained the whole creation of these archangels. For thy praise and thy glory, I beseech thee to send thy Archangel Raphael of the first rank of the angels, that he may come to me and instruct me concerning things about which I design to ask him. Nevertheless not my will, but thine, be done through my love and thy love, O Mother Goddess, Diona/Nerthus, she-who-is-our-lady."

She struck the ground again with the wand, which was made

of hazelwood and copper, and fitting for the summoning of Raphael. Then she cast upon the fire aloes and mace, then benzoin, styrax, and other things that she had chosen for Raphael.

She took a palm branch and sprinkled it with the wine, swept the Circle with it and said, "I invoke, conjure, and command thee, O Archangel Raphael, to appear. Show thyself invisibly or visibly, as be thy choice, in this holy Circle. Come in fair and comely face without deformity or guile, by the name of Nerthus and by the name of Njord. Be here with me and do unto me no harm."

She raised her right hand and drew down the light of the moon and the stars, drawing power from them with her bare hand. Then, with the light of the night, she drew the sigil of Raphael and sealed it with an emerald.

Then she waited.

A wind came up off the river and it blew around the East Tower. There was the sound in it of birds, wind, snow, and rain and all things that are of the air, and Elizabeth knew that Raphael was with her. She knelt down in the Circle and took out from the tabard a pair of ivory dice. She rolled them back and forth in her hands and prayed to the Mother Goddess, Nerthus, to be with her. Then she said unto the Breath-of-Raphael that was in that place, "I will dice with you, mighty Raphael, and my stake shall be that of my ancestor, William the Lucky. I stake my kingdom, my husband-to-be, and my children-to-be. Yea, all my future happiness I do stake against thy ring, and I will dice you for it!"

She waited for some indication of acceptance on the part of the archangel. There was naught but the sound of the east wind blowing through the roofless room.

Elizabeth raised aloft her right hand with the dice in it and put all of her *own* power into that hand. She took naught from the stars or from the moon, nor from the Goddess or any other impersonal thing. All the power was hers and hers alone, as it should have been at Great Yermouth.

And she cast the dice.

The dice rolled across the Circle and came to a stop at the very edge of the first of the triple eight rings. Elizabeth had rolled upon one a five and upon the other a six. She looked at the eleven and sighed, then said, "O great Raphael, roll and beat me if you can, for that is my number. If you roll less the ring is mine; if you roll more, all is yours."

She waited, but the dice did not move nor did the angel cause them to be any number lesser or greater than they were.

So at the first light of dawn, Elizabeth got to her feet, rubbing the cramps from her legs. She faced the east, where the sun rose, and she genuflected deeply unto the east, and she did say, "O Archangel, great Raphael, because thou hast diligently been in my Circle and not answered my demand, I do hereby give you leave to go out from me. Depart, I say, and be thou willing and ready to come again whensoever duly requested and conjured by the sacred rites of magic. I conjure thee to depart peacefully and quietly. May the peace of the Goddess continue forever between thee and me."

As she bowed herself again unto the east, a tear fell from her eyes and dropped upon the ring finger of her right hand, and it sparkled there on her skin like a jewel. The dawn light caught it and made it gleam with the glow of copper and emerald. Then the drop faded away in the sunlight and there was nothing upon her hand. Elizabeth left the Circle without answer or aid from the Archangel Raphael.

Chapter 29

"True Thomas, as I recall, you promised I would be queen by Midsummer," Elizabeth said, "and lo, it is Midsummer Day and I am *not* queen." She stood in one corner of the forecourt of the Palace of Witchdame and watched the preparation of the improvised tiltyard. There would be no room for elaborate pavilions or reviewing stands. There would be only the tilt and a fence to keep back the crowd. But then, this tourney did not require elaborate preparation.

Thomas the Mage had stood talking with Menadel, Jackie, and Doctor Mittron. He turned at the sound of his princess's voice and listened with great attentiveness to her words. "But my lady," he protested, "it is but the early morn of Midsummer Day, and there are many hours yet to go before the day is over. I have taken the oracles three times and they *have* said you will be queen this day. More than that I cannot do."

"I am inclined to agree with Thomas," said Menadel. "I

have consulted what oracles I believe in—the Mother Goddess and the Archangels Michael, Uriel, and Gabriel, and they all say you will be queen."

Elizabeth shrugged and turned away from the small group of supporters. She was very aware that one name had been left out, but there was little point in commenting on it. The princess felt like the bottom of a herring barrel—musty, wet, and decaying. She had sluiced her entire head in a bucket of water to soak some sense into her sleep-sodden wit. Her eyes felt as if all the sand of Araby were scratching at them, and her tongue was as thickly furred as the back of a cat. She felt thoroughly miserable. She had been wise enough not to eat breakfast, not even a small pint of ale, but her stomach rumbled uneasily.

"What I'm going to be on Midsummer Day is dead!" she muttered. "I fear I listen too much to the words of others and believe in nothing. That is a grave sin—but I know what Prince Eblis is, I know he means to destroy me, and here I am about to let him do it, all on the word of the Goddess and the Flame. Ah, me, but I do want to *believe!*"

She watched young Thomas Seymour and her other grooms bring her armor over to her corner of the forecourt. One of the grooms led in the magnificent white horse from the West, the great barbary stallion, Jibriel. Elizabeth smiled a little at the sight of the magnificent animal, and she went over to stroke its nose and bury her hands in its magnificent mane.

"Hello my lovely, my sweet one," she murmured into its neck in a voice so low that only the horse could hear her. "You and I will have an interesting day, my dear, and if I fall to my destruction I'll know you cannot be blamed."

The horse's ears twitched and he turned his head to bump gently at her chest. His eyes were large and dark and Elizabeth could read concern in them. He nibbled at her wet hair, tugging it playfully, and she gave him a hug about the neck and took from him what reassurance she could.

"Saddle him well, Tom," she said, "and make sure that all is in readiness, for I will not be shamed this day by my horse or its barding. If I fail I want the fault to be mine alone."

Doctor Mittron came over to admire the horse. His long slender fingers caressed the animal's forelock and he smiled at it in obvious pleasure. Elizabeth was much amazed that

Jibriel allowed such familiarity from a stranger. "Do not fear, my lady," Mittron said. "This horse and I will do all that we can for you, and there are others who support you. You do have the Mother Goddess behind you, and that is no small thing. And I think that even Sulis, though he has his mind on many more important things, does bless you. As Menadel has said, you will have the backing of three of the archangels, and even now the Mother Goddess debates with Raphael the importance of defeating the Prince Azazel."

"Azazel?" Elizabeth said, turning to face Doctor Mittron. "Why do you call him Azazel? I thought his name was Prince Eblis."

"I call him by it for I know that is what he is: Azazel, seducer of mankind, standard bearer to the great one who is lord of the Nether Regions. After Lord Ashmedai fell, Azazel was first of the angels who fell after him. He is the mighty prince of demons! I beg you to go froth into this tourney using all the power and magic within you, for you will need it."

Elizabeth shook her head. "No," she said firmly, "I have never in my life used magic to win a tourney. My honor forbids it, chivalry forbids it. I cannot—"

"Chivalry be damned!" Michael Mittron said. "Do you think this is some pleasant Sunday afternoon tourney where the ladies will throw roses at you and the men will clap politely? Azazel will not be polite, nor will he abide by his honor, for he has none. He will use all the power that is his to command from the Nether Region itself. If you would rather go to your grave a proper chivalrous knight, so be it. But I think you are a fool. A living queen is better for Englene than a dead chivalrous princess. Consider this, and consider it quickly, for the time has come for you to gird yourself for this conflict."

Elizabeth stared at the doctor open-mouthed, amazed that someone of his rank would dare to speak to her in this manner. Then she threw back her head and laughed, for what he had said was quite right. Chivalry had no part in this battle. She was *not* fighting a being who believed in chivalry. "So be it," she cried aloud. "Death and destruction to Eblis who is the demon Azazel! So mote it be."

Michael Mittron grabbed her shoulder and squeezed it firmly. "So it *will* be!"

* * *

To aid her, Elizabeth wore the bronze armor that had been given her by the Mother Goddess. Garbed in that power she rode Jibriel out to one end of the forecourt to face the demon who called himself Prince Eblis.

Eblis was clad all in black; his horse was coal black and barded with red trappings. The ostrich plumes in Eblis's helmet were red and the tabard he wore over his armor was scarlet. He was a blazing coal that had come from the Nether Regions. Elizabeth was sure that beneath his helm his eyes blazed like those eternal coals.

The court was crowded behind the fence, packed together in an uncomfortable mass. Elizabeth could see her Aunt Marguerite with Guenhwyvar, close by the south corner where Jackie, Menadel, Doctor Mittron, and Thomas the Mage had gathered, and she smiled as she saw an old woman clad all in green join the princess and kiss her hand. Nerthus had come; that fact gave confidence to Elizabeth and melted a little of the ice in her belly. She sat waiting politely as Prince Eblis/Azazel issued challenge, and it was much as she had expected.

The Prince of the Nether Regions called aloud in a ringing voice, "I, Prince Eblis of the Bene Elim, do hereby challenge the Princess Elizabeth of Englene to a battle of three courses. We fight for a lady's earrings, the land of Englene, and her life!"

There was a loud outbreak of questions, exclamations, and cries from the courtiers. Eblis silenced it with a gesture of his hand. "We will talk no more of rings and archangels," he shouted. "This battle and this alone decides who is ruler of Englene. It is a battle to the death and I say to you prepare yourselves to acknowledge your new king."

Elizabeth leaned forward and patted Jibriel's neck. "Insufferable braggart!" she said, and was pleased when the animal snorted in agreement with her.

Then there was a blast of trumpets from the musicians, and the herald stepped forward and repeated the challenge. A tourney of three charges, a tilt to the death for a lady's earrings, the kingdom of Englene, and the princess's life. There was silence. The crowd had absorbed the information, and looking first to Elizabeth and then to Eblis, they realized that they did not know where their loyalties lay. They could only stand and watch as the first course was engaged.

Elizabeth hefted the heavy cypress lance and tested its balance in her hand. She knew the iron lance-head was sharp and vicious, capable of breaking through even plate armor if enough force was applied—and she intended to apply such force. It was, as Michael Mittron had pointed out, no Sunday afternoon tourney. At the signal, the two horses and their riders moved toward each other, thundering down the forecourt with only the tilt to protect them or their animals.

Elizabeth watched Azazel with great care. Her every instinct was alert to the slightest indication of how he would swing his lance. She saw from the movement of the lance socket and shaft, and his gauntleted fist, that it would be high. That was a mistake.

Reining Jibriel sharply toward Eblis, she couched her lance tightly, grate to lance rest, and came in under his staff, catching Eblis's lance close to the vamplate and shattering it as her own lance-head glanced off his gorget.

The two horses passed each other with a rending of the tilt and a clanging of metal armor, so close had they been to one another. Elizabeth sat her horse firmly and well, but Eblis had been rocked by the blow.

Turning, she watched him ride to the end of the forecourt and even without seeing his face she knew how angry he was. She rode back to Tom Seymour to take the next weapon for the second course. It was a morgenstern, that great iron ball covered with spikes affixed to a sturdy oak handle. It fitted into her locking gauntlet as if it had been there all her life. She flexed her arm muscles and waited.

Michael Mittron came to the side of her horse and reached up to touch her armored thigh. "Go with peace, my lady, and with *my* blessing," he said in a voice of quiet authority.

Puzzled, Elizabeth lifted her helm and turned to look at him. As she did she smelled the scent of full-blown roses and remembered a forest glade and a sacred Circle. She looked deeply into his blue eyes and knew that this was the man who had been with her at Avebury and at the Heartwoods. She saw a light burning in his eyes, a flame as different from the fires of Eblis as any light could be. It was a warm and comforting thing, and in that moment she *saw* his simple saffron robes turn to cloth of gold and felt upon her face the shadow of mighty wings; and she knew that this was the Archangel Michael, and that he was pledged to her for all eternity. In his eyes she could see his soul, and knew then that he loved her greatly, even beyond the love of human, witchlord, or angel.

There was nothing now to fear. The man that was meant to be her consort was with her. No demons' threat would ever quench the love and desire in his eyes, nor would death separate them. Elizabeth rode forth for the second course, and Michael's shadow rode with her.

The morgenstern required close work. Elizabeth carried in her left hand her large battle shield with the arms of Englene upon it and with her right she tried to batter at the figure of Prince Eblis with her morgenstern as he blocked her with his black and red dragon shield and his mace. They were closely matched and the blows were swift and sure. Their horses attempted to savage each other, Jibriel slashing out with his steel-edged hooves, cutting at the black destrier's legs.

Eblis tried a feint with his shield; Elizabeth debated responding to it and the fraction of a second pause was enough for Eblis to send his weapon crashing across Elizabeth's right hand, smashing her locking gauntlet and causing the flesh over her knuckles to break and bleed.

But it was not just her hand which bled. There was a shriek of agony from the black destrier, as with one blow Jibriel flayed open its side, exposed and broke its ribs. The black horse foundered and started to fall, so Eblis, savagely tearing at the animal's mouth, disengaged from the battle and spurred his stricken horse to the end of the field. The second course was over and Eblis's anger was a palpable thing in the forecourt.

Elizabeth rode back to Michael so that he might examine her hand. Her locking gauntlet had been totally destroyed; Tom Seymour started off to fetch another, but Michael raised a hand to forestall him. "No," he said, "I will provide a glove for the princess."

He took her injured hand in his and raised it to his lips, kissing away the blood and hurt until it was whole again. And then he said, "Take my gauntlet and wear it in battle as a token of my love."

"But it will not fit!" Elizabeth protested. "Your hand is far larger than mine."

*   *   *

The Archangel Michael held out to the princess a mailed glove of solid gold, and he said as he expertly fitted it over her hand, "The glove will fit, and that within the glove will fit as well."

Elizabeth felt his hand shape the glove to her fist. Then on her ring finger she felt something constrict, and she knew even as it touched her hand that it was a ring of copper and emerald. She started to exclaim at it, but Michael forestalled her. "Say nothing until the moment is come. The Goddess convinced Raphael that he would not manage to throw a greater number than yours. He has conceded that eleven has won."

Elizabeth laughed aloud in triumph. She *would* win! The day had changed to one of brightness, and out of the gloom salvation had come. "Tell me, O great Prince of Princes, how did the Goddess convince the mighty Lord Raphael that he would not win the cast?"

"I told him that cast as he would from now until the end of eternity he would never throw higher than a ten. *I* would see to it," the Mother Goddess said from behind her. Nerthus's voice was firm and amused; she had all the time there was to dice with an archangel, for *all* time was hers.

Elizabeth saw that Prince Eblis/Azazel had chosen his final weapon, a broadsword, and knew that he intended her death. This third pass might well be the last of the battle, but Elizabeth felt a quiet confidence that she would win. She took from Tim Seymour her great broadsword with its sixteen good spells upon it and prepared to ride down and destroy Azazel.

And as the Princess Elizabeth of Englene rode into battle for the third course, the Archangel Michael raised his hands to the heavens and called upon the Lords of the Watchtowers: upon his own power as Lord of the South; upon Gabriel, Lord of the West; upon Uriel, Lord of the North; and, most important, upon Raphael, Lord of the East. And the Towers of the Palace of Witchdame were completed.

They rose brick upon brick until they formed the great square of the sigil, the square within the Circle of the moat. Then the shadows of the four Towers met in the center of the forecourt to form the cross of the sigil, and around all of Englene flared the blue fire of the Circle of Elizabeth's quest, and in each of the four quadrant points that she had visited rose the blue fire of the Lords of the Watchtowers. The square within the Circle and the Circle within the square were completed. The sigil of the princess who ruled Englene was done.

Eblis saw, and knew what the sigil meant. With a cry of rage he struck out at the princess with a bolt of red fire. Her sword sundered, its two pieces and its sixteen spells useless to her. She turned back to fetch another and did not see what the demon did.

For there in the middle of the sigil, the standardbearer of the Nether Regions revealed himself as he was. The handsome golden haired prince of the Bene Elim grew; his black armor stretched and formed scales, the red of his ostrich feathers ran as blood down his belly as the thing he was grew and grew until its head towered even with the four Watchtowers. There in the forecourt of the Palace of Witchdame was a fearsome dragon, a beast which made the dragon of Bamborow seem like a child's toy.

Its scales were black and irridescent, its belly bright red—red as its flaming eyes. Its jaw was long and serpentlike and its teeth sharp as steel knives. Its breath was fire and its tongue a darting sword. Its every step caused the ground to shudder, and the sight of its eyes was enough to turn the courtiers still as the bodies in the royal waxworks.

There was silence in the forecourt. Elizabeth sat her horse and considered what she might do. She took a deep breath and said aloud, "Azazel, be gone from this place. I command thee in the name of the Mother Goddess! For I say unto you this day, the God is with me, the Goddess is with me, and the four archangels are with me. With their aid, I, Elizabeth of Englene, will encompass your death!"

Azazel laughed, but there was a false note to his laughter, for he felt about him the chains of power Elizabeth had forged with the sigil.

Now Michael brought forth the sword. He put Uryan into Elizabeth's hands, still clad in its green brocade. Elizabeth took the sword and cradled it like a child against her body while she removed the glove of Michael and tucked it into her helm so all might see that she wore his token and fought in his name.

Then with slow, prancing steps, the horse Jibriel—he who was the Archangel Gabriel—stepped out to do battle with the mighty prince of the Nether Regions. Elizabeth ripped the green brocade from the sword that was made from the wood of the Tree of Life and Death which grew in the Garden of Beginning.

And the great sword of the Archangel Uriel burst into Flame.

Azazel saw the ring, the sword, and the Flame. Fear touched him and he cried aloud for Ashmedai's aid. But the Lord of the Nether Regions had abandoned his lieutenant.

Elizabeth rode rapidly, a la jineta, at the stunned dragon-demon. She brought the mighty destrier at a full gallop toward the dragon-demon's belly. She ducked low beside the horse's neck to avoid the fiery breath of Azazel, and Jibriel's mane covered and protected her from Fire and Flame. Jibriel came to an abrupt halt and reared, resting his weight on his back legs in the levade. Then he leapt upward in the courbette.

Elizabeth struck. Her flaming sword entered the belly of the demon and the Flames of the sword met the Flames of the Nether Regions.

There was a sound as if the very Ethereal, Earthly, and Nether Regions had rent. A great shriek of despair, anger, and pain filled the air. The Flames of the sword Uryan consumed the flames of the Nether Regions, and as Elizabeth pulled the sword from the demon's belly, she saw the creature had turned to ash from its heel to its head. A mighty wind came out of the Ethereal Regions and blew the ashes of Azazel to dust, spreading it to the four corners of the earth, and the demon was no more.

The tenor bell in the palace chapel rang out; Queen Dianne's bell sang of her daughter's triumph, and all the other bells of Witchdame answered with a *Te Deum* for the new queen.

Queen Elizabeth of Englene, true queen of the lands her ancestors had ruled, sat upon the mighty horse Jibriel; in her hand was the sword Uryan; on her finger was the ring Raziel; and on her helm was the golden glove, love token of the Archangel Michael. No one who had lived upon the earth had ever possessed all the power she had at that moment. At her command the universe would roll up like a scroll and be no more. At her slightest wish kingdoms would vanish. At a touch of her finger mountains would tremble and rivers dry up. At the flash of her eye the seas would boil. She knew her power and knew, in that moment, she could challenge the power of the Goddess herself.

And she heard a small quiet voice. The Archangel Michael said, "My sister, my love, think that thought but once. For on the day that you think it again, you will lose all and your desolation will be greater than that of the demon Azazel, and your star will fall shrieking from the Ethereal Regions, and I will turn my back and do nothing. Remember Ashmedai!"

Elizabeth considered the archangel's words and knew he spoke a truth. She knew that the power she held was hers in trust, and must be used only for the good of Englene. For there was a balance between the Nether Regions, the Earth, and the Ethereal Regions which must be kept. She, Elizabeth, Queen of Englene, was that balance.

And it was so

Appendix

A CHRONOLOGY OF THE KINGS AND QUEENS OF ENGLENE
(1066–1535)

1066	Sweyn Forkbeard (human king, killed at Goddess Field when witchlords invaded)
1066–1088	Andrew I of Pleasance (younger son of King Philip of Pleasance) m. Gunhilde, daughter of Sweyn Forkbeard—no issue m. Matilda of Pleasance
1088–1105	Geoffery I of Englene (son of Andrew I) m. Kathrine of La Bonne Terre sacrificed at the Heartwoods
1105–1155	William I the Lucky (Ringstealer) (son of Geoffrey I) m. Anne the Fair
1155–1156	Henry I the Short (son of William I) m. Ursula of Burgundia

1156–1189   James I Woodwitchbane (son of William I)
             m. Eleanor of Aquitaine (died in
                childbirth)
             m. Gurtruda Gibbetch

WAR WITH THE WOODWITCHES 1182–1193 (James I
  killed by woodwitch magic, 1189)

1189–1216   Richard I the Wellbeloved (son of Henry I)
             ends war with woodwitches, 1193
             m. Berengaria of Navarre

1216–1220   Isabele I Englene's Curse (Daughter of
                Richard I)
             m. Geoffery of Burgundia

CIVIL WAR WITH GEOFFERY II 1217–1220

1217–1223   Geoffery II Sans Terre (son of James I)
             m. Philipa of Espania

1223–1273   Edward I the Peace Maker (son of
                Geoffery II)
             m. Joan of the Rhine

1273–1278   Richard II the Great Beast (son of Edward I)
             m. Elenora (Regina, Englene),
                greatgranddaughter of Isabele and
                Geoffery, Duke of Burgundia;
                considered by some to be the
                rightful queen; murdered her
                husband, 1278

1278–1279   Elenora (Regent)
             executed by the Great Coveyne at her own
               request for the murder of Richard II

1279–1291   Richard, Duke of Sudfolke (Regent)
             bastard half-brother to Elenora

1279–1327   Andrew II the Boy King (son of Elenora)

1327–1370   Richard III the Good (grandson of Andrew
                II, son of Andrew's second son,
                Richard, Duke of Eboric)
             m. Anne of Warwicke

1370–1401   Edward II Middleham's Joy (son of
                Richard III)
             m. Queen Jane of Gaeland, joining
                Gaeland to Englene

1401–1413   William II the Unlucky (son of Edward II)
             m. Isabele of La Bonne Terre

1413–1420   Isabele II the She-Wolf
             killed her husband, William II; executed
                 by the Heartwoods, 1420
1420–1461   Edward III the Handsome (son of William II)
             m. Katherine of Espania (died in
                 childbirth)
             m. Anne of Hever (died in childbirth)
             m. Jane of Wolf's Hall (divorced)
             m. Anne of the Rhine (died in childbirth)
             m. Catherine of Nordfulc (divorced)
             m. Catherine the Fortunate (survived the
                 king)
1461–1471   William III the Weak (son of Edward III by
                 Katherine of Espania)
             m. Queen Elphame of Faerie
             killed in Faerie by Things
1471–1478   Henry II the Hopeless (son of Edward III by
                 Katherine of Espania)
             m. Joan of Gaeland (no issue)
             sacrificed at the Heartwoods, 1478
1478–1514   Edward IV the Just (son of Edward III by
                 Anne of Hever)
             m. Elizabeth of La Bonne Terre

EDWARD DIVIDED THE KINGDOM BETWEEN HIS
    TWIN SONS

1514–1528   Robert I the Younger, King of Gaeland (son
                 of Edward IV)
             m. Renee of La Bonne Terre
             eaten in Faerie by a Thing
1514–1535   Richard IV the Unready, King of Englene
                 (son of Edward IV)
             m. Dianne the woodwitch
             father of Elizabeth